Amazon Reviews of Kevin Craver's Novels

"Grabbed me by the throat and did not let go. I felt this was a far more realistic depiction of decline and disaster than almost any other [post-apocalyptic] story I've read."

"This book is what life is going to be if we don't open our eyes. It has it all—suspense, action, humor. Once you start reading you will not put it down."

"The author knows both prepping and military tactics and blends them masterfully into a fantastic, very realistic story."

"I absolutely loved every minute of this adventure."

"The story is so powerful and realistic that I soon became part of the feeling of danger, the horror of conflict, the sadness of lives lost, the pain of betrayal."

ALL WE'VE LOST

THE UNRAVELING: BOOK THREE

Kevin Craver

ISBN e-Book: 979-8-9882166-7-4

ISBN Paperback: 979-8-9882166-8-1

Library of Congress Control Number: 2025911077

First Edition, 2025

Printed in the United States of America

Cover design by Christian Bentulan

Created with Atticus

For the record, this book was proudly written by a human being. No AI software was used at any time to develop, write, or edit this work. By buying this book, you support actual *homo sapiens* authors who do honest work. Buy human—don't give your money to douchebags who ask an AI to write a book for them and get paid because they're too lazy or stupid, or both, to do it themselves.

Books by Kevin Craver

The Unraveling Series

Big Sky Fallen

Cascadia Rising

All We've Lost

Contents

Disclaimer

Thank you very much for purchasing this novel, and generously contributing to the Kevin Craver Margarita Fund. Seriously, I know that every dollar counts these days, and I appreciate from the bottom of my heart that you're willing to spend some of your hard-earned money on my work.

All We've Lost is the third novel in my Unraveling series, after *Big Sky Fallen* and *Cascadia Rising*. I'm a firm believer in "one and done" stories where you don't have to read a ten-part series and four thousand pages to see the hero get the girl in the end and find out how many babies they end up making; no offense is intended to any of my fellow post-apocalyptic author brethren. Having said that, while *All We've Lost* is written to stand on its own, reading the other books will increase your understanding and enjoyment of this one.

Before we embark on this newest adventure together, I once again need to cover my fourth point of contact in this extremely litigious society in which we live.

All We've Lost is a work of fiction. Aside from the mention of a handful of public and historical figures, any resemblance of fictional characters to any individual, living or dead, is purely coincidental.

This novel follows several groups of twenty-somethings and adolescents as they try to make their way home following the collapse of civilization. However, this is *not* a book written for the young-adult (YA) market, and its themes—plus a generous helping of the words George Carlin said you can't say on TV—make it inappropriate for young readers.

I've always been a stickler for accuracy in my novels to the point of having to stop myself from spending hours going down rabbit holes—if I write that there's an Exxon gas station at the corner of Second and North Front streets in Townsend, Montana, that's because it was there when I wrote the chapter. However, in a departure from my previous works, several of the locations in *All We've Lost* have been altered or fabricated—besides being necessary to move the story along, it would be a douchebag move on my part to write fiction about real towns full of real people doing horrible things.

While *All We've Lost* is set in a post-apocalyptic world where law and order have disintegrated, the rule of law still exists at the time of this writing—and given the results of the recent presidential election, it looks like Americans are ready to go back to the good old days when we actually locked up bad guys rather than the toothpaste in the supermarket. With that in mind, there are a number of activities described in this book that will get you locked up as well if you're dumb enough to try them, including but not limited to breaking and entering, going AWOL from the military, rigging lawn and garden decorations to explode, theft of government property, threatening to shoot your mayor or other municipal officials in the ding-ding, and other no-nos. Likewise, there are several things in this book, such as the ownership of modern sporting rifles (what our corporate media call "semiautomatic assault-style weapons") and high-capacity magazines, that are legal in some jurisdictions but not in others. Please consult your applicable laws.

In conclusion, you and you alone are solely responsible for your own actions and their consequences. The author is in no way culpable for any damage, injuries, or death if this fiction book encourages you to do something shit-all stupid in real life. If you wish to use my novels as some sort of instruction manual to cause trouble or do harm, please seek professional help.

Now that you've asked your doctor if *All We've Lost* is right for you, I hope you enjoy it.

For Margene Pappas, Sir Georg Solti, and John Williams, for lighting the fire of music in a young boy's soul

and for Frank Bibb, who kept it burning

PART ONE

You take people, you put them on a journey, you give them peril, you find out who they really are.

—Joss Whedon

CHAPTER 1

GERMANY

Army Sergeant Martin Crenshaw grimaced as he checked his watch, his groan drowned out by the polite applause of his fellow cavalry scouts at the end of their new battalion commander's speech. He and his team had an hour left to tough out the unit's "mandatory fun" summer picnic before they would be released to their own time—after which they would drive back to Rose Barracks and let the drinking begin in earnest to celebrate his impending discharge.

Soldiers and their spouses gabbed while their children frolicked on the mammoth playground at the Wild Bavaria Outdoor Adventure and Recreation Facility in Grafenwoehr that Martin's unit—Outlaw Troop, Fourth Squadron, Second Cavalry Regiment—had chosen for its get-together. A sip of his Kapuziner wheat beer on the cloudless July day returned a short-timer's smile to his face, and a contentment that only a soldier who had ever counted down the days until returning to civilian life could ever know. He would miss Germany and the beer, though; while the brew in his native Wisconsin was exceptional, thanks in no small part to all the German immigrants who had settled there, he thought he had died and gone to heaven when he transferred to the Second Cav, which was stationed in neighboring Vilseck.

The tall pines that hid Bavaria's beautiful mountains from view swayed in the wind as Martin strolled to the two members of his fire team and the driver of their squad's Stryker infantry fighting vehicle. By a quirk of fate or divine whim, all four of them hailed from different parts of Wisconsin, giving them the unofficial moniker of "Team Cheesehead" among the rest of the platoon.

"How's it going, sergeant?" Specialist Josh Czernik, a thin young man with close-cropped blonde hair, asked with a salutatory hoist of his red plastic cup.

"That's a dumb question to ask a guy who's gettin' out," Josh's teammate, Specialist Theo Carlvin, retorted—the muscular black man downed the rest of his beer in one impressive gulp. "Hope you didn't fill up, sergeant, 'cause I'm firin' up the grill the moment we get back. We're eatin' good tonight." Martin grinned—Theo's barbecue was legendary.

"Sure you don't wanna reenlist, sergeant? Misery loves company, after all," Specialist Patton Childress said, threading his fingers through thick black hair that always just barely met Army regulation. Patton, the squad's driver, had a knack for getting into trouble; he had just been promoted back to specialist after being busted down to private first class.

"Never been so sure of anything in my life," Martin groused, wiping the sweat from his high-and-tight haircut with his free hand. "When the new battalion commander introduces himself by stating what his pronouns are, like ours just did, it's God's way of telling me to get out while the gettin's good. You assholes are on your own." Martin had joined the Army to follow in his father's and older brother's footsteps, and to give his life some sorely needed direction after his dream of playing college football fizzled after flunking out halfway through sophomore year. But it didn't take him long after stepping off the packed cattle car for his first day of basic training at Fort Benning, Georgia, to realize that his old man's repeated warnings about the military going woke and being unwelcoming to conservatives and patriots weren't just the rantings of an old man who watched too much Fox News. That disdain for the very people who traditionally made up a large chunk of the military didn't bode well for its numbers, and it showed—Martin's recruiter had practically kissed his feet when he signed the enlistment papers. Empty spots in unit rosters were a routine problem throughout Martin's time in the service.

"Got a job lined up when you get back to Fort Living Room, sergeant?" Theo asked. "Folks on the news won't shut up about the bad economy." Martin shook his head—he planned to spend a month or so taking it easy before finding work in his hometown of Elkhorn, a small village about an hour southwest of Milwaukee.

"Let's save Sergeant Crenshaw's exit interview for later and focus instead on the debauchery to immediately follow this dog and pony show. Speaking of which, is Ann-Katryn bringing any friends?" Josh asked Patton, referring to his stunningly beautiful German girlfriend. Josh's hobbies included role-playing games, science fiction and superhero movies, and other nerd fare; his inability to meet ladies without significant assistance could thus be inferred. Patton muttered no as Josh scanned the crowd until he spotted Ann-Katryn Müeller sipping from a clear Owala water bottle while chatting with her fellow German and American civilian employees who supported US Army Europe's mission. "Water?! Dude, is she feeling OK? Normally, she'd be six beers deep by now and drinking you under the table . . ." Josh trailed off as he noticed the blood drain from Patton's haunted face.

"Ho-lee *shit*," Theo said, his jaw dropping as the unspoken revelation dawned on them.

"Tell me about it," Patton croaked. "How do you say 'broken rubber' in German?"

"Verdammt Scheiße—mein Kondom ist kaputt," Josh dutifully answered. "Sorry," he added, catching Theo's and Martin's disapproving scowls. "You know me—if I have knowledge, I gotta share it."

"Which is why you couldn't get laid in a morgue," Patton grumbled before turning to Martin. "Sergeant, I know it's asking a lot, but please don't say anything—First Sergeant Dominguez is gonna fuckin' kill me when he finds out."

"You're not my soldier, and I'm about to become a fat and happy civilian again, so your secret's safe with me," Martin reassured him before polishing off his drink. "But trooper, you need to do right by her, and you need to have a plan—preferably not one you're pullin' outta your ass when you're locked up at parade rest in Top's office."

Patton exhaled with relief. "Thank you, sergeant," he said, draining his beer. "I need another. And another. And another."

"We all do," Theo said, leading the way to the row of kegs underneath a shaded wooden picnic shelter.

Martin brought up the rear of the four-man beer detail as it made its way through a small delegation invited from the recently arrived 167th Infantry Regiment of the Alabama Army National Guard; the "Fourth Alabama" had been federalized and deployed to Vilseck, Grafenwoehr, and the Joint Multinational Readiness Center at nearby Hohenfels, as a show of force after Russia's repeated threats against the Baltics and other Eastern European members of NATO. The pulsing *buzz* of Martin's smart phone informed him of a news alert from American Forces Network Europe that both the London and Euronext Paris stock exchanges would be closing early following three consecutive days of thousand-point losses on the New York Stock Exchange. Martin didn't know anything about banking or economics, but he knew shit hitting the fan when he saw it.

Theo let Patton fill up first. "Too bad you're ETSing, sergeant—you're takin' off right before things get interestin' around here."

"You may be right on that one," Martin muttered.

MICHIGAN

Melinda Hodgson didn't stroll down the beautiful wooded path at the Interlochen Center for the Arts so much as she glided on air.

The past month of her six-week summer camp at the world-renowned arts education school, nestled in the isolated woods of the northern "mitt" of Michigan, had been the greatest experience of her seventeen-year-old life. She smiled as she passed a wooden practice hut where a Japanese boy was playing Vivaldi on his violin like a master—creativity and art seemed to resonate from every building, every tree, and every rock. Melinda tightened her grip on her flute case and sheet music, quickening her pace in eager anticipation of her practice session at The Music Center with the principal flutist for the Chicago Symphony Orchestra, one of Interlochen's many guest instructors.

She almost dropped her folder as she fumbled to take a welcome but inopportune call from her mother back in Elkhorn—her parents, neither of whom were musicians, had moved heaven and earth to nurture Melinda's talent upon being told by one music instructor after another that she had the makings of a virtuoso.

"I can't put all this into words—I never wanna leave!" Melinda gushed, telling her mom that she had learned more about music in the past month than she ever had up to that point.

"Well, unless you marry a millionaire or rob Fort Knox so you can attend year-round, Dad'll be coming to pick you up in two weeks," Mom replied with a chuckle—Melinda had worked two summer jobs to save up the tuition. "I'm glad you're having so much fun—we miss you."

"Miss you too, Mom—gotta go," Melinda said, ending the call. The path from the summer camp cabins opened up to the main campus and a back-and-forth sea of students dressed in Interlochen's uniform of light-blue collared shirts and navy-blue shorts, with the color of their belts and socks denoting their field of study. Melinda made a mental note as she passed the Dennison Recreation Center to walk a few miles on the treadmill before dinner; while she wasn't fat, she struggled with her weight, and silently envied her skinnier classmates who could eat whatever they wanted without consequence.

A cluster of students talking animatedly in what sounded like Chinese caught Melinda's attention, their anxiety and fear understandable regardless of language. She wondered if they were worried about the new strain of flu in China that she had heard about two days prior on Interlochen Public Radio while she waited for her friend and cabinmate Dulcy Bowers's live on-air performance of Paganini's "Caprice No. 24." Melinda felt a pang of sorrow for the foreign students—*if China seals its borders like the news said they might to prevent a repeat of COVID-19, how're they gonna get home? Poor kids*, she thought.

She grinned ear-to-ear as she approached The Music Center—a beautiful glass- and wood-paneled building that had been designed with music and performance in mind—and darted through a front door considerately propped open by a younger student's trombone case. Melinda was living a dream she never wanted to end, but when it did, she would return to Elkhorn High School to enjoy her senior year with lifelong friends before heading off to college to forge a future making music and teaching it to others.

Or maybe even coming back to this wonderful place to teach, Melinda told herself as she hustled down the hallway to her practice room, her dream life playing out in her head.

WISCONSIN

The gravel of the unpaved country road crunched under the tires of Donna Moran's old but reliable Ford pickup truck as she turned onto the driveway to her farmstead, quickly disappearing into the thick woods.

She clicked off the AM news station with a scowl as a former Treasury secretary turned cable news talking head predicted an "imminent" default on the national debt; the soundbite came on the heels of a report about growing unrest and bank runs sparked by rumors that the president would soon announce the emergency closing of all banks nationwide.

"Looks like our day of reckoning from decades of overborrowing and overspending has finally come. And what's gonna happen when that strain of H7N9 avian flu going around in China makes it here?" she said before pursing her lips in annoyance—she had just turned seventy in June, and had become cognizant of the fact that she talked to herself too much. Donna raised her window as her truck crawled along the winding driveway, slowly cutting off the cool breeze coming from the line of menacing thunderstorms edging closer on the western horizon. "Got here just in time before the sky opens up," she said before biting off a curse with the realization she was talking to herself again. She craned her neck at the tarp-covered truck bed packed with last-minute supplies she had bought from the Costco in Bellevue, a forty-five-minute drive from her rural farmstead near the border with Michigan's Upper Peninsula. *Got our money's worth while our money's still worth anything,* she said—silently, this time—before resignedly wondering whether she had just made her last-ever shopping trip.

Donna bounced in her seat with a bump in the road as the woods ended to reveal an apple orchard leading to a beautiful red farmhouse and rustic red barn set amidst green and golden fields. To her customers, it was Moran Farm, a family-owned agri-tourism business; to the trusted friends now descending on her property with all possible haste, it was simply The Compound—a place they would ride out a societal collapse like the one Donna feared was playing out before her eyes.

The first thunderclap from the approaching squall rumbled as Donna pulled in front of the farmhouse that she and her late husband, John, had bought upon retiring after thirty-five years of practicing medicine in the Chicago suburbs, and leaving the high taxes, corruption, and crime of neighboring Illinois once and for all. A pot-bellied man with a bushy gray beard and wearing a white beekeeping suit strolled to the truck as Donna stepped out—while her hair had grayed, her physique was that of a much younger woman who still had a lot of living to do, courtesy of the nonstop work that homesteading entailed.

"Calling Doctor Howard, Doctor Fine, Doctor Howard!" Al Leonard joked in a nasal monotone, talking into a pretend intercom.

"For duty and humanity!" Donna exclaimed with a sorely needed laugh—the Three Stooges reference Al busted out whenever he saw the retired doctor never got old. "So, how're our bees doing today?"

"Great, as always, Doc—they told me to tell you hi."

"Grandma!" a young man's voice called out from a nearby aluminum pole barn, followed by a dog's friendly bark. Donna warmly smiled as her eighteen-year-old grandson, Ethan, galloped toward her with his golden retriever, Buck, in tow.

"You're just in time—I need help lugging this stuff inside," Donna said, mussing Ethan's jet-black hair as Will, her son and Ethan's father, rounded the corner. Ethan was strong and devilishly handsome, having inherited the best features from his Anglo father and half-Mexican mother. "Anyone else make it here while I was gone?" she asked her son as she stooped to scratch Buck's head.

"Frank and Krista finally pulled in 'bout an hour ago in their monster Winnebago—that's the last of our Iron Point people," Will said, referring to the small town about three miles from the farmstead where several of the retreat's families lived. "That leaves the Burkes and the Menendezes. The Burkes got a long haul from Minneapolis—hope they get here before things get outta control."

"And before we gotta quarantine 'em in case this flu's the real deal," Al interjected, "and not more corporate media horseshit meant to scare the hell out of ev'ryone for views and clicks."

Donna's blood turned to ice with the grating tone of the Emergency Alert System rising from the farmhouse's all-hazards radio over the stiffening winds. Her heart began to pound as Will and Ethan fished their buzzing smart phones from their pockets with matter-of-fact indifference; her anxiety over the worsening situation aside, Donna was a child of the Cold War—and like anyone who grew up under the Damoclean sword of nuclear holocaust, the emergency alarm tone, even its harmless weekly tests, still made her hair stand on end.

"Weather service just upgraded the watch to a warning," Will said, eyeing the black sky as a much louder thunderclap underscored his words. "Looks like a bad storm's coming."

"No truer words have ever been spoken," Donna muttered, undoing the bungee cords holding down the truck tarp while hoping the storm didn't knock too many apples from the trees. "Let's get this stuff inside before we get soaked to the bone."

CHAPTER 2

UNITED KINGDOM

"Wait! *Stop!*" the middle-aged woman sitting behind Kara Westman in the armored Escalade screamed at the driver as the main gate of RAF Lakenheath streaked past their left-side window. "You missed the turn—*go back!*"

"We didn't miss anything!" the driver yelled without taking his eyes off the road, riding the bumper of an identical black Escalade as their convoy reached the end of their desperate dash to the American-controlled air force base northeast of London to evacuate the lucky dependents who had been sheltering at the US Embassy. "We're taking the back way in through the delivery gate, ma'am—takes us straight to the tarmac!" Kara, who was losing her battle with car sickness, anxiously leaned in to peek through the front windshield before a tight high-speed turn on the winding English road forced her to close her eyes and swallow hard to keep from throwing up.

"The gate!" the lead driver's voice screeched from the encrypted dashboard radio, which had crackled nonstop with the convoy's comm traffic since the harrowing trip began. "Tell 'em to raise the damn arms—they got ten seconds before we mow through!" Kara grasped the Escalade's roof handle with a sickly moan as the driver peeled hard left into the base, slamming on the brakes as he weaved around the concrete barriers that had been placed in the access road to slow any potential intruders. She caught a glimpse of the US Air Force base guards, clad in full protective gear and their faces covered with sinister-looking black M50 gas masks to protect them from the killer pandemic flu that was tearing through the UK and the rest of the world.

The convoy straightened out and picked up speed past the gate. It tore onto the taxiways, passing several large concrete bunkers housing the ultramodern fifth-generation F-35A Lightning fighter jets of the 48th Fighter Wing, before blowing past Base Ops to brake in a large semicircle on the main runway near the monster C-130J Super Hercules transport plane waiting for them.

Kara stumbled out of the Escalade, dropping to all fours to violently puke up her breakfast on the tarmac. A reassuring pair of hands held back her strawberry blonde hair as she heaved for what seemed like forever, struggling to catch her breath as she rose on shaky legs.

"You OK, miss?" the driver asked from behind mirrored sunglasses. Kara nodded, barely managing to gurgle a thanks as he picked up her hiking rucksack that her inconsiderate fellow passengers had knocked to the ground. "Sit tight with everyone else until you're told to board," he ordered before striding away.

Kara nervously ran her hands through her hair as she fought to chase away thoughts of the nightmare sights she had witnessed—mobs rampaging through London, several close calls as the convoy weaved through streets to find a safe way out through the rioting and burning, and health workers in orange protective suits and respirators tossing body bags into the back of a truck that was stacked full of them like cordwood. She shivered, despite the summer sun bearing down on her and the heat rising from the runway. *This is happening all over the world—how is America gonna be any safer?* she asked herself.

The sight of the embassy's ten-man Marine security detail fanning out into a perimeter around the convoy reminded Kara of the one task she had to do upon her safe arrival at Lakenheath. She yanked her iPhone from the back pocket of her jeans and fired off a terse text message to her father—the two-star Army general who had called in every last favor he was owed in US European Command to get his only child on one of the last planes out of the disintegrating country. It was supposed to be the other way around—he had planned to fly over at the end of the month to visit Kara, who had completed her first year at the prestigious London School of Economics. She had spent the summer living with a classmate in the trendy borough of Shepherd's Bush when the call from her father a week prior turned her life upside down.

You're up late, Dad—it's, what, three a.m. in Seattle . . .

Listen to me very carefully, her father interrupted in a tone of voice that chilled her to the bone; it wasn't his proud-father-doting-on-his-princess voice, or the stern tone of Major General Jack Westman, Deputy Commander of United States Army I Corps, but the voice of a man scared out of his wits. *Drop everything and go straight to the Embassy. Pack one bag with what you need and go right now. Call a taxi, and wear a mask—whatever you do, don't take the Tube. Stay away from crowds. I'm getting you back home.*

You mean, all this stuff on the news? Kara asked, mind racing—the BBC had been reporting nonstop about the deepening financial crisis, and some sort of flu in China, but her young life had been one big roller coaster ride of endless economic problems and the COVID-19 pandemic. Wouldn't this all sort itself out, like it always had before? *Dad, you can't be serious—fall semester's starting soon!*

Now, Kara, her father cut her off, his command voice returning. *Don't tell a soul. This is life or death—yours. The embassy knows you're coming. Do you understand me?*

Kara hastily crammed what she could into the large rucksack her dad had bought her for a month-long hiking trip to Switzerland, barely managing to zip it shut. She obediently followed her father's orders, save for the one about keeping quiet—she told her roommate everything, and advised her to grab her mother and high-tail it out of London to her grandmother's house in the West Country. Her trip to the embassy was uneventful, but the glittering futuristic cube on the south shore of the Thames quickly became a fortress—and her prison—as the world fell apart. The economic malaise exploded overnight into a US default on the national debt, dragging the world's economies down with it. Then the H7N9 virus arrived—far more contagious than COVID and hundreds of times deadlier—and slashed its way through London and other international travel hubs, cutting down young and old alike.

An incoming phone call from her father snapped Kara back to the present. "Dad!" she yelled over the loud drone of the cargo plane's engines, jamming a finger into her other ear. "I'm here at the base. How'd you get a call through?"

"Never mind—thank God you made it," her father said over the frenzied sounds of activity around him. "That plane's gonna fly you to a place called Joint Base Andrews, outside of DC. It's secure there—that's where they keep Air Force One."

"Dad, I know what Andrews is."

"Don't interrupt," her father admonished. "Text me the moment you land—if you can't get through, tell them who you are and ask them to patch you through to me. I'm working to get you on another flight to join me here at JBLM."

"But I heard the West Coast is getting hammered really bad," Kara stammered—her father's current duty station of Joint Base Lewis-McChord was sandwiched between Seattle-Tacoma and the Washington state capital of Olympia.

"We cordoned ourselves off and we're keeping everyone out. You'll be safe here." The shrill voice of a young man—or woman, Kara couldn't tell—informed her father that he needed to jump on an urgent conference call with Pacific Command. "Honey, I have to go. Get on that plane, and contact me when you land at Andrews."

"I'm scared, Dad," Kara whimpered, voice trembling.

"You'll be here with me soon. You can do this, Princess," her dad reassured her before ending the call.

Kara wiped her eyes as a pudgy man in civilian attire waved his arms and hollered to order the new arrivals to line up with their travel documents ready. She unzipped her rucksack to retrieve her passport, which peeked out from behind a photo of her and her parents from her father's promotion ceremony to general—her mother would be dead from pancreatic cancer six months later. At six feet tall, Kara and her dad towered over her mom. She had been a force to be reckoned with on the high school basketball court—she had played on two teams, courtesy of her father's change of station from Fort Carson, Colorado to JBLM—but Kara had spurned a basketball scholarship in order to pursue an academic path.

She hoisted her rucksack onto her back and got in line, only to be asked to set it down so the flight crew's loadmaster could weigh her and her luggage separately. A heavyset woman behind her—the histrionic lady from the Escalade—ignored the loadmaster's prompt and handed him a "don't weigh me" card. He gave it a glance and handed it back with barely hidden contempt. "Ma'am, I'm not gonna say your weight out loud. Please step on the scale."

"Asking me my weight is insulting and offensive," the woman huffed while trying to keep her two antsy children still. "Do you know who my husband is?"

"I don't got time for this," the jumpsuit-clad loadmaster responded, his eyes narrowing to slits. "I gotta account for every ounce of weight so we don't end up going into the drink. Step on the scale or stay in England—your call." The woman grudgingly acquiesced as Kara grabbed her bag and followed the thin line of Air Force personnel guiding her and the other passengers up the plane's cargo ramp.

She groaned with disappointment at the sight of the uncomfortable webbed seats unfolded from both sides of the plane's fuselage—a sight she remembered from her umpteen guided tours of cool military hardware as an Army brat. Kara scooted down the thin gap between the seats and the pallets of supplies tethered to the floor before finding the frontmost unoccupied seat next to an unassuming plainclothes bureaucrat; *this is gonna be a long flight*, she groused, silently praying that the entitled Karen and her rugrat kids wouldn't end up sitting next to her.

The C-130J's ramp raised, slowly replacing the bright summer day with sterile white lighting. The plane taxied to the runway, its four six-rotor Rolls Royce AE-2100 propeller engines roaring to full power to lift the Hercules into the sky towards home—and an uncertain destiny.

CHAPTER 3

GERMANY

Martin and his team combed the woods for three hours before finding the body of their fellow cavalry scout who was shot trying to flee post.

The young Hispanic soldier sat upright against a spruce tree, his face serene in death despite clutching his blood-drenched abdomen, as if he had died content that he spent the last moments of his short life free, and not imprisoned on a military post far from home while the world ended.

"Poor bastard—I was kinda rootin' for 'im," Theo grunted; they had picked up the trail of disturbed foliage and blood and followed it for more than a kilometer through the woods surrounding Rose Barracks. "Looks like he gave it his all, though."

Martin stared transfixed at the first dead body he had ever seen up close outside of a funeral home. "Liver shot," he muttered, saying out loud what a lifetime of hunting with his father had taught him the moment they first spotted the soldier's dark red blood smeared on a bush. "What a way to go. Any of you recognize him?"

"He was a driver in Palehorse Troop, I think," said Patton, who had been assigned to Martin's team as a rifleman when the brigade's eight-wheeled Strykers were mothballed to conserve precious fuel. "Saw him a coupla times during vehicle training."

"Want me to call it in, sergeant?" Josh asked, grasping the hand-held SINCGARS radio strapped to the shoulder of his load-bearing tactical vest.

"What's the fuckin' rush, dude?" Patton chided. "Can't wait to get locked back up in the barracks or put on some other shit detail?"

Martin let his M5 battle rifle hang free on its harness as he knelt to unzip the dead soldier's backpack. "Hold off, Josh," he said, and after a second of rummaging tossed four purloined MREs into the grass. "Not to be a ghoul, but this poor soul's not gonna be needing these anymore, and I don't know about all of you, but I've been starving since they cut our rations to stretch out the food."

A refreshing breeze rustled through trees spaced out with German meticulousness, bringing instant relief as the team popped off their Enhanced Combat Helmets and sat down to eat just out of sight of the corpse. While his teammates eagerly tore into their rations, Patton grabbed a black burner smartphone from one of his magazine pouches—a pre-collapse fallback he had purchased to be able to talk to Ann-Katryn after his phone had been taken away as punishment for some minor offense. He glanced at the screen and tossed it to the forest floor with disgust.

"Anythin'?" Theo asked.

"*Nichts,*" Patton replied, dejectedly reaching for his lunch. "No bars, no 5G, no nothin'."

"I'm sure she's all right, dude—her and the baby," Josh optimistically said as he stuffed his main course into the MRE's water-activated flameless ration heater.

"Hope you're right," Patton murmured, sliding the phone back in his vest.

"Don't get careless with that, trooper—you get caught and it's my ass, too," Martin said with his mouth full. The post commander had shut off access to what was left of the internet and ordered all smart phones, tablets, and laptops confiscated to keep the steady stream of bad news from destroying what remained of morale and unit cohesion. Martin, who wasn't in the mood to do the Army any favors after his discharge was postponed "for the duration of the emergency," had allowed Patton to keep the phone, on the condition that he shared with the team all information pertinent to their respective Wisconsin hometowns.

Theo's hometown of Milwaukee, like every other major US city, was being torn apart, as was Patton's native Kenosha, which was sandwiched between Milwaukee and Chicago's far-north suburbs. Green Bay, and its suburb of De Pere where Josh had grown up, was faring little better. Patton hadn't been able to find anything about Elkhorn; its close proximity to Milwaukee down Interstate 43 didn't imbue Martin with much optimism about how his family and friends were doing. With both American Forces Network television and the American Forces Radio station in Grafenwoehr off the air, their only source of information was the Army rumor mill, sprinkled with whatever snippets could be gleaned from the BBC and the handful of other English-language news services that were still operating, at least intermittently.

"Wonder if it's true what those Fourth Alabama boys said about all of us getting shipped back to CONUS?" Josh said as he tore open a packet of jalapeño cheese spread and slathered it on a cracker. The National Guard soldiers were very anxious to return home with the reports that Alabama was among a handful of states openly talking secession in the wake of the federal government's bungling of the response to the economic collapse and the pandemic.

"Hope so—pro'bly the only way I'll ever get back to the States at this rate," Martin muttered.

"Hope not, sergeant—I'm not leavin' Ann-Katryn here to die so I can shoot looters in what's left of Chicago or wherever," Patton retorted. "Besides, someone told me they overheard someone in S-2 sayin' they wanna keep Second Cav right here so's the Russians don't take advantage of the situation and invade."

"Well, Top still doesn't know 'bout you becomin' a daddy," Theo said, cracking open his MRE's small bottle of hot sauce with his teeth and emptying it into his chicken and noodles. "Maybe they can work somethin' out if we end up goin' home—I mean, they gotta be shippin' back families and dependents if they're shippin' *us* back, right?"

"That'd go over great," Patton snorted. "'Hey, First Sergeant Dominguez, sorry to bother you while you're dealing with Armageddon and all, but I wanna bring along the local I knocked up.' Besides, I'm calling bullshit on us getting sent home—Army's way too ate-up at this point to be sending anyone anywhere."

"How can you be so sure?" Josh asked.

"Well, for starters, we just stole our lunch off a fucking corpse 'cause the Army's having trouble feeding us," Patton said, his voice dripping sarcasm. "*And* they stopped paying us, which doesn't matter, because the dollar's worthless now."

The whine of a loudspeaker cut Josh off before he could respond, followed by a booming authoritative voice speaking German echoing through the woods. "'Go back to your homes. We have nothing to spare for you,'" Josh translated without being asked.

"Someone's trying to get in at Gate 5? That's weird," Martin said, stuffing his MRE trash into its plastic pouch. The team sat only a few hundred meters away from the isolated access gate along the "tank trail" connecting Rose Barracks with Tower Barracks in Grafenwoehr through the massive forested training area between them. Guarding Gate 5, which was about five kilometers from Vilseck proper, was much easier duty than the handful of times the team had to help reinforce the main gate to post. It was especially hard on Josh, who could understand the desperate locals, some of them obviously sick, screaming that their kids were starving.

Martin and his men rose one by one as the unmistakable chant of an angry mob carried on the breeze.

"That ain't someone—that's a lotta someones," Theo anxiously said.

"'We want food,'" Josh translated. "This doesn't sound good . . ."

"*Halt! Oder Wir schießen!*" the loudspeaker blared. Josh didn't need to translate the one phrase every soldier deployed to Germany was required to learn for sentry duty—stop, or we'll shoot.

Martin threw on his helmet and zipped up his tactical vest. "Gear up, troopers," he ordered as the faceless soldier repeated the ominous warning twice more over the growing chants. "We're a little too close for comfort—"

The team flung themselves to the dirt with the roar of a chain of explosions.

"*Is everyone OK?!*" Martin screamed over the rumble of the blast rolling away into the forested hills.

Theo breathlessly grabbed for the helmet that had flown off his head. "Holy shit, sarge, those were the fuckin' Claymores!"

Josh's eyes went wide with the creepy silence that had set into the woods. "Did they just blow all those people away?!" he managed to ask before a deluge of automatic weapons fire cut him off.

"Childress! Get the fuck back here!" Martin screamed as Patton tore away, sprinting through the forest toward Gate 5. "God-*dammit*!" he cursed, pursuing him with Josh and Theo in tow. Patton, who barely passed the Army Combat Fitness Test's two-mile-run on account of putting in the bare minimum effort, ran like a man possessed, leaping over roots and dodging branches like a parkour *traceur*. Martin barked Patton's name twice more as they pursued him through the woods.

The trees thinned out as Patton scrambled up a small but steep incline overlooking Gate 5—and stopped dead in his tracks at the sight before him when he reached the crest. Martin leaped to roughly tackle him, almost causing them to roll down the hill. "What the *fuck* is your malfunction?!" Martin roared, red-faced, into Patton's ear as he pinned him face-down in the dirt. "You tryin' to get us all fuckin' killed?"

Patton racked with sobs underneath Martin as footfalls in the weeds announced the arrival of Josh and Theo, who dove for cover on both sides of them. "Oh, dear Jesus," Theo gulped.

Martin raised his head to find a sea of dead and dying civilians scattered before the heavily reinforced checkpoint through the thinning smoke of the Claymores. With the click of a detonator, a soldier had set off the gate's chain of antipersonnel mines, each of them blasting out seven hundred steel balls in wide arcs to mow down the mob before they could storm the gate and bring the H7N9 flu onto post. Martin hastily rolled off Patton and scanned the carnage through his rifle's advanced M157 fire-control scope; at least two hundred people—mostly adults, but teenagers and some children as well—lay where they had been cut down, several of them still moving. Many were missing limbs or were bleeding out; the corpses closest to where the mines had been staked were little more than butchered pieces of vaguely human remains. The checkpoint's soldiers were still in their foxholes, weapons at the ready, except for a sergeant behind a concrete barrier frantically radioing in for instructions.

"Some of 'em are still alive!" Josh exclaimed from behind his rifle scope. "They gonna do anything for 'em?"

"With what?" Theo spat.

"They musta tried to muscle their way through the checkpoint," Martin whispered, his anger over Patton's insubordination evaporating with the horror of the scene in front of him—and with the realization why Patton had done what he did. "Hey, trooper," he softly said, rubbing Patton's back. "I'm sure Ann-Katryn's not down there."

Patton buried his face in his hands, silently praying to a God he wasn't sure existed that his team leader was right.

CHAPTER 4

OVER THE ATLANTIC

Kara glanced up at the Air Force medic sliding down to her from atop the stacked pallet of supplies anchored down the middle of the Super Hercules cargo plane.

"How ya doin', miss?" the handsome black kid yelled over the dull roar of the plane's engines, his voice muffled by the orange foam earplugs Kara and the other passengers had been handed to protect their hearing.

Kara cracked a sardonic smile. "The world's ending—I'm doing pretty lousy, all things considered," she yelled back, kicking her feet against the pallet in front of her. "That, and there's no effing legroom on this flight."

"Ain't nothin' I can do 'bout that," the medic said, smiling back, "but I can take care of your air sickness. The Dramamine working?"

"Yes, thank you—then again, I don't have anything left to throw up."

"I can do somethin' about that, too," the young man said, tossing Kara a vacuum-packed foil square of MRE crackers. "These an' water, and you'll be fine. Let the medicine do its thing and grab some z's. No better way to kill the time on a ten-hour flight in a four-fan trash can."

Kara nodded her thanks as the medic scrambled back over the mountain of boxes to check on other passengers. *Ten hours*, she moaned to herself, wiping the sweat from her brow before reaching down to re-wrap her hooded sweatshirt around her freezing feet—the peculiarities of the C-130J's environmental system made the air by the floor cold as ice, and the air at head level hot enough to fry an egg. She cautiously sipped from a plastic water bottle as she stared down both sides of her row of webbed seats; the civilians, like her, were awake and nervous, while the airmen and the embassy's Marines were zonked out—some sleeping in their seats, others sprawled atop the pallets of cardboard MRE boxes and duffel bags that made for an uncomfortable but functional mattress. Kara had always been envious how her father, and the handful of military boyfriends she had kept secret from him, were able to sleep anywhere, anytime, at a moment's notice. *And sleeping means you're not worrying about your loved ones*, she thought with a shudder.

Besides being scared spitless and uncomfortable as hell as the plane tried to freeze and parboil her simultaneously, Kara was bored out of her mind. In her haste to get to the embassy, she had packed only one book that she was now thoroughly tired of, and she didn't dare listen to music or her handful of saved podcasts on her iPhone; she needed to have enough juice to call her dad when she landed, and had no idea when, or if, she would have an opportunity to recharge it.

The bureaucrat in the seat next to Kara gave her an apologetic look as he sat back down, forcing her to lean back and shift her long legs to make room for his pudgy frame; the man had made at least a half dozen trips to the flight deck at the behest of the well-dressed woman two seats down, who Kara recognized as one of the embassy's senior foreign service officers. Rumors had swirled among the diplomatic staff and the sheltering American expatriates that both the ambassador and the deputy chief of mission had abandoned ship at the start of the crisis under the guise of returning to Washington for "urgent discussions"—the ambassador and her family had been flown by helicopter directly from her official Winfield House residence to a waiting private jet at Heathrow without even saying goodbye.

The FSO rose to meet the co-pilot who had followed the runner back to his seat. "No news still?" the official hollered over the turboprop engines. Kara clandestinely slid a foam plug from her ear to eavesdrop.

"Bad news, unfortunately," the co-pilot answered, rubbing the nape of her neck under her olive drab flight suit. "We're being diverted from Andrews." Kara's heart began to pound with the realization that a large wrench had just been thrown into her dad's plan to get her home.

"*What?*" the FSO incredulously blurted. "You've gotta be kidding! To where?"

"Dover."

"*Delaware?!* Why?"

"They said it's not safe with all the rioting in and around DC."

"Miss—" the FSO snapped before stopping herself. "Sorry, um, lieutenant . . . it's vital that I brief the president on the diplomatic situation. The prime minister's dead, and the UK doesn't have a clear line of succession like we do. The king's supposed to ask another Parliament member to step up and take the reins, but . . ." Kara quickly turned away as the FSO glanced around. "But the flu killed the king and the whole damn royal family, too. Is there any chance you can just say 'fuck it' and set down at Andrews?"

"Negative, ma'am," the co-pilot shot back, shaking her head. "We got special permission to fly back after NORAD shut down US airspace, but they're not screwing around. They doubled the ADIZ—the Air Defense Identification Zone—out to four hundred miles, and issued a one-time notice that any plane deviating from its pre-approved flight plan'll be shot down."

"Dammit, lieutenant, Dover Air Force Base may as well be in fucking Alaska for all the good it's gonna do me!" the FSO fumed. "Our closest ally—the one we're gonna hafta rely on big-time to help American citizens trapped in Europe—has no functioning national government, and I can't call it in because your bird's satellite comms aren't working!"

"Ma'am, I don't know what your runner's been telling you, but our SATCOM and HF radio are working just fine. The problem's that no one's listening."

"What do you mean?"

Now it was the co-pilot's turn to look around for eavesdroppers. "We've been able to talk to other inbound planes and get snippets here and there, but command and control's gone dark—Air Combat Command, USNORTHCOM, the Pentagon, you name it. Rumor has it that all of Washington DC's burning, and they're evacuating whatever's left of Andrews." The FSO barely had time to catch her jaw from dropping before the co-pilot delivered the hammer blow. "We also heard that the president, vice president, and the house speaker caught the flu and died, too—you may not have anyone left to brief."

The FSO stood in mute shock as the co-pilot stepped back. "If you'll excuse me, ma'am, we got a plane to fly, and we're heading into some nasty weather, so keep your fella outta our way. If we hear anything, I'll let you know as soon as I can," she said before disappearing around the corner to the flight deck stairs.

Kara nervously re-inserted her earplug with a one-fingered shove and waited for the air-sickness pills to knock her out and temporarily escape the reality that her life was now in serious jeopardy.

CHAPTER 5

MICHIGAN

Melinda vacuously stared at the fireflies flickering in the dark woods to the chorus of frogs and crickets singing farewell to the setting sun—a welcome sound that drowned out the distant cries of Interlochen's stranded children.

She had all but spent the past three days sitting on the shaded bench near her cabin, save for using the bathroom or eating her one meal a day from Stone Cafeteria's dwindling food supply, still served by a handful of dedicated workers concerned that the remaining students had nowhere else to go. Melinda would drag herself to the bench with the sunrise to stare blankly into space, sip water and repeatedly check her phone for a text from her parents, shoo away Dulcy or anyone else who tried to check in on her, and occasionally spare a thought about whether she was losing her mind. When darkness came, she would plod back to her bunk, charge her phone, and toss and turn all night until waking up to repeat the ritual.

Interlochen had tried locking down with the governor's declaration of a state of emergency, but stopping the flood of older students fleeing in their cars, and hysterical parents braving the ongoing collapse of society to get their kids, was as futile as trying to stop a tsunami. It was only by the grace of God that none of them had brought the killer H7N9 flu with them, but God's mercy had not extended to Melinda being among the lucky students whose parents came to bring them home. As the dim sunset finally faded into night, Melinda briefly wallowed in the comforting fantasy of Mom, Dad, younger brother Steven, and sister Mallory arriving to get her. She checked her phone one last time, and again it mocked her—no emails, no texts, and no service bars on account of overloaded cell towers going down across a hysterical and dying nation.

I can't just sit here forever, Melinda told herself, unaware of whether she had said it in her head or out loud. *Or maybe I can. Just sit here, day after day, until I die.*

The computerized monotone voice of the Emergency Alert System blared from a radio in a distant cabin, repeating the presidential message declaring a nationwide state of martial law and a dusk-to-dawn curfew. It faded into static, only to come back weaker as the naïvely hopeful listener scanned the FM band. "It's on all the stations, moron—same as yesterday, same as the day before. Turn that shit off!" a teenage boy's angry voice snapped; the radio fell silent, returning the night to nature's symphony. Interlochen Public Radio had risen to the challenge in the early days of the crisis, relaying news and information as best it could until the president activated the alert system and the staff jumped ship to fend for themselves. Melinda's stomach growled as she began shambling back to her cabin—hunger had been a constant companion since the dining hall had cut back their meals, but she didn't want to dip into the food stash she had squirreled away.

Her phone loudly chimed, and Melinda leapt as if she had been pinched in the rear. She yanked the phone from her pocket, her heart racing at the sight of the word bubble icon letting her know she had a text message.

> **Are you there, Mel?**

"Mom!" she exclaimed and excitedly sat back down, typing wildly as relief rushed over her like a drowning woman being tossed a life ring.

> **YES I'M HERE!**

Melinda silenced her notifications with a nervous glance around her, realizing she could quickly find herself mobbed if her fellow campers realized that she had a phone that had gotten through to someone.

> **Oh, thank God! Are you OK?**

> **YES!**

> **I'm more scared than I've ever been, but I'm OK.**

> **Is everyone else OK?**

> **Are you still there Mom?**

Please don't let me lose the signal, Melinda silently pleaded as another minute passed. The elation Melinda felt when she saw the pulsating ellipsis indicating that her mother was typing a response was immediately replaced by cold dread—Mom had been hesitating because she had bad news. *Oh God oh God oh God oh God* Melinda thought, panic swelling inside her.

> **Mallory died yesterday. Your dad and Steve are sick, too.**

Melinda shrieked, pulling her hair with clenched fists, screaming again and again into the darkness until sobs overcame her. She gingerly picked up her phone, now her sole tenuous connection with what was left of her family, as if it was made of porcelain.

> I have no words.

> Are you sick, Mom?

> No. Not yet.

> I'm coming home. I'll find a way.

"There she is!" Melinda heard in the distance as the bobbing of a smart-phone flashlight heralded the arrival of Dulcy and their cabinmate Anja, both of them armed with wooden sticks to defend themselves. "We heard screaming—are you all right?"

Melinda looked up at her friends, the glow of her phone in the pitch black of the new moon illuminating a face twisted with anguish. "Yes. Please leave me alone. *Please.*" Out of the corner of her eye, the message thread shifted to announce a reply from her mother as her concerned friends headed back to the cabin.

> NO! It's not safe here. We're being overrun with all the people fleeing Milwaukee and Chicago.

> The police are gone. Everyone who can has left already.

> You're safe in the middle of nowhere. We'll come get you when this is all over.

"Mom, are you *kidding me?*" Melinda angrily shouted as she typed.

Everything's over! FOREVER!!!

I'm coming home.

STAY WHERE YOU ARE. Give me your word, Mel.

OK.

Do what you have to do to live, Melinda. Do you understand me?

Melinda silently nodded her acquiescence, choking back another sob as she made her mother this last promise.

Yes.

I'm never gonna see you again, am I?

Don't say that. Yes, you will. Oh, honey, I wish I could hear your voice.

Same, Mom.

Gtg—my battery's almost dead and the power's been out more than it's been on. I'll try to text tomorrow. I love you, Melinda.

Love you too. Bye.

For now.

For now.

Melinda cradled her head in her hands and struggled to process the news—the hope that had swelled inside her when she finally heard from her family had shattered her instead. *Your kid sister's dead*, she said to herself. *And Dad and Steve will be joining her soon.* Melinda rose to her feet, quickly steadying herself on the bench's backrest as she fought the urge to pass out. *Mom's gonna die, too. And when that happens, you'll be all alone in a world of corpses.*

"All alone in a world of corpses," she mumbled aloud, throat burning from her screams, as she staggered back to her cabin with no thought but to crawl into bed and never wake up.

Dulcy's petite, athletic frame eclipsed the soft light of the open cabin door. "Melinda, what happened?" she barely managed to ask before Melinda collapsed in her arms, weeping as she shared the awful news with the remaining four girls in their cabin, who joined them in a hug to console their friend.

"You get the night off from watch—I'll take your shift," Dulcy said, helping Melinda to her unmade bottom bunk; with Interlochen's campus safety officers and counselors long gone, their cabin had joined with several others to create a night guard roster to patrol their immediate area for thieves and other trouble. Melinda barely grunted her gratitude, expending what little energy she had left to plug in her phone. The power shut off a second later, throwing the cabin into darkness and eliciting a distant scream from a frightened child; the lights flickered back on, then off again, then back on—dimly at first, but slowly returning to normal.

Melinda fell asleep to her phone's friendly chime that it was once again recharging, her last conscious thought pondering how long they had until the lights went out for good.

CHAPTER 6

GERMANY

Theo's snarling face was the last thing Patton saw through his night-vision goggles before they flew off his head with a violent shove to the concrete floor.

Patton barely had time to push himself up on hands scraped raw from breaking his fall before Theo yanked him to his feet and punched him in the face, a red flash of pain briefly interrupting the darkness as Martin and Josh circled to to cut Patton off from making a run for it.

"Goin' somewhere, motherfucker?" Theo growled, ripping the backpack from Patton's shoulders and flinging it away, almost catching Josh in the breadbasket.

"What's it to you?" Patton snapped at his teammates, their silhouettes just barely visible as his eyes began to adjust to the black that enveloped Rose Barracks with the outside lights turned off to save energy.

Martin violently shoved Patton against the wall of the baseball field dugout where they had caught up with him and foiled his attempt to go AWOL. "No one goes over the wall on me, slapdick," Martin seethed, grabbing handfuls of Patton's civilian clothes. "I got half a mind to turn you over to the MPs to be shot, but I don't want your kid growin' up without a dad—even a worthless piece of shit like you who'd fuck his buddies to save his own skin."

"Is that what you think I'm doing? Saving my skin?! It's more dangerous out there than it is here!" Patton spat. "I got a text from Ann-Katryn—she and her family are OK, but they're runnin' outta food. I gotta get to 'em."

"So what's your plan when you get there, high-speed?" Martin yelled in his face, tightening his grip. "That is, provided you don't get a bullet in your gut like that poor bastard from Palehorse Troop!"

"I got no fucking clue—I haven't thought this out past 'get to Ann-Katryn.' But lemme turn that question on you, sarge—what's *your* plan? Stay here 'til you die?" Patton challenged. "Because that's what's gonna happen to you. You think this is all gonna blow over and they'll let you ETS like you were supposed to? Your term of enlistment's officially 'from now on'—you just don't realize it!"

Martin savagely punched Patton in the stomach and dropped him to the ground.

"You wanna beat the shit outta me 'til the MPs hear the racket and lock all four of us up, have at it!" Patton gasped, staggering to his feet against the dugout's rough wall. "But that's not gonna change the fact that I'm right and you know it!"

Theo towered over Patton, tendons popping as his large hands balled into fists. "If you don't keep your fuckin' voice down, an ass kickin's exactly what you goan' get," he threatened.

"You got any idea of the pickle you put me in, shithead?" Martin snarled, seizing Patton by the collar. "We're not gonna rat you out—we'll get ourselves in trouble, too, the way things are goin'—but if we keep you around, I gotta know I can trust you, and right now, I can't. You're just gonna bail and screw us all the first chance you get!"

"Unless we all bail together," Josh blurted.

"Shut the fuck up!" Martin barked without looking at him.

"Josh . . ." Theo growled through clenched teeth.

Martin's talon grip on Patton went slack with Theo's admonition to Josh to keep quiet. He turned to face the duo; their faces, outlined in neon colors through Martin's next-generation night-vision goggles, wordlessly revealed their unspoken conspiracy.

"Are you two fucking insane?" he asked, dumbfounded.

"We've been talking about it since the day those guys in S-2 let slip that the rumors were true, and that we're being kept here to rot to stop a Russian invasion that'll never come because Russia's just as dead as the US," Josh said. "Our cities are burned, with God knows how many dead, and Alabama and Texas are openly talking secession. So what are we defending now? Patton hasn't said anything that Theo and I haven't said to ourselves—we can stay here, abandoned to die, or we can roll the dice and take our chances."

Patton groaned with pain as he stooped to grab his night-vision goggles and backpack. "And you buddy fuckers weren't gonna bring me in on it?" he grumbled, massaging his sore jaw.

"That's right, fuckhead," Theo shot back. "Your riskin' our asses by runnin' off half-cocked is Exhibit A as to why."

"Sergeant, we weren't gonna leave you high and dry—you've always had our six," Josh said to Martin, who stared in disbelieving silence. "We were gonna ask if you wanted in, hoping you'd say yes on account of Uncle Sam giving you the Big Green Weenie. We were just waiting for the right time—and well, Patton may be a stupid asshole, but he just gave it to us."

"Our best shot to bail's comin' up fast, sarge. Unlike this fuckin' oxygen thief here," Theo said, pointing at Patton, "we got us a plan. It'll be even better if you come with us—and Patton too now, I guess. With adult supervision, he should be a'ight."

Martin sat on the dugout bench and ran his hands over his head as if to jump-start a brain that had gone numb. "I got no idea what to say."

"How about 'I'll do it,'" Patton cautiously ventured, his head beginning to throb with the haymaker Theo had thrown him. "You can turn us all in, or you can look the other way and act surprised that we deserted—neither option'll make you look good. Or you can join us and risk it all. Maybe, miracle of miracles, we'll somehow make it all the way back to Wisconsin. And if we don't, at least you'll die free and standing on your own two feet."

A pregnant pause filled the dark dugout. "So, sergeant," Theo said, "what's it gonna be?"

CHAPTER 7

DELAWARE

The muggy mid-Atlantic summer humidity clung to Kara like a wet blanket as she walked on rubbery legs down the C-130J's ramp onto Dover Air Force Base's gigantic flight line.

She squinted into the gorgeous red sunset dominating the western horizon as an enlisted airman in full protective gear slapped a white cloth mask in her hand. "Make sure it covers both your nose and mouth—keep moving!" he yelled, the voice amplifier attached to his M50 mask making him sound robotic as he motioned Kara toward the massive base operations building. Looping the mask's elastic behind Kara's ears brought back unpleasant memories of the COVID-19 pandemic that had unnecessarily ruined far too much of her generation's childhood.

Kara woke up her iPhone to see if her father had responded to the text she had fired off the moment the plane's wheels hit the runway. Nothing. She pulled up the message telling him she had been diverted to Dover, and discovered to her horror that it hadn't gone through; she sent it again with a frantic stab of her thumb.

A line of airmen, their gas masks and camouflage-patterned protective suits giving them an almost reptilian appearance, shepherded Kara and the other passengers along to the whine of distant police and fire sirens; a column of smoke climbed from the direction of the nearby state capital from which the base got its name, its oily blackness contrasting the colors painted by the setting sun as if someone had torn a strip from the sky. Floodlights sprang to life ahead, illuminating a series of white plastic tents and a fire truck from the base's crash fire rescue unit at the flight line's edge. Personnel clad in colored hazmat suits with built-in face shields like extras in a pandemic disaster movie buzzed about. Yellow tape cordoned off the entire area, and more ominously, its perimeter was patrolled by masked Security Forces personnel armed with M4 rifles.

"May I have your attention, please?" a man in a dark red hazmat suit called out at the head of the line, the bullhorn held up to his faceplate's voice box emitting an ear-splitting screech. "I need the men to line up to my left, and the women to my right—young children can stay with the parent of their choice. We need to decontaminate you before you proceed to quarantine—this is for our safety, and the safety of everyone on base. Place your luggage and other personal items in the designated area behind me before following the white line to the first tent . . ."

I can't be quarantined! I need to get out of here and on the next plane, Kara's inner voice screamed, panic rising inside her as the powering up of pumps and the *hiss* of pressurized water drowned out the whines and groans of the passengers who realized they would have to strip naked and be hosed down. Kara dropped to a knee and pretended to fiddle with her rucksack to let the remaining people behind her pass to give her time to reason with the man with the bullhorn. She could see through the man's faceplate that he was older, with white hair—a doctor, perhaps—and red, baggy eyes that revealed long hours worked with little rest. "Excuse me, sir, but I'm supposed to be getting on another plane . . ."

"Miss, I'm sorry, but our orders are clear," the man flatly cut her off, the sharp edge to his tired voice revealing in no uncertain terms that he was in no mood to deal with any nonsense. "Anyone entering base, regardless of who they are or where they came from, has to be decontaminated and quarantined. No ifs, ands, or buts."

"My dad's a general—Major General Jack Westman, U.S. Army," Kara anxiously said. "He's sending a plane to take me to Joint Base Lewis-McChord. I can't be stuck in quarantine—"

"Get in line and proceed to decontamination," the man sternly ordered, gesturing to two nearby Security Forces guards, "before I order them to use force to do the honors—and you won't be the first. I'm not gonna let the H7N9 flu kill everyone on base because of one young lady with a vivid imagination and a tremendous sense of entitlement."

Kara swallowed hard, fighting the urge to cry as she began making her way to the women's line behind a middle-aged mother comforting her young son and daughter. She had just set down her rucksack in the luggage pile when a Humvee wheeled to a stop at the edge of the decontamination area with a flash of headlights and a squeal of brakes. "Westman!" an Air Force first lieutenant in fatigues yelled as she hopped out the doorless passenger side, her voice muffled by her mask. "Kara Westman! I'm looking for—"

"Westman! Right here!" Kara hollered, frantically waving her arms.

"You got ID?" the lieutenant challenged in a thick Boston accent. Kara yanked out her passport and handed it to the woman, who after the briefest of glances lifted up the staked tape marking the decontamination area's limit. "Grab your shit and get in the back of the Hummer—we don't got much time."

Kara snatched up her rucksack and darted under the tape without a second thought. "Hold it right there!" the man in charge of decontamination bellowed behind her, striding with a pronounced limp with the two guards in tow. "*No one* breaks quarantine—you stop right now before I order these men to shoot!"

The lieutenant whipped out a piece of paper as the guards brought their weapons to the ready and trained them on Kara, who froze in her tracks just shy of the Humvee. "Orders come straight from the top! She's not entering base—I got fifteen minutes to get her on a bird outta here!"

The man snatched the paper from her hand and gave it a quick read. "Looks like I'm officially outranked," he grumbled, his armed entourage lowering their weapons to Kara's immense relief. "But lieutenant, if you fuck this up and she gets on base and infects your family and everyone else you know, that's on you." The man spun away and headed back for the decontamination line.

Kara climbed inside the Humvee, barely having enough time to fasten her seat belt as the enlisted driver gunned the engine and peeled off the moment the lieutenant sat back down. The Humvee picked up speed, tearing down the flight line past dozens of mammoth military transport planes parked along its tremendous length toward another Hercules being prepped for takeoff.

"Thank you," Kara told the lieutenant as they both alit. "I never liked flying—I get airsick if I look at a picture of a plane—but I've never been so glad to catch a flight in my life." She enthusiastically slung her rucksack on her back. "But if there's a bright side to this horrible mess, it looks like I won't be doing any flying for a long time once I get to Seattle."

"About that, Miss Westman," the lieutenant apologetically started, the sympathy in her voice contrasting her sinister-looking "Darth Vader" gas mask. "We don't got any direct flights to JBLM. This'll get you to Scott."

"What?" Kara yelped. "Where's Scott?"

"Scott Air Force Base, Illinois. Near St. Louis."

"*Illinois?!* I gotta get to my dad!"

"Sorry, Miss Westman, but this is what we got. That reminds me," the lieutenant said, fishing a folded paper from her pocket and handing it to Kara.

Kara wiped her eyes as she read the terse message. I'M TRYING TO GET YOU A FLIGHT TO JBLM. CHECK IN AT FLIGHT OPS WHEN YOU LAND AT SCOTT. STAY STRONG, HONEY. WE'LL MAKE THIS HAPPEN. LOVE, DAD.

"At least this'll get you one step closer," the lieutenant reassured Kara as she handed her a Kleenex. "You got no idea how lucky you are—it's been days since I've been able to reach my parents and brothers in Massachusetts."

"You're right—I'm sorry," Kara blubbered, dabbing her eyes before lowering her paper mask to loudly blow her nose. "I hope your family's OK."

"The news said Boston's outta control and that lotsa people are dying from the flu, but they're in Fitchburg, more than an hour away—hope that's far enough."

Kara leaned against the Humvee while the driver excused himself to stretch his legs, griping about there being far too few places on base to smoke a cigarette. She lowered her mask, edicts be damned, to enjoy fresh air while she could before enduring another miserable cargo plane flight. The Hercules and its flight crew appeared dim to the point of shadow against the backdrop of the setting sun lighting up the western sky.

"That's one beautiful sunset," Kara said to make idle conversation. "It's so big. Never seen one like it."

"And you never will again," the lieutenant quipped, pointing straight west. "That's the sun. *That,*" she continued, slewing her arm left along the glowing horizon, "is Baltimore burning to the ground. And *that's* Washington, DC. Or what's left of it."

Kara stared, aghast, as the Hercules's engines began to warm up with a long ascending whine.

CHAPTER 8

WISCONSIN

The precocious freckled young boy led Donna by the hand through the farmhouse to the ham radio room where Al Leonard sat, hunched forward and pressing his headphones into his ears.

"Grandpa! I got her, just like you—" Kyle loudly proclaimed before Al demanded silence with a finger to his lips. The boy beckoned Donna to come close with comical exaggeration. "Grandpa's got something to tell you, but we gotta be quiet," he whispered in her ear.

Donna kissed the boy's freckled forehead and mussed his mop of sandy blonde hair. "Thank you, Kyle—you can run along," she said, sending him off to play outside with the other children. She smiled wanly at the sight of Al working the ham radio, her mind flashing back to a heart-wrenching old movie about a small California town that had survived a nuclear war, and how a kindly old ham radio operator, to whom Al bore more than a passing resemblance, was their only link to what was left of the outside world. She offered a silent prayer that their story would have a happier ending than the townspeople in the film.

"So what's so important that you had Kyle tear me away from breakfast?" Donna asked the moment Al signed off.

"Looks like the reports we heard are true," he said, rising from the leather office chair and shuffling to a large acetate map of Wisconsin and its immediate surroundings; the map, like the national and world maps dominating the wall, were plastered with notes detailing news and rumor that Al and the handful of The Compound's ham operators had picked up. Just over the Illinois border, near the city of Byron and its nuclear power plant, he plastered a sticky note with the word MELTDOWN scrawled in blood-red marker.

"Mother of God," Donna intoned. "We're not in danger, are we?"

"We're fine. Byron's more than three hundred miles away, and the winds aren't gonna blow straight north. But not everyone's gonna be so lucky," Al explained, his wrinkled hand drawing a black plume of radioactivity hooking northeast from the plant.

"Right over Milwaukee and Chicago," Donna said with a whistle. "So besides carrying H7N9, all the fleeing people could be coated in fallout as well. You sure about this?"

Al peeked out the door for Kyle or any other young ears. "The poor guy I just talked to is downwind—he just signed off so he and his wife could crawl into bed and die. Let's just hope that the cordon the new governor threw into place to keep these poor souls out holds." Donna's finger followed a thick red marker line cleaving southeastern Wisconsin from the rest of the state. The feds had marshaled a large military force at Fort McCoy to restore order to Milwaukee and the state capital of Madison, but it quickly found itself without orders when Washington, DC fell silent. Lieutenant Governor Kristina Weber, who had stepped up with the governor's death from the flu, took command of the force along with the state National Guard and made the critical decision to deploy them in a rough line along the Wisconsin River east to Lake

Michigan just south of Sheboygan to stem the tide of potentially contagious refugees.

"I don't wanna stoke panic, but if reactors can melt down in Illinois, they can melt down elsewhere," Al said, lowering his voice. "You may wanna have that fancy dosimeter you bought when Russia invaded Ukraine placed outside, just in case either of Minnesota's reactors go full China syndrome, too."

Donna took a step for the door. "Well, I think I'm gonna get back to my now-frigid oatmeal with what little's left of my appetite, provided Buck hasn't already eaten it," she said. "That is, unless you're not yet done ruining my morning."

"I'm not, sorry to say," Al said, sticking another note to the map. "I also confirmed the rumor that the Air National Guard blew up the I-94 bridge over the St. Croix River to keep us from gettin' flooded with sick people fleeing the Twin Cities. That could explain what happened to the Burkes," he gruffly said of the Minneapolis family that had never made it to The Compound.

"Damn," Donna sighed. "I told Mike and Joanna to get a move-on and not wait 'til it was too late."

The black MURS radio on Donna's hip lit up with a *chirp*. "Big Mama, you there, over?" came the agitated voice of her son, Will, on the dedicated frequency for Donna to handle the thousand issues a day that came with being the matriarch of a post-apocalyptic survival retreat.

Donna's pulse quickened; she could not recall a single time that her radio—a constant, twenty-four-hour companion—had brought her good news. "Yes, I am—what is it?"

"Mom, you ready for this?"

"Spit it out, son."

"Ashley's here at the front gate."

The blood drained from Donna's face as Al's jaw went slack with the news that her long-lost daughter had returned.

"Family, too, or just her?" Donna asked, fighting to keep her composure.

"Just her. Sweet Jesus, does this mean . . ."

Donna strode down the hallway and through the kitchen past her half-eaten breakfast that Buck was eyeing with a swish of his tail. "Keep her there, and tell the sentries to stay alert in case this is some kind of trick," she ordered, hating herself for believing her estranged daughter capable of duplicity. "I'm heading over with the QRF right now." Her stride became a dash the moment she stepped through the screen door, bolting for the nearby pole barn where the compound's quick-reaction force stood ever-vigilant in the event of a problem that required an armed solution.

The QRF's olive-drab pickup truck tore down the gravel driveway moments later, with Donna crowded in among the four-member team in full combat gear. She wiped her eyes with her thumb and forefinger as the thoughts of what to say and do gave way to a horrible question dominating all else.

Oh, God, where's my granddaughter?

CHAPTER 9

MICHIGAN

Dulcy followed the soothing melody of Melinda's flute to the concrete patio overlooking Green Lake.

Her nose wrinkled at the odor of the trash can at the entrance, its contents scattered about the plastic dome lid that had been unceremoniously tossed aside. *Probably some desperate soul looking for something to eat*, Dulcy thought, shooting a glance behind her at Stone Cafeteria, which had closed for good the day before with no food left to serve; one of the patio's blue rocking chairs had been thrown through the glass pane next to the cafeteria's locked door. A ring-billed gull strutted among the refuse, briefly shaking a grease-stained wrapper before giving up and flying off to join others wheeling over the lake.

Melinda stopped playing at the sight of Dulcy's shadow falling across the patio with the morning sun behind them. "Knew I'd find you here," Dulcy said. "Mozart?"

"Debussy, actually," Melinda corrected her. "But I can play something from *Flute Concerto No. 1* for you, though, if you'd like."

"I'd like," Dulcy said, easing herself into a nearby rocking chair as her friend began to flawlessly play from memory. She applauded at the end of the three-minute piece, as did a young man who had been strolling barefoot along the beach below them, and Melinda thanked them both with an exaggerated bow.

"Beautiful view to practice by," Dulcy said, leaning on a stone pillar holding the metal handrail. "Acoustics could be better."

Melinda watched the boy continue his lonely trek down the lake shore. "Well, the practice rooms aren't what they used to be, now that the power and AC went out for good. Great if you're into hot yoga, though."

"It's not much cooler out here," Dulcy said, wiping the sweat from her brow and eyeing a line of storm clouds growing on the western horizon across the lake. "Hope the rain blows through early and doesn't ruin the concert." Interlochen's remaining students, like the musicians on the *Titanic*, had decided several days earlier to hold one final performance before going their separate ways to face whatever God or fate had in store for them; while the handful of Interlochen's small neighboring towns had grudgingly agreed to take in the young kids, older students like Melinda and Dulcy would have to fend for themselves.

"The weather'll hold. It has to," Melinda said, bringing her flute back to her lips and continuing where she had left off with Debussy.

"Save something for the show," Dulcy said.

Melinda lowered her flute with a sigh. "This is probably gonna be the last concert I ever play," she resignedly said as a great blue heron stalked for a mid-morning snack in the shallow water amid the reeds. "May even be the last time I ever play at all if this is the end for me. And if this is gonna be my final performance, I'm making darned sure it'll be my best."

"Don't say that."

"I don't see any music festivals happening anytime soon—and if what they said on the radio is true about every major city being gone, I'm guessing that means their symphony orchestras are gone, too. You know," Melinda continued, biting off a bitter laugh, "all I could think about before everything went to hell was staying at Interlochen forever. Mom always said to be careful what you wish for. Did you find a bike last night?" she asked, eager to change the subject.

"A real beaut," Dulcy said—she had snuck out in the middle of the night to steal an abandoned bike chained to a rack since the collapse with a pair of bolt cutters appropriated from a supply shed left unlocked by a careless groundskeeper. "First light tomorrow, I'm heading to my dad's house in Mackinaw City—should only take me a few days." Like Melinda, Dulcy had held out hope that her father would come for her, but now realized that her fate was in her hands. While Detroit, Lansing, and everything south of Saginaw and the Tri-Cities were a write-off, the trickle of news Dulcy had heard was that the upper mitt of Michigan and the Upper Peninsula were all right; in the grim mathematics of the collapse, the millions of deaths meant less likelihood that she would run across trouble in this new lawless world.

"Good luck," Melinda said with a forlorn smile. "I'll miss talking to you."

Dulcy placed her hands on Melinda's shoulders and looked her in the eyes. "It doesn't have to be that way. I stole *two* bikes last night—one for each of us. Come with me."

Melinda's lip quivered; she opened her mouth to speak, but no words came.

"I know your mom told you to stay, but you haven't heard from her since. That's because your parents aren't coming—not because they don't love you, but because they can't," Dulcy said, reciting the speech she had practiced in her head since stashing the bikes in the woods. "The government's not coming to rescue you either, because the government doesn't exist anymore. If you stay . . ." Dulcy stopped to compose herself as her voice cracked. "If you stay here, you'll die. You'll waste away, all alone, or someone bad will find you and kill you. Please don't choose death over a fighting chance at life—I'm begging you."

Melinda grabbed Dulcy and hugged her tightly as they both racked with sobs. The text from her mother flashed in her mind like a neon sign—*do what you have to do to live.*

"My dad's cool—my kid sister's a pain, but what'cha gonna do?" Dulcy tearfully said, wiping her eyes as Melinda blubbered a laugh. "I can talk him into letting you stay with us. If I'm wrong and your folks *are* coming for you, they'll have to stop in Mackinaw once they cross the bridge—no way they can go around Lake Michigan through whatever's left of Chicago and Gary." Dulcy's hometown sat at the southern end of the five-mile-long Mackinac Bridge that connected the UP with the mitt of Michigan.

"You have yourself a deal!" Melinda proclaimed with a sniffle, shaking hands to make it official before they laughed and hugged once more.

A low rumble of thunder from the approaching storm rolled across the lake. "My phone ran outta juice, so I have no idea what time it is, but we got a bit before the concert—let's pack what you need, pool together whatever food we've scrounged, and see if we can rustle up any more. Then again," Dulcy said, gesturing at the seagulls combing the shore, "if *they're* having a hard time finding human food, I don't think we'll have much better luck—we'll probably be gnawing on twigs by the time we get to Mackinaw."

"Well, I've always wanted to lose some weight. Looks like I have my chance," Melinda joked.

Dulcy pointed to the cafeteria's shattered glass pane. "I hate doing this, but seeing as how somebody already let themselves in, let's start here and see if there's anything edible that anyone missed."

Melinda followed her friend up the grassy incline to the dining hall, nervously peeking around for nonexistent cops before dismissing her naïveté with a rueful snicker. A fire had kindled inside her, torching the hopelessness that had resigned her to a fate of languishing at Interlochen until the end came. She wasn't done living yet.

The afternoon performance would be her best ever, Melinda said to herself as her sneakers crunched on the broken glass leading into the stuffy heat of the shuttered building. She once again had a purpose in life—and a reason to go on.

CHAPTER 10

WISCONSIN

Donna's tears flowed silently as the QRF's pickup truck navigated the winding gravel drive past the apple orchard toward The Compound's heavily guarded front gate—and the daughter she hadn't seen in almost a decade.

She tried her best to think about the good times—when Ashley was a beautiful, caring, and intelligent high school girl ready to make her mark on the world. Then she got accepted to Harvard, where the Morans paid a small fortune for the university to scramble her brains and send them back an insufferable, humorless leftist who couldn't stand her parents and their conservative values. Ashley had married a fellow traveler—a beta-male weasel as unbearable as she had become—and gave Donna and John their only granddaughter, Sonia. Two weeks after they got to hold their grandchild in the hospital for the first and only time, Ashley sent her parents and brother a terse email disowning them because their "abhorrent" views made her feel unsafe, and telling them in no uncertain terms to stay clear of her and her daughter.

The truck skidded to a stop at the edge of the woods separating the farmstead from the county road. "We gotcha covered, Big Mama—if there's trouble, it won't be trouble for long," said the QRF leader, Gunnar Nolan, a dangerous-looking former Airborne Ranger who had seen action in Iraq and Afghanistan, before leading the four-member team into the forest to reinforce the perimeter security.

Donna walked the rest of the way to find Will standing vigil in full combat gear, his Daniel Defense AR-15 rifle at the low ready. She chased away one final pleasant thought of Ashley dancing at her first ballet recital—*the daughter you knew is dead*, she steeled herself, muttering a quick prayer for strength as she rounded the thick metal gate at the end of the drive and forced herself to look at the pathetic figure standing in the road. Ashley was barely recognizable, her hair dyed pink and shorn short with some sort of tattoo on her neck and a barbell nose ring through her septum. Her dirty clothes, and mosquito bites covering a face and arms reddened by sunburn, revealed that Ashley had had a very rough go of things.

"Hi, Mom," Ashley weakly offered.

"Ashley . . ." Donna ventured, voice trembling, "where's Sonia?"

"I don't know," Ashley barely managed before breaking down. "She was with her dad in Milwaukee when everything started falling apart. David was supposed to bring her back 'cause it was my turn to have custody, but he never showed up, and I couldn't get a hold of him . . ."

Donna's hand slowly rose to her mouth; Ashley took several cautious steps toward her estranged family before a flick of Will's rifle stopped her in her tracks. "That's close enough—you could have the flu or something else that could get us all sick," he said authoritatively.

Or she could be covered with fallout from that meltdown, Donna kept to herself, silently hoping that Ashley hadn't been condemned to one of the most agonizing deaths known to man. "Do you feel sick? And over the past few days, have you thrown up, or had diarrhea, or had any unexplained skin rashes or hair loss? Tell the truth." Ashley shook her head. "What happened to you, and how'd you get here?" Donna asked, struggling to stay focused as her thoughts dwelled on her granddaughter.

"It was hell, Mom," Ashley started. "The riots started in Madison right when the economy started tanking and the banks closed—there were no cops in sight."

"Looks like you got what you voted for," Will jibed.

"Will! You're not helping," Donna snapped. Her son pursed his lips and fell silent, but kept his eyes, and his rifle, on his sister.

"Then the flu came. I realized getting here was my . . . my one shot at survival," Ashley stammered. "I took 39/90 north, but the highways were jammed to a crawl, the gas stations were closed, and—and after a while, people were dying right in their cars. I finally ran outta gas outside Antigo, and had to walk the rest of the way here. Took me three days, with no help—towns are setting up roadblocks to keep 'the city people' out, and one flat-out shot at me. Mom? Can you help me?"

Donna's heart sank, her daughter's voice no longer that of an entitled, sanctimonious adult, but of her scared child pleading for aid. "We can give you some supplies," Donna said, taking a deep breath to steady herself. "But you can't stay."

Ashley recoiled as if she had been slapped. "What?!"

"This isn't just your crazy mom's farm—it's a survival community we created with friends and their families to give us a fighting chance in the event of a collapse like what's happening right now. We all agreed that no one would bring any uninvited guests, and everyone's followed that rule. I've had grown men cry like babies in my arms because they felt guilty about coming here with their families and leaving their parents and grandparents to *die*!" Donna said, voice rising. "What am I supposed to do? Tell them all that Empress Donna rewrote the rules because I can, and that they can go pound sand if they don't like it?"

"I'm your *daughter*!"

"Now that it matters," Will spat. "You disowned her on account of her voting record—sorry, no takebacks."

"You're really gonna bring that up at a time like this?" Ashley indignantly screeched.

"Abso-fucking-lutely!" Will thundered. "We're a team, and your toxic personality and shitty attitude are gonna be one great big monkey wrench thrown into the works that'll get us all killed. I'm not putting my son's life at risk for you—sorry, not sorry."

"Do you know how to garden?" Donna asked Ashley. "Can you shoot a rifle? Can we put our lives in your hands and trust you to stay awake on guard duty at night in the cold and rain? You and I both know the answer to that."

"Mom . . ."

"I've got dozens of families counting on me now. I can't risk their lives for one person, even if it is my daughter. Fathers, mothers, children, and grandchildren—like the one you heartlessly cut out of our lives! *Over politics!*" Donna screamed. "When your father was on his deathbed, all he talked about at the end was how much he missed you and how he wanted to see you and Sonia one last time. And you didn't even bother to return my calls when I told you he was dying!"

"You can't . . ." Ashley sputtered.

"Yes, we can," Will sternly cut her off. "You got no idea what you did to Mom and Dad. And to me. I hope Sonia's OK, and we'll pray every day for her safety. But as for you, this is what you chose. If you hadn't let Harvard Yard turn you into a brainwashed NPC, you and Sonia'd be here, safe, with us. Remember that."

"But I'll die out here!" Ashley screamed in desperation.

With a signal from Donna, Gunnar emerged from the woods and wordlessly tossed a drawstring bag at Ashley's feet. "There's food, water, and medicine in there, along with a water purifying straw and instructions on how to use it," Donna said. "Iron Point's about three miles down the road, and from what we've been hearing, they sound more accommodating to refugees—maybe they can help you. You have a lot of growing up to do, Ashley. If you make it through the winter and learn how to think about people other than yourself, come back here and we'll reconsider."

"And if I sneak in? You'd really shoot me?" Ashley challenged.

"We wouldn't have to," Gunnar sneered, his voice dripping contempt. "These woods are filled with booby traps—they start out with noise-makers, flares, stuff to scare people off. Then they get really nasty. You'd be dead before you got within sight of us."

Ashley stood silent for a long moment before scooping up the bag. "You'll be sorry for this."

"I'm sorry for a great many things," Donna said, pointing down the road. "God be with you." Her daughter grumbled a slew of bad words and stormed away, her indignant march becoming slumped and defeated as she disappeared around the bend.

"You all right, Mom?" Will asked, breaking the uncomfortable silence.

"No, I'm not," Donna tiredly answered, still gazing after her wayward child.

"Permission to speak freely, Big Mama?" Gunnar asked.

"Always."

"Letting her go ain't very smart. If she goes blabbin' about our little survival Shangri-La, we could end up with every hungry soul within a hundred miles beatin' a path to our door."

Donna turned to Gunnar, her eyes leaden with pain. "Young man, if that was your daughter, and I asked you to kill her to keep our existence a secret, could you do it?" His silence answered the question.

"Let's round up the QRF and head back," Donna ordered, turning off her radio. "Will, I'm gonna tune out for a little bit—you think you can switch over to my frequency and be the honcho for a spell?" He nodded, hugging his mother before she followed Gunnar around the gate.

Will melted back into the woods, meandering around two hidden trip flares to make his way to the well-concealed LP/OP where he had spent the past four hours before Ashley appeared. Will radioed in for a replacement to finish the last two hours of his shift as the older man sharing the foxhole with him took a long pull of water from his military surplus green plastic canteen. "Who in the hell was that?" he asked.

"Just some nobody," Will truthfully answered.

CHAPTER 11

GERMANY

"I'm sorry ya cain't get any news 'bout your hometown," the Alabama National Guard sergeant in charge of his half of the sentry detail told Martin, checking his wristwatch for the umpteenth time since the midnight start of their shift. "Believe me, I know how ya feel."

Damn, this guy loves to talk, Martin complained to himself in the dark; their two fire teams were assigned to guard the entrance to Gate 5, where two weeks prior, Martin and his men had witnessed the slaughter of townspeople trying to storm their way onto post. "My family's in Vance," the sergeant droned on in his thick Southern drawl, "which is offa I-20, right smack dab between all the scared shitless people in Birmingham an' Tuscaloosa. I don't wanna think 'bout what's happenin' with all the refugees flowin' through town."

The sergeant checked the time yet again, his nervous face glowing green from his wristwatch's night light. "Got a hot date or something?" Martin asked. "It's not even 0300 yet. Our relief doesn't come 'til zero six."

"Just tryin' to stay awake. A coffee'd go down real nice right 'bout now—a real coffee, not that freeze-dried MRE shit."

"Amen to that—haven't seen real coffee in weeks," Martin agreed, rising to stretch from their position behind the concrete barrier next to the prefab guard shack. He clicked the ENVG-B night vision goggles strapped to his combat helmet over his eyes. "I'm gonna check on my boys—be back in a flash."

"Hurry up and get back so's I can take a leak," the sergeant said to the back of Martin's head, sneaking another peek at his watch.

Martin strode down the road, his surroundings glowing with bright funky outlines through the futuristic night vision system that was light years ahead of its predecessors; aside from the faint glow from the handful of lights that remained on at Rose Barracks, the loss of grid power with the collapse had made nighttime dark as pitch. The stench of the vile port-o-johns that the local pumping company had long stopped servicing assaulted Martin's nose as he knelt down at the foxhole where Theo and Josh had been watching the entrance.

"How we doin'?" Martin whispered.

"Readier'n I've ever been to do anythin'," Theo whispered back from behind the position's imposing black M240B heavy machine gun. "Twenty minutes, an' we make our move."

"Change of plans—we go in five."

"What gives?" Theo nervously asked.

Martin scanned around for prying ears. "These yokels are up to something. Their sergeant's been checkin' the time every other minute, and he's jitterier than Josh reachin' second base for the first time with a real live girl. I don't like it."

"That'd explain the little geek who keeps botherin' us," Josh said, shooting a glance at the foxhole manned by the Alabama soldiers on the other side of the road. "Their runner's come over twice in the past half hour offering to take watch on the 240 so we can take a break and stretch our legs."

"Maybe we should take 'im up on his generous offer. Split 'em up," Theo grunted.

"Do it," Martin hissed. "Remember, we're still on the same team—no fuckin' anyone up unless it's absolutely necessary." Theo and Josh grimly nodded their understanding as Martin rose to his feet, adrenaline erasing his near-constant backache from the omnipresent weight of his rifle and plate carrier vest. He stopped under Gate 5's deactivated floodlights—they were only turned on for the very rare times when traffic passed through—and fished a cheap civilian FRS radio from his pocket, looking around once again for eavesdroppers before thumbing the transmit button.

"Patton?"

"Here."

"You in position?"

"Affirmative."

"Timetable's changed. We're going now."

"Roger that. Moving."

"Counting on it. Out."

Martin quietly unclipped his M5 rifle from its three-point chest harness and tried to act calm as he walked back to the guard shack and the Alabama sergeant eagerly awaiting his return.

"About damn time—my back teeth are swimmin'," the sergeant managed to say before Martin closed the distance with blazing combat speed and violently butted his rifle into his stomach. While the sergeant's tactical vest stopped the blow from knocking the wind out of him, it didn't prevent him from being thrown flat on his ass.

The hapless sergeant looked up the moment he got his bearings to see Martin's rifle aimed squarely at his chest. "Move and you're dead," Martin growled.

Patton materialized to the sergeant's left to put him in a crossfire, his rifle likewise aimed at his vitals. "I'd believe him, if I were you."

The muffled *pop* of a CS gas grenade followed by the hissing release of its noxious contents came from the direction of the foxholes a second later. *"What the—?!"* one of the Alabama soldiers screamed before being overcome by coughing and retching.

"What the *fuck* you doin'?" the sergeant yelled.

"Gettin' the hell outta here," Martin shot back. "Toss your rifle and sidearm my way—slowly, or they're gonna hafta send out a detail to find your brains."

"Y'all are desertin'?!" the sergeant asked in disbelief.

"Very astute, Cap'n Obvious," Martin snarked as Theo and Josh trotted to them. "Your rifle and sidearm. Now."

"Easy there, hoss," the sergeant said, slowly raising his hands. "Listen—it's just fine by us if you're tuckin' tail . . ."

A strobe-like flash lit up from behind the trees in the direction of Rose Barracks, followed by a deafening *boom* and the cacophony of small-arms fire.

"We wanna go home, too!" the sergeant continued, interrupted by the racket of the Alabama National Guard's mutiny. "We were s'posed to take y'all outta action, but now we don't gotta. Now could ya stop pointin' your boomstick at me?"

"I'll be damned," Martin incredulously said, cautiously lowering his rifle as he stared at the explosion's plume rising over the treetops, glowing red with the fire it had started. A duller, more distant flash lit up the northeastern sky from the direction of Grafenwoehr, followed by the chatter of gunfire rising from Tower Barracks. "The whole fuckin' Fourth Alabama's in on this?"

"Damn straight," the sergeant confirmed, the thunder of the second explosion punctuating his answer as he dusted himself off. "If ya hadn't heard, Alabama's leavin' the Union, and the gov'nor wants us back home where we belong. We ain't stayin' here to die for the Germans or anyone else."

"How you guys gettin' back stateside if you pull this off?" Martin asked.

"That's way above my pay grade. Same way y'all are, I guess—dumb luck an' the grace o' God."

"Excuse me, um, sergeants?" Patton interjected, the desperate sarcasm in his voice cutting like a knife through the distant gunfire. "All this is absolutely fascinating, but we're gonna be continuing this lovely discussion in the stockade if we don't move out."

"Start 'er up!" Martin ordered, turning to Theo as Patton dashed for the armored Humvee parked behind the guard shack. "You got the 240?"

"Ours and theirs—already loaded 'em up, along with the ammo," Theo answered. "All that's left in our foxhole is a PFC who's enjoyin' some sleepytime."

"You didn't hurt my guys, didja?!" the sergeant exclaimed.

"Nope, but they're gonna be hating life for a while—tear gas is a bitch," Josh said, whipping the soldiers' three confiscated M5 rifles off his back and dropping them in a pile. "You can give 'em these back, with our humble apologies."

"We were s'posed to grab the Humvee and the 240s," the sergeant said as the Humvee's engine roared to life, Martin and his men raising their night vision just in time as its headlights lit up the dark.

"You're lucky we're letting you keep your rifles. Shoulda gotten the drop on us first, buddy—you snooze, you lose," Martin unapologetically retorted as the Humvee skidded to a halt behind him. Martin climbed into the front passenger seat as Theo and Josh squeezed into the back, which was stuffed to its hard-shell roof with purloined supplies. "Good luck, Johnny Reb. Hope you get home—I mean that."

The sergeant flashed a defeated smile. "Same to you, Billy Yank," he said as the Humvee weaved around the barriers and disappeared into the black.

CHAPTER 12

MICHIGAN

Melinda's fingers danced like sprites on the keys of her flute, her double-octave chromatic scale joining the hundred disjointed melodies of her fellow stage musicians warming up for their farewell concert.

She stared out in awe at the audience that had packed the four-thousand-seat Kresge Auditorium. Students had reoccupied Interlochen Public Radio to spread word of the performance until the power had gone out and stayed out, and people had poured in by school bus and convoy from neighboring small towns and as far away as Traverse City, taking a gamble that the pandemic had burned itself out before reaching rural Michigan. After the show, Interlochen's remaining young children would leave with the audience, leaving Melinda and the other high school kids to find their own way.

A steady breeze blew from Green Lake through the open-air venue, bringing some relief from the early afternoon heat; the storm clouds that had threatened to rain out the orchestra's swan song performance had harmlessly blown over. Her instrument warmed up and ready to go, Melinda scooted forward in her folding metal chair and adjusted her music stand for the hundredth time.

Musicians fell silent as the lead violin player stood up and took a bow to the audience's applause, signaling that the show was about to begin, and the first chair oboe played B-flat for the orchestra to tune. The crowd leaped to its feet as the conductor of the Interlochen Orchestra crossed to center stage to the stomping of the musicians' feet—an old tradition by which the performers could applaud while holding instruments. With a warm smile and a bow, Emil Jorgensen acknowledged the hodgepodge band with a sweeping of his arm to the audience's deafening roar.

"Thank you! Thank you all for coming out!" the old man enthusiastically hollered in his Scandinavian accent over the din, waving his hands for quiet as the audience slowly returned to their seats; the auditorium's phenomenal acoustics made it easy for him to be heard despite the sound system not working. "We hope you enjoy our show, and please bear with us—after all, we're sight-reading most of our selections this afternoon. This may be the most talented group of young musicians ever assembled, but we're only human, so we apologize in advance for any sour notes!" he joked. Emil and a handpicked group of older players had spent the better part of an evening combing the voluminous archives of the Fennell Music Library by flashlight to select their pieces. He had ruled that every selection had to be uplifting, with nothing warlike or foreboding—requests for Verdi's "Dies Irae" or Carl Orff's "O Fortuna" were immediately rebuffed, not the least reason for which was the fact that they had no choir.

The wizened conductor slicked back his mane of white hair and stepped onto the conductor's podium. Dulcy turned quick enough to give Melinda a wink as Emil theatrically tapped his baton on the stand.

This is gonna be one hell of a show, Melinda said to herself excitedly as she raised her flute to her lips.

Their first selection was the minute-long "Interlochen Theme," a passage from a symphony that the composer had partly written at the camp, and had graciously allowed to be used as its official anthem. The handful of noisy young children who had resisted their parents' efforts to keep quiet during Emil's introduction had fallen silent. "Music hath charms to soothe the savage beast," he said *sotto voce* to the musicians before looking to a young Chinese clarinetist who couldn't have been more than twelve—and with a point of his baton let him rip with the solo introduction to Gershwin's *Rhapsody in Blue* as if he had composed it himself.

The ninety-minute concert flew by for Melinda and the other performers as the shattered world around them disappeared, leaving only the music. Gershwin led to *The Cowboys* by John Williams, followed by the final movement of Dvorak's *New World Symphony*. Melinda's worries melted away as she played piece after piece, her universe consisting solely of the orchestra and its audience.

"This last song of the evening is more big band than orchestral," Emil said as a trombone player placed her horn on a stand and walked to the front of the stage, "but it's from the heart—and when this is all over, we hope to see you back. Feel free to sing along." With a voice gifted by God Himself, the young woman led the band in a performance of the World War II-era song "We'll Meet Again," and a surprising number of audience members knew the words. Melinda's heart beat harder as she sang the chorus; the concert would soon end, and when it did, the outside world—a world of plague and death with no help to turn to—would come crashing in at full speed and squeeze her in its deadly embrace.

The audience's roaring ovation quickly gave way to calls for an encore thundering across the auditorium, with Melinda and her fellow performers loudly and tearfully joining in. As long as they were on stage, they were alive, and not cast out to fend for themselves; every song they played was an extended lease on life.

Emil jokingly shrugged in acquiescence to the audience's wishes, eliciting another roar of applause as he turned to the performers for another go—returning to John Williams for *The Raiders March*, followed by the finale of Stravinsky's *The Firebird*. And with Emil's apology to the string players for having to sit it out, the slapdash orchestra's disproportionate brass and wind members tore the roof off with "Stars and Stripes Forever."

Calls for yet another encore, echoed even louder by the orchestra, boomed once again as Interlochen's president crossed the stage to take his place by the conductor, politely calling for silence.

"As much as Dr. Jorgensen and our students would like to play for you forever, and I think I speak for everyone here when I say they'd love to do exactly that . . ." the kindly middle-aged man said, pausing as the players cheered and hooted their approval, "we need to ensure that all of you have time to get home before sunset—with the lights out, we don't want any of you driving at night and getting hurt. That, and as talented as these kids are, they can't read music in the dark," he added to the audience's polite laughter. "For those of you who volunteered to take in the remaining young children whose parents, um, couldn't pick them up, we'll be walking them straight from here to your buses at the welcome center near the exit. And on behalf of myself and their parents, I simply say, God bless you . . ."

He paused, fighting a losing battle to keep his composure. "Ladies and gentlemen, it's been an honor performing for you for what hopefully won't be the last time. At the start of each summer camp, we assemble the children in these very seats, and I tell them all to make art and make friends." He turned to the students, tears streaming. "As you leave here, I task you to keep making art. Keep making music, and keep making friends. May each of you be a candle that lights this darkness—and wherever it is you go, may God be with you and keep you safe." The crowd rose in one last ovation as Emil and the president stepped back to recognize the orchestra, which leaped to its feet as one as the duo joined hands to end the performance with a sweeping bow.

***

Melinda and her fellow older musicians spent the next half hour saying tearful goodbyes and interrogating one another about their plans, trying their best to stretch out their time in a final but futile effort to stave off reality crushing their lives. Many, like Melinda and Dulcy, had some kind of a plan to get home or at least survive, but others didn't. A violinist from Hungary resignedly shrugged, wishing with a wan smile that she had had one final chance to perform Bartók before wandering away.

Dulcy grabbed Melinda's attention with a squeeze of her arm. "I'm heading back to finish packing," she said, clutching her violin and bow. "I'll whip us up a five-course meal tonight to celebrate heading out in style."

"What's really for dinner?"

"Fritos and Easy Cheese," Dulcy quipped. "And gooseberries from a patch in the woods I found when I was stashing our bikes."

"You sure they're gooseberries and not something poisonous?" Melinda asked half-seriously. "Don't kill us out of the starting gate."

"I pick 'em all the time with my dad and sister. You can try some of our jam when we get home—it's the best thing you've ever tasted," Dulcy said before exiting the stage and walking up an empty aisle, brushing the backs of the folding seats with a free hand.

Melinda caught a glimpse of Emil's white hair as he disappeared through one of the cavernous auditorium's exits. Her disappointment over not being able to thank him and say goodbye quickly turned to alarm upon noticing that he had left his wallet and baton on the conductor's stand—items that would be impossible to replace in a post-collapse world. *What if he needs his driver's license to prove who he is or something*, she silently fretted as she snatched them up and hopped down from the polished wooden stage to run after him, apologizing as she barely avoided plowing into a trumpet player. She squinted and shielded her eyes as she bolted into the light of the late afternoon sun, blinking away the dazzle before spotting the old man strolling down the wooded path past the Interlochen Bowl toward the camp cabins.

"Dr. Jorgensen! Dr. Jorgensen!" Melinda called out until Emil stopped and turned, grinning as she fought to catch her breath—stooped over, she matched his diminutive height. "Sir," she panted, holding out his belongings, "you forgot these."

"Thank you, my child, but I won't be needing them," he replied, folding Melinda's hand around his baton with wrinkled fingers. "Do with the wallet what you will, but I'd like you to keep this."

"But—"

"I won't be needing it anymore."

"Are . . . are you sure?" she stammered.

"I'm sure," Emil affirmed. "May I ask what you're going to do, young lady?"

"Try to make it home to Wisconsin. My friend and I are biking out in the morning."

"You'll make it—I have a good feeling about you. When this is all over, don't let my gift sit in a box somewhere. Use it to make music and light the dark, like the president said. Can you do that for me?" he sweetly asked. Melinda bit her lip and nodded as Emil dug into his trousers to check the time with a tarnished pocket watch. "Now, if you'll excuse me, my lovely wife is waiting for me at our home on the lake, and I don't want to be late."

"I can't think of a nicer way to spend the day," Melinda said. "Forgive me, sir, but I remember hearing that she passed."

"Four years ago—right after we bought the house."

"Oh," she blurted, realizing what he had admitted he intended to do without saying the words. "I'm sorry."

"Don't be—reunions are happy occasions. Remember what I said about that baton, now," Emil said and continued walking.

"Sir?"

Emil stopped again.

"You're headed my way—why walk alone? Would you mind a little company?"

The old man stood as upright as his age allowed. "Who am I to turn down a charming young lady? I don't think Margaret will mind."

With a smile, Melinda slipped her hand through the crook of his arm as they strolled down the path toward the summer cabins.

CHAPTER 13

GERMANY

The few brave locals who had cautiously ventured from their homes to gawk at the sounds of battle from Rose Barracks scurried back indoors at the sight of the headlights of the Humvee tearing down Vilseck's narrow streets.

Patton's frustration over having to drive with his protective mask on quickly turned to despair at the sight of the piles of trash and scampering vermin that defiled the once beautiful German town. He tightly rounded a corner anchored by a pharmacy looted long ago by desperate towns-people, gagging with disgust as he swerved to avoid a corpse in the road, scattering the rats that had been enjoying the bonanza.

"Damn," Josh grunted, grimacing behind his mask at the grisly sights flashing past their headlights like a slideshow of horrors. "This is how the Black Death got started—if the flu doesn't kill everyone, the diseases the rats are carryin' sure will."

Patton drove up onto the lawn of the home that Ann-Katryn shared with her parents and slammed on the brakes, thrusting his passengers into their seat belts and almost causing a box of MREs to fall into Josh's lap. "Keep your smart-ass observations to yourself, egghead!" Patton snarled, killing the engine. With the headlights off, the only illumination came from the dim glow of fires from Rose Barracks coloring the horizon a sickly yellow.

Martin ordered Theo to mount one of their M240B machine guns atop the Humvee and keep watch. "You got fifteen minutes, no more," he told Patton, grabbing his tactical vest one-handed and pulling him close to be heard through his mask over the distant chatter of gunfire. "I get the final say if she comes with—if she's been exposed to the flu, no deal. I'm not risking us all for one person."

"Fair enough," Patton said as Theo pulled the long black machine gun through the Humvee's hatch, seating it in the rotating turret ring with a metallic *clack*.

"And I'm coming in with you, because I don't completely trust you."

"Sergeant, I dunno how Ann-Katryn's parents'll—"

"It's my way or no way at all," Martin cut him off. "I'm glad you found true love, but you'll lie your ass off to my face if it means taking her along—because I'd do the exact same thing if I was in your shoes. *Doveryai, na proveryai.*"

"Huh?"

"'Trust, but verify'—something from the Cold War my high school history teacher made me write a hundred times, in Russian letters, because I mouthed off to him in class. Let's go, trooper," Martin ordered, falling in behind Patton. While Martin never liked school, he had always liked history teacher Eric Jaeger; Martin had emailed him the moment he got his orders for Vilseck, and Mr. Jaeger, an Army veteran himself whose parents had met while his father was stationed in Germany, had sent back an elated response. Martin had just enough time to hope that he and everyone else in Elkhorn were all right before Patton pounded on the front door.

"Ann-Katryn! It's me! Open up!"

No response. *Bam bam bam*, Patton pounded again. "It's Patton! *Please open up!*" he yelled with growing desperation, his rubber mask sucking to his face as he gulped air with the effort. He stepped back and raised his M5 rifle to shoot the lock when an older man's voice timidly called from inside in German-accented English.

"Patton, is that you?"

"Of course it's him, Papa! Let him in!" Ann-Katryn elatedly vouched, her voice sounding to Patton like a choir of angels lifting a heavy weight from his soul.

"Are you sick?" her father asked.

"No—we've been locked down since this whole thing started. Are you?"

"No. We have done the same."

"May we come in, *Herr Müeller*?"

"We?"

"Me and my sergeant—he's not sick either. I'll explain, but we don't have much time. Please."

The oaken door creaked open with the clicking and sliding of locks, and Ann-Katryn bounded into Patton's arms.

"Inside. Quickly," Dietrich Müeller urged, ushering his daughter and their unannounced guests with his free hand, his other hand clutching the polished wooden stock of a Blaser R8 bolt-action hunting rifle. While Ann-Katryn looked little worse for the wear aside from not wearing makeup, Dietrich's usually well-trimmed salt-and-pepper beard had grown bushier and unkempt, and he had lost a noticeable amount of weight. "We were awakened by the gunfire from the base," he told Martin as he leaned his rifle against the wall to lock the door. "What in the devil is going on?"

The sergeant's eyes bore straight into Dietrich's through the plastic shield of his protective mask. *"Das Ende,"* Martin coldly replied.

***

"No! I forbid it! Our son is dead, and you want to send our daughter away with these *soldiers*? Dietrich, have you lost your *mind*?!"

Martin stood as an uncomfortable spectator as Ann-Katryn's mother, Heidi, shrieked at her husband; while he spoke almost no German, her fury over the idea of entrusting Ann-Katryn's life to a gaggle of American deserters needed no translation. He had unmasked and had instantly regretted it, as the stink of trash, body odor, and funk from a house that had sealed itself off for a month added significantly to his unease. Patton had once told him that Ann-Katryn's mother had never been thrilled about American servicemen, much less her daughter dating one; unlike Dietrich, Heidi had grown up in the post-Soviet former East Germany, and therefore had no experience living among thousands of brash young GIs driven by a desire to drink themselves blind and screw anything that moved.

"I am an adult, Mama—this is not your decision to make!" Ann-Katryn angrily interjected.

"Hush," her father ordered in English. "Please go to your room—take Patton with you—and pack a bag with what you need."

"Are you *insane*?!" Heidi screamed at her husband as Ann-Katryn and Patton ran down the hall. "Konrad's lying dead at university, and there he will rot—we will never even get to bury him! And you want to send our only remaining child, *and our unborn grandchild*, out into this chaos? They will die, too!"

"They will die for sure if they stay here," Dietrich calmly replied.

"The announcer on the radio said the pandemic is ending!" Heidi pleaded, stabbing her finger at the red Eton shortwave radio on the living room table. "We just have to hang on! Like after the war!"

"The pandemic is ending because it is running out of people to kill—that is what the BBC announcer said, and I have not been able to pull in the BBC since. Deutche Welle is gone, too, because our *Deutschland* is gone," Dietrich said. "And the only reason we rebounded from the war was because of the bottomless generosity of the Americans—who right now are killing each other a couple of kilometers from here because America is splitting up and the reservists want to go home." Dietrich rolled up his sleeve to reveal a dirty bandage wrapped around his forearm. "Soon, the only thing left in Vilseck will be the rats, like the one that bit me and almost bit Ann-Katryn. The Americans are not going to save us this time, Heidi. No one is."

"Nein!" Heidi wailed, grabbing her graying hair as Dietrich took her in his arms. "I can't—I just can't . . ."

"There is nothing here for Ann-Katryn but death. Leaving with these soldiers is her only hope."

***

"When are they coming out?" Josh hissed, nervously eyeing the front door before continuing to scan the surrounding block of dark houses, the colorful view through his night vision reminiscent of the old *Predator* movies. "This is some damned spooky shit."

"Tell me 'bout it," Theo muttered from behind the machine gun. The fury of the fighting at Rose Barracks had tapered noticeably. "I wonder who won."

"Does it matter? The only thing that matters is getting outta here—with or without Patton and Ann-Katryn," Josh said. "Don't you dare tell him I said that."

"Was thinkin' the same thing."

Martin burst out the door, striding toward the Humvee with his mask back on and Patton, Ann-Katryn, and her family in tow. "We're poppin' smoke, boys, and we're heavy one *fräulein*. Theo, stay where you are on The Pig. Josh, grab a case of MREs and bring it inside for the Müellers."

"No offense, sergeant, but that ain't a good idea," Theo objected as Josh reached in through the back door. "What we got's all we got, and now we got five mouths to feed—six if ya count the baby."

"What we got's not gonna last us all the way back to the States by a longshot," Martin retorted. "We're gonna hafta forage and trust in God if we wanna get home. This may not be the smartest thing to do, but it's the right thing to do."

Heidi bawled as she embraced her daughter, who looked alien in the spare gas mask that Patton had fitted to her. "Your food gift is very generous, but we cannot accept it," Dietrich told Martin as Josh trotted by with the box.

"Yes you can, sir," Martin replied. "Hopefully help is coming, and this'll help get you through 'til then."

"I'll take care of Ann-Katryn and keep her safe, *Herr Müeller*," Patton promised, shaking Dietrich's hand. "You have my word."

"Danke," he said, slipping his arm around his inconsolable wife's shoulders and caressing the side of Ann-Katryn's masked face. "Be well, *mein Blümchen. Gott sei mit Ihnen allen.* Now go, before the Americans start looking for you." Ann-Katryn nodded, tears pooling under the rubber of her mask, before running for the Humvee with the team and

jumping into Theo's vacant seat as Patton gunned the engine and tore away into the night.

Martin gave the OK to unmask the moment they drove past the red-slash sign announcing the end of city limits. "Keep driving west—we gotta get as far as possible before dawn," he ordered Patton; while the revolt by the National Guard soldiers was an added bonus—with luck, it would be days or more until they were discovered missing, if at all—Martin wasn't about to take any chances. He rolled down his window and peeled off his mask to be rewarded with a blast of fresh air that caressed his sweat-soaked face.

Ann-Katryn gasped with relief as she pulled her mask up over her head, wincing as one of the straps painfully snagged a loose strand of blonde hair. "Thank you all," she said over the growl of the diesel engine shifting into a higher gear. "I don't know what more to say."

"You don't have to say anything," Martin said with a forced smile. "Welcome to the team—you, and your future bundle of joy."

"If you do not mind me asking, what is the plan?" she cautiously ventured, leaning to glance out the windshield as the headlights cut into the darkness of post-collapse Bavaria.

"You're looking at it, honey—get you and take off," Patton said without turning around.

"And pray," Martin added. "Pray like we've never prayed before."

CHAPTER 14

MICHIGAN

Melinda hastily scrawled the last-minute letter to her parents by the light of the morning sunbeam blazing through the stuffy camp cabin's window.

I hope you're not reading this, because that would mean we missed each other. I left with my friend Dulcy Bowers to stay with her dad in Mackinaw City. We're sticking mostly to US Route 31 and the lake shore—I drew a map of our route, with the address, on the back. If I have to move on from there, I'll leave a note with them. I miss you all so much, and I'll see you soon. Love, M.

Melinda capped the souvenir pen she had bought at the Interlochen gift shop for her late younger sister, and shoved it in her backpack next to her smart phone, which for all she knew contained the only pictures she would ever have of her family, friends, and life before the collapse. And, for the hundredth time since packing the night before, she moved her clothes to make sure she had packed her flute and Emil Jorgensen's baton, carefully wrapped in an old shirt.

Melinda licked the envelope shut, almost reverently laying it on the mattress before slipping on her backpack and taking one last look around the cabin, dust motes floating in the morning light. She stared forlornly at Anja's saxophone at the foot of her bunk, remembering how her cabinmate had wept like a lost soul upon being forced to abandon it; Anja had set out on foot after the concert with six other students, hoping to eventually reach her parents in Bardstown, Kentucky. *Please, God, let us all make it home*, she silently prayed before stepping outside into fresh air pleasantly tinged by the light summer rain that had passed through before dawn.

Dulcy straddled her ten-speed bicycle, a pack on her back and her violin stowed along with the meager provisions they had been able to scrounge in twin black canvas panniers strapped behind her seat. "You ready?"

"Let's do this," Melinda chimed, sneakers squishing on the wet walking path as she climbed onto her bike. "Thank you for giving me a few minutes to write that letter."

"No problem—I don't think you need to worry about your parents coming here after all this time, but better safe than sorry," Dulcy said. "You sleep any last night?"

"Not a wink," Melinda excitedly replied, feeling as exhilarated as she had the day that she and her dad loaded up the car to drive to Interlochen.

"Me neither, but I got a feeling that sleep's not gonna be a problem tonight for either of us," Dulcy said. "Try to keep up with me."

"Try? I'll do my best not to leave you eating my dust!" Melinda shot back.

With a playful *ring ring* of her handlebar bell, Dulcy stuck out her tongue and took off down the path, forcing Melinda to start after her with a wobble.

The duo took the scenic route out of Interlochen, its neglected landscaping doing little to detract from the campus's beauty. They offered a ring of the bell and a friendly one-handed wave to each of the handful of souls still remaining; Melinda wondered if their plan was what she had originally intended to do and stay, come what may.

Dulcy and Melinda whizzed by the beautiful rubble masonry Bonisteel Library which housed Interlochen's music repository—at more than one hundred thousand items, it boasted one of the world's largest performing ensemble collections. A small group of faculty, students, and townspeople had shut off the utilities and were doing what they could to board up and seal off the building, their labor a testament to the hope that it would one day reopen for musicians to discover its treasures, regardless of whether the collapse was a hiccup in the story of civilization or the start of a new Dark Age.

Melinda knew in her soul that it would be the former, and that somehow she would return to Interlochen when civilization rose from the ashes. Her heart soared as she slid into a higher gear to catch up with her friend.

CHAPTER 15

GERMANY

"How you take it, sergeant?" Josh called over his shoulder as he tended to a steaming canteen cup of freeze-dried coffee cooking over a heating tab.

"Let's not get into the habit of yelling in the field," Martin called back from the Humvee. "But as long as you just killed noise discipline, I'll take cream and sugar, please."

Josh tore open the packets from his MRE's accessory pouch and dumped them into the tin cup, stirring with a plastic spoon until the stubborn powdered non-dairy creamer finally dissolved. He rose with a groan, shifting dirt with his boot to smother the blue fire of the trioxane flame tab as the morning sun filtered through the thick, dark woods of Veldenstein Forest, where the team had holed up to catch their breath and figure out their next move.

Martin studied a Michelin map of Germany, one of several he had laid across the Humvee's hood, while Theo continued his vigil behind the M240B in the cupola. "Here you go, sergeant—best coffee in the world," Josh said, handing the drink to Martin. "Kinda sorta hot Taster's

Choice, served in the same cups we shave with. Just think of the stubble and Barbasol as extra vitamins."

"Shaving every day's not something we're gonna worry about anymore, until we get so bushy that our masks won't seal," Martin said, sipping the coffee with a grimace and setting it down so as not to spill it on the maps or the Eton emergency radio that Ann-Katryn's father had gifted them. "Same goes with our haircuts and clothing—GIs stick out in Germany like a sore thumb, and we gotta start thinking about blending in."

"With an armored Humvee and a bunch of cool Army gear?" Josh wisecracked.

Martin snorted and took another pull of the lousy coffee. "Go easy on me," he said, cocking his head at Patton and Ann-Katryn, who were asleep in each other's arms under a poncho liner on the forest floor. "Like Romeo over there told Juliet back in Vilseck, I'm making this up as I go."

Josh glanced at the couple and lowered his voice. "I'm glad we rescued her, sergeant—it was the right thing to do. But I'm just gonna say this plain—I got a bad feeling she's gonna be a fifth wheel," he admitted.

"That's where you're wrong, trooper," Martin said, returning to studying the maps. "What you call a fifth wheel, I call an invaluable asset—a native guide. My granddad served in Vietnam—he was in the bush and saw some shit, lemme tell ya—and the native attached to his unit got them outta more than one scrape alive. You speak German, thank the stars, but to the survivors we're gonna hafta deal with, you're still an *Ausländer*. Ann-Katryn not only knows the lay of the land, but she's also gonna be able to open doors for us that you can't."

"And what do we do seven months from now when she's ready to pop?"

"Throw her a fuckin' baby shower—we'll cross that bridge when we get to it," Martin snapped.

The singing of unfamiliar birds welcoming the rising sun punctuated an uncomfortable silence. "Sorry, sergeant," Josh offered.

"No worries," Martin said, choking down the last of his coffee and handing Josh back the cup. "If you, Theo, or Patton have an idea, or wanna tell me I have shit for brains, I wanna hear it. We gotta start thinkin' as a team if we're gonna get through this alive."

"That'd be a first if Patton gets himself a thought of any kind," Theo muttered from behind the machine gun. The trio's laughter brought some much-needed relief, and caused Patton to briefly stir before falling back asleep. "So, sarge, what's the plan?"

"Head west and take it one day at a time is the best answer I got right now," Martin answered, returning to the map to war-game out the ultimate field problem he had been presented. They had two ways to get back to CONUS—by air or by sea. To their west lay the two US Air Force bases at Ramstein and Spangdahlem; Martin had almost zero hope that they were operational at all, much less offering flights, which left reaching the coast and finding a boat—*talk about crossing a bridge when we get to it*, he dejectedly thought as his finger migrated across a map of France and the Low Countries. The English Channel was more than nine hundred kilometers away, and reaching it meant navigating a maze of back roads to avoid what was left of cities in what had been one of the most densely populated regions of Europe. That would take a lot more time, which also meant burning far more gas and eating far more food than they had.

The main advantage they had was their training, Martin reassured himself. They were cav scouts, military occupational specialty nineteen delta—the eyes and ears of the Army. Their job was to recon ahead to clandestinely gather information about the enemy and the terrain they controlled; short of the Special Forces, there was no MOS more qualified to take on the challenge of making their way home in a post-apocalyptic world.

"We'll head here, to Ebermannstadt, and see if it's safe to cross Autobahn 73 and squeeze between Nuremberg and Bamberg," Martin decided, tracing his finger northwest from their location near the village of Neuhaus an der Pegnitz. "Theo, Josh is gonna relieve you so you can grab some chow, but eat it now and taste it later, 'cause we're gonna be pullin' up stakes as soon as I tell Patton where to drive." He tossed Josh the square hand-crank emergency radio over the Humvee's hood. "Until further notice, you and Ann-Katryn are takin' turns monitoring the radio for any information you can gather. We're flying blind out here, and that by far's the biggest thing that could get us killed."

"You got this, Josh," Theo ribbed as he scrunched his huge frame to exit through the Humvee's passenger door. "You crank that radio like you yank your own crank ten times a day, and you'll do jus' fine."

Josh popped up through the turret as Theo grabbed a tan MRE pouch from the open box in the back. "Hey, sergeant—you were serious about ignoring AR 670-1 from now on?" he asked, referring to the regulation prescribing the Army's uniform and grooming standards. Martin looked up to answer before staring, dumbfounded, at the sight of Josh pinning a replica *Star Trek* comm badge onto his unzipped tactical vest.

"You gotta be shitting me," Martin said with a sardonic laugh—he had once caught Josh wearing it under his Class A uniform at the annual ball, and spent the following morning smoking him while nursing a four-alarm hangover. "What was it I told you? If I ever caught you wearing that on your uniform again . . ."

"You'd shove it so far down my throat that I'd have to give myself a prostate exam to beam up," Josh finished his sentence as he patted the gold and chrome insignia. "Don't get me wrong—I'm honored to join you all in this Twilight 2000 live-action role-play, but *Star Trek*'s my first love."

"And it's gonna be your only love," Theo said with a mouthful of cold MRE chili. "Don't ever ask why you ain't gettin' any."

Josh shrugged. "Well, I was gonna pin a peace symbol on my vest and write 'born to kill' on my helmet, but that's already been done."

"We're all gonna die," Martin muttered under his breath as he stepped over to wake Patton.

CHAPTER 16

ILLINOIS

"Ohmigod!" Kara exclaimed the moment she noticed her iPhone's 5G icon flash on, then off, then back on again.

"What? What is it?" Senior Airman Alexia Rios barked as she scrambled about her Scott Air Force Base dorm room, hastily stuffing clothes into the camouflage-patterned individual protective equipment bag on her unmade bed.

Kara flew to the window to keep the weak signal, thumbs flying over her phone's tiny screen to fire off a last-ditch message to her father, who had repeatedly tried—and failed—to fly her the rest of the way to Joint Base Lewis-McChord. *There are no flights left. We have to get out of here before the rioters come. I'll try to get a hold of you when I'm somewhere safe. I love you, Dad,* Kara hurriedly typed before stabbing the send button with a prayer that the message went through.

"Get the hell away from the window, you dumbass!" Alexia shouted before Kara dove for cover with the *pop pop pop* of nearby gunfire, her phone tumbling onto the room's rough brown carpeting. Gunshots had been a constant background noise in the week since Kara had flown into Scott, as St. Louis and its crime-ridden Illinois suburbs barely twenty miles to the northwest had fallen into lawlessness and chaos. It had grown louder and closer with each passing day—and now the criminals and gangs were making their way onto post, drawn to the potential plunder like a pack of wolves descending on a wounded animal.

Alexia grabbed another bag of survival gear from one of her roommates who had gone AWOL and violently shoved it into Kara's chest, almost knocking her back to the floor. The young Hispanic member of the Air Force Security Forces hoisted her bag over her shoulder, shrugging to adjust the load over her ballistic-plate tactical vest and the M4 carbine rifle and pistol magazines strapped across its front. "It's time to fuckin' leave," she said, her voice dripping with annoyance over having to babysit a general's little princess who wouldn't make it five minutes without someone to hold her hand.

Their footfalls echoed as they thundered down the concrete stairwell to the empty and ransacked common area of the Shiloh Dorms enlisted barracks, just in time to find Airman First Class Reed Finley smashing the glass of a vending machine with the butt of his rifle. "Surprised no one else thought of this—we need all the food we can get," Reed excitedly said as he chucked handfuls of candy and chips into a two-ply trash bag. Rampant inflation that had driven the cost of the snacks to more than twenty-five dollars an item had quickly made them unaffordable on enlisted airmen's salaries; a row of similarly vandalized machines revealed that Reed had been busy while Alexia and Kara packed. Reed handed Kara the loot and led the way through the front door.

Reed's silver Honda Civic was one of only a handful of vehicles left in the dorm parking lot, which made it easy to spot the three young men wearing low jeans, white tank tops, and red bandanas on their foreheads making a beeline for the car, crowbars and baseball bats in hand.

"Step away!" Reed ordered as he and his partner raised their rifles.

"What'd you say, mother—" one of the hoods arrogantly challenged, fearlessly striding toward them and reaching for a pistol tucked into the band of his jeans.

"Gun, gun, gun!" Alexia and Reed hollered in unison, shooting all three men repeatedly until they dropped. Kara shrieked and hit the ground, the parking lot's fresh black sealcoating burning her skin like a hot iron.

Out of habit, Reed almost grabbed for the nonexistent radio on his shoulder to report shots fired to the nonexistent dispatcher at the empty police station. The duo watched the downed criminals like hawks to Kara's whimpering chant of *oh God oh God oh God* before the thug who had challenged them, his shirt soaked with blood, made one last futile attempt to reach for his gun. Alexia and Reed thumbed their safeties and fired into the man, ending him. Alexia slid her bag to the ground one-handed, her rifle still aimed at the bodies. "Gotcha covered, Finley—grab my shit and start the car! Stay clear of 'em in case they got the flu!"

Reed snapped up her bag and ran to his Civic, popping the trunk. "Get your ass up, *güera fresa*," she growled back at Kara, "or stay here on the ground—doesn't matter to me either way." Kara sprang to her feet, averting her eyes from the grisly sight as she threw the bags of food and gear in the trunk next to her college rucksack and scrambled into the back seat. Reed sped out of the parking lot the moment Alexia jumped into the front passenger seat, pulling into a tight turn onto Enlisted Drive to the car's repetitive chime reminding them to fasten their seat belts.

"Thank you for not leaving me behind," Kara uncomfortably ventured, rolling down her window for relief from the car's summer stuffiness and the lingering pungent smell of cordite from the rifles.

"Don't thank me—thank Reed," Alexia responded, shifting her rifle to point toward the floor. "Bringing you along was his idea."

"And don't thank me just yet," Reed muttered, warily eyeing a lone civilian vehicle passing by on the deserted road. "Save it for after I manage to get us outta here in one piece."

Kara allowed her mind to wander with the first somewhat quiet moment since sunrise, when the two airmen assigned to look after the general's daughter banged on her door at the base's guest facility. *Thank God!* she had proclaimed, all but jumping for joy the moment Alexia told her to grab her stuff. *I was so worried Dad would never get me a flight out to JBLM!*

He didn't, and you don't, Reed had said, stopping Kara in her tracks. *You don't understand—we gotta bail. The chain of command's completely broken down, everyone's goin' AWOL, and we're about to get overrun by all the trash streaming outta St. Louis.* Kara had stared back in slack-jawed disbelief, words failing her. *We're punchin' out, and you gotta come with us if you wanna live.*

Reed drove by the base commissary and post exchange, where a growing mob was streaming out through shattered glass panes with whatever they could carry—only several hundred meters from the abandoned police station. "Oh, damn—Reed, get us outta here!" Alexia breathlessly said.

He floored the accelerator, tires squealing as he turned south onto Scott Drive toward the Belleville Gate leading off base. "Jesus Christ," he gasped at the sight of a pack of ne'er-do-wells streaming into the street at the gate to stop them; the road was lined with cars of previous victims intercepted before they could flee, their doors and trunks flung open. "Oh Jesus . . ."

"Mow through!" Alexia ordered, leaning out her window with her carbine and opening fire, downing two and scattering the rest.

Alexia tucked back inside as the car flew past the gate, Kara ducking with a scream to the sound of the thugs emptying their guns as Reed tore out of Scott Air Force Base and into the cornfields and woods of southern Illinois.

CHAPTER 17

GERMANY

Patton scanned the thick woods on both sides of the hiking path as he and Ann-Katryn walked toward the gasthaus nestled in the foothills of the Rhön Mountains.

The pleasant aroma of a fireplace greeted them as they drew closer to the stone inn that looked as if it had been plucked from a Brothers Grimm story and plopped down just outside the tiny town of Hacksrode, a clump of houses north of the former US military town of Schweinfurt. The well-maintained path ran past the inn, one of many that catered to a nation of hikers and cyclists.

"I'm nervous," Ann-Katryn fretted under her breath, eyeing the smoke curling from the stone chimney into the overcast sky.

"Don't be—all we're doing is nicely asking the owners if they're willing to barter for fuel and food," Patton said. His holstered Sig Sauer M17 handgun sat uncomfortably under his civilian light jacket, but he felt naked without his rifle; the fact that his buddies were covering them from a nearby rise in the woods offered little solace. "Just enjoy the walk."

"That is funny advice coming from you, *meinen Schatz*," Ann-Katryn responded with a nervous snicker. Patton snorted at the jab; while

Ann-Katryn loved going on *Volksmarches* like any self-respecting German, Patton couldn't stand them, griping every time she dragged him along that the Army offered him all the walking he needed without having to do it in his free time as well. He smiled wistfully with the memory of their last walk before the collapse—during which they snuck into the woods and had the fun that resulted in her delicate condition.

Patton pretended to adjust the civilian rucksack on his back as they neared the gasthaus so he could clandestinely toggle the transmit key for his concealed FRS radio. "We're comin' up—whaddya see?" he muttered out the corner of his mouth.

"Still nothing, except for the fella loading stuff into the Mog," Josh's voice crackled into Patton's earbud, its cord hidden by his collar and his shaggy black hair. The squat, olive drab Unimog truck and the young man loading it came into view as Patton and Ann-Katryn left the path and cut through the beer garden.

"Got it—keep your eyes peeled. Out," Patton said, relieved that they would be able to introduce themselves in full view of their overwatch, without having to step inside. "You're on, babe—you got this," he reassured his girlfriend.

The tall young man, his blonde hair sheared to a crewcut and wearing a jacket patterned with the German military's unique brown-mottled *Flecktarn* camouflage, had just locked the Mog's tailgate upright when he noticed the duo with a start. He strode toward them as Ann-Katryn nervously waved, as if to intercept them as far away from the truck as possible.

"Entschuldigung Sie bitte . . ." Ann-Katryn began as Patton did his best to follow along, recognizing snippets he had picked up from her and from his time in country. The man towered a head over both of them, reeking of beer and his bloodshot eyes darting nervously about—Pat-

ton's skin began to crawl with his sixth sense's screaming alarm that something wasn't right.

"Nein," the man hurriedly declined the moment Ann-Katryn finished her proposition, showing his palms as if to push them away. *"Wir brauchen nichts . . ."*

"He says they do not need anything and are not interested in trade," Ann-Katryn translated for Patton.

The man grew agitated with the realization that Patton was an American, and almost certainly a serviceman. *"Ihr müsst alle gehen,"* he insisted, pointing back to the trail and waving away with his other hand as if he was shooing a stray cat. *"Raus von hier!"*

"He's telling us to leave," Ann-Katryn anxiously said.

"I figured that out myself," Patton shot back. "Tell him—"

"No, *Amerikaner*—leave now!" he forcefully bellowed in English.

Patton grabbed Ann-Katryn's arm, stepping back with her to keep a safe distance. "Can you just hear us out for a damn minute—"

"Hilfe!" came a muffled shriek that cut through the argument like a knife. A terrified young woman, bound and gagged, darted through the delivery door screaming for help as a disheveled man brandishing a military rifle stumbled outside and angrily chased after her—he crumpled to the ground a second later as rifle fire from the team overwatch tore through him. Patton drew his Sig Sauer, body-checking Ann-Katryn out of the line of fire and shooting their interlocutor three times in the chest before he could drunkenly fumble a pistol from his coat pocket.

"Move move move!" Patton hollered, pulling Ann-Katryn to her feet and grabbing the hostage's arm to bolt for the safety of the woodline, roughly dragging the women down into a cut in the forest floor as a bullet whizzed by his head. Josh's agitated voice chattered into Patton's

ear demanding a status report as the team returned fire to keep their attackers' heads down.

"You speak English?" Patton hollered in the hostage's face as he yanked the gag from her mouth.

"A little!" she hysterically responded, grabbing the lapels of Patton's windbreaker the moment Ann-Katryn untied her. "You have to help! They came last night! My fam—"

"Shut up and listen!" Patton cut her off, forcefully prying the young lady's hands from him. "How many bad guys, and how many hostages? *Wiefiel?* Quickly!"

"Seven! They have my mom, dad, and brother!" she wailed before ducking as a bullet ripped into a nearby tree.

"Patton, SITREP, goddammit!" Martin's voice screamed into Patton's earbud.

"Does that include the two we just shot?" Patton asked the woman.

"Yes! *Do something!*"

Patton hurriedly relayed the information, his booming adrenaline-fueled voice piercing the oppressive silence that had settled over the battlefield; neither side had ammo to waste, and the team had to be extra cautious differentiating targets from hostages. Receiving Martin's hasty plan with a grunt, Patton quickly peeked over the lip of the cut before yanking the quick-release straps of his rucksack and re-drawing his Sig Sauer.

"You two, stay here—*bleib hier*," he emphasized to the innkeeper as he rose to a squat. "And stay down!"

"What are you *doing*?" Ann-Katryn cried with fear.

Patton quickly kissed her. "I'll be back."

He sprinted along the edge of the woods, Ann-Katryn and the freed hostage covering their ears as the Humvee-mounted M240B machine gun tore up the ground around the gasthaus with a thunderous roar to cover his advance. Patton leaped into the open to meet Martin and Theo as they stacked along the rough-hewn stone wall next to the ajar delivery door, rifles raised.

Patton found his rifle strapped across Martin's back. "We go when you're ready—speed, surprise, and violence of action," Martin hissed as he took position behind Theo and reached up to grab the large man's shoulder with his non-firing hand. Patton pulled back his rifle's charging handle just enough to ensure that it had a round chambered, and fished a spare magazine from Martin's tactical vest before stacking behind him to bring up the rear; the soldier at the end of the stack, regardless of rank, always gave the order to go in urban combat, lest the lead soldier charge inside before everyone was ready.

Theo shifted on the balls of his large feet, his boots grinding pebbles into the hard soil. "Oskar?" a shaky voice called out from the ajar door. "Oskar? *Bist du das?*"

"Any fuckin' time, Childress," Martin quietly growled through gritted teeth.

Patton passed along the order to go with a squeeze of Martin's shoulder, the trio charging single-file through the doorway—and almost headlong into two of the armed intruders. Theo brought his rifle up and planted three rounds into the man in front of him, moving to the far wall of the small storage room as Martin peeled left to shoot the second man in the chest and head, spraying the wall behind him with gore. *"Clear!"* all three soldiers hollered in unison from separate corners of the room before wordlessly stacking by the wooden door leading to the next room, with Martin now taking the lead and Theo bringing up the rear. *Four down, three to go,* Martin silently tallied, quietly eyeing the door as he ever so slightly twisted the knob to ensure it was unlocked. *No hinges visible—it opens in*, he took note, praying their enemy hadn't barricaded the door while silently cursing that the presence of hostages prevented him from lobbing a frag grenade in first; the supplies they had stolen from Rose Barracks hadn't include flashbangs.

With a squeeze of his shoulder, Martin flung open the door and barreled through, Patton and Theo on his heels to move out of the "fatal funnel" of the doorway as fast as possible.

Ann-Katryn hugged the young innkeeper as she screamed with the second round of gunfire that had erupted from inside the gasthaus scant seconds after the first. *"Freeze, motherfucker!"* Theo's deep bass voice echoed from inside, followed by more shots.

"Runner out the back!" Patton called out as a bald young man in a leather jacket burst into the open from the gasthaus's far side, wildly brandishing a handgun and frantically scanning his surroundings before deciding to make a run for it. He made it ten meters before Josh stitched him from buttocks to head with a burst of machine-gun fire.

***

Patton moaned with delight the moment he slid the first forkful of crispy roasted pork knuckle in dark beer gravy into his mouth. The gray clouds that had blanketed central Germany for three straight days had parted by dinnertime, and the innkeepers, elated not to be dead, feted their rescuers in the umbrella-shaded beer garden with the best meal they had eaten in a long time.

Killing the bandits was only the beginning of a long day for the team. They buried the bodies in the woods with the help of the men of Hacksrode, and unloaded the stolen provisions from the Unimog truck back into the storage room. Martin agreed to give the bandits' weapons to the innkeepers and villagers, save for four Heckler & Koch HK416 military rifles the team kept for themselves because it fired the NATO standard 5.56-millimeter round; Martin considered them insurance in case they ever ran out of the M5's exotic 6.8-millimeter ammo.

As for what to do with the loot the bandits had stolen from previous victims, the people of Hacksrode chose to split the food and other perishables amongst themselves, but hold onto the other valuables for safekeeping in the extremely unlikely event that the rightful owners ever came forward to claim them. However, Martin decided to take several rolls of silver coin, and several small gold coins still in their plastic protective slips, as payment for their services in case they ever needed hard currency—while the economic crash had rendered the US dollar and the Euro worthless, precious metals would hold their value as a universally accepted medium of exchange as they had since time immemorial.

Patton drained the last of his Erdinger wheat beer and looked over at Ann-Katryn, who picked unenthusiastically at a simple plate of *späetzle* dumplings—the nausea of her early pregnancy, and the grisly events of the day, had stolen her appetite. "How you doin', babe?" he asked, taking her hand under the table.

"All right," she said, sipping a glass of water. "But it should be me asking you this."

"Why do you say that?" Patton asked, savoring a forkful of gravy-covered potato dumpling.

"Have you ever killed anyone before today?"

"Nope—first time. Their first time, too, I think," Patton said, gesturing at the rest of the team. Josh and Theo were wordlessly wolfing down their food, while Martin, between bites, was giving Hacksrode's *bürgermeister* a crash course on how to build defenses to protect their town against any future unwelcome visitors. The mayor had grudgingly agreed, in exchange for the weapons and training, to spare enough diesel fuel to top the team off.

"And you are fine with this?" Ann-Katryn asked, troubled.

"It's what we're trained to do. I killed that guy before he could kill me—otherwise, he would've killed you and the baby or done God knows what to this poor family." He popped another forkful of *Schweinshaxe* into his mouth. "There're two kinds of fighters: the quick and the dead. You act on instinct or you die—you don't have time to think."

"But you do now."

"You're absolutely right," Patton said, a wry smile crossing his face. "And I think I'm gonna order another beer." No sooner had Patton held up the empty glass than the young lady they rescued strode to put another in his hand with a grateful smile. "Thank you," he said, taking a sip.

"No, sir, thank you," the woman replied.

Ann-Katryn leaned in and kissed Patton. "What she said."

CHAPTER 18

MICHIGAN

The bushes at the forest edge behind the darkened mom-and-pop sporting goods store rustled with Dulcy and Melinda's sneaky advance.

"I don't know if I can do this," Melinda nervously whispered over the chorus of crickets in the night, her heart threatening to pound out of her chest.

Dulcy swatted a mosquito on her neck—they had run out of repellent the day before. "I don't like stealing any more than you do, but we're out of options. It's this or we die of starvation or exposure."

The girls' plan to follow Route 31 straight to Mackinaw City got shot to hell within hours of leaving Interlochen. They had made it to Elk Rapids, a small town covering the tiny isthmus between Elk Lake and the Grand Traverse Bay arm of Lake Michigan, before being stopped at a roadblock by half a dozen armed townspeople who forbade them from passing through. The girls' pleas were cut short by a shot fired into the air and a final warning to turn around or face the ultimate consequence. It became a pattern repeated at town after town; residents worried about the H7N9 flu and criminals running wild wouldn't let them through, and each detour took Dulcy and Melinda farther away from their destination, forcing them to burn calories that they could ill afford to waste.

But water, or lack of it, had become the biggest threat to their survival—and in the heat and humidity of summer, they were losing it fast. Dulcy and Melinda were barely able to pack what they thought would be just enough to get them the 120 miles to Mackinaw City, if they rationed it; one of God's practical jokes on mankind was making the most vital necessity for human life besides air a bulky and heavy item to transport. While northern Michigan was blessed with an abundance of fresh water, the duo couldn't drink any of it for fear of getting sick with a waterborne illness.

The girls had stumbled across the sporting goods store outside of the small town of Elmira later that day. While it appeared boarded up and abandoned, they had pedaled by while two men armed with shotguns loaded several boxes from inside into a pickup truck. Curious, the girls left the road and watched as the men locked up and cautiously replaced the chains and plywood covering the front door before driving away. Dulcy and Melinda had spent the next day casing the store from the woods, and discovered that the back door had a window that could be broken so they could reach the lock. What's more, the men had not returned since.

"Let's go," Dulcy muttered in the darkness, parting the bushes before Melinda grabbed her arm.

"Wait," Melinda blurted. "I have a really bad feeling about this."

"Mel! We're running out of food and water, and we don't have camping stuff—we're one rainstorm away from getting drenched and sick," Dulcy anxiously hissed, her annoyance with once again having to reassure her travel companion adding a sharp edge to her words. "We don't have anything of value to trade that these guys would want, except for something that neither of us would be willing to give them, if you catch my meaning." The gurgling of Melinda's empty stomach rumbled in the still of the night as if to second Dulcy's argument. "My point exactly—your gut just vetoed your conscience. Now let's do this and scram—in and out."

Melinda followed Dulcy at a crouch to the back door, the cold dew clinging to the weeds of the unkempt back yard soaking through her jeans. They ducked down, backs to the cinderblock wall, on both sides of the battered door, its brown paint faded and peeling with age. Melinda reached into the laundry bag she had brought to carry off their loot and pulled out a softball-sized granite rock, nervously fumbling it into Dulcy's hands. Dulcy nervously exhaled, rising up just above the weeds to make sure the coast was clear before leaping to her feet and striking the window with the rock as hard as she could, the loud *bam* echoing in the night.

"Geez!" Melinda bleated.

"*Sssssh!*" Dulcy hissed, rising again to strike the window, the crack of glass rewarding her for her effort. "One more and I think we're in business. Be ready with the towel—I don't wanna cut myself to pieces reaching in to unlock the door!" Dulcy shot to her feet again, and Melinda flinched with the ear-splitting *crack* that followed.

"The whole world heard that!" Melinda whined, fishing the towel out of her bag before realizing that Dulcy had crumpled to the ground, clutching her throat with a horrific, sickening gurgle as blood spurted through her fingers.

Melinda had just enough time to scream before a flash from the woods heralded another thundering *crack*, and searing pain burned her cheek as if she had been slapped. She dropped the bag and ran for all she was worth back the way they came; Melinda had barely made it into the forest before tripping on an exposed root, sending her flying before landing flat on her stomach and knocking the wind out of her.

"The other one's gettin' away!" a man's excited voice called out as Melinda gasped for breath, struggling to keep moving.

"Let 'er go," another man said. "You'll roll your ankle chasin' after her—ain't worth it."

Melinda slithered behind a large tree, fighting the urge to puke. She watched as the two men emerged from the woods and into the weeds toward where Dulcy lay, their silhouettes just barely illuminated by starlight.

"Thank God you wanted to check on the shop, li'l brother!" the man with the deeper voice said. "Those two woulda robbed us blind."

They stopped dead in their tracks at the sound of Dulcy's grotesque gurgle rising like a wounded animal. "Holy shit, this one's still alive," the shrill-voiced younger brother said before the powerful beam of his Maglite flashlight sliced through the darkness. Melinda slapped her hand over her mouth at the sight of Dulcy's blood-soaked hand reaching out to them over the weeds. "God-*damn*!" the man gawked.

"Turn that damn thing off! You're lightin' us up like a beacon!" admonished the older brother, who was armed with a long rifle.

The flashlight winked off, returning the macabre scene to darkness. "She's just a kid!"

"A kid who was gonna steal the food we need to survive the winter," the older brother dispassionately retorted. "Dad built this business with his bare hands—I ain't gonna let our families starve to death 'cause every big-city asshole thinks they can help themselves to our stuff."

Dulcy moaned, blood rattling in her throat. "So whatta we do 'bout her?" the younger brother asked.

"Put her outta her misery."

"You for real?!"

They're gonna kill her, Melinda realized, paralyzed by fear. *Ohmigod ohmigod ohmigod . . .*

"What're we supposed to do? Drive her to the fuckin' hospital that's been closed since the flu started?" the older brother argued, ignoring Dulcy's loud gurgle in support of the idea. "Hell, our criminal lovin' governor'll probably lock *us* up instead of her! B'sides," the gunman continued, "I know a goner when I see one, sorry to say—I saw shit like this all the time in Iraq. She's *all* fucked up."

"I can't believe we're doin' this!" the younger brother whined.

"I don't like it any more'n you, but I ain't gonna let her lie here'n suffer," the older brother said, drawing his handgun with the *snap* of his holster's fastener and taking careful aim between Dulcy's eyes. "Miss, I'm sorry about this, and I'm sorry you made this horrible choice." Dulcy weakly gurgled one last time before the yard flashed with the *coup de grâce* that ended her life.

"Lord, ain't this some mess," the younger brother groaned. "Whadda we do with her?"

"Leave her 'til morning when we got some light an' we can give her a proper burial. I ain't no monster—she'll get dignity in death. Hey, li'l brother, ya understand why we had to do this, right?"

"Yeah, I do," he resignedly answered. "But that don't mean I gotta like it."

Melinda lay motionless until Dulcy's killers trundled back into the woods. After waiting for what seemed like an eternity, she rose up on all fours, violently threw up what little food she had in her, and blindly crashed through the forest back the way they had come as fast as her legs could carry her.

CHAPTER 19

ILLINOIS

Reed pulled over along a lonely, cornfield-lined stretch of State Route 158 and killed his engine, silencing the one radio station left on the air as it played prerecorded emergency instructions on a loop for whatever remained of St. Louis. He jumped out to give his Civic the once-over, swearing at the sight of several bullet holes in his trunk and a shattered brake light.

"Damn," Reed spat, running his finger around one of the holes. "I thought I heard us take a hit. Fuckers."

"Small price to pay," Alexia said, pointing back the way they came at the tendrils of smoke rising from Scott Air Force Base. "Anyone who couldn't get out is about to have a real bad day."

"There's a lotta that going around," Kara muttered, staring transfixed at the long black smear along the northwest horizon from where St. Louis and its suburbs were burning.

Reed walked over to his passengers—while solidly muscled, he was five foot eight and stood shorter than both of them. "We went AWOL in the nick of time, but that leaves the question of what the hell we're gonna do next."

"We're not AWOL—we were forced to abandon our post because we couldn't hold," Alexia snapped. "As far as I'm concerned, that means we're still in the Air Force, which means we report to surviving military authority."

"What surviving authority?" Reed asked incredulously. "If Scott Air Force Base is gone, I'm betting every other Air Force base is gone, too. We're on our own."

"No, we're not," Alexia shot back as she crawled across Reed's front seats to look in the driver-side door map pocket. "Right before the internet and phones started goin' down, I got a message from my ex-boyfriend at Whiteman saying they're OK—they got a lotta muscle shipped to 'em when the shit started hittin' the fan to help guard the B-2 bombers and the nukes. Whiteman Air Force Base isn't that far away—just the other side of Missouri—and it's one hella better plan than wanderin' the wastelands and livin' off the Hefty bag of Funyuns and Prime you boosted from the vending machines." She opened his glove box, which was empty aside from an old energy bar wrapper and his auto insurance card. "Where you keep your maps?"

"Here," Reed sheepishly replied, fishing his smart phone from his pocket. "No 5G, so no Google Maps."

"Are you fucking serious?" Alexia screeched, jumping out of the car and getting in his face. "You don't got a fucking paper map in your car?"

"OK, boomer!" Reed roared, hands balling into fists. "Maybe you should walk back to Scott and get the maps outta your piece of shit car that wouldn'ta made it five miles—"

"Excuse me!" Kara interrupted with a shout. The airmen turned to her, their red faces masks of fury. "I have a fifty-state pocket atlas in my rucksack—don't ask why, I just do. Here's my proposition—I give you the atlas, you two take me to this Whiteman place, and you both earn the eternal gratitude of a two-star general for saving his only daughter. And you," she continued, pointing at Alexia, "stop calling me Spanish names that I can only assume translate to 'stuck-up white bitch' or something similar."

The airmen looked at each other and back at Kara as the high-pitched screech of a summer cicada rose and fell. "Works for me," Alexia said with something resembling a grin as Kara strode to pop the trunk.

They spent several minutes flipping between the maps of southern Illinois and Missouri on the Civic's sun-baked hood, Reed's finger tracing a line from the border to the air force base southeast of Kansas City. "Two hundred thirty miles straight shot—thank God I snuck into the fuel point last night to top off," he confessed; illegally filling up a personal vehicle with government gas was a great way to end up in the stockade. "The only problem is . . ."

". . . that we can't take the direct route because St. Louis is gone," Alexia finished her partner's thought. "And that ain't our only problem—there aren't a whole lotta places to cross the Mississippi." She set her finger on the river just west of their location. "How about we cross at I-255 and loop around the city?"

"No way—you watch the news before it all went off the air? The interstates were nothin' but huge traffic jams. Besides, that's still way too close to St. Louis for comfort," Reed argued, tapping his finger to their south. "Our best shot is the Route 51 bridge at Chester, but that's fifty miles in the opposite direction—if we can't find a place to beg or steal gas, we'll be rolling into Whiteman on vapors."

"Think you can get us there, airman?" Alexia asked with an optimistic smile.

"Reckon I can, if you can be my GPS," Reed answered, handing her the atlas.

"I have an idea before we go," Kara said, walking to the farm field's edge to begin ripping ears of corn from their stalks. The trio went back and forth until corn crammed every nook and cranny of Reed's trunk.

"We're gonna get pretty tired of eatin' corn every day," Reed said as the trio stared down at their handiwork, their personal effects covered with cornsilk.

"I think I can officially speak for every surviving Mexican when I say you'll get used to it," Alexia joked.

"And it beats getting tired of starving," Kara remarked.

"I see your point," Reed said, slamming the trunk shut and brushing his hands. "Let's roll."

CHAPTER 20

MICHIGAN

Melinda hugged her knees, rocking back and forth as the rays of morning light started filtering through the trees.

She had only just stumbled upon the small clearing where she and Dulcy had stashed their bikes after a long and desperate night of wandering in circles through the woods. Exhausted and overwhelmed, she knew she had to get moving, and fast, but couldn't convince her body to comply. *I would've wasted away and died at Interlochen it hadn't been for Dulcy*, she said to herself. *She saved my life, and now she's dead.* Melinda spent another half hour staring blankly at the clearing's small pond as the temperature and humidity climbed with the morning sun, not caring about the possibility of the store owners coming after her to finish the job.

This wasn't your fault. You didn't want to rob the place, her conscience pleaded with her. *Dulcy would want you to keep going.*

"She'd want me to keep going," Melinda murmured to herself as she staggered to her feet, a stabbing pain in her calf threatening a charley horse before disappearing as quickly as it came. Her face stung to the touch, and she walked to the pond's edge to check her reflection in the water. An angry but superficial pair of cuts crossed her cheek from where the ricochet from the gunman's near miss nicked her with spalling from the cinderblock wall.

Melinda then realized that the reflection staring back at her was sprayed with Dulcy's blood.

Jumping back with a scream, Melinda yanked a change of clothes from her backpack and tore off her bloody shirt as if it was radioactive. She fell to her knees, dirtying her new outfit as she furiously dug a hole with her bare hands to bury her incriminating garments like a criminal on the lam. The job finished, she hammered the turned earth with balled fists and shrieked again in anger and desperation before snapping her mouth shut like a steel trap. *Do that again and they'll find you and kill you*, she silently berated herself as her outburst echoed into the woods. *Then you'll have a nice little grave right next to Dulcy's. Get away from here.*

Melinda lifted Dulcy's bike, the kickstand slightly sinking in the soft earth as she adjusted the seat for her height. She tore open the panniers to quickly inventory what was left of their supplies, selfishly realizing that Dulcys' death had given her a stay of execution from hunger and thirst. Suddenly ravenous, Melinda devoured their last chocolate brownie Clif bar and washed it down with a cautious gulp of water.

Her heart sank at the sight of Dulcy's violin and bow as she grabbed the road map to double-check the next leg of her journey. She would get to Mackinaw City and deliver Dulcy's worldly possessions to her family—and in exchange, get food, water, and as many nights as possible with a roof over her head. She hated herself for her selfish motive as she threw on her backpack and cautiously weaved the bicycle through the woods to the country road.

Melinda briefly panicked as she struggled to get her bearings before realizing that she needed to head east, and that the sun rose in the east. Squinting into the sunlight, she fished a pair of sunglasses from her backpack's front pocket and set them on her wounded face.

"I'm so sorry, Dulcy," she said with a ragged sigh before pushing off.

CHAPTER 21

The Iron Point squad car—one of only two the village police department had—rolled slowly by the half dozen well-armed people waiting at The Compound's entrance.

Police Chief Milo Beecher stared in disbelief at a trio of ceramic garden gnomes propped up on cinderblocks on the shoulder of the road, each of them flipping their middle fingers in front of a plywood board with GO AWAY spray-painted on it in bright orange letters. "This is gonna go just great," he muttered from the front passenger seat. "Looks like Donna and her new tenants are sendin' us a message."

"Let's send 'em one of our own," Village President Budd Alworth retorted from the back. "Park right in front of their little display to show that threats aren't gonna get 'em anywhere."

"If I'd known they sold lawn ornaments like that, I woulda got me one," the patrolman driving the cruiser arrogantly chuckled as he shut off the engine, glancing out of ingrained habit at the empty dashboard bracket for the laptop computer, which was useless with the loss of 5G internet.

"You and me both," Alworth said, pulling his slacks up to his protruding paunch; while he was far from starving, he was now using the actual notches of his belt rather than the extra one he had poked with a leather awl. He turned to find Milo pulling his M4 carbine out of the trunk. "Is that necessary?" he asked under his breath.

"You see what these lunatics are carryin'? They look like they're about to drop into Normandy," Beecher shot back. "Don't tell me how to do my job, Budd."

"Fair enough," Alworth conceded. "Let me do the talkin', and no sudden moves—let's see if we can do this with the carrot rather than the stick."

Donna watched the trio slowly make their way toward them—while she wore her trademark button-down flannel shirt and jeans, she had brought along her son, and Gunnar and his QRF, in full battle gear as a show of strength. "At the next Compound Council meeting," Will grumbled with a scowl, "I'm making a motion that we officially name the entrance 'Bad News Point.'"

"I'll second it," Gunnar quipped.

Donna curtly hushed them as the balding, portly village president offered his hand. "Hey, Donna—glad to see you an' your family are makin' it through the troubles all right."

"Same to you," Donna replied. "Let's get whatever this is over with—you didn't burn precious fuel just to pay us a social call."

Alworth pulled an envelope from his back pocket and handed it to Donna with a flourish. "It's my privilege to officially welcome you into the Village of Iron Point. This is a copy of the resolution passed at last night's board meeting officially annexing Moran Farm into village limits, as well as a copy of the governor's emergency decree allowing us to inspect your property to determine what supplies you have."

I hope you're happy, Ashley, Donna silently cursed her exiled daughter—she was the only possible way that Alworth and his cronies could have learned about their survival retreat.

"I gotta hand it to you, Donna. We were always glad to have you and your farm as neighbors—you always had the best watermelons around—but you and your friends might be exactly what Iron Point needs to make it through the winter," Alworth said, his politician's shit-eating grin disappearing as Donna handed him back the envelope without opening it. "Aren't 'cha gonna read it?"

"Nope—and my watermelons are gonna do even better next year, courtesy of the great big heap of bullshit you just delivered us," Donna flatly answered—in Wisconsin, municipalities wanting to annex land had to jump through a gauntlet of hoops that included court hearings and a voter referendum. "This is about as legal as me declaring myself queen."

"Well, I'm sorry, Donna, but that emergency decree the governor signed at the start of the crisis suspending peacetime laws makes it legal."

"You mean our *former* governor?" Donna sneered. "Our former governor who caught the flu and died because he went to a fundraiser after issuing stay-at-home orders for everyone else? That moron?"

"It doesn't matter," Alworth testily replied, annoyance growing over the challenge to his authority. "What matters is that you comply."

"I think it's time for you gentlemen to leave," Donna said.

"So you survivalists or preppers or whatever are just gonna sit on your huge pile of food while the children of Iron Point starve?" Beecher angrily challenged.

"What part of 'leave' do you tyrants not understand?" Gunnar growled.

"Donna, you don't got a choice in the matter! We're talkin' national catastrophe here, and everybody's gotta do their part—includin' you," Alworth declared, pausing to let the gravity of his words sink in. "We can do this the easy way, or the hard way."

"I was about to say the same thing—but unfortunately, you've already decided to choose the hard way," Donna said, fishing a pair of foam plugs from her shirt pocket and stuffing them in her ears.

"What're those for?" Alworth warily asked.

"For this."

The garden gnomes exploded with a thundering *ka-boom*, shredding the squad car with shrapnel and forcing the unwanted visitors to hit the dirt for dear life. The QRF descended on them like a raptor on a squirrel, disarming the chief and the patrol officer as hoots and cheers rose up from the farm. "That . . . was . . . *awesome!*" Will's son, Ethan, exclaimed in the distance.

Beecher leaped to his feet, his uniform disheveled and dirty as his patrol officer helped the village president off the gravel road. "Are you fuckin' *crazy*, lady?!" he screamed, wild-eyed.

"Like a fox—it's amazing what you can do with ball bearings, fertilizer, and Tannerite, isn't it?" Donna said with a wicked grin as she pocketed her earplugs.

"You heard Mom—vamoose," Will ordered, shaking his head to get rid of the ringing in his ears. "Sorry you gotta walk, but I wouldn't try starting your engine—you might finish what the gnomes started." He took an exaggerated sniff of air that was heavy with the smell of gasoline dripping from the squad car's punctured tank.

"You assholes got no idea what you just started," Alworth snarled, his crimson face matching the spots of blood on his arms and short-sleeve dress shirt from diving onto the gravel road. His anger quickly turned to fear as he flinched with the loud *ping* of a rifle bullet piercing the red township fire district sign across the street.

"Whatever you start, we'll finish. You show your faces here again, and our marksmen'll blow off one of your appendages—and your wives'll weep when they find out which one. Except for you, Jabba," Gunnar sneered at Alworth. "If *you* can't even find your dick under all that blubber, I don't reckon we'll be able to, either."

Donna pointed down the road. "That was a warning shot, gentlemen. The next one won't be. Start walking."

The group watched the officials slink away like Ashley before them, their shoes crunching on the loose rock. "We thought we wouldn't hafta deal with city people and government commissars out here in the middle of nowhere, yet here we are," Gunnar spat, the scowl on his face communicating to Donna what he didn't have the nerve to say out loud—her act of mercy toward her daughter, no matter how understandable, had gotten them into this fix.

Will sighed. "Before the collapse, we proudly flew the 'thin blue line' flag at my house to support law enforcement. And now we just assaulted two cops and blew up their car."

"They wanna disregard their oaths to uphold the Constitution, they ain't cops," Gunnar retorted, signaling for the QRF to head back up to the farm. "Big Mama, we need to send a detail to push that squad car outta here so it doesn't give attackers cover and concealment."

"Will, round up some strong backs and make it happen," Donna ordered as they walked around the iron gate. "But don't push it *too* far away—a smashed cop car will scare people off more than lawn decorations flipping the bird ever could."

"Agreed," Will said, falling in behind his mom and the QRF. "Besides, with no more Home Depot, we're fresh outta gnomes."

CHAPTER 22

MICHIGAN

Melinda squeezed her brakes so hard that she almost dumped her bike.

She shook her head to ensure that the young child sitting at the edge of the lonely country road wasn't a mirage, a jabbing pain driving into her temples like icepicks from hunger, thirst, and fatigue rewarding her for the effort. But the boy selling lemonade at the end of his driveway was as real as she was.

The boy eagerly eyed his prospective customer as Melinda cautiously walked her bike to the young entrepreneur, who sat at a folding table decorated with a colorful homemade sign offering lemonade for a dollar a cup. "Hi," he ventured from behind shaggy blonde locks, his face and arms red with sunburn. "You thirsty?"

"Very," she said, peeling her sweat-drenched t-shirt from her skin under the baking noontime sun. "A dollar, huh?"

"Yup!"

Melinda's eyes went wide at the sight of ice cubes floating in the pitcher—which meant that the young man's home had power. "If I pay you for the whole pitcher, can I stand here and drink it?"

The boy's sunburned face lit up. "Wow, really? Sure!" he exclaimed, pulling a paper cup from the top of his stack and carefully filling it from the condensation-soaked vessel, an ice cube tumbling down with a small splash. Melinda's mind raced with questions—none of this made any sense whatsoever—but all she could think about in the moment was her thirst and her dangerously low supply of drinking water. She unzipped her backpack and handed the boy a twenty-dollar bill from Emil Jorgensen's wallet, which for whatever reason she had decided to keep. The boy happily shoved the now-worthless currency in a Mason jar as Melinda downed the glass in a gulp and eagerly set it down for a refill, the powdered drink mix and sugar doing little to mask the mineral tang of well water.

"Thank you," Melinda said after downing her fifth straight cup. "What's your name?"

"Jimmy."

"My name's Melinda. I'm very happy to meet you. How old are you?"

"Eight and a half," the boy answered proudly.

She looked down at the money jar, which was empty save for her payment. "Was I your first customer today?"

"My first customer ever."

Melinda set her cup on the table for a reload. "Jimmy, are your mom and dad here? May I talk to them?"

He shook his head. "They told me to stay away from them until they got better."

Melinda just barely suppressed the panicked urge to leap back and cover her nose and mouth. "How long ago was that, Jimmy? Do you remember?" she nervously asked.

"Right after Uncle Alex and Aunt Jenny came here to stay with us—once the bad things started."

She breathed a sigh of relief with the realization that the boy would have gotten sick by now if he had been exposed to the flu. Jimmy took a wary step back as Melinda took a knee in front of him. "You shouldn't be out here all by yourself. It's not safe," Melinda said. "Where are your mom and dad now?"

"The guesthouse out back—that's where they're all staying."

"Can you show me?" Melinda asked, skin crawling. "We'll, um, stay far away."

"Well, OK," he hesitantly replied, snatching up his money jar. "No one's gonna steal my lemonade?"

"No. I promise."

Melinda walked her bike up the driveway toward the large house; its roof was covered with solar panels, and another large panel glistened in the sun in the front yard. "This is Uncle Alex's," Jimmy said, running his hand down the length of a tan camper hitched to a large black Ram pickup truck. "They came from the city to stay with us, but they got sick, then Mom and Dad and Brittany—that's my big sister—got sick, too."

Jimmy led Melinda around the garage into the side yard, where a horrible, sickly sweet stench hit her like a hammer. One step into the backyard was all she could manage—behind a huge overgrown garden rustling with wildlife that scattered at their approach sat a small guesthouse surrounded by roiling clouds of flies.

"They told me not to come near so I wouldn't catch it," Jimmy said.

Melinda scurried back around the corner, gasping for air fouled by the reek of decomposition and forcing herself not to scream for the boy's sake. "Have you been alone all this time?" she asked, just barely stifling a gag as she fought to keep down the lemonade sloshing in her belly like a waterskin.

"Yeah," Jimmy said, not even acknowledging the smell.

"Can I come inside? I don't think your parents would mind. You can show me your toys."

"OK!" he exclaimed. "Can you help me take down my lemonade stand first?"

"Sure," she answered, her soul leaden with a bottomless pity as she watched Jimmy tear away and gallop down the driveway.

***

Jimmy enthusiastically guided Melinda by the hand through the comfortable, air-conditioned house, his tour quickly revealing how the little boy had managed to survive for so long on his own.

His parents had been preppers, and had chosen this quiet rural corner of Michigan to set up their homestead in the event of a catastrophe. The solar panels and battery banks they had installed to power the house weren't connected to the grid, Jimmy explained; his dad spurned the opportunity to collect a monthly check from the utility company for generating power in exchange for keeping their independence in case the grid went down. The boy's knowledge for someone his age went far deeper than hero worship of his parents, Melinda thought while Jimmy talked her through the living room bookcase full of preparedness and homesteading books—it was obvious that his mom and dad had begun pounding self-sufficiency into his head at an early age. Several books about raising children with autism caught her attention. *Jimmy or his sister?* she silently wondered.

Jimmy led her to the basement, and with the flick of a light switch revealed a main room packed floor to ceiling with food. "Holy cow," Melinda whispered, gawking at row upon row of shelves of cans, boxes, and jars.

"Mom says we have enough to last years. The green metal boxes aren't food—they're bullets for the guns," Jimmy said. "Dad keeps 'em locked up and I'm not allowed to touch 'em—he says one day, when I'm ready, but I'm not ready yet."

Melinda eyed an open box of Mountain House freeze-dried meals that still had the shipping label attached to it. "Callahan," she read aloud. "Is that your last name, Jimmy?" He nodded. "Is this what you've been eating since your parents went out back?"

"Yeah. I can add the hot water. Mom doesn't let me cook anything without her help."

Melinda's gaze returned to the doe-eyed boy trying hard to impress his guest. Foreseeing the collapse, his parents had moved heaven and earth, and had spent untold riches, to protect the people they loved—only to perish on account of a family member bringing the plague to their front door.

"You're a very smart and resourceful little boy, Jimmy Callahan." The boy beamed with pride as she reached into the box and grabbed a foil pouch of chicken fajita filling. "How's this stuff taste?"

"Good, but everything tastes good when you're hungry—Mom says that all the time."

"Jimmy, what's your favorite thing to eat in the whole world?" Melinda asked, returning the pouch where she found it. "If you could eat anything you wanted, what would it be?"

"Spaghetti," he answered without hesitation.

"And here I thought you'd give me a challenge," Melinda said as she scanned the shelves and quickly located dried spaghetti and home-canned meat sauce. She smiled warmly as she spied home-canned apples, canned butter, and shortening. "And how about apple pie for dessert?"

"Wow, really, Minda?" Jimmy cheered, jumping up and down with excitement.

"Really!" she answered with a laugh over his response and the cute way he butchered her name. Melinda's stomach loudly growled in anticipation, but filling her own belly was the furthest thing from her mind—she wanted to make this poor, lonely boy the best meal he'd ever eaten.

"Then we can play with my toys?" Jimmy asked. "I just got the Bluey house for my birthday!"

Melinda handed him the spaghetti and shortening to take upstairs. "You got yourself a playdate."

***

The skies, which had begun to grow dark in the afternoon, had finally opened up about half an hour after Melinda and Jimmy crawled into his bed.

Jimmy had insisted that she stay with him as thunder rattled the house and lightning flashed through the thin curtains; he confided in her that he had hidden under his bed alone the handful of times that thunderstorms had blown through since his family locked themselves away.

Melinda set aside the illustrated children's Bible that Jimmy had asked her to read from as sleep began to take him. Had she not come across Jimmy, she would be outside—hungry and soaked to the bone, trying desperately to collect rainwater so she could stay alive for a couple more days. Instead, she was warm, dry, and after taking an actual bath, felt normal for the first time in a long time. She would have to think about her next steps in the morning—but for now, in that moment, she was all right.

"Minda?"

"Yes, Jimmy?"

"Mom and Dad aren't gonna get better, are they?"

"*Sssssh.* Get some rest," Melinda whispered, stroking his hair until he fell asleep.

The storm died down, leaving the patter of steady rain and Jimmy's tiny snores. Melinda stared around the room, a shrine to the children's cartoon *Bluey* that was illuminated by a night light shaped like the precocious blue heeler. She hadn't slept since yesterday afternoon, when she and Dulcy had tried to grab a few hours' rest in the muggy shade before the break-in that claimed her friend's life, but she laid wide awake.

Her gaze fell back to the Bible, and the smiling cartoon Jesus on its bookmark. *I've never stepped foot in a church outside of weddings and funerals, and I got my friend killed trying to steal. And here I am, lying in a warm bed with a full stomach while Dulcy's lying in an unmarked grave. Why, God? Why am I being rewarded?* she silently asked.

An electric chill ran through her from head to toe under the covers. *So you can save this boy,* came her answer.

Melinda fell into an exhausted and dreamless sleep.

CHAPTER 23

GERMANY

Martin, Theo, and Josh weaved silently like phantasms through the bumper-to-bumper graveyard of dead vehicles choking Autobahn 66 northeast of Frankfurt, the setting sun casting long shadows onto the woods around them.

Theo set a square military fuel can next to a sleek BMW, grimacing at the sight through the window of the body of a young girl buckled into her safety seat. He violently pried open the fuel door with a crowbar, dropping it to the asphalt with a ringing *clang* before jamming a sharpened rod down the filler neck to hold open the flapper. The anti-siphon screen punctured with a *pop*, and Theo fed the tube of the Arnold 490 siphon they had found during a recent foraging mission to suck out whatever diesel the car had left. Despite stringent European Union environmental regulations, the Germans loved their diesel cars, which made finding fuel for the team's Humvee much easier than it otherwise would have been.

Martin opened the rear hatch of an SUV, a wall of stench from decomposing people and food rewarding him for his effort as he hurriedly tossed a dozen cans into a drawstring bag before staggering back with a retch. Gasping for fresh air, he looked back at the traffic jam that seemed to go on forever from the jackknifed semi that had blocked both lanes; the median guardrail and the woods had prevented panicked drivers from going around. *So they stayed here until the flu killed them*, Martin thought, skin crawling.

He made sure he still had eyes on Josh and Theo before moving farther down the jam to find more opportunities to forage—and leaped out of his skin as he spooked a pack of badgers that darted out from the open door of a Volkswagen sedan where they had been dining on the corpse of the driver.

"Jee-zus!" he shouted as the badgers scampered back into the woods.

"You OK, boss?" Theo called out from behind a nearby minibus, weapon at the ready.

"Doin' just great!" Martin called back, turning away from the gruesome view. "Just collecting canned sausages and PTSD, that's all."

A wet *splat* announced Josh losing his battle with keeping his dinner inside him where it belonged. "We got enough stuff—let's get the fuck outta here," he gurgled, wiping his mouth on his sleeve.

Martin silently ordered Theo and Josh to rally to him with an overhead wave of his hand; they would make their way back to Patton, who was providing overwatch from the Humvee, and then displace to bed down before setting out again at first light. Their route plan looped north around Frankfurt, giving it a wide berth before hooking west to thread the needle between the dead city and the Rhine-Ruhr metropolitan region, one of the most densely populated areas of Europe that, if the handful of radio reports that Josh and Ann-Katryn had been able to pick up were accurate, had descended into a wasteland of death and anarchy.

They had just started down the autobahn before the sight of two American soldiers coming up from the other direction stopped them cold.

"What're you guys doin' on this detail—" a male soldier loudly inquired before the trio dove out of sight behind the nearest cars.

"Sarge!" Patton radioed in. "I got eyes on two bogeys headin' up the autobahn your way—they appear to be alone."

"No shit!" Martin answered, releasing the transmit button just long enough to wave off Josh and Theo to spread out and find cover. "Be ready to lay down fire if we need to break contact! Out!"

"Sandwich!" the soldier called out, waiting for Martin to give the password match to his verbal challenge.

Martin made sure Theo and Josh were in position to shoot back if it came to that. "You guys Americans?" he bellowed, peeking around from behind an Audi to scan for movement.

"Sandwich!" the man repeated.

"We don't know your challenge and password—we're doin' our own thing!" Martin shouted. "If you guys are cool, we can be cool, too, and we all can be on our way without anyone gettin' hurt. How about it?"

His proposition echoed away into the racket of birds and insects singing with the sunset. "OK! We're comin' out!" the man hollered in agreement. "No funny business, 'cause we got an overwatch that'll cut you down if you try anything stupid!"

"So do we!" Martin responded, rising with Theo and Josh to find the two soldiers—a man and a woman—standing on both sides of a boxy white van.

"Where you coming from?" the man asked, hands off of his chest-harnessed rifle as a sign of goodwill.

"Vilseck! How 'bout you?"

"Ansbach!"

"Sounds like we pounded some of the same turf gettin' here," Martin said, lowering his rifle.

The soldiers cautiously approached Martin's team. "What'cha doing here?" the man asked, stepping over a beaten-up suitcase between the lanes.

"Same thing as you, it seems—scrounging for anything useful," Martin answered, moving forward to meet in the middle and scaring off a tribe of magpies that had been strutting amongst the cars.

"Yeah, this is some fucked-up shit," the man said, shaking hands with the team. "Worst shopping trip ever. Aldi this sure as hell ain't."

"Got that right—never thought I'd miss the commissary," Martin said, noticing the man was a buck sergeant like him. "Martin Crenshaw, Elkhorn, Wisconsin."

"Clayton Kirchhubel, Omaha, Nebraska—my friends call me 'Alphabet.' Original, huh?" Martin introduced Theo and Josh with a chuckle over Clayton's nickname, which the Army practically issued to any soldier with a last name longer than eight letters.

Clayton introduced his companion, Specialist Kira Cooke, who eyed the round Second Cav unit patch on Martin's left shoulder through her black military glasses. "We heard about what happened at Vilseck," she said. "We were worried for a minute that you guys belonged to the Nasty Guard unit that shot it up."

Josh shook his head. "Negative—Outlaw Troop, Fourth Squadron. We bugged out the moment that shitshow started. You're the first American faces we've seen since."

Kira looked at Clayton, who gave her the nod of approval to make the offer. "Wanna come with us and see a lot more?" she asked.

CHAPTER 24

MICHIGAN

"*Wheeee!*" Jimmy excitedly squealed as his bike picked up speed down the small hill.

"Careful!" Melinda called out from behind, her ten-speed wobbling as its hitched two-wheeled trailer loaded with supplies hit a rock. She welcomed the cool wind on her face as she coasted after Jimmy down the incline—after days of rain, the humidity as the sun reached high noon was overbearing, even by Michigan standards.

They had set out for Mackinaw City at sunrise, four days after Melinda had met the orphaned boy. She had spent her first full day catching up on rest, playing with Jimmy, and cooking him whatever he wanted to eat. He woke up bawling the next morning, begging her not to leave. Melinda cried as she hugged him, gently telling him that his family was dead, and asking if he wanted to come with her.

Can't you just stay here with me? he had asked, sniffling and wiping his nose on the back of his hand.

I need to get back to my family, she answered, powering up her phone just long enough to show him a family photo taken the day before she had left for Interlochen—the pain of seeing her dead sister cleaved her heart like a knife. *You can be a part of it if you want,* she promised with forced optimism that she had any family left. *You'll never be alone again.*

Jimmy's eyes met Melinda's. *Can I say goodbye to Mom and Dad and Brittany?*

Later that afternoon, during a lull in the rains, they held a makeshift memorial service in the front yard—the Callahans' final backyard resting place was out of the question. *I'll take care of him,* she silently promised his parents in prayer as Jimmy, clutching his Bible, said a heartbreaking farewell. And with that, they walked hand-in-hand back inside to begin packing.

Melinda had briefly pondered taking Jimmy's uncle's truck and camper before surrendering to practicality; besides the fact that she had only just learned to drive, she realized that the truck would become useless the moment they hit a traffic jam of abandoned vehicles. That wouldn't be a problem for their bicycles, which could simply weave around any obstructions. Fortunately for Melinda, the Callahans had loved biking, and she quickly found a bicycle-mounted trailer and larger panniers that would allow them to haul more than they otherwise would have been able.

They packed the trailer full with camping equipment, as well as the large cylindrical metal Berkey filter from the kitchen counter, which Jimmy explained would make any water poured into it safe to drink; she crammed the rest of their available space with as much freeze-dried and dehydrated survival food as she could fit. Another way the Lord had blessed Melinda was that Jimmy's mother was almost exactly her size; while it was sweltering hot outside, autumn would be upon them before they knew it, and a voice inside her told her to pack as many winter clothes for the both of them as she could. She searched in vain for Jimmy's birth certificate and other vital documents, but found a photo album that she carefully fit into one of the panniers next to Dulcy's violin—she wanted him to remember his family.

Jimmy had cried when Melinda broke it to him that he would have to leave almost all of his toys behind. Melinda sat cross-legged in the playroom for moral support as the boy, one by one, whittled down his collection into a small pile of absolute favorites that he could fit in his backpack, plus the stuffed Bluey doll that he slept with every night.

Melinda wasn't counting on reaching Mackinaw City by the end of the day, but they were making better time than she thought they would. She began scanning ahead to find a secluded place where they could eat a quick lunch, again calling out to Jimmy to be careful as he deftly navigated a maze of tree branches felled by the summer storms.

Optimism swelled inside Melinda that they would be able to make it all the way back home to Elkhorn. Finding Jimmy and the mountain of supplies his parents had stashed away was far more than luck or coincidence; Melinda and her family had never been religious, but something way beyond her understanding was in motion—something that had a vested interest in their survival.

She rose on the bike and pumped the pedals to catch up with Jimmy, the rattle of the metal Berkey filter reminding Melinda of her good fortune.

PART TWO

*If you can't fly, then run. If you can't run, then walk. If you
can't walk, then crawl. But by all means, keep moving.*

—Martin Luther King Jr.

CHAPTER 25

WISCONSIN

Ethan blinked the sweat from his eyes as he finished tying a tripwire to the noisemaker nailed to the maple tree in the deep woods behind The Compound. "How's that?" he whispered to Gunnar, who watched over Ethan's shoulder as they baked in the oppressive summer heat.

Gunnar carefully ran a finger along the wire strung across the deer path; any intruder trying to take the easy way to infiltrate the retreat through the thick forest would set off the blank twelve-gauge shotgun shell nested in the discrete metal tube. "Looks like you got the hang of it, kid," he said, wiping his brow under his camouflage boonie hat—a storied and salt-ringed souvenir from his rotation with the First Ranger Battalion through the Jungle Operations Training Course in Hawaii.

Ethan stood, swinging his Rock River Arms LAR-15 rifle off his back. "How many more we stringin' up?" he asked, leaving a smear of green camouflage face paint on his sleeve as he wiped his forehead.

"Six," Gunnar answered as the two other members of their detail—Justin and Jane Christensen, newlyweds several years separated from the Marine Corps—rose from the thick brush around them. "Then you graduate from noisemakers to booby traps."

"Closest I'll ever get to learning a trade," Ethan ruefully joked; he had decided before the collapse to go to trade school and become an electrician rather than get a four-year degree and be saddled with a lifetime of student loan debt—especially after seeing how college had scrambled his Aunt Ashley's brain.

Gunnar slapped Ethan on the shoulder. "On the bright side, this is an apprenticeship you'll never forget," he said as the boy and the Christensens lined up behind him to move out to set another noisemaker. "We're gonna be passin' by some pretty dangerous traps, kid—stay right behind me, OK?" Ethan silently nodded and followed Gunnar, trying his best to move silently by rolling his feet heel to toe as he had been taught. He nervously scanned his surroundings as they began trudging downhill, taking full advantage of the on-the-job training in small-unit tactics that, in a world without law and order, could one day mean the difference between life and death.

The odor of cigarette smoke tickled Ethan's nose—an out-of-place scent in the humid summer woods. Before he could say a word, Gunnar grabbed the shoulder strap of his tactical vest and roughly yanked the young man to the ground.

"Quiet!" Gunnar hissed as the Christensens also hit the dirt, noiselessly slithering on their bellies for cover behind the trees dotting the wooded slope. Ethan crawled after Gunnar to one of the many boulders sprinkled throughout the forests of northern Wisconsin by the Ice Age glacier that had carved out its distinct topography. The loud cracks of fallen branches snapping under clumsy, careless feet echoed through the woods ahead, the pungent stink of tobacco growing stronger. "Stay down and keep still!" Gunnar quietly ordered Ethan before scooting

to the boulder's edge, sighting his SCAR-H rifle downhill. *Four-man recon*, he told himself, knowing its size just by the sounds it was making crashing through the forest.

A heavyset bearded man wearing flannel and carrying a shotgun came into view about fifty meters ahead, followed by three men armed with a variety of weapons. The bearded man tripped on a log and fell, cursing loudly to the laughter of another, and to the admonishment of a lanky, reedy-voiced man nagging them to keep quiet. *Amateur hour*, Gunnar silently chided as he toggled his headset radio with the switch taped to the front handle of his rifle to order the QRF to the edge of the woods in case the intruders were the vanguard of a larger group.

Ethan peeked around the boulder as the bearded man brushed the dirt and mud from his shirt before continuing up the deer path, making it two steps before one of The Compound's traps swallowed his leg to the knee. The man dropped his shotgun and screamed in agony, clutching his leg and trying to pull it out of the trap, only to scream even louder with the effort. Two of his buddies began shooting indiscriminately into the woods over their comrade's howls, and the lanky man had barely managed to scream at them to stop before Gunnar, Justin, and Jane opened fire. Ethan gawked as he watched the lanky man's chest explode in puffs of red and pink—the bearded man had time for one more blood-curdling shriek before he was permanently silenced by the bullet that blew off the top of his head.

The racket of the brief but violent gunfight rolled away as Gunnar radioed the QRF to move to his position. "Advance to contact?" Justin yelled in his husky voice.

"Negative—wait 'til backup arrives in case there's more of 'em! Let 'em bleed out," Gunnar barked, leaving unsaid that the standard tactic of mowing through an ambush site to double-tap the bodies wasn't particularly smart in a forest bristling with traps like the one that had snared the intruders' point man. Ethan stared in morbid fascination at the grisly sight of blood pumping in weakening spurts from the trapped man's demolished head.

The QRF leader appeared out of nowhere and slid next to Gunnar. "Where the hell you get off havin' all the fun without us, Big G?" said Lukasz Mankiewicz, a former SWAT sniper and Gunnar's second-in-command.

"Cover us—I think they're alone, but stay sharp, just in case," Gunnar ordered before shaking Ethan's booted foot to get his attention. "You OK?"

"Yeah."

"C'mon," he said, rising to his feet, weapon at the low ready. "You're bound to see shit like this sooner or later—may as well get it outta the way."

Gunnar cautiously led Ethan and the Christensens down the slope to the grisly scene, where the adults peeled off to search the dead. Ethan hesitantly peered into the pit trap as Justin searched the pockets of its victim's blood-sodden shirt; a bed of stakes had pierced the man's boot, and rows of them along the small pit's walls had mutilated his leg, further tearing into his flesh with his futile attempts to escape. Ethan realized with dread that one of his first jobs when the collapse started was to sharpen wooden stakes and harden them with fire—while he hadn't shot his rifle that day, he had played a role in killing the man.

A wisp of smoke rose from the cherry of a cigarette next to the corpse of an overweight man in hunting coveralls. "Careful, buddy—those things'll kill ya," Jane joked, extinguishing it with the toe of her boot as her husband took a knee to search the body.

"You're a barrel of laughs, hon—you should take your act to the Catskills," Justin said, wiping gore from his leather glove with disgust before retrieving the dead man's shotgun.

"She's right, though—it's what gave these clowns away," Gunnar said, yanking a notepad from the pocket of the lanky man's body. Gunnar studied the corpse for a moment—his blood-spattered face twisted in a confusing mix of surprise, fear, and pain—before recognizing him as the Iron Point police officer who had driven the chief and the village president to deliver their ultimatum several weeks prior. "Warned you not to come back, dickhead," he snorted as he thumbed through the pad, quietly deciding not to share with the group that they had just shot and killed a cop, albeit a crooked one.

Justin, who like his wife wore his old Marine Corps digital camouflage uniform, slung a battered bolt-action rifle from one of the dead over his shoulder and offered his hand to pull Jane to her feet. "I don't like this."

"What's there to like?" Ethan incredulously asked, wrinkling his nose at the stink from the dead men's loosening bowels.

"What the hell are these guys doin' here?" Justin said, ignoring Ethan's remark. "There's nothin' but miles of forest between the back of The Compound and Iron Point—and we nailed up God knows how many signs warnin' trespassers what was waitin' for 'em. These losers weren't innocent hunters trying to bag a deer."

"You got that right," Gunnar spat, tossing Justin the notepad, which was opened to a crudely drawn map of the path and the locations of two previously planted noisemakers. "We're being scoped out."

CHAPTER 26

MICHIGAN

Melinda slowed to a halt along the deserted stretch of Mackinaw Highway and scanned the skies upon hearing the distinctive buzz of a drone.

"Cool! Minda, look!" Jimmy excitedly yelled, his bike wobbling as he let go of the handlebars and pointed excitedly ahead. She lifted her sunglasses, following Jimmy's finger to the tiny black blob hovering above the trees ahead of them against the cloudless summer sky. Mackinaw City lay just a few miles up the road—and if there was a drone, there was someone in town piloting it.

"You have great eyes, Jimmy," Melinda said, playfully mussing Jimmy's sweaty mop of hair.

"I'm gonna ask Santa for one," the boy proclaimed.

Melinda smiled. "Let's go," she said, pedaling forward.

The drone kept pace with them as they biked north across the I-75 overpass, the highway below them eerily empty save for a single SUV in the northbound shoulder, its doors flung open and luggage scattered about. Two lines of concrete barriers had been hastily laid across the off-ramp to keep cars from exiting—and just past the interchange, three hand-painted signs had been staked in the right-of-way like an old-fashioned Burma Shave ad for refugees who hadn't yet caught the hint that the townspeople weren't rolling out the red carpet.

ROADBLOCK AHEAD—BE PREPARED TO STOP

MACKINAC BRIDGE IS CLOSED

TRESPASSERS AND CRIMINALS WILL BE SHOT

Jimmy stopped, mouthing the words as he read. "They're not gonna shoot us, are they?" he asked, voice rising with fear.

Melinda nervously squinted at a wall of concrete barriers blocking the northbound lane half a mile ahead, shimmering in the summer heat. "No—don't worry. But stay right behind me and don't say a word. Can you do that for me?" Jimmy zipped his lips shut with an exaggerated gesture.

The duo weaved around rows of orange construction barrels that had been staggered in both lanes to force approaching vehicles to slow to a crawl—*and to make it easier to shoot the driver*, Melinda realized with a shudder. She braked at a stop sign bolted to a construction barricade about a hundred feet from the roadblock; a dozen townspeople took positions behind the protective wall near an abandoned truck stop, rifles trained on the newcomers.

"State your business!" a portly older man cradling a shotgun yelled out to them. The drone's buzz faded as it flew away to continue patrolling the two-mile-wide headland on which the village sat, jutting into the strait where Lake Michigan and Lake Huron met.

"I need to speak with Nathan Bowers. I have news about his daughter, Dulcy," Melinda yelled back.

A young woman Melinda's age sprang up from behind the wall like a jack-in-the-box. "You know Dulcy?" she excitedly asked.

"Get down, Samantha! For heaven's sake, use your head before some bad guy blows it off!" the man admonished. He leaned his shotgun against the barrier wall to consult a checklist of residents who had been out of town when the collapse hit; Melinda stared past the weeds on the far side of the road at a row of cars that had been unceremoniously dumped in a casino parking lot, their windshields shattered and hoods pockmarked with bullet holes.

"They came to cause trouble—I hope for your sake that you didn't," the man warned as he scanned Dulcy's information. "So how do ya know her?"

"We were bunkmates at Interlochen when all this started. My family didn't come for me—Dulcy said we could come stay with her."

"We're not lettin' outsiders stay, no exceptions. But fortunately for you and your little travel companion," the man said, his demeanor taking a softer tone, "your story's startin' to check out. What instrument does Dulcy play?"

"Oh, for heaven's sake!" a heavyset sunburned woman in a short-sleeved shirt scolded the man, slugging him in the arm. "Sorry about my friend here, young lady—he's watched too many war movies." Another sentry rose to his feet and laughed, his two teenage sons following suit.

"That's OK!" Melinda said, relieved that she had passed the test. "Violin—she played the violin."

The teenage girl's pretty face fell. "Um . . . you said 'played.' Past tense," she said, voice beginning to tremble. "Where's Dulcy?"

"I think it's best if I, um . . . talk to her dad," Melinda answered, lip quivering.

The woman wrapped her large arms around the girl as she broke into sobs, the rest of the guard detail standing in respectful silence. Melinda loudly sniffled as she fought back tears, the girl's pain ripping open wounds that would never heal.

"Jesus, Mary, and Joseph," the man sighed, calling over the younger of the two boys. "I need you to escort these two to the police station and tell 'em to bring Reverend Willis along. Half the damn town listens in on the CB now," he said, shaking his handheld Midland radio as he wordlessly beckoned Melinda and Jimmy to walk their bikes around through the truck stop. "I call this in, and this poor girl's dad's gonna hear it first from a dozen gossips who get off on givin' people bad news."

The teenager slung his bolt-action rifle across his back and jogged to a ten-speed bike laying in the shaded overgrown grass behind a weathered billboard advertising a cross-lake ferry service. "Follow me—police station's only a mile or so up the road," he told Melinda as they pushed off. "Stick to me like glue—lotta people around here aren't too keen on seein' unfamiliar faces."

"Can I talk now?" Jimmy asked Melinda, pumping his pedals to keep up with the older kids.

"It's OK."

"Is your friend in heaven with Mom, Dad, and Brittany?"

"Yes, she is," Melinda bit off, the road ahead blurring with her watering eyes.

CHAPTER 27

GERMANY

The packed Humvee rocked in the rutted woods like a boat caught in choppy seas as Patton followed a ground guide to park in the middle of the displaced soldiers' camp.

"We cut and ran, just like you guys," Kira said, climbing over laps to exit into the fresh, cool forest air as Patton killed the engine. Soldiers buzzed around them in the night, red-lens flashlights illuminating their tasks like fireflies dancing in the woods. "Clayton and I were part of a convoy of Strykers evacuating Ansbach to consolidate into Hohenfels. When we saw our chance, we peeled onto a side road and took off."

"Lotta our buddies had the same idea—half a dozen other Strykers split off and came with us," Clayton said as he stretched, beckoning the men to follow. "We stumbled across Colonel Stirling and The Lost Boys two days later and joined up. Strength in numbers."

"The Lost Boys?" Ann-Katryn asked, confused.

"Some ancient movie—never seen or heard of it. The colonel's something of a movie buff—he decided we needed a name right about when he shanghaied me as his driver and personal dogsbody," Clayton explained. "I wanted to call us 'The Last of Us,' but I guess that struck a little too close to home." He trailed off as Ann-Katryn doubled over and slapped a hand over her mouth. "You all right, miss?"

Ann-Katryn took a deep breath, hands on her knees as the urge to vomit started to subside. "I do not know why you Americans call *Schwangerschaftsübelkeit* 'morning sickness' when you feel like this all day."

"Probably 'cause it's a lot easier to pronounce," Kira said, gently taking Ann-Katryn by the arm and pointing to a boxy M997A3 Humvee ambulance, the red cross on its side barely visible in the dark. "We have some medics with us—maybe they have something that can help. At the very least, if you're expecting, a checkup wouldn't hurt."

Ann-Katryn silently nodded her consent. "We'll catch up with you guys later," Patton said, following Kira and his girlfriend to the aid station.

Clayton led Martin, Josh, and Theo past Strykers and other Army vehicles tucked into the woods until they reached an M1130 Stryker command vehicle parked under camouflage netting. A tall, imposing man wearing the eagle insignia of a colonel ducked out and descended the ramp to meet them, the soldiers coming to attention but following the tradition of not saluting in what was essentially a combat zone.

"At ease," William Stirling commanded in a Texas drawl, the men relaxing as he gave the newcomers a quick once-over. "So, these are the soldiers you ran across in the *stau*?" he asked Clayton, using the German word for traffic jam that GIs stationed in Europe had long ago adopted as their own.

"That's affirm, sir."

"I was told there were five."

"No, sir—four soldiers and a civilian," Clayton reported. "The civilian's got morning sickness, and she and the father are at the aid station."

Consternation briefly flashed across Stirling's face. "Well, as much as I don't like the idea of addin' another dependent with a bun in the oven to our flock, I'll deal if it means getting four able-bodied soldiers—that is, if you're willing to join us." He stepped in front of Martin and looked him square in the eyes. "What's your plan, sergeant?"

"Get back to the States, sir," Martin sounded off—while he and his team had loosened military courtesies, he wasn't about to talk to a full-bird colonel like they were drinking buddies. "Either find a flight and catch it, or get to the coast and find a boat."

"Goin' home's our plan, too," Stirling said. "There's just under three hundred of us now—more than two hundred military and just under a hundred civilian dependents. We've been collectin' people like a snowball rolling downhill since this whole mess started. So, you guys are Two ACR, huh? What's your MOS?"

"Nineteen delta, sir—all four of us!" Theo said.

"Cav scouts—hallelujah!" Stirling exclaimed, waving his hands in the air like a worshipper at a tent revival. "You boys are literally the answer to my prayers—thank you, Jesus! We haven't been moving nearly as fast as I'd like, because we got no idea of the conditions ten klicks ahead of us at any given time—and the slower we go, the more we burn through food and fuel that are becoming harder and harder to get. Seein' as how we got a mutual goal, y'all wanna be our eyes and ears?"

Martin turned to Theo and Josh. "How about it?"

"Too lazy to walk, too stupid to fly—*recon!*" Josh cheerily replied.

"We're in, sir," Martin told the colonel.

"Out-freaking-standing! Welcome to The Lost Boys," Stirling said, welcoming them with a strong handshake and asking them their names and their hometowns, smirking with amusement upon learning that the entire team hailed from Wisconsin. "I'll let you in on the big plan—a boat's comin' from CONUS to ship us home."

"Holy shit! Really, sir?" Martin exclaimed.

Stirling nodded. "The chain of command's been fed through the wood chipper, but it looks like there's two competin' factions remaining—the smart one that wants to get as many overseas soldiers as possible back home, and the shit-all stupid one that wants to keep what's left of us deployed in the event that whatever's left of Russia, China, Iran, or wherever, try to take advantage of the situation. The 'bring our boys and girls home' faction sent the boat, and we're gonna catch it."

"When and where, sir?" Josh asked.

"Dunno yet—we just know it's coming. But when it does, and it finds a deep-water port that's still in one piece and has enough living dockworkers to run it, we wanna be ready," Stirling answered as Kira returned from the ambulance. "Get some sleep, get something to eat, and Sergeant Crenshaw, report to me first thing in the morning so we can put your team to work scouting us a route. Understood?"

"Yes, sir!"

"We can talk more tomorrow, but Top and I gotta make the rounds and check in on everyone," Stirling said before disappearing into the darkness.

Martin stifled a yawn as he turned to Kira. "How's Ann-Katryn?"

"They're looking at her now, sergeant—I'm sure she's fine. She's hardly the first woman who's ever caught pregnant."

"Thanks. And I don't know how the rest of this unit is, but you don't hafta stand on ceremony and address me by rank if you don't want to," Martin said.

"Most of us are like that, except for addressing the commander and first sergeant, and a handful of officers and NCOs who still have a stick up their ass about it," Clayton said. "After all, what're they gonna do—give people Article 15s when they can come and go as they please? Anyway, let's welcome you in style by crushing a few beers."

Theo grinned ear to ear at the invitation. "You guys loot a Class Six store or somethin'?"

"On our last foraging trip to the *stau*, I found a coupla cases of Bitburger in the trunk of some poor soul who didn't need it anymore—I guess he didn't wanna face the end of the world sober," Clayton said. "It ain't cold, but it doesn't matter, because it's Bitburger."

Josh unzipped his tactical vest with a contented sigh. "A coupla brews and a night of uninterrupted sleep without having to keep one eye open sounds great."

Kira's laugh floated on the night air at the sight of his Starfleet comm badge catching the moonlight. "What school'd you earn *that* from?" she ribbed.

"Well, actually, it's . . ."

"Save the explanation—my parents met at a *Star Trek* convention," Kira cut him off. "And they weren't done geeking out by a long shot, because they named me after Colonel Kira from *Deep Space Nine*." She pointed down a line of vehicles. "Every coupla nights, a few of us get together and watch reruns—they probably already started without me. Wanna come?"

"Save some of those beers for me, guys," Josh said without looking back, eagerly following Kira's lead.

Theo started laughing the moment the duo walked out of earshot. "Remember that time we went clubbin' in Munich, just before the shit hit the fan, an' Josh totally struck out with that frau who threw her drink in his face?"

Martin chuckled. "That was some funny shit."

"I told 'im—" Theo said, struggling to continue, "I told 'im it'd be the end of the world before he ever managed to hook up!"

"You hit that nail on the head!" Martin howled, Clayton joining in with The Lost Boys's newest recruits.

"Last laugh might be on your friend, though," Clayton said, wiping his eyes. "Kira's a born-again Christian—he wants to try anything, he'd better have a ring in his pocket. Bad luck for him, I guess."

"But good luck for the gene pool," Theo said, catching his breath. "It's bad enough that Patton's breedin'—last thing we need are any little Josh Czernik fuck trophies runnin' around."

"Ain't that the truth," Martin laughed again. "Now Alphabet, I recall you sayin' something about beer."

CHAPTER 28

MICHIGAN

Nathan Bowers clutched Dulcy's violin, twisting its polished neck with a trembling hand.

Melinda and Jimmy sat in silence, the police chief and the pastor who had escorted them having respectfully taken their leave; Dulcy's younger sister, Esmeralda, had dashed to her room shrieking the moment the horrible news left the kindly pastor's lips. Melinda had blubbered through tears to tell the grief-stricken father what had happened, holding Jimmy's hand as she relived the trauma of watching Dulcy's execution and barely escaping with her life.

The heartbroken father stared at the violin, rocking back and forth in his wheelchair to the ominous *tick tock* of a grandfather clock that matched the ornate woodwork of a study lined floor to ceiling with bookshelves crammed with old tomes.

"I . . ." Melinda barely managed to stumble. "I can't tell you how—"

Nathan held up his hand to silence her. "You don't have to. You were faced with a choice of stealing or starvation. If anyone's responsible, it's me," he croaked, weakly slammed his fist on the wheelchair's armrest. "I was leaving for Interlochen to bring her home when I totaled my car. I got distracted by my phone—I thought Dulcy had gotten a text through—just long enough to slam head-first into a tree. I'm lucky to be alive," he spat, laughing bitterly as he ran his hand over a bald spot ringed by thinning brown hair. "I could've saved her, but for my carelessness. You didn't kill her, young lady. I did."

"Minda, can I play with my toys?" Jimmy interrupted, tugging at her shirt. With her silent nod, he went to the corner near a vintage globe resting in its wooden stand and pulled his Bluey action figures out of his backpack.

The scuffed wooden floor creaked as Nathan set the violin on a desk crowded with leather-bound books. "Did Dulcy ever tell you how she got her name?"

Melinda shook her head no.

"No surprise—she hated it," he said with a reminiscing grin. "Her full name was Dulcinea. Cervantes—*Don Quixote*. Dulcy's mother picked the name to celebrate me landing my professorship in literature. 'Oh, my lady Dulcinea del Toboso, perfection of all beauty, summit and crown of discretion, treasure house of grace, despositary of virtue, and finally, ideal of all that is good, honorable, and delectable in this world . . .'" Nathan trailed off, hands shooting under his thick black glasses. Melinda stood helplessly, feeling like an accessory to Dulcy's murder as her father's grief filled the room.

"You and the boy can stay in the guest room for a few days, but that's it, unfortunately—city rules," he mumbled, loudly blowing his nose into a pocket handkerchief. "Sorry to be so blunt."

"That's very generous—thank you," Melinda softly replied. "We brought our own food—we won't impose."

Dulcy's father stared forlornly at Jimmy innocently playing with the Heeler family, framed in the sunlight beaming through the study's lone window. "Actually, thank *you*—you didn't have to come here and bring this news to me. I could've spent the rest of my days not knowing what happened to her. But you came, and at great personal risk to you and the boy. I didn't catch his name."

"Jimmy," Melinda said, briefly recounting the story of how she found him.

Nathan gave an approving smile. "'Ideal of all that is good and honorable in this world,' indeed. Dulcy had very good taste in friends."

"I don't deserve that, but thank you."

"As for your plan to get back home, you might want to be sitting down for what I'm about to tell you," Nathan said, gesturing to the worn black office chair behind her. "You saw the sign coming into town that the Mackinac Bridge is closed?"

"Yes," Melinda said, sitting down for the first time that day, her heart racing once again—now it was Dulcy's father's turn to be the bearer of bad news.

"St. Ignace—the town on the UP side—has blocked it off at their end. They've straight-up turned the toll gate into one big barricade like *Les Misérables*, and they're shooting anyone who won't take no for an answer. The Yoopers are scared out of their wits about a bunch of trolls from the Mitt bringing in the H7N9 flu, or refugees from Detroit storming across the bridge to wreak havoc."

"But we gotta get across!" Melinda protested. "We're not sick, and we're not staying—we're just passing through!"

"I know, but they're not letting anyone in. No exceptions."

"We can't get across, and the police chief said we can't stay, so, what—we wander the wilderness until winter comes and we *die*?" Melinda raged before lowering her voice with a glance at Jimmy, who stayed occupied by his toys. "What're we supposed to do?"

They sat in silence for a minute before Nathan's face lit up ever so slightly, wiping away his guilt-ridden stare. "I think I have an idea."

"What is it?" Melinda asked.

"Let's talk later," Nathan said, scooting back his wheelchair. "Esmeralda needs me, and we need time to grieve as a family. You and Jimmy will stay with us tonight. Then tomorrow morning, we'll try to talk my neighbor into helping you on your way."

CHAPTER 29

With a belch of thick black exhaust, the filthy yellow Randolph County plow truck backed off the road just enough to let Reed's car onto the bridge crossing the Mississippi River into Missouri.

Kara tried not to cough as the fumes rolled in through her window along with dust from the drought that had been hammering southern Illinois, further adding to the car's stifling discomfort; Reed had decided to keep the air conditioning off to maximize their gas mileage. Hot wind blew out the noxious exhaust as Reed picked up speed, but replaced it with the odor of all the things that lived and died at the river's edge. Behind them, the plow truck lurched forward to once again block off the bridge from any refugees fleeing St. Louis down I-55.

The trio had spent two days in the small riverside town of Chester—*home of Popeye the Sailor*, Kara mockingly said to herself. While the break had given them time to collect themselves, and the townspeople were friendly and willing to share—Reed had even managed to wheedle enough gas to top off—they had heard enough unsolicited stories about hometown hero E.C. Segar and his spinach-powered cartoon character to last a dozen lifetimes. Most importantly, a local ham radio operator had managed to confirm that both Whiteman Air Force Base and Joint Base Lewis-McChord were still standing, although he had no luck getting a message through to either.

The Mississippi had swollen its banks and was lapping up to the railroad tracks following the river's edge, courtesy of heavy summer rains farther upriver. The window breeze battered Kara's face, her feet shifting uncomfortably among the extra plastic shopping bags of drought-stunted sweet corn the people of Chester had gifted them; for survivors across the Midwest, corn was going to be breakfast, lunch, and dinner for a very long time.

"Aaaaand, welcome to Missouri!" Reed cheerfully called over his shoulder to Kara as they passed the sign demarcating the state line at the river's mid-channel. "Let's get you home!"

Alexia pointed ahead at a mob of seagulls and crows flapping around a red SUV blocking the centerline. "I see it," Reed said, easing off the accelerator as Alexia readied her rifle; he tersely ordered everyone to raise their windows the moment he realized that what he thought was heat shimmer from the road was in fact swarms of flies. Reed crept into the oncoming lane and the thin shoulder strip, just barely squeezing by the derelict vehicle and the family of five decomposing in the summer heat, their slack-jawed faces, pecked repeatedly by scavenger birds, barely visible under a wriggling layer of maggots.

Kara lunged for a plastic bag from the floorboards, dumping its corn with barely enough time before violently throwing up her breakfast. "Sorry," she gurgled, bracing for a dressing-down from Alexia as Reed sped away from the grisly sight.

"Don't be—damn near puked myself," Alexia grunted, lowering her window to gulp the hot but fresh air. "That fuckin' sucked."

"Especially for those poor souls—let's hope we don't see anything like that again," Reed said as the fields and woods of Missouri raced toward them.

Unlike Chester, which was built on a high bluff, the Missouri side of the river was flat floodplain, and therefore at the mercy of Old Man River; a verdant green strip of grass lining the edge of its flooded bank sharply contrasted the drought-parched, sun-baked yellows and browns inland. With the federal government and the Army Corps of Engineers gone, there were plenty of towns along the Mississippi that had survived the collapse, but wouldn't survive the next attempt by the mercurial river to wash them off the map. There was no town on the Missouri side of the bridge, which meant no roadblock of armed and paranoid townspeople to bull their way through; that would come at the small city of Perryville, ten miles down the road. Smack on I-55 ninety minutes south of the charred remnants of St. Louis, the town had borne the brunt of panicked survivors who hadn't been cut down by the flu or their fellow man—the people of Chester had warned Reed that Perryville was very unwelcoming to strangers as a result.

They had just entered the woods beyond the farm belt lining the river when Reed slowed down with a curse. "Again?" Kara nervously groused, staring at a nasty head-on collision between a sedan and an SUV at a T intersection up the road. Unlike the SUV on the bridge, the accident and its debris had completely blocked off both lanes and the shoulders.

"Hang on, everyone—it's gonna get a little bumpy," Reed warned as he slowed to ease his Civic off the road and onto the grassy strip between the shoulder and the woods.

"Reed . . ." Alexia cautioned, her sixth sense and a military career of writing accident reports sounding alarms in her head. She had just barely asked herself how a car traveling the vertical of a T intersection could get into a head-on with a car on the cross when she noticed a flash of sunlight glinting off the barrel of a rifle sticking out of a concrete drainage pipe. *"Ambush!"* she screamed, fumbling to get her carbine up and over the glovebox. *"Floor it!"*

The woodline came alive with masked gunmen as Reed stomped on the gas, clenching the steering wheel with an iron grip to keep from losing control on the rocky weeds. An obese man with a bandana over his face rounded the roadblock, his black AR-style rifle pointed squarely at Reed and finger on the trigger. The bandit's eyes went wide with terror before Reed plowed into him and caused his shot to go wild; Kara shrieked and ducked with the crash of glass as the man's body shattered the windshield before rolling off to hit the ground. Reed almost skidded out to avoid hitting a concrete bridge rail before wrestling his car back onto the road and speeding away to the cracks of gunfire and the *thunks* of rounds puncturing his trunk.

"Goddammit!" Reed hollered, contorting himself to see through the smashed glass as he involuntarily flinched with the withering pot shots. "Everyone OK?"

Kara's mindless scream answered his question—he took his eyes off the road just long enough to see Alexia slumped forward, her seat belt holding her upright as her chest above her ballistic tactical vest grew sodden with blood.

CHAPTER 30

GERMANY

The outline of the small cinderblock pumping station building, and the trio of red deer stags grazing in the tall grass around it, glowed bright orange in the night-vision binoculars strapped to Martin's helmet.

"Right where the colonel said it'd be," he said in the dark from the small rise where his team and a nine-man infantry squad were watching the nondescript structure, which sat in a clearing along a lonely stretch of road through the thick forest of the Saar-Hünsruck Nature Park. The fueling station had been constructed as part of Europe's crash program to beef up its war infrastructure following Russia's invasion of Ukraine, and was connected to the NATO Pipeline System laid during the Cold War to supply alliance forces in the event of a Soviet invasion. But it was about to serve a function that military planners never envisioned—refueling a convoy of what could quite possibly be USAREUR's sole remaining unit as it continued on its quest to evacuate the Continent altogether.

The squad leader, Staff Sergeant Nick Alger, eyed the cav scouts, who appeared as spooky apparitions in his night vision. "You guys got us covered?" he whispered.

"Roger that," Martin assured, eyes glued to their objective. "The moment it's secure, we'll radio Actual to bring everyone up to top off. You think you Big Dead One fellas can handle the walk?"

"Fuck you," Nick grunted at Martin's jab—he and his squad from the First Infantry Division had hooked up with The Lost Boys after making it across much of Poland and Germany following the collapse of the Army garrison at Forward Operation Station Poznan. Nick pushed himself up on his hands to rally his squad—and dropped right back down upon seeing a human figure emerge from the woods. "Movement!" he hissed. "Eleven o'clock, two hundred meters."

"Got 'em," Martin confirmed as the glowing silhouette was joined by a second, then a third. The figures, toting rifles and decked out in military gear, froze at the sound of the spooked bucks bounding into the woods before continuing single-file across the clearing. The two bringing up the rear each took a knee to pull security while the line lead knelt at the side of the pump building.

Patton shifted his weight behind the team's bipod-mounted M240B machine gun. "Light 'em up?"

"Hold fire—they could be friendlies lookin' for a fill-up like we are," Nick ordered—although Martin was Patton's team leader, Nick was the one leading the mission. "But if this gets hot, only take out the fellas watchin' the road—I don't need you accidentally blowin' up the gas station."

The figure at the building unslung a satchel from his shoulder and pulled out a small bundle that he unwrapped before angrily spiking it to the ground. *"Pizdyets!"* he hollered, his angry outburst echoing through the woods.

"Zatknees! Shto nye tak?" one of his buddies yelled back.

"What're they sayin'?" Martin quietly asked Josh.

"No idea—whatever it is, it's not German," he whispered from the far side of the line.

The man angrily dumped the satchel's contents, unwrapping two more bundles. *"Nyet!"* he roared, hurling them into the clearing. "Nyet, nyet, *nyet!*"

His tantrum solved the mystery of their nationality—and sealed their fate. *"Open fire!"* Nick barked, bullets tearing into all three intruders before they knew what hit them; the machine gun's roar hammered Martin's eardrums as Patton mowed down the men by the roadside with two bursts, the last man's helmet flying off his head as it burst like a melon.

"Second squad, advance to contact by teams—*follow me!*" Nick hollered, jumping to his feet. "Cover us!" he ordered Martin as Theo reported the enemy contact on the SINCGARS radio strapped to his back.

***

Colonel Stirling stared with contempt at the blood-smeared bodies stripped to the waist in the dreary gray of the overcast German sunrise. The three dead men had been wearing German Bundeshwehr uniforms complete with proper kit, but the Cyrillic tattoos they sported gave away their true origins.

"Good shootin', boys," he told Martin and Nick over the rumble of the station generator and the engines of The Lost Boys's vehicles as they queued to refuel from the six pipe-mounted nozzles lining the road. "We woulda been SOL if they blew this up."

"Not with this shit they wouldn't have, sir," Nick said, tossing Stirling a paper-wrapped wood block.

The colonel twirled the block in his hand with a mischievous grin. "Well, I'll be damned," he chuckled.

"What's going on, sir?" Martin asked, puzzled.

"During the Ukraine War, front-line Russian soldiers discovered the hard way that many of their explosives had been replaced with wooden blocks because the corrupt oligarchs in charge of procuring it pocketed the cash instead," Stirling sniggered. "Tough luck for Ivan and his comrades here."

"And for us, too, sir," Nick spat, gesturing at the bodies. "We got enough to worry about without havin' to watch out for Spetznaz."

"No way these jokers were Spetznaz," Stirling retorted, referring to the Russian military's ruthless and feared special forces. "A commando wouldn't have made the rookie mistake of not doing a pre-combat check of his demo charges before moving out. My guess is that Putin had these losers, and others like 'em, infiltrate Europe among all the Ukrainians fleeing the war and the Russians dodgin' the draft—ol' Vlad royally fucked the puppy starting that war, but the old KGB coot knew a thing or two about covert ops. We gotta stay vigilant, but if these jokers wanna die for their dead country by fighting our dead country, let 'em. This battle ain't ours—our mission is to catch that last boat home." Stirling absentmindedly tossed the wood block onto the nearest corpse, Martin grimacing as it caught the dead man between his lifeless eyes with a *clonk*. "How your men doing, Sergeant Crenshaw?" the colonel asked.

"Never better," Martin said, watching his team in the lead refueling slot. Josh topped off their Humvee as Patton and Theo lined up and unscrewed their spare fuel canisters. Ann-Katryn stepped from the rear driver-side door, yawning and stretching under a military-issue wool blanket. She turned away to watch the vehicles filling up behind them, and the rest of their convoy curving around the bend into the woods waiting for their turn.

"That's good to hear, because it's gonna be a long day for y'all, sorry to say. Once you're green on fuel, I need you to scout ahead to Allenbach, and then head south to recon a small town called Schönenberg and prepare for our arrival," Stirling said, ripping open the Velcro map pouch of his tactical vest and beckoning Martin to follow. "We need to be ready if we're gonna run across any more armed resistance, so we're gonna take a little supply detour to play it safe. I'll brief you and your men."

"Yes, sir," Martin tiredly said, falling in behind the colonel.

"Whaddya want us to do with the bodies, sir?" Nick asked.

"Fuck 'em," Stirling said, not bothering to turn around. "Let 'em rot."

CHAPTER 31

MICHIGAN

"I've known Spence and Caroline a long time, but this won't be an easy sell—let me do the talking," Nathan told Melinda as he rolled his wheelchair through the empty parking lot of Mackinaw City Marina. "Then again, you haven't said a word since we left the house."

"I'm too nervous—that, and I've been thinking about Jimmy," she admitted.

"He's in good hands, don't you worry—before the collapse, if you needed someone to watch the kids for date night, you called Esmeralda."

"It's not that," Melinda said, helping Nathan over the curb onto the small walkway leading into the marina. "This is the first time we've been apart since I found him, and I can't get the little guy out of my mind."

"'Each the other's world entire.'"

"Say what?"

"Cormac McCarthy—*The Road*. Great book, but I wouldn't read it, if I were you—it's a little too real-life right now. Coming through—move it or lose it!" he yelled at a herring gull in his way as he rolled his wheelchair onto the marina's main dock. The seagull defiantly bellowed out a haughty, screeching challenge before taking off, Melinda ducking with a yelp as it buzzed over her head, riding the stiffening onshore breeze.

"Jeez, I hate those things!" she groused. "Rats with wings!"

"Any of your teachers ever torture you by making you read *Jonathan Livingston Seagull*?" Nathan asked.

"Never heard of it."

"Consider yourself fortunate," he muttered as he wheeled down the length of the dock, which was crammed to capacity with boats, from barely seaworthy rust buckets to luxury yachts and everything in between. Skippers and their families, who had fled from elsewhere with no clue what to do next, aimlessly milled about. Melinda grimaced at the whiff of sewage—the marina had suspended its pump-out service with the collapse, and more than a few of the boats's heads were full. The duo passed by a tattooed, bearded man wearing an Iraq War veteran hat and cradling an AR-15 rifle—one of the locals deputized by the police chief to maintain order with the influx of refugees who would soon be ordered to leave.

Nathan rolled up to a pristine Tiara 44 Coupe tied up at the last berth before the fuel station at the dock's edge, which was guarded by four men armed with rifles and shotguns. He waved to a middle-aged man in jeans and a flannel shirt standing on the boat's transom next to the dinghy strapped to the aft. "Howdy, neighbor! Nice to see you out and about," Spencer Myers cheerily said, pushing a wisp of gray hair out of his face. "What brings you out here?"

"I stopped by your house, but no one was home—Phyllis down the street said you and the missus were getting ready to store *Sweet Caroline* for winter."

"Or forever, the way things are going," Caroline Myers said as she stepped through the glass salon doors onto the aft cockpit to join her husband. "Shame to put her up so soon, but we don't wanna risk leaving her tied up for any of these out-of-towners to mess with." Caroline's friendly smile evaporated upon laying eyes on Melinda, who to her looked like just another refugee looking for an opportunity to cause trouble. "Who's this?"

"A friend of Dulcy's who needs a huge favor," Nathan said, the uttering of his daughter's name rending his heart.

"Dulcy?!" Caroline yelped. "Did you hear from her? Is she OK?"

"She's dead," Nathan flatly replied.

"Ohmigod," Caroline gasped, hands flying to her mouth as her husband closed his eyes and lowered his head. "Oh, I'm so sorry . . ." she stammered, stepping off the boat to wrap her arms around Nathan and cry over his shoulder. Melinda choked up, her pulse racing in anticipation of the huge ask that Nathan was about to make on her and Jimmy's behalf.

"This is Melinda," Nathan said, wiping his eyes. "She was Dulcy's cabinmate at Interlochen—they were making their way back here when Dulcy, um . . . when Dulcy was killed. She came here to let me know—she didn't have to do that—and along the way saved a young boy who lost his entire family and would've died alone. She's a good kid who's trying to get back to her family in Wisconsin, and she needs—"

"A boat ride across the Strait," Spencer finished his sentence.

"They'd bike over the Mighty Mac if they could," Nathan said, cocking his head at the five-mile-long bridge stretching through the thin mist to the Upper Peninsula barely visible on the horizon, "but they can't, 'cause St. Ignace isn't letting anyone through. Could you two take 'em across? It's not like they're patrolling the waters."

"I wish that were true," Spencer said, stepping into the cockpit and turning up the dashboard-mounted Icom marine radio to full. An authoritative voice repeated a terse announcement over the Channel 16 emergency frequency that any boats approaching the coast would be turned back or fired upon. "They got control of the Coast Guard's response boats at the St. Ignace installation, and they're not fooling around." Spencer pointed across the harbor inlet to a moored blue and white tourist ferry, its side pockmarked with bullet holes above the water line and most of its windows smashed. "Coupla well-heeled people from Grosse Pointe waved gold under the skipper's nose—as in real gold—to ferry 'em to sit out the apocalypse on the Big Tourist Trap," Spencer continued, referring to Mackinac Island six miles north-northeast. "Skipper got his ear shot off, and one of his passengers caught a bullet in the shoulder and almost died. I dunno what the hell the Yoopers think they're gonna do when winter comes and people can just snowmobile across the strait—maybe they think everyone'll be dead or outta gas by then."

"I'm not asking you to run a blockade to drop 'em off right at the St. Ignace dock," Nathan protested. "Take 'em a few miles up the coast to someplace quiet so they can be on their way. You know these waters better than anyone. Besides, GPS still works, right? It's not like the satellites got sick."

"Nate," Spencer blew noisily as he stepped onto the dock, "I can't tell you how heartbroken we are about Dulcy. Your daughters were the closest we'd ever get to having kids of our own, and I'm gonna miss opening our windows to listen to her practice the violin—it was like a free concert every night. You and I go back a long way, old friend, but you're asking us to risk our lives." Spencer looked to Caroline for support, but his gaze was met with a face he knew well—concern mixed with disappointment. It would be three against one.

"She needs our help," Caroline said softly. "It'd be wrong not to."

"Honey, this collapse or whatever is just getting started," Spencer argued. "We survived the flu, but winter's coming, and I don't know how much food there is to go around—I can't say with any degree of confidence whether we'll still be alive come spring. You and I are living on borrowed time right now without running the added risk of getting shot."

Caroline smiled wanly, slipping her hand into her husband's. "Spence, I've been living on borrowed time every day after two bouts with breast cancer, and chemo that almost killed me both times. It's why I'm always so melancholy when it's time to put *Sweet Caroline* into storage—I never know if it's gonna be my last boating season. Sorry to say, the way things are looking, I think this is it. And I'm perfectly fine dying for a noble cause, rather than waiting for the cancer to come back a third time and finish me off." She looked at Melinda. "She's one of the good ones, Spence. If we only get one last boat trip before we starve or freeze, let's make it count for something."

Spencer silently stared at his wife to the squawking of gulls and the racket of a husband-wife quarrel from one of the refugee boats farther down the pier. "I'd like to say you win, but we have a problem that love and rainbows can't fix—we don't have the gas to get *Caroline* out and back, and we can't buy more." He thumbed at the neighboring fuel point and its armed guards with a frustrated shrug. "They're only taking ammunition and precious metals as payment, now that the dollar's nothing more than toilet paper. I got five rounds of .30-06 left in the box I bought twenty years ago for the rifle I pulled outta mothballs to join the neighborhood watch, and we don't have any gold or silver, short of our wedding rings and my fillings."

"That's where you're wrong," Nathan said, his back flaring with pain as he dug into his jeans pocket with a grimace to flash a one-ounce US

Silver Eagle coin. "This oughta be more than enough to cover the cost of filling up. And this," he continued, flipping his fingers to produce a five-dollar gold coin in a protective plastic sheath, "is for your trouble smuggling two passengers and their bikes across the Strait."

"I can't let you do that, Mr. Bowers," Melinda gasped as Nathan grabbed Caroline's hand and pressed the coins into them.

"Yes, you can—keep quiet, please," Nathan said flatly.

"Nathan . . ." Caroline protested.

"You're agreeing to do something dangerous for a total stranger. You're taking this payment. End of discussion," Nathan cut her off. "This is real money that'll go a long way."

Spencer took the coins from Caroline, inspecting them as they sparkled in the noontime sun. "We won't turn down the silver—we need fuel to do this for you. But are you sure you wanna part with the gold?"

"I already parted with it, and I'm not taking it back. Use it for food, supplies, or buy the Dixie Saloon and go into the brewpub business—whatever you want," Nathan said. "Maybe if I had had half a brain, I could've paid someone to drive down and bring Dulcy home. I couldn't be there for my daughter, but I—we—can help her friend and the boy she saved."

Spencer pocketed the coins with a conspicuous glance around—flaunting gold and silver in a lawless society was an invitation for trouble—as Caroline sniffled and dabbed at her eyes with her sleeve. "OK, young lady . . . Melinda, is it? You and your little friend got yourselves a boat," Spencer said. "I know it's short notice, but you think you two can be back here at sunset with your stuff? NOAA and the Weather Channel are history, but the barometer and my trick knee are telling me it's gonna rain later—it could make for choppy waters, but it'll also make sneaking you across without being detected easier."

"Thank you so much," Melinda said, energetically shaking Spencer's and Caroline's hands.

"Don't thank us just yet. Now, if you'll excuse me, I've gotta negotiate a fill-up with the big guys with the guns," Spencer said, nodding back at the fuel station. "I know one of 'em—we'll be ready."

"And so will your passengers," Nathan said, spinning his wheelchair around to return to shore.

"Mr. Bowers?" Melinda meekly ventured halfway down the dock. "Um . . . thank you, too. That was very generous of you."

"You can thank me by making it home," Nathan responded without looking back. "Find your family. Live happily ever after—for yourselves and for my Dulcy, who'll never get the chance."

The duo didn't say another word the entire trip home.

CHAPTER 32

MISSOURI

Reed shot to his feet the moment the surgeon tiredly walked into Mercy Hospital Perry's foyer, the sunset flooding through the lobby windows bathing him an eerie crimson that almost matched the bloodstains on his scrubs. The surgeon's haggard face gave away that Alexia was still alive—even as a rookie cop, Reed knew the look of a man bearing the news of death when he saw it—but likewise didn't inspire confidence in her prognosis.

"How is she, doc?" Reed anxiously asked as Kara rose from her padded chair, sweaty clothes clinging to her skin from the lack of air conditioning.

"Alive, and I'm sorry to say that that's the best answer I can give you," he wearily replied with a light Indian accent. "The bullet went through the upper right side of her chest, and the bleeding collapsed her lung. We couldn't take an x-ray because we don't have power—I had to operate by the light of a lantern—and I made a lucky guess as to where to insert the thoracotomy tube to drain the air and blood to re-inflate it."

"She gonna make it?"

The surgeon peeled off his cap and scratched a face roughened by several days' worth of stubble. "I don't know. She lost a lot of blood, and we have none to give her, so an IV is the best I can do. She's going to be very susceptible to pneumonia, or opportunistic infections from our inability to maintain a sterile operating field. In short, it's in God's hands—and if she does pull through, she has a very long road to recovery."

"Thank you," Reed said, running his hand through his hair, which had grown since the collapse to just barely meeting Air Force regulation.

"You can stay the night in the waiting room," the surgeon said, gesturing toward the main staircase at the far end of the foyer. "We'll see how she is in the morning."

Reed sighed resignedly as the surgeon took his leave—he and Kara had nowhere else to go. His car, belching smoke and trailing sparks from running on a tire rim, had managed to limp to the roadblock cordoning off Route 51 at the Perryville city limits before breaking down. The militia, a mixture of civilians and National Guard infantrymen from the local armory, loaded Alexia onto a golf cart and took her to the hospital, disobeying their orders to keep people out rather than let a wounded airman die.

Kara sniffled. "What're we gonna do?" she whimpered.

"I'm workin' on it, starting right now," Reed said, grabbing his rucksack from the tile floor. "The mayor and police chief wanna talk to me about where we've been, and everything we've seen and heard. Hopefully, once I tell them about our heroic odyssey to get you home to your two-star general dad—who just might reward this town handsomely with food and aid—they'll be amenable to giving us a hand."

"What, you're gonna leave me here?" Kara nervously protested.

Reed jerked his thumb at a pair of good ole' boys armed with hunting rifles strolling outside past the lobby. "Kara, this is probably the safest you've been since this whole mess started. They got the hospital on twenty-four-hour guard to keep out the druggies dying for a fix. Why don't you take the doctor up on his offer and catch some sleep in the waiting room?"

"Can't I come with you?"

"If it's all the same, I'd like you here with Alexia." Reed fished a peanut butter Clif bar and a stick of beef jerky from a side pouch of his rucksack. "Dinner's on me—besides, all our food's still sittin' in what's left of my car. I hope," he said, tossing the packages to Kara. "Was saving these for a special occasion."

"Thanks," Kara said—she was ravenous. "I guess not being dead counts as a special occasion."

"Not special enough," Reed grumbled, throwing his pack onto his back with a grunt before reaching for his rifle leaning against the chair. "Because Alexia deserved one hell of a lot better than this."

Kara stood silent as Reed pushed open the glass door and exited into the evening twilight.

***

"Kara?"

A hand gently shook Kara awake, her eyes struggling to adjust to the waiting room, pitch black save for a sliver of light from the hallway reflecting off the wall-mounted flatscreen TV.

"Reed?" she groggily asked as she slowly sat up from the row of cushioned seats with a yawn. "Wha . . . whatizzit?"

"Alexia's dead."

"Oh, no," she gasped in disbelief, Reed's words jolting her awake.

"I checked on her after I got back from city hall, and . . . she must've passed in the night. Screamed for the one nurse on staff, but, um, there was nothing they could do."

"Oh, God," Kara said as he sat next to her, cradling his head in his hands. "I'm so sorry."

"I am, too. She was . . . she was something else. I really liked her, but never said anything—woulda been too much of a hassle, being in the same squadron and all," he confessed, forlornly running his thumb along the raised engraving of one of Alexia's dog tags, its metal surface catching what little light filtered into the room. "I wanted to tell her after we punched out from Scott, but there was never a good time. And now there never will be."

"I'm sorry, I really am," Kara softly repeated, silently berating herself for not feeling worse about it than she did; while she genuinely felt bad about her death, and was very frightened about only having Reed left to help her, Alexia had made abundantly clear to Kara in both word and deed that she considered her dead weight. And, she hated herself for thinking, they now could get moving instead of waiting for months while Alexia convalesced. "What do we do now?" Kara cautiously ventured after a respectful pause.

"They're gonna bury Alexia in the afternoon with everyone who died of the flu," Reed answered. "Then we're gonna get outta here and continue mission to Whiteman. We got a ride."

"Really?" Kara excitedly exclaimed before tempering her inappropriate, if understandable, enthusiasm. "They decided to help us?"

"No—city's got nothing to spare, and the mayor flat-out said that he doesn't give a shit who your father is. Believe it or not, I bought a used car, courtesy of Senior Airman Alexia Rios."

"I don't understand."

"I traded the doctor his new Camry and a full tank of gas for Alexia's rifle and magazines," Reed said matter-of-factly. "We need a set of wheels, and he realized he needed a way to protect his family, so we made a deal. Doc said he was a real anti-gun guy before all this—nothing like the end of the world as we know it to make you see the error of your ways. Hope he's got a kid who played a lotta Call of Duty, 'cause I think he's gonna shoot his own foot off before he ever shoots a bad guy," he snorted.

"Thank you," Kara said, gently putting her hand on Reed's shoulder.

"Don't thank me—thank Alexia. You know, it's funny—we had to take my car because hers was a piece of junk, and her last act on this earth was to buy me a new one," Reed sadly chuckled as he laid down on a nearby loveseat. "I'm gonna take my own advice and try to grab some rack while I can. Sorry I woke you up," he mumbled, and was asleep seconds later.

Now wide awake, Kara slid her iPhone from her rucksack and slipped out of the waiting room, the relative cool of the tiles on the soles of her feet a welcome contrast to the stuffy heat that nightfall had done little to ameliorate. Kara turned it on, painfully jamming her eyes shut with the white welcome screen that lit the dark hallway around her before dimming to its nighttime setting.

No WiFi, no 5G—were you really expecting to get a signal, you jackass? she silently admonished herself. Kara glowered at the half-empty battery icon before affording herself a few minutes to scroll through pictures with her parents—the three of them together, and then just her and Dad after Mom had passed.

She closed out the photo album and opened her messages, scrolling past a dozen failed attempts at contacting her father to the last text that had successfully gone through, right before she, Reed, and Alexia bugged out of Scott. Kara thought a moment before her thumbs danced on the glass.

I'm safe in Perryville MO. We're heading for Whiteman AFB tomorrow to try and catch a flight. See you soon!

She hit the send icon and stared at the screen, knowing the text would bounce back; sure enough, the red exclamation point and the "not delivered" message appeared moments later.

Reed's snores began echoing down the hallway. Kara allowed herself an optimistic smile about their chances—they were only a few days away from Whiteman, if that.

"See you soon, Dad," she said, turning her phone off and slipping back into the waiting room to try and go back to sleep.

CHAPTER 33

MICHIGAN

Jimmy nauseatingly moaned, face-down in his folded arms, as *Sweet Caroline* crossed the choppy waters of the Straits of Mackinac in the middle of the dark and overcast night. While the storm that Spencer had predicted earlier in the day made for a rough ride, the rain had let up the moment they left port shortly after two in the morning.

"Stay with us, little guy," Spencer said from behind the ship's wheel, his anxious face lit by the display of the Garmin open-array radar and GPS he was relying on to navigate. The death of the US economy meant the shipping lanes through the straits were empty, which made navigating the channel without running lights only slightly less of a dangerous challenge.

Melinda and Caroline grabbed the table of the forward corner lounge to steady themselves as Spencer spun hard to port to compensate as the boat ran into one of the Strait's many tricky and unpredictable currents, which flipped direction every couple of days with Lake Michigan's and Lake Huron's never-ending tug-of-war to reach equilibrium. "Sorry—hang in there," he grunted.

"Where we at?" Caroline asked, rustling the trash bag she had ready in case Jimmy lost his dinner.

"Far side of St. Helena Island," he said, tightening his grip as a gust of southerly wind buffeted the port windows; the island's leeward side facing the Upper Peninsula coast had long been used as a storm shelter by boaters, but Spencer wasn't taking any chances being spotted.

Caroline stood long enough to gaze out the window into the darkness. "Shame the lighthouse is out—it's so beautiful."

Spencer checked the map display. "Suits me just fine, given our situation. You have the conn, honey—we're almost at the drop-off point," he said, sliding down the cockpit seat to let his wife behind the wheel so he could slip into a red drysuit and neoprene anti-slip boots. He exited the sliding glass door onto the rain-slicked outdoor salon, the drysuit negating the cold, wet chill. Steadying himself against the rocking boat, he scanned the nearby Sand Dunes Beach and the thick woods beyond with a pair of thermal binoculars. There was nobody around, which was precisely why he and Caroline had chosen the long stretch of beach far from the summer homes that dotted the UP coast.

The grumble of the boat's twin Volvo Penta diesel engines throttling back greeted Spencer as he stepped back inside. "We're here," Caroline said, turning to face him. "Coast clear?"

"Yup," Spencer curtly replied. "How's the current?"

"Someone up there likes us—I can hold position," she answered. "I'd feel better if we were able to drop anchor."

"Me, too, but if it turns out we're not alone, we'll have to slip away in a hurry," Spencer told his wife before taking a knee next to Jimmy. "Just a little longer and we'll have you on dry land, OK, buddy?" He looked to Melinda as he slipped a pair of night-vision goggles over his eyes and clipped a handheld marine radio to his shoulder. "Get your life vests on and be ready the moment I get back from dropping off your stuff."

Spencer stepped back outside and turned on his goggles, the aft of his boat lighting up in a pea-soup green. He made his way to the Newport Baja inflatable dinghy strapped to the swim platform, and pulled the children's bicycles and backpacks from *Sweet Caroline*'s transom storage hatch to carefully lay them on board. Revving up the Honda outboard motor, Spencer piloted for shore as fast as conditions allowed, dragging the cargo onto the wet sand and shoving a green glow stick through Melinda's front spokes so he could find the landing site again. He pulled the dinghy back into the surf and returned to *Sweet Caroline* holding station offshore.

It had taken longer than Spencer would have liked to get his passengers on board, with Jimmy giving them a scare by almost slipping into the drink. Jimmy clung to Melinda as Spencer piloted toward the glow stick beckoning them to shore, a fine mist beginning to fill the sky from the low clouds. Spencer shook his head to clear the droplets blurring his view as they reached the beach, nervously realizing that his goggles were dimming, and fast.

"Get into the woods and outta the rain," Spencer advised Melinda as she hitched the trailer to her bike by the light of the glowstick. "Come sunrise, get on Route 2 and head west—thataway, lake on your left," he said, pointing down the beach. "I don't think the locals are gonna hassle you two—I'm guessing St. Ignace was doing their own thing with sealing off the bridge. In case I'm wrong, keep your heads down and your mouths shut—your lack of their very peculiar dialect'll give you away sure as anything."

Jimmy unexpectedly hugged Spencer, almost knocking him off balance. "Thank you, mister."

"Yes—thank you so very much," Melinda said, joining in.

"Don't mention it," Spencer said, voice thick. "Caroline and I were never able to have kids. If fate had been kinder, I'd like to think they would've been like you. When all of this is over, you're more than welcome to visit and get a boat ride in much better weather. Good luck—and get home safe."

"Good luck to you, too," Melinda said, shaking his hand as she started to shiver with the wet chill.

"Looks like I'm gonna need it," Spencer muttered, keying his marine radio to call his wife as he dug a trench in the sand with his heel to bury the glow stick. "I'm coming back, hon, but I need you to turn on the running lights—my night vision's on the fritz."

Sweet Caroline sprang into view seconds later, its outdoor lights bathing it in an ethereal blue—Melinda thought the boat was much farther out than it actually was. "Get back here fast," Caroline's voice crackled. "We got a contact, bearing one eight zero. Might be nothing, but if it isn't, I just lit us up like a Christmas tree!"

"On my way," he said, grabbing the dinghy's perimeter rope and towing it back into the water. "Get into the woods!" he yelled to the kids before starting the motor.

Melinda guided Jimmy off the beach, her calves burning as they slogged through the wet sand to reach Route 2. She pulled Jimmy's bike the rest of the way to the shoulder, looking up just in time to see *Sweet Caroline*'s lights wink out, once again shrouding the boat in darkness. Melinda mouthed one more thank you, and a silent prayer for their safe return to harbor before jumping with a start at what sounded like a distant gunshot coming from the water. The mist became a drizzle as they dragged their bikes through more sand and beach weeds before reaching the cover of Hiawatha National Forest.

***

The drizzle had become a downpour shortly after Melinda finished setting up their two-person tent.

She held Jimmy on their rolled-out sleeping bags as raindrops pelted their waterproof shelter, a tiny battery-powered lantern acting as a night light to soothe the boy after their harrowing ride. Melinda grimaced with the annoying *buzz* of a mosquito flying outside the air vent; after two days of actual baths, she didn't relish going back to slathering herself with insect repellent.

"We should try to get some sleep before the sun comes up," she said, reaching to switch off the lamp.

Jimmy grabbed her arm. "Can we keep it on? Please?"

"Sure," Melinda agreed, stroking his wet, shaggy hair—she had tried to give him a haircut during their time with the Bowers family, but he had steadfastly refused. "Are you OK?"

Jimmy shook his head. "I miss Mom and Dad. I wanna go home."

"I know," she said, a lump rising in her throat. "When we get to my house, you can join our family. And we'll never be apart."

Jimmy clutched his stuffed Bluey doll. "Ever?"

"Never ever. Cross my heart."

"Can I have some Swedish Fish?"

"Sure—you've had a long day," Melinda said, reaching to unzip her backpack, remembering with a pang of guilt that they hadn't brushed their teeth before bedding down. She stared, perplexed, at a small Mason jar peeking out from an old kitchen towel atop her belongings. She unwrapped it to discover a container of Nathan's black gooseberry jam with a handwritten note taped to it.

Just think happy thoughts and you'll fly—Peter Pan, Nathan had scrawled.

"I will," Melinda whispered huskily, making herself a silent promise not to open it until she and Jimmy were safe at home—or wherever fate landed them if her home was no more. She gingerly rewrapped the jar and continued digging for Jimmy's sweets.

CHAPTER 34

GERMANY

With the finesse of a surgeon, Josh tuned the Eton radio in an attempt to pull in the distant broadcast in what sounded like Italian—he didn't speak a word of it, but it was the only thing he could find on the shortwave band on the sunny afternoon. Despite his best efforts, he couldn't coax the signal from the electromagnetic swirl of empty static.

He defeatedly set the radio next to him on the Humvee's hood and checked the time, silently cursing his inability to fall asleep before his team's all-night mission.

"You look like a man with a problem," Kira said, appearing from the woods where The Lost Boys had set up a perimeter shortly after arriving outside the abandoned town of Schönenberg.

"I got a million problems, but you're not one of them," Josh cheerily replied. "What brings you calling?"

She patted her low-slung M4 carbine. "Clayton and I just got back from foraging duty in the village. Believe it or not, the local market's back room was fairly well-stocked, and the colonel sent a detail to clean it out," she tiredly muttered. "Can I join you for a bit before I try to catch some sleep? My feet are killing me."

"That depends," Josh said with a smirk. "Find anything good in town?"

Kira theatrically pulled a bag of Haribo Primavera strawberry marshmallow candy out of her leg cargo pocket. "This oughta cover my admission," she said, tossing it to Josh and climbing up next to him, peeling off her helmet to reveal a messy bun of brown hair held back by umpteen bobby pins. "*Star Trek*'s cancelled this evening, if you hadn't already figured it out. Too bad, too—it's the DS9 episode where the Obsidian Order and the Tal Shiar get tricked into attacking the Dominion homeworld and get wiped out."

"It's gonna be a long night," Josh mumbled with a mouthful of candy. Under cover of darkness, Josh and his team would join other soldiers in breaking into the abandoned Miesau Ammo Depot—the largest military ordnance depot outside the US—and swiping as much small-arms and vehicle ammunition as they could. "Colonel isn't taking any chances with unwelcome surprises after we zapped those Russkies at the fuel point."

"Shouldn't you be trying to catch some rack?" Kira asked as Josh loudly yawned.

Theo's loud buzzsaw snore rose from nearby in the woods where the rest of the team had sacked out. "With that racket?" Josh joked, handing back the bag. "Actually, I've been thinking about my mom—hoping she's still alive. Where you from, if you don't mind me asking?"

"Akron," she flatly answered. "And I already know that Akron's toast, so I try not to think about it at all."

"Sorry."

"Me, too. I've had more than my share of sleepless nights—then again, maybe we're all trapped in a nightmare we can't wake up from."

Josh tapped his Starfleet comm badge and looked to the sky. "Computer, end program!" he called out to Kira's laughter. "This holosuite program sucks—I'm totally asking Quark for my money back."

"Thanks. I needed that," Kira chuckled, picking up the hand-crank radio. "Any news?"

Josh's hands brushed against Kira's as he turned it back on and straightened the antenna. "I was trying to pull in something called Redoubt Radio. It's out in Idaho or Montana—they relay whatever information they find," he said, scanning the band again. "Mid-day isn't the best time to pull in shortwave, but I don't have anything better to do." The Italian broadcast faded in and out, followed by the staticky, garbled ramblings of a fire-and-brimstone preacher quoting from Revelation in a thick Southern accent—before the collapse, religious programming had been one of shortwave's few remaining mainstays as governments slashed or eliminated their services in the internet era.

His scan stopped with the prerecorded *ding-dong* of a large bell coming in loud and clear. *"Dyevyat, tree, syem, chitirye, dva,"* a deep Slavic voice intoned. *"Dyevyat, tree, syem, chitirye, dva. Katya, Nadia, Volodya."* The hair on Josh's arms stood on end with a creepy chiming tune from what sounded like an antique music box.

The bell tolled again. *"Nula, dva, adeen, pyat, vosyem,"* the voice continued.

"This is weirding me out," Kira said with a shiver as the speaker repeated the new sentence. "What is it?"

"No idea," Josh said, turning the radio back off.

CHAPTER 35

MICHIGAN

Sparks from the campfire danced into the purple evening sky as Melinda played the flute for her first audience since Interlochen.

Jimmy sat enthralled, their gracious hosts clapping and swaying while Samuel, the nineteen-year-old eldest son of eleven children, accompanied Melinda on the guitar. *Soothe the savage beast indeed*, she said to herself as she glanced at her young charge, the words of the late Emil Jorgensen echoing in her head as she and Samuel finished their rendition of the Dave Matthews Band's "Say Goodbye"—her salt-of-the-earth listeners preferred rock to classical.

Melinda and Samuel held hands and took a bow as the family's applause and hoots rang out into the night. "That was awesome! I'd love to play more, but unfortunately, guard duty calls," Samuel said, handing his father the guitar and grabbing his bolt-action .30-06 rifle as his younger siblings scattered to get in some playtime before bed. "Elias, remember you got midnight to sunup—be ready to relieve me!" he called after his teenage brother as he followed the flock.

Jimmy scooted to Melinda and laid his head on her lap the moment she sat on the well-worn camp log abandoned by the kids; she rubbed his back, contentedly staring at the half moon dancing on Lake Michigan's tranquil waters. The stormy night from their stomach-churning boat crossing had cleared into a beautiful, albeit humid morning, and Melinda and Jimmy had made great time following US Route 2 westward as it hugged the picturesque shoreline. They ended up at a rest area outside the village of Naubinway, where they ran into the Barksdales, a Christian missionary family that graciously welcomed them to spend the evening under their protection. Hailing from eastern Tennessee, the family had been spending the summer traveling the upper Midwest and preaching the Gospel when the collapse hit.

Esther, the family matriarch, sat across from the duo after checking to make sure the older children were keeping an eye on the younger ones. "Miss Hodgson, the Lord gave you a wonderful gift," she said, the fire illuminating her tired face and thin brown hair that poked out from underneath a red bandana.

"And you honor Him by using it to bring people joy," her husband, Caleb, added.

"Thank you so much—and thank you for your hospitality," Melinda said, cautiously setting her flute behind the log. "The venison was delicious."

"You're very welcome," Esther said. "And we're sending you and your little angel off tomorrow morning with as much smoked meat and trout as you can carry to help you on your way. Sorry to say, you two aren't gonna find much Christian charity out there—present company excepted."

"Oh, I know that firsthand," Melinda snorted.

"Young lady, you don't know the half of it," Caleb said, scratching his thick graying curly beard. "It's dog-eat-dog."

Melinda glanced down to make sure Jimmy was asleep—the long day and his full belly had zonked him out. "I'd appreciate anything you can tell me about what to expect up ahead."

"You can expect a lotta unfriendliness to strangers like yourselves," Esther said. "The news, before it went down for good, was full of horror stories of country folks gettin' overrun by people fleein' the cities and suburbs like the Golden Horde. And even though the UP got spared from the flu—pro'bly because it killed everyone long before they could make it this far—everyone's scared spitless of outsiders bringin' it in."

Melinda fought back a flash of anger, remembering town after town that had denied her and Dulcy passage, putting them on a path that resulted in her friend's death. "I just wanna get home, and I have no idea if I have a home or a family at all! We also gotta deal with this nonsense out here in the middle of nowhere?!"

"There's no 'middle of nowhere' anymore, hon," Esther continued, making sure their small children were too far away to hear. "There's a lotta riff-raff causin' trouble—even out here in the willywacks. Radio says there were prison breaks all over the place when the you-know-what hit the fan, and those convicts have been formin' gangs and runnin' wild with no police to stop 'em. And that's on top of all the addicts trying to find their next fix, and good people turnin' bad outta desperation—*and* the gazillion or so illegals those fools in Washington let in when they erased the southern border and rolled out the red carpet."

Caleb tossed a log onto the fire to ward off the lake-effect chill that had become more pronounced with sunset. "Fella on the CB the other day said there's a huge biker gang that's been terrorizin' people up and down the Wisconsin-Michigan border, right where you two're headed. It's by the grace of God Almighty that you made it this far—from here on out, you need to be *very* careful about who you trust. We'd give you a gun to protect yourselves, but sorry to say we don't got one to spare."

Melinda shuddered as Caleb's warning laid bare the reality of her and Jimmy's predicament. Her extraordinary luck since cheating death—finding Jimmy and his family's deep larder, making it across the Straits to the UP, running across the Barksdales—had made her overconfident, as if the men who killed Dulcy would be the only bad people they would run across. She had never liked guns, and she and her hunter father had had more than a few dinner-table arguments about gun control; she naïvely didn't give it a second thought at Jimmy's house when he told her the family's firearms were locked away. Like a nervous child realizing at school that she had forgotten to pack her homework, she anxiously wished she and Jimmy could teleport back to his house and try to find a gun, even though she didn't have the faintest idea how to use one. Gun control, Melinda now realized with dread, was a luxury belief made possible by civilization—and with civilization gone, she and Jimmy would be at the complete mercy of anyone who was armed.

She glanced at the children of the Barksdale clan, playing tag and zipping in and out of the tents that had been set up along their large white Highland Ridge Open Range recreational vehicle; Samuel sat armed vigil on the hood of the Ram truck towing it. "Well, you know my plans—what're you folks gonna do, if you don't mind me asking?"

"You're lookin' at it," Caleb answered with a wry grin. "We'd never make it back to Tennessee. Even if we had the gas, there's a lotta no man's land between here and home—and that's not countin' northern Illinois and southern Michigan glowin' in the dark 'cause Illinois let their nuke plants melt down."

"What?!" Melinda exclaimed, causing Jimmy to briefly stir.

"That's what they're sayin'," Esther said. "Anyway, looks like this is gonna be our home for a while. The hunting and foraging 'round here are good, and we're gonna dig in—literally. Gonna build earth lodges, just like the Plains Indians did, then store up as much food and firewood as we can to last the winter, and trust that the Good Lord sees us through."

"Just as he'll lead you through the wilderness to green pastures, Melinda Hodgson," Caleb added.

Melinda sheepishly smiled, remembering God's mercy in leading her to Jimmy and his family's supplies. "I hope so."

"But don't forget what we told you," Caleb said, stoking the campfire with a stick. "America, may she rest in peace, became Satan's playground long before the collapse. Without law and order, there's nothing stoppin' the bad guys—there're some grade-A predators out there, and they're runnin' riot. The Lord made sure we crossed paths, but from here on out, you need to grow eyes in the back of your head."

Esther excused herself to round up the children and get them tucked in while Melinda spent the better part of an hour extracting every scrap of information she could from Caleb pertinent to the conditions ahead. She hoisted Jimmy in her arms and carried him to their unfurled sleeping bags, the muscle aches and saddle soreness that had plagued her at the start of her journey long gone. Jimmy woke just long enough to clutch his stuffed Bluey before falling back asleep.

Melinda lay down next to him, exhausted. But sleep refused to come.

CHAPTER 36

MISSOURI

The abandoned house's muggy, stale air was a welcome break from the constant smell of burning.

Kara and Reed had first noticed it driving through the unincorporated town of Banner, and into the largest of the nine tracts of woods that made up Mark Twain National Forest. The odor still hung in the air ten miles down the road, where they had stopped to forage for supplies at an empty town consisting of a dozen homes and a convenience store.

Reed crept down the prefab home's tiny hallway, methodically clearing it room by room, his M4 carbine at the low ready. Kara followed several steps behind, the three cans of food that had been left on the store's shelves rattling in her plastic shopping bag. Although she had inherited Alexia's handgun, it stayed on her belt holster—while General Westman had made sure that his daughter knew how to shoot, he had never taught her close-quarters combat.

An empty dresser and a single bed stripped to the mattress greeted Reed as he swept into the last room. "All clear," he declared as a formality, dust wafting in the sunlight filtering through the window. "Whole damn town up and left."

"Which means they had a reason," Kara fretted.

They returned to the small kitchen, where Kara searched in vain through the bare pantry and cupboards while Reed thumbed through a notebook that had piqued his interest the moment they made entry through the smudged sliding glass door that the owners in their haste had left unlocked. He realized it was a ledger of news and events that the author had collected by CB radio since the collapse.

"Vibranium burning? Viburnum?" he quizzically read aloud as he attempted to decipher the author's atrocious handwriting and grammar. "Ranger Station in Potosi says fire is spreading everywhere, caller in Springtown said. Sky west of Bixby black with smoke." Multiple entries referenced news from something called Redoubt Radio; *whatever it is, it must be broadcasting on some other band*, Reed said to himself—they hadn't picked up any FM or AM stations since bugging out of Scott Air Force Base.

Kara picked up a NOAA all-hazards weather alert radio from the counter, its glowing red light indicating that it still had battery power. "Maybe this'll help," she said, clicking it on and dialing through its six preset emergency frequencies, all of them silent. "Or maybe not," she muttered, shutting it off and shoving it in her shopping bag.

Reed skipped to the final entry, dated the previous day. *I hope all the stupid St. Louis big-city assholes who didn't bother to put out their campfires are happy, because they burned us out! Thanks a lot, fuckers!* the author angrily scrawled.

"Everyone had a reason to bug out, all right," Reed said, tossing the notebook onto the yellowing table. The smell hanging in the air was a forest fire—a big one, by the homeowner's account—and it likely stood between them and Whiteman Air Force Base.

***

Reed and Kara shoveled the Dinty Moore beef stew and corned beef hash they had foraged into their mouths by the light of the backyard fire pit, their anxiety doing nothing to curb their enthusiasm for eating something other than corn.

"Is staying the night a good idea?" Kara asked, her foot tapping the pistol belt she had taken off to sit comfortably in the cheap plastic lawn chair. "I don't think it's safe."

Reed tossed his plate and plastic spoon onto the fire. "It's the least worst option," he explained, picking up the Missouri state atlas that the surgeon in Perryville had given him with his Camry, the towns mentioned in the homeowner's radio log circled with red marker. "If we try to navigate all these back roads in the dark, we could end up lost or trapped by the fire—or ambushed. After what happened to Alexia, I don't wanna take that chance."

Kara gestured to the western horizon, which glowed an angry red long after the sun had set. "That could come up on us pretty quick," she said, shuddering with the memory of watching from Dover Air Force Base as Washington, DC and Baltimore burned.

Reed gave an exaggerated sniff to illustrate the fact that the smoke had lifted. "I think we're OK for the time being. Look on the bright side—this'll be the first time since leaving Scott that you'll get to sleep in an actual bed." He stood and stretched before stooping to grab his rifle leaning on the log bench. "Get some rest. I got first watch," he said, disappearing around the corner of the house to stow the atlas in their car parked in the garage.

Kara stared into the night sky, thinking about her father and wondering whether any of the friends she had made at the London School of Economics were still alive, when a loud crack echoed from the side yard.

"Reed?" she called out. No answer. She slowly rose, walking with a slow and cautious crouch to the corner of the house. "Reed? Are you—"

Her words caught in her throat as she found herself facing four young Army soldiers, their rifles trained on her, and Reed sprawled on the ground at their feet, blood oozing from his head. "Don't move," one of them growled, grasping for her like a hawk descending on prey.

CHAPTER 37

MICHIGAN

Melinda's pounding heart threatened to burst from her chest as she and Jimmy followed their guides in the dark, walking their bikes along the railroad tracks at the edge of the closed town of Maristippi.

The point man in the lead raised his fist to silently order the group to freeze—one of the arm signals the good Samaritans smuggling the kids through town had taught them. *What is it? Did we get found out?* Melinda anxiously wondered, forcing herself to keep her cool for Jimmy's sake.

Caleb and Esther Barksdale had warned Melinda about Maristippi back at their camp in Naubinway. Like St. Ignace, the villagers had sealed off the small coastal town to outsiders by barricading Route 2 and digging some crazy defensive works, courtesy of residents who belonged to the local National Guard combat engineer unit which had ignored its deployment orders. Detouring around town meant days of travel on a maze of meandering backroads through Hiawatha National Forest, and fording a river with no crossings. However, the pastor of the Assembly of God church outside city limits deemed the town leaders' decision a grave injustice, and had enlisted his most trusted parishioners to smuggle people through—another valuable nugget Melinda had learned from the Barksdales. The timing of their arrival was serendipitous—they came the afternoon before the parishioners had Maristippi's all-night roving patrol, and therefore could be shepherded through town right away.

Melinda almost jumped with Reverend Alex Korhonen's soft but firm grasp on her shoulder. "Dis is the hard part, where the tracks cut across the main drag like we talked about," he whispered in a thick UP accent, her nose wrinkling with his bad breath. "Dere's no lights 'cause the power's out, but we're not takin' any chances—we gotta move fast and quiet. Remember, if things go wrong, we'll raise a ruckus so you can follow the tracks outta town fast as you can." He bent down to face Jimmy. "Remember—quiet as a mouse." Jimmy gave an exaggerated nod.

Up ahead, the point man gestured to move out with a forward roll of his arm. Melinda looked to Jimmy, wincing with the sound of her bike tires crunching the crushed gravel ballast from the railroad tracks. A breeze temporarily displaced the chemical smell of what the locals jokingly called "Yooper cologne"—the insect repellent they had doused themselves with to ward off the Upper Peninsula's legendarily horrendous mosquitoes. She shivered with the cool wind, and its foreboding reminder that each day brought them closer to winter.

The darkened town to their left and the spooky woods to their right absorbed light like a black hole; their sole illumination came from the dim, hazy band of the Milky Way arcing overhead, and the two tiny patches of lime-green "cat eye" luminescent tape sewn to the back of the point man's old Army patrol cap. Melinda fixated on the glowing green slits bobbing in front of her, nervously breaking eye contact just fast enough to make sure that Jimmy was following along. The cat eyes lifted higher in the black as the point man stepped up from the railroad easement to the town's main street.

"Here we go," Alex whispered. "Once we cross, keep followin' the tracks down into the weeds past the road."

Melinda wheeled up the incline to the two-lane street, silent except for the *tick-tick-tick* of her ten-speed's gears. She had just made it across when the *ring ring* of Jimmy's bike bell pierced the quiet. Melinda froze in horror, blood turning to ice water in her veins.

"Are you *serious*, kid?" the point man hissed.

"I'm sorry!" Jimmy loudly apologized, stopping in the middle of the road. "Mom and Dad always told me when I cross the street . . ."

"Quiet! For heaven's sake!" one of their escorts snarled under his breath.

Alex darted to Jimmy, grabbing his arm with his free hand. "It's all right, son—c'mon," he whispered, pulling him across so fast that Jimmy lost his balance, sliding with his bike down the far side incline into the railroad gravel.

"Owwwwww!" Jimmy screamed, clutching his knee.

"Oh, God!" Melinda gasped, lowering her kickstand and squatting next to him. "Jimmy, get up! We gotta go!"

"It huuurts!" he wailed as Melinda roughly hoisted him to his feet and righted his bike.

"Miss, shut him up or we're all cooked!" the escort bringing up the rear demanded.

"Who's dere?" a deep voice called out from down the empty, darkened street.

"Shit!" the point man spat. "Rev'rend, we gotta move!"

"Jimmy, *sssssssssshhhhh!*" Melinda desperately pleaded, firmly planting his hands back on his handlebars.

"Dat you, Rev'rend Korhonen?" the booming voice challenged again. Melinda covered Jimmy's mouth so hard that she worried she had slapped him.

Alex gritted his teeth, cursing their bad luck of having been stumbled upon by Maristippi's insomniac police chief—he had to act, and fast, lest his parishioners and their innocent charges end up behind bars, or worse. "Stay right where you are, chief—it's not safe!" he hollered.

"I heard a kid!" the chief yelled.

"For God's sake, stay put and take cover!" Alex hollered before raising his Remington 780 twelve-gauge shotgun into the air toward the woods and firing. Jimmy screamed through Melinda's hand as he covered his ears, his bike falling back to the ground as the reverend racked the slide with a loud *cha-chunk* and fired again.

"We got 'em on the run! Into the woods on the far side of the tracks!" Alex hollered, laying the groundwork to lead the chief and the posse he would soon raise on a wild goose chase back the way they came. "We got this, chief—get to the fire station and raise the alarm!"

"Hold in place—I'll be back wit' da cavalry!" the chief yelled, voice cracking as his footfalls echoed away.

"We're screwed!" the point man railed over Jimmy's whimpering.

"No we're not—hush that talk," Alex sternly reprimanded. "You all know the plan—lead 'em away, just like we practiced!" He lifted Jimmy's bike back up and anxiously knifed his hand down the railroad tracks out of town, the faint starlight reflecting from Melinda's frightened eyes. "Move your butts right now—they don't fool around with trespassers! God be with ya! *Go!*"

"Jimmy!" Melinda urged as she pried the boy's hands from his ears, startling him as if he had just noticed she was there. "How's your knee? Can you walk?"

"It hurts!" Jimmy whined.

Melinda lifted him by the armpits onto his bike and grasped the neck of his handlebars. "Hold on!" she said, grabbing her bike with her other hand and striding as fast as she could alongside the tracks, the bike trailer bouncing on stray rocks from the railroad bed. Jimmy's hands shot to his ears again with the *boom* of Alex's shotgun as he hollered out fake orders to his men to repel Maristippi's nonexistent invaders and cover the children's escape.

***

"Ow! Ow! Oweeeeeeeee!" Jimmy cried, his leg bucking in Melinda's grip as she dribbled peroxide on the gash in his knee.

"I'm sorry, but I gotta clean this out—you need to be a big boy, OK?" she pleaded, the early sunrise peeking through the woods allowing her to work without a flashlight.

"I hate that stuff! It stings really bad!"

"I know, but it'll stop. Now *sssssh*," Melinda said with a nervous edge to her voice; her worries about the locals giving chase had given way to concern over Jimmy's cut getting infected—a potentially life-threatening complication in a world without doctors. Melinda stuffed the peroxide bottle back into the on-the-go medic aid bag Jimmy's survivalist parents had prudently assembled in the event they had to evacuate, and slathered the wound with a packet of Bacitracin ointment before covering it with a large flexible bandage. "We'll change this again when we stop for lunch, and again before bed," she said, carefully rolling his jeans back down.

Jimmy stared, red-eyed, at the inch-long tear of his pants. "I'm sorry, Minda," he whimpered.

"You fell down—you didn't do anything wrong, OK? You have nothing to be sorry for," Melinda reassured him as she tore open a packet of ibuprofen. "We've got a long way to go today, and this'll help keep it from hurting—can you swallow pills?" Jimmy nodded in the affirmative and washed one of them down with a gulp of water. Melinda lifted him to his feet from the dead log that had served as her examination table. "How's it feel?"

"It still hurts, but just a little."

"Exercise'll do it some good," she said, pocketing their medical trash to bury later. "We're gonna get far away from this awful town before we eat breakfast, just to be safe."

Melinda and Jimmy weaved their bicycles through the forest toward nearby Route 2; morning twilight was slowly giving way to a beautiful dawn, and its promise of a day of great travel weather. "What's that smell?" Jimmy disgustedly asked the moment they exited the woods for the thickets of waist-high weeds marking Route 2's unmown right-of-way.

"Let's get outta here," Melinda gagged, picking up the pace with a retch, the unmistakable stench of decomposition bringing back the horrid memory of the guest house where Jimmy's family had died. She burst through the weeds first, screaming in terror the moment she laid eyes on the source of the stink.

"What's that sign—" Jimmy managed to say before Melinda roughly grabbed the wide-eyed boy and his bike and pointed him down the road.

"Don't look! Ride!" she yelled over the sound of her bike and trailer crashing to the asphalt.

Jimmy started to turn toward her the moment he straddled his bike, but Melinda forcefully pointed his head forward. "I said *don't look*! I'm right behind you!"

They tore down the road as fast as they could pedal, Melinda keeping pace behind Jimmy to block his view in the event his curiosity got the better of him. Three corpses, bloated and putrid in death, and wired to trees along with a spray-painted plywood sign informing travelers of the fate that awaited trespassers in Maristippi, blankly gazed after the children through eyeless sockets until they rounded the bend out of sight.

CHAPTER 38

GERMANY

Martin and Clayton lugged the heavy crate of shoulder-fired AT-4 anti-tank rockets out the door of the concrete ammunition bunker into the cool night air, squinting as they stepped into the blinding headlights of the transport truck illuminating the scene of their heist.

Clayton almost tripped over the acetylene blowtorch that had been swiped from an abandoned auto repair shop in order to burn through the metal door of the bunker, one of four hundred dug into the thick woods of Miesau Ammo Depot. Martin wiped the sweat beading under his helmet with his forearm, tightening his grip on the crate's rope handle as they speed-walked for the Light Medium Tactical Vehicle, passing half a dozen men trotting back to the bunker to make off with more.

Colonel Stirling watched with approval as a detail handed the purloined crates up to Theo, who stacked them in the back of the boxy armored truck; he had worried that they would find the bunkers empty, and every last round of the depot's more than twenty-five-thousand tons of ammo shipped off to Ukraine or some other ally. Stirling checked the time—0320 hours—and breathed a little easier for being ahead of schedule; turning on the LMTV's headlights to speed up their work was a risk, but an acceptable one, given that there was no one else around.

His new executive officer, Major Diego Villa, made a beeline for Stirling from the bunker, which was illuminated from the inside with red flashlights and green glow sticks reminiscent of a Christmas display. "We're lookin' good," reported Villa, who had joined The Lost Boys the week prior. "Hope we won't need to fire any of this off in anger."

"It's just insurance, that's all—I wanna make sure we can put up a fight if we have to," Stirling said, looking northeast over the treetops behind the bunker. "Too bad we can't just drive to Ramstein and catch a flight home."

"Woulda been great," Villa muttered—Ramstein Air Base, fourteen kilometers away, was a burned-out shell, as was the gutted Landstuhl Regional Medical Center where the major had been stationed. Ramstein's fleet of transport planes had been quickly appropriated at the start of the collapse—some of them under dubious pretenses—to fly dependents and lucky soldiers back to the States, including Villa's wife and three children.

"I'm sure your family's safe," Stirling said, sensing the thoughts of the XO he was still getting to know.

"Hope so," Villa muttered.

The two officers stepped over to the LMTV as Martin and Clayton set down the case for Patton and Josh to hand up to Theo. "How y'all doin'?" Stirling asked.

"Good PT, colonel!" Theo said, his large biceps swollen with the manual labor.

"Could be better—I sure could use a cold one after this," Patton grunted. Stirling was about to agree when the woods shook with a tremendous explosion, followed by another, and then another.

"What the fuck was that?" Theo gasped, gawking with the work detail that had stopped in its tracks as the sky over the treetops began to glow.

"That had to be Ramstein," Villa said, aghast.

"Turn those damn headlights off!" Sterling barked at the LMTV's driver. As the bunker again returned to darkness, a series of flashes flickered through the trees from the direction of Landstuhl.

"We're under attack!" Josh cried out as the sounds of the explosions reached them.

"No fuckin' shit, Sherlock! Keep goin'!" Patton shot back, grabbing a box of rifle ammunition to hoist up to Theo.

"Leave it! Let's go!" Villa shouted at the work detail before sprinting toward the bunker door, repeating the order as he passed by dumbstruck troops. "Saddle up and let's get outta here!"

The sky lit up with blinding white as a glowing fireball rose above the forest. *"Get down!"* Martin screamed to his men as he hit the dirt to the piercing shriek of the woman soldier on the detail with them. Theo leaped from the LMTV's tailgate, hitting the ground with a roll the moment the deafening shock wave reached them.

Martin staggered to his feet, staring in horror at a rapidly dimming mushroom cloud, a shower of incandescent white sparks racing skyward around it. "Did . . . did we just get nuked?" he stammered, the blast overpressure messing with his balance.

"No—if that was a nuke, we'd be blind, deaf, and burning," Stirling mumbled, popping his ears with a pained grunt. "Miesau's used to destroy old ammo, and whoever's doin' this must've found a nice big fat pile of it. Let's move!"

The soldiers scrambled onto the trucks to the steady racket of ordnance cooking off in the distance, the flames engulfing Miesau bathing the woods with blood-red light crisscrossed by dark shadows.

***

Two dozen soldiers and civilians huddled around the Eton radio on the hood of Martin's team's Humvee, listening in stunned disbelief.

"If you're just joining us on Radio France, amateur radio operators are reporting attacks on military bases and critical infrastructure across France and the Continent," translated Corinne Roberts, a dumpy civilian employee who had taught French at the Wiesbaden American High School, her monotone a stark contrast to the announcer's agitated, rapid-fire diction.

This must've been what 9/11 was like for Mom and Dad, Martin thought, fighting a losing battle to stay awake despite the steady stream of horrible news. Colonel Stirling had ordered The Lost Boys to put as much distance between them and the US Army's Kaiserslautern Military District as possible; Martin's team had led the convoy on back roads through the night and into the following afternoon, when they took refuge in the Steinbachtal woods north of the ruins of Saarbrücken, near the French border.

"Bomb and guerrilla attacks have been reported at Lyon-Mount Verdun Air Base, Mont-de-Marsan Air Base, and the ballistic nuclear submarine base at Ile Longue," Corinne continued. "Mass shootings have taken place at emergency food distribution centers at Marseilles, Lyon, Arles . . ."

Patton comforted Ann-Katryn as she dabbed her bloodshot eyes with a handkerchief while Corinne translated second- and thirdhand reports of attacks throughout what was left of Germany. Kira nervously slid her hand into Josh's as another civilian dependent quietly ushered away her ten-year-old daughter from having to listen to any more.

Corinne frowned with a burst of static that briefly drowned out the French announcer. "It sounded like she said something about Russian infiltrators."

"Hell, we coulda told them that," Sterling's gruff voice called from behind the group, which parted to let him through. He glanced at Theo, who sat in the Humvee's front passenger seat, his right ankle wrapped with a compression bandage from leaping too enthusiastically from the LMTV. "How's the leg, Carlvin? We gonna hafta amputate?"

"Doc hooked me up with some Ranger candy—I'll be fine, sir," Theo said, shaking a small bottle of 800-milligram Motrin pills—the Army's standard-issue miracle cure for everything from sprains and fevers to sucking chest wounds.

"Helluva day," the colonel continued, taking off his patrol cap to rub his gray high-and-tight haircut.

"Looks like not all the Russkies got issued wood blocks after all," Patton snorted.

"That's for damn sure," Theo agreed. "Colonel, why're the Russians even doin' this? America's gone, Russia's gone—this don't make no sense. It's like beatin' up a corpse."

Stirling shrugged—the limited intelligence they had pulled in since the collapse indicated that the flu had devastated the Russian political and military leadership just as badly as it had its American counterpart. "Russians do what they're told, when they're told to do it, even if it makes zero sense. Maybe this date was set before the shit hit the fan, or maybe some dyin' general decided people weren't sufferin' enough and gave the order outta spite—I dunno. We'll probably never know."

"How did they even give the order?" Ann-Katryn nervously asked.

"Radio—it's the only thing still workin'," Stirling answered. "Maybe a numbers station, or something as simple as a code phrase, like in the movies. *The Longest Day, Red Dawn*—the original, not the shitty remake." Patton did a double-take at the sight of Josh's and Kira's eyes going wide and jaws dropping as if they had seen a ghost.

"No offense, colonel, but thanks for the nightmare fuel," Martin tiredly mumbled. "You all can rock me to sleep tonight."

"Sorry to be the bearer of even more bad news, Sergeant Crenshaw, but sleep ain't gonna be on your itinerary tonight," Stirling said. "Take a walk with me back to the Stryker—I got a job for you."

Martin mumbled a curse as he turned off the radio, which Josh promptly snatched up. "Show's over folks," he said to the gaggle before turning to his team. "Grab some rack while you can, boys—and try to grab some for me, too."

Josh anxiously motioned Kira to follow him behind the Humvee as the audience dispersed, making sure Martin and the colonel were out of earshot. "Kira," he whispered, "do you remember that weird broadcast from yesterday—"

"No, I don't," Kira hissed, scared out of her wits by the possibility that they had heard the attack order and didn't think to pass it along. "I don't remember a thing, and neither do you! Because it never happened."

CHAPTER 39

MICHIGAN

Melinda jokingly revved her handlebar grip with a *vroom vroom*, staring with Jimmy down the empty strip of US Route 8 on the beautiful summer morning.

"Last one into Wisconsin's a rotten egg!" she exclaimed without taking her eye off the Menominee River bridge half a mile up the road. "You ready?"

Jimmy aped Melinda with a *vroom vroom* of his own. "Ready!"

"On your mark . . . get set . . ."

Melinda suddenly took off with a maniacal cackle. "Hey! *Cheater!*" Jimmy yelled to her back as she tore away, her bike trailer rattling as she picked up speed.

She flew toward the state line, her excitement erasing the frustration of having to take a lengthy detour. Melinda had hoped to follow the shore of Green Bay and cross over at the twin cities of Menominee, Michigan and Marinette, Wisconsin. But they heard rumors from the townspeople manning the roadblock at Escanaba that their path via State Route 35 was crawling with bandits like the Barksdales had warned about. Melinda and Jimmy were forced to keep following Route 2 inland to the small and friendly town of Norway, where they spent the night before starting south.

Melinda raised her fists in triumph the moment she crossed the bridge, cheering like crazy as she flew past the Wisconsin state line sign and coasted into the paved rest area next to it. Jimmy's anger at Melinda's perfidy evaporated at the sight of her jumping up and down and screaming with joy like the Green Bay Packers had just won the Super Bowl. The boy barely had time to put down his kickstand before Melinda grabbed his hands and whirled him in a circle, her laughter echoing into the forested river valley.

"You cheated, Minda!" Jimmy protested through his giggles as Melinda dropped to her knees and kissed the ground.

"Sorry!" Melinda said, unslinging her backpack and fishing out a pack of Skittles. "Will this make it up to you?" she barely managed to ask before Jimmy snatched it out of her hand. He greedily poured the candy in his mouth as Melinda drained her Owala water bottle, making a note to herself to bed down for the night near an open water source so they could fill their Berkey filter and top off.

She gazed over the tall weeds down the right-of-way, rehashing the plan for the next leg of their journey; they would spend the next several days traveling south, coaxing whatever information they could from the handful of small towns scattered throughout northern Wisconsin's vast hilly forests, before looping around whatever remained of Green Bay toward Lake Winnebago. Melinda knew that crossing northern Michigan and the UP, for all its challenges, had been the easy part of their journey; she and Jimmy would have to find a route to safely pass between Milwaukee and Madison, with no guarantee of what, if anything, they would find in Elkhorn. At the finish line, Melinda realized, the duo could discover that their problems were only just beginning.

"Let's go!" Melinda told Jimmy, chasing away the depressing thought as he mounted his bike, pocketing the candy wrapper and wiping the colored dye from his lips with the back of his hand. She closed her eyes and stared into the sky, feeling the sun on her face. *Mallory, Dulcy, if you're listening, we could really use a guardian angel. If not for me, then for him*, she silently prayed before they shoved off.

***

The sky had grown leaden by mid-afternoon. After several minutes trying to ride against a stiffening wind that threatened rain, Melinda decided to stop for the day before they got soaked to the bone. A small, weedy roadside clearing in the thick coniferous forest lining US Route 141 promised an opportunity to find a secluded spot deep inside the woods to set up camp—although they had not run into a soul since crossing the state line, Melinda wasn't taking any risks.

She had just turned to tell Jimmy to stop when a thick metal wire sprang from the road and snapped taut, snagging the front of her bike and flinging her over her handlebars. Melinda hit the asphalt hard, a sickening wet *snap* in her left arm heralding the worst pain she had ever felt in her life.

She barely had time to clutch her broken arm before a meaty set of hands yanked her to her feet and began dragging her away. Jimmy slammed on his brakes, his eyes saucers of fear at the sight of the group of men leaping out of the weeds. *"Go!"* Melinda screamed at him before a man in a patch-covered leather vest grabbed him and plucked him from his bike.

Melinda's captor wrestled her into the tall grass and yanked her backpack to the ground, unspeakable pain wracking her arm as her wrists were roughly pinned behind her. *"No! Let him go!"* she shrieked as the man with the vest bearhugged Jimmy from behind—and dropped him the moment the boy sunk his teeth deep into his beefy arm.

Jimmy ran for the woods as the man grasped his wounded limb and swore. "Get after the little fucker, you jackass—we need 'em both!" Melinda's captor managed to holler at his bumbling accomplice before she grabbed his crotch with her good hand and gripped and ripped for all she was worth. The man howled in agony as Melinda broke free, only to be violently shoved to the ground by a scraggly young tough. Fat raindrops began to pelt her like icy needles as she looked up at a trio of bikers towering over her, the burly, bearded man in the middle clutching his injured groin.

"Fucking *bitch*!" he hissed through clenched teeth, slowly drawing a large serrated knife from a belt scabbard as Melinda desperately tried to crawl away with her good arm. "I'm gonna love usin' you to send your stupid friends a message," he taunted, unfastening his belt as the skies opened up into a downpour. "And don't you worry—he's gonna work just fine . . ."

Three bullet holes suddenly blossomed from the man's chest as gunfire erupted from the woods on the other side of the road. Melinda screamed as a round caught the young tough squarely between the eyes, blowing the back of his head open.

"Holy shit!" the surviving biker shrieked like a girl, diving into the weeds next to Melinda—and looking up long enough for her to kick him in the face. *I gotta find Jimmy!* she screamed in her head, crawling one-armed through the rain-slicked weeds as the biker bucked on the ground, his broken nose bleeding like a faucet through his fingers. *The woods—he ran into the woods!* She leaped to her feet, holding her arm as

steady as she could as she bolted at a crouch for the treeline, blinded by the rain.

"Get down, lady!" a young man's voice called out in the distance over the firefight. She winced with the *zip* of a round whizzing by, turning on the run the moment she reached the relative safety of the forest to see a biker wildly shooting back at their unseen attackers before collapsing in a hail of bullets. Melinda tripped on a root, hit her head against a rock, and all went black.

***

"Minda!" Jimmy screamed at the sight of the man carrying her soaked, limp body out of the woods, her broken arm strapped to her chest with a makeshift splint.

"Get 'em both to the ORP! We'll be along in a few mikes!" Gunnar Nolan boomed over the downpour, knifing his hand back across the road. "I'd rather the boy not see this!"

Jane Christensen grabbed Jimmy's arm to keep him from running to Melinda and stumbling across the grisly aftermath of their successful ambush scattered amongst the weeds. "She's gonna be OK—she's coming with us," she reassured him, gently wiping his mop of soaking wet hair out of his face before helping him lift his bike.

Gunnar scowled at their lone prisoner, on his knees with his hands atop his head, the rain mixing with the blood from his broken nose to turn the front of his white t-shirt a washed-out red. "What're you gonna—" the prisoner nervously asked before he was interrupted by a gunshot that put one of his wounded buddies out of his misery.

"That answer your question, shitbag?" Lukasz Mankiewicz sardonically asked, the former cop savoring the impending application of frontier justice. The prisoner started to beg for mercy before Lukasz shut him up with a tap of his rifle butt to the back of his head.

The Compound's twelve-person ambush party scoured the scene like army ants, searching the dead for anything of intelligence value and stripping them of weapons, ammo, and their boots. Justin Christensen handed Gunnar a patch he had cut from the vest of the man who had grabbed Jimmy—a red clenched fist with bloody horns emblazoned with the words DEVIL'S WARRIORS.

"More of Iron Point's new friends—like we didn't already know," Justin spat as two other men walked the last of the gang's choppers from the woods to a heap in the middle of the road. Gunnar caressed the homemade thermite grenade stuffed into one of the pouches of his tactical vest; he couldn't wait to melt the gang's bikes into slag with the simple mix of aluminum powder and iron oxide poured into a cola can.

Gunnar wiped the rain from his wristwatch and blew three blasts from the black plastic whistle tied to his tactical vest with parachute cord. *"Three minutes!"* he bellowed. "Ethan!"

Ethan Moran trotted up, his olive drab and loam camouflage face paint streaked from rain and sweat. Gunnar glanced at the prisoner, who was barely older than the young man. "Yours if you want it, kid."

"Aw, c'mon!" the prisoner pleaded with Ethan's determined nod, his swollen nose giving his pathetic begging a comically nasal tone. "This was my first job—I never did nothin' to nobody before this!"

"So you don't qualify for the Devil's Warriors health and dental plan yet? Looks like this is gonna be out-of-pocket then, asshole," Gunnar sneered. Ethan began to raise his rifle to the man's chest before Gunnar stopped him with a hand on the barrel's black Picatinny shroud. "We wasted enough rifle ammo on these motherless fucks today. Use your sidearm, back of the head. Let their buddies know it's personal."

"Well, I'd love to stay and chat, shitbag, but that's my cue to move," Lukasz taunted, stepping away from behind the condemned as Ethan circled around. "You got no idea how hard it is to get brains out in the wash."

"Don't do it, man," the prisoner blubbered, his nose bubbling blood and snot. "Lemme go—I'll leave and never come back. Swear to God! Please, I'm beggin' ya," he sobbed at the sound of Ethan drawing his .45-caliber Glock from its Kydex holster with a plastic *click*. "Please! I got a family!"

"So did I once," Ethan spat before pulling the trigger.

CHAPTER 40

MISSOURI

Tom Bergan yanked the chocks from the wheels of his four-seater plane, staring helplessly at the wildfire descending on his family farm.

The wall of flame consuming Mark Twain National Forest shot into the sky like a curtain of destruction behind the ridge overlooking the historic Bergan Farm that had been in his family for more than a century and a half—and would soon be nothing more than a smoldering pile of ashes. His Cessna 172S Skyhawk SP was ready to fly, rolled out from its small hangar onto the farm's grass runway, and packed with the family's bug-out bags and what few keepsakes they could safely transport without overloading her. The Bergans were doomsday preppers who had stockpiled enough food and supplies to last to the Second Coming, every last bit of which was about to be incinerated—but they prudently had a Plan B to fly to his younger brother's ranch in Killeen, about six hundred miles away as the crow flies. Tom silently thanked God for giving him the forethought to have his onsite tank of avgas topped off once it was obvious the economy was about to crash.

"Diane! We gotta go!" Tom hollered toward the farmhouse to his wife over the growing roar of the approaching conflagration and the winds being sucked in to feed it. He solemnly took one last look at the rustic red home, the fields and hills where he had played as a child, and the small family cemetery where his parents, grandparents, and seven older generations of Bergans had been buried. The sage words of his late mother after a tornado had toppled their old grain silo echoed in his head—*things can be replaced. People can't.* Tom silently promised his ancestors that he'd one day return to rebuild, reassuring himself that he had made sure to pack their deed to the land.

The towering flames leapt higher over the ridge, fear gripping Tom with icy fingers—the fire was racing uphill and would be upon them soon. He was about to shout again for his family to get their asses in gear when Diane bolted out the front door clutching their granddaughter, Ava. Tom spun toward the hangar to tell his son Jasper to get moving when he found himself facing a crazed and disheveled man in a military uniform pointing a handgun at his chest.

Reed stared daggers at the farmer with his one good eye, the other swollen shut and crusted with blood. "Your gun," he hoarsely commanded, nodding at the .45-caliber Glock 21 on Tom's hip. "Set it down and step away from it. Slowly. No sudden moves."

Tom did as he was told. "Take it easy, son," he said in his gruff, fatherly voice as the stranger stifled a cough. "Eeeeasy. Whaddya want?"

Reed gestured toward the red and white Cessna. "A ride. You're gonna fly me and my friend to Whiteman Air Force Base," he croaked, his throat on fire from days of breathing smoke. "You know where that is?"

"Yes, I do," Tom cautiously answered. "But that ain't happening."

"Wrong answer!" Reed mindlessly yelled, the pain shooting through his throbbing head angrily reminding him of getting jumped at the abandoned house he and Kara had found. The four young privates who had gone AWOL from basic training at Fort Leonard Wood had robbed them blind, taking their car and his rifle and leaving them only their rucksacks—and in their haste, Alexia's handgun that Kara had left by the backyard fire pit.

"Honey, what's—" Diane called out before rounding the back of the Cessna and freezing at the sight of Reed, who wildly aimed his handgun back and forth to cover them. "Oh my God!" she blurted as six-year-old Ava screamed.

"It's gonna be OK," Tom nervously reassured them. "Listen, stranger, I got enough room for my family. We can't fit any more—we'd be too heavy to take off."

"You better figure it out!" Reed screeched, voice cracking. "I don't wanna hurt you, but I will if I have to, and nobody'll be going anywhere!" He cocked his head back without taking his good eye off the Bergans. "Kara! Let's *go!*"

Tom watched as a haggard young woman timidly stepped out from behind the hangar, gawking at the sight of the approaching fire. "I can do you better," he tried to reason with Reed as calmly as he could. "There's a pickup truck in the garage, full tank of gas, and a house full of survival food. It's all yours. I give you the keys, you let us go, and you and your friend load up with whatever you can carry and split before the fire gets here."

"She's the daughter of a two-star general—they're lookin' for her!" Reed raved like a madman, tasting salt from the blood beading in his parched throat. "Get us to Whiteman and they'll give you whatever you want—food, fuel, a new farm, anything! *Kara! C'mon!*" he screamed, his bloodshot eye glowing red. *"Don't just stand there—"* he managed before doubling over, struggling to keep his gun trained on Tom as he wracked with coughs, his tortured lungs unable to take any more.

Kara had barely taken a hesitant step forward when Tom's adult son strode from the shadows of the darkened hangar, leveling a pump-action shotgun at Reed. Her warning came out as a pitiful croak as Jasper fired, shredding Reed's head and neck with double-aught buckshot before racking the slide with lighting speed to blow Reed's chest open as he fell.

She sprinted for the woods, fueled by nothing but adrenaline and terror after days without food, the screams of the woman and her granddaughter punctuated by shotgun blasts as Jasper tried to pick her off on the run. Kara bolted into the bone-dry forest, frantically looking behind her to see if Reed's killer was chasing her before she found herself running off a cliff and plummeting into a deep ravine.

CHAPTER 41

WISCONSIN

The melodic chatter of birdsong pierced the silence. Then came the welcome sensation of warmth and comfort, and a refreshing breeze carrying the laughter of children playing.

We're safe, a disembodied voice reassured from the darkness of unconsciousness. *Wait—were we not safe before?*

Then came the pain—a dull ache rising from all around. *No, we weren't. We were in danger. We got hurt.* The sounds of frolicking kids grew louder. *There was a child with us.*

Fear began to rush in like a rider cresting the first drop of a roller coaster. *We were biking and the rain was coming and then all of a sudden—*

"Jimmy!" Melinda screamed, sitting upright before the most agonizing headache she had ever felt slammed her back down to the bed as if she had sprinted head-first into a brick wall.

"Easy there, honey. You've had an exciting past couple of days," a matronly voice reassured her.

Melinda squinted, the morning light drilling into her eyes like icepicks, just long enough to see an older woman peeling back a thick set of curtains and opening another window. "My apologies—it's hotter than an oven in here," she said as a breeze began flowing through the room. "Can't really be helped, though—without the blackout curtains, we'd shine like a beacon at night with everyone's power out."

"Who are you?" Melinda groaned. "Where am I?"

"My name's Donna, and you and Jimmy are safe as our guests. He's just an absolute darling—we turned on *Bluey* for him, and he thought he'd died and gone to heaven. He's been worried sick about you."

"Oh, thank God," Melinda gasped with relief. She cautiously opened her eyes to find her left forearm wrapped in a pink plaster cast. "What happened?"

"You had the misfortune of running smack dab into a trap some scumbag lowlifes set for unsuspecting travelers like you," Donna said, crossing to the ornate dresser to grab a glass of water and two ibuprofen. "Fortunately, they had the misfortune of running smack dab into an ambush we set up for scumbag lowlifes. Can you sit up for me?"

Melinda rose with a grunt, her headache returning with a vengeance. "This'll help, but you're gonna be feeling not so hot for the next few days," Donna said as her patient slowly washed down the pills. "My official diagnosis is a mild TBI and hematoma, and a distal fracture of your left radius—in layman's terms, you got a concussion, a goose egg, and a broken arm. Don't worry, we'll have you playing the piano again in no time."

"I play the flute, actually."

"So you never heard that one, huh? Tough crowd, tough crowd," Donna quipped, taking the empty glass and nonchalantly grabbing Melinda's wrist to check her pulse.

Melinda laid back down, the throbbing in her head subsiding. "You a doctor?"

"Retired—but just when I thought I was out, the Four Horsemen of the Apocalypse pulled me back in."

"And Jimmy's OK?"

"Aside from being in desperate need of a haircut, he's fine," Donna said. "We thought he was your little brother until he told us how you found him. It sounds like you have quite a story to tell—I can't wait to hear it once you're up to it. You hungry?"

"My head says no, but my stomach says yes."

"One stack of pancakes coming up," Donna said with a smile, heading for the door. "And I know a little waiter who's gonna be happy as heck to see you."

CHAPTER 42

GERMANY

A light morning rain drummed on Colonel Stirling's helmet as he descended the Stryker's ramp toward the two French Army officers waiting for him at the once-open border.

Martin and Staff Sergeant Nick Alger fell in behind him as he walked to meet the French soldiers standing behind a lone concrete construction barrier that had been dropped in the middle of the lonely country road cutting through the rolling hills and woods of German Saarland and French Lorraine. Behind them stood four enlisted French infantrymen standing vigil in front of a hulking six-wheeled VBMR Griffon armored personnel carrier blocking both lanes.

The officers took their hands off the HK416 rifles strapped across their tactical vests and snapped Stirling an open-palmed salute. "Good morning, Colonel—thank you for agreeing to see us," said a tall, bearded man wearing the three black bars of a company commander. "Captain Lucien Borgeau, First Infantry Regiment."

"The pleasure's mine," Stirling said, returning the military courtesy. "Your English is excellent, by the way."

Borgeau acknowledged the compliment with a nod. "I studied in America—New York University. Your accent . . . Southern?"

"Texas—close enough," Stirling corrected. "Well, I know you didn't invite us for coffee and croissants, so say what you gotta say."

"Fair enough," Borgeau said. "The border is closed to all American units. You and the others cannot cross."

Others? Stirling caught, filing the nugget of information away for later. "You couldn't have just said that on the radio and saved us some gas?" he snorted—the fact he had known what was coming didn't make him any less pissed off.

"I understand your frustration, but I have my orders," Borgeau responded, gesturing to the infantry squad and the APC as rainwater dripped from the metal bracket for his night vision. "In person, you can see that we, as you Americans say, 'mean business.'"

Stirling had known from the start that crossing into France would present problems. While the situation in France was a shitshow like the rest of the world, it was less of one; the nation had fared better than the United States and the rest of Europe. France immediately sealed its borders and withdrew outright from the Schengen free travel agreement at the start of the pandemic, and mobilized the military and police to crack down—hard—on unrest. Stirling had still been confident that The Lost Boys could slip across the border and make their way to the Channel coast for pickup before anyone was the wiser—until the Russian terror attacks ramped France's paranoia up to eleven.

"Captain, to be very clear, we're just passin' through," Stirling said. "This is our only way, given that Belgium and The Netherlands are too torn up. We just wanna go home."

"I am sorry, colonel, but as an officer, you of all people should understand that I am not here to negotiate my orders—you will have to find another way," Borgeau said. "I do not know what you expect to find on the coast of *La Manche*, but the Tunnel has been sealed. Besides, England has all but collapsed, like Germany—you and your men would find the *rosbifs* even less accommodating than us."

"Damn," Stirling spat with feigned anger to keep his interlocutor in the dark about their true intentions in the unlikely event they knew about the ships coming to get them. *Time to bait the hook*, he said to himself. "Have the other American units been told about this?"

"If you are being told, I can only assume that your remnant units near Saarbrücken are being told as well."

Gotcha—so there are *more of us.* "Is this how your government treats allies?" Stirling challenged.

"Colonel," Borgeau continued, shifting on his feet, "France has problems of her own, and that was before those Russian sleeper cells launched the most brutal attack on my homeland since the Second World War. Put yourself in our place—if I wanted to cross from Quebec through your sovereign territory to the Atlantic coast on a gamble to find a way home, your government in Washington would forbid it as well, *non*?"

"Maybe your betters should try putting themselves in our place, instead," Stirling said.

"I sympathize with your plight, Colonel. But understand—if you cross the border, you will be dealt with."

"Thank you for your candor," Stirling said, offering a salute.

"Bonne chance, Colonel," Borgeau said as he and his lieutenant saluted back.

Stirling and his security detail walked back to their waiting Stryker, which Clayton had parked next to the blue European Union sign welcoming visitors to Germany. "Now go away, or I shall taunt you a second time," Stirling seethed in a mocking, over-the-top French accent.

"We gonna miss the boat home, sir?" Nick asked.

"Negative, soldier—convoy hasn't set sail yet," Stirling reassured him without looking back; while the ships themselves had been marshaled by whatever was left of the chain of command, finding enough sailors for even skeleton crews had continued to present a challenge. "But when they arrive, we'll be there, come hell or high water." He spun to face Nick and Martin, throwing a military five-finger point in their faces. "And let me be clear—you two animals blab about this little setback to anyone, and you *and* your men will be in charge of diggin' every last latrine from here to home. We trackin'?"

"Loud and clear, sir," Martin said. They continued their walk to the Stryker, the morning rain lightening to a drizzle. "As long as we're sworn to secrecy, permission to speak freely?"

"Shoot."

"What the hell do we do now?"

"I'm workin' on it," Stirling replied as he signaled Clayton to start the engine. "In the meantime, our little snail-eating friend back there let slip that there's more of us out there—and we're gonna find 'em."

CHAPTER 43

MISSOURI

Kara was too dehydrated to shed tears over her impending death.

The last thing she had seen before blacking out from the pain of her shattered left leg and arm was the Bergan family making their escape from the wildfire, their Cessna Skyhawk banking over the deep ravine in which Kara's broken body lay. She had been awakened twice since by earth-shaking explosions as the fire reached the farm's diesel and aviation fuel tanks.

And now, the monster had found her.

The voracious blaze, its blinding red and deepest black reminiscent of a medieval painting of hell, descended the ravine toward her, devouring everything in its path with a freight-train roar. *Oh God, this is it,* she whispered through cracked and bleeding lips, her voice a casualty of the smoke and the unforgiving furnace heat.

She yanked the quick-release straps of her rucksack with her good arm and weakly rolled out of it, pain shooting through her broken leg, which had swollen against the fabric of her jeans like a sausage. Furiously yanking it open, she fished out her iPhone and turned it on, squinting at the brilliance of the approaching fire as she waited for the main screen to appear.

The phone's top bar informed Kara for the final time that she had no WiFi or 5G—finding a signal in the Missouri Ozarks would have been problematic even before the collapse. Undaunted, she began composing a final message to her father. *I'm about to die in a forest fire. I'm trapped and there's no way out*, she pecked one-thumbed, mouthing the words as she typed, her broken limbs throbbing with each heartbeat. *I'm sorry. I tried the best I could, and I know you did, too. Two airmen from Scott named Reed Finley and Alexia Rios died trying to help me. Please try to let their families know.*

Kara fumbled the phone with the thunderclap of another explosion from the burning farm, frantically scooping it back up and blowing the film of dirt and ash from the screen. *Mom and I will be waiting for you. I love you, Dad*, she finished, taking a ragged deep breath of searing hot air before pushing send. *Please, God, go through*, she silently prayed. *Please grant this one last miracle for me.* Her heart sank with the red exclamation point telling her that the message hadn't been delivered. The ground shook with the falling of a large flaming tree as she tried again, with the same result.

She angrily tossed the phone away, her ruined throat denying her the ability to scream in frustration as she rummaged one last time through her rucksack to dig out the photo of her and her parents, her father's newly-pinned general stars on his shoulders. She dropped it twice with her trembling hand before sliding the picture from its frame, staring desperately into it as if it were a portal through which she could escape. Her face and arms began to blister as if a hot iron was being pressed to them, the radiant heat of the approaching inferno forcing her to jam her eyes shut as the corners of the photo began to curl and shrivel.

Kara's last coherent thought as agony began to overwhelm her was for her poor father, who would never know what happened and would never stop looking for her.

CHAPTER 44

WISCONSIN

It was a miracle what a bath and a good night's sleep could do for the spirit, Melinda mused as she checked her appearance in the guest room's wood-frame cheval mirror.

Melinda had done a double-take the moment she saw her reflection, her still-aching head punishing her for the theatrics. She knew she had been losing weight since Interlochen, courtesy of her progressively looser-fitting clothes, but the young woman staring back at her was thin. She had comically lifted her t-shirt to stare at her flat stomach when a knock at the thick oaken door startled her.

"Come in," she blurted, giving her hair one last run-through with her hand. She beamed at the sight of Jimmy bounding to her.

"You ready to eat? The food's great!" Jimmy boisterously declared, wrapping his arms around her waist.

"You bet, little guy," she said, hugging him back as her eyes met those of a handsome, dark-haired young man, dressed in jeans and a t-shirt like her, and a military-style rifle slung over his shoulder.

"Good morning," he said, the floor creaking with the footfalls of his work boots. "I'm Ethan—Donna's grandson."

"Melinda Hodgson—pleased to meet you," she said, awkwardly shaking his hand with an embarrassed grin for the forearm cast covering half of her palm.

"Like Jimmy here said, let's grab breakfast."

"Sounds great," Melinda said. "No offense to your gracious hospitality, but I've been going stir crazy in here."

The aroma of bacon carried on the morning air the moment they stepped out the farmhouse's squeaky screen door and headed toward the small pole barn that served as an open-air mess. Melinda grinned at the sight of two dogs padding toward them through the thinning late summer fog that had started to burn off with the rising sun. The golden retriever sniffed Melinda and sat in front of her, wagging his tail as Jimmy pet him.

"Buck's not gonna let you pass until you scratch his head," Ethan remarked as she happily complied.

Melinda thumbed at Buck's companion, who seemed indifferent to the new human's attention. "What's the German shepherd's name?"

"Reaper's a Belgian Malinois, actually—he belongs to Gunnar, our chief of security. He fell in love with them in the Army 'cause they keep 'em as MP dogs."

"He said they call 'em 'maligators,'" Jimmy chuckled.

Melinda watched as the dogs walked away. "Reaper likes you—you still have all four of your limbs," Ethan said, beckoning them to continue on. "Let's go—I'm starving."

The trio grabbed silverware and plastic trays from a small stack. "Mornin', kids!" said Al Leonard, his bushy gray beard covered with a hairnet, as he spooned bacon, scrambled eggs, and hash browns onto Jimmy's tray from a battered green military-surplus mermite can. "I've already met this little chowhound," he told Jimmy with a smile, "so that must make you Melinda. Pleased to meet'cha."

"Al here's our ham radio operator, and he's the best there is," Ethan said as Al started slapping food onto his and Melinda's trays. "Nice to see you out in the daylight for once—sorry it took KP to do it."

"Watch your mouth, kid, before you find yourself volunteered to help clean up," Al joked, pointing a spatula at the water-filled tray of dirty dishes and the covered bin of table scraps awaiting transport to the compost heap. "Melinda, when you're settled in, feel free to stop by the radio room and we'll try an' track down your loved ones. Where you from?"

"Elkhorn—it's a small town near Lake Geneva," Melinda answered, unnerved by Al's jovial face dropping upon hearing her answer. "We were on our way there when we got ambushed."

"I see," Al cautiously replied. "Well, like I said, we'll give it a shot," he said, excusing himself to serve a late arrival.

The trio took over an empty picnic table after stopping to pour themselves orange drink from a faded yellow Coleman jug. Melinda attacked her food with gusto, trying her best to ignore the stares of the handful of other armed diners—some of them discreet, others not bothering to hide their concern that she and Jimmy would be two more mouths to feed.

"Do you mind if I get some of my questions answered now?" she asked Ethan.

"Go for it."

"What *is* this place?"

"My grandma's farmstead," Ethan explained with his mouth full. "Before the collapse, she and my late grandpa and us grew produce and raised meat to sell to rich city and suburban folks. It used to be called

Moran Farm, but now we just call it The Compound. Grandma got into doomsday prepping when I was a kid and slowly turned it into a survival retreat for trusted friends—I was reading prepper authors like James Rawles, Jim Cobb, Charley Hogwood, and Doctor Bones and Nurse Amy when all my friends were reading Harry Potter."

Melinda was about to say that she had never heard of any of them when the patter of feet in the dewy grass announced Al's grandson Kyle running up to Jimmy and tapping him on the shoulder. "Wanna play?"

"Yeah!" Jimmy said, leaving his empty tray and darting after Kyle toward the large red barn behind the Moran home.

"Be careful!" Melinda called after him.

"Don't worry," Ethan reassured her. "He's safe, and they know not to leave the sight of any grownups."

"I can't help it—Jimmy means the world to me."

"I know. Grandma told me about how you found him and took care of him. I'm in awe of you."

"Jimmy may be all I have left," Melinda sighed. "I noticed your friend's face when I told him where Elkhorn was—that wasn't the face of a man who has good news to share."

"I'm sorry," Ethan softly replied. "I know what it's like to lose someone, believe me."

"Ethan, I'd really like to meet everyone who rescued us so I can thank them personally," Melinda asked, desperate to change the subject. "Could you help me?"

"Sure—we can start right now, if you'd like. You're welcome," Ethan said with a grin at her surprised look, gesturing to the couple sitting at the adjoining table. "And Justin and Jane were there, too."

"Don't mention it!" Jane said, hoisting her Yeti coffee cup in salutation as she and her husband picked up to leave.

Ethan popped the last morsel of breakfast into his mouth and washed it down with the rest of his orange drink. "When you're done, I'll take you to the QRF—sorry, our quick reaction force—and introduce you to Gunnar and Lukasz. You already met Gunnar's dog."

Melinda smiled warmly. "Thank you. Jimmy and I owe you our lives—we're lucky that you and your friends happened along when you did."

"Luck had nothing to do with it," Ethan said, looking down at his empty tray. "We didn't just 'happen along.' We set up an ambush to kill those men. They attacked you two because they mistook you for being with us. Had we not been there . . ."

"What's going on?" Melinda asked with a shudder.

"There's a nearby town called Iron Point that wants our stuff for themselves," Ethan said. "They tried to annex us, and we told 'em to go to hell. They were easy to handle at first, but they allied themselves with a really bad motorcycle gang—they're called the Devil's Warriors, and they're monsters. One of our members from town agreed to go back to spy for us. She never returned. My dad volunteered to sneak into town to find out what happened to her. We intercepted a radio message that they caught him." He blew out a ragged breath, pausing as a young girl checked in with her mother at a nearby table before running off to attend to her assigned chores. "They drove by the front gate and tossed out a duffel bag with our spy—cut up into pieces. I have no idea if my dad's alive or dead."

Melinda placed her hand on his. "Oh, God, I'm so sorry."

"We weren't lying when we said you and Jimmy are safe here," Ethan said *sotto voce*. "But you've stumbled into the middle of an end-of-the-world feud."

PART THREE

Confront them with annihilation, and they will survive; plunge them into a deadly situation, and they will live. When people fall into danger, they are then able to strive for victory.

—Sun Tzu

CHAPTER 45

"One more time," Ethan spoke in Melinda's ear as she steadied the red dot of her rifle's scope on the paper target. "Breathe, relax, aim, then squeeze. You got this."

Melinda shifted her weight on a bed of autumn leaves, tucking in her left elbow to compensate for her cast before holding her breath halfway though the exhale and slowly squeezing the trigger. The Windham Weaponry SRC 5.56-millimeter rifle bucked in her hands, her shoulder taking the recoil as the report disappeared into The Compound's thick woods.

"Cease fire," Ethan ordered, pulling orange foam plugs from his ears as Melinda safed her new weapon with a *click*. "Let's see how you did," he said, offering his hand to pull Melinda to her feet. "But first . . ." He slid his arms around her waist and kissed her, which she happily reciprocated. They had officially become an item two weeks after her arrival; Melinda had earned more than a few dirty looks from the handful of teenage girls who resented that the newcomer had reeled in The Compound's best catch.

Melinda reached back to stop his hand from sliding down to grab her rear. "Whoa there, cowboy," she ribbed before kissing him again.

"Can't win 'em all," he said with mock dejection as they slung their rifles. They held hands down the well-worn path through the scythe-trimmed weeds to the target frame, the woods ablaze with the brilliant reds, oranges, and yellows of mid-October. Their matching heavy flannel shirts, standard attire for autumn in far northern Wisconsin, staved off the chill of the overcast early afternoon.

Melinda's muscles ached from the nonstop labor she had put in since Donna cleared her for duty. Eager to earn her keep and repay The Compound's generosity, Melinda had jumped in with both feet to make herself useful; she and Jimmy enthusiastically pitched in to help prepare for winter, from hauling firewood to the nonstop labor of bringing in and preserving the harvest—and digging defensive works to repel a potential Iron Point invasion.

Ethan whipped out a pen to connect Melinda's most recent three-shot group into a triangle, which joined half a dozen other triangles clustered around the center of mass of the target's black silhouette. While most of the shot groups were tight, Melinda's most recent had a shot that was several inches apart from the other two.

"You're getting the hang of it—your scope's officially zeroed—but you're still jerking the trigger," he said, tapping the errant bullet hole with his pen. "Remember—squeeze the trigger with the meaty part of your finger, not the tip. It should be a surprise when the rifle fires."

"Sorry," Melinda offered as Ethan tore the target sheet from the frame.

"Don't be," Ethan said, fishing a handheld MURS radio from his pocket to inform the CQ that The Compound's small firing range was no longer hot—meaning any gunshots heard from that point forward would be fired in anger. "You're doing great for a girl who never fired a gun in her life before." He pulled a honeycrisp apple from his cargo pocket and sank his teeth into it with a satisfying crunch before offering it to Melinda. "Enjoy the fresh ones while they last. Don't worry—we've canned and dried enough to last us clear 'til next season."

"Oh, I know," Melinda said with a smile as she took a bite—picking apples was her and Jimmy's favorite chore.

They strolled back to their firing position to police up Melinda's spent cartridges to be reused the next time The Compound's armorer reloaded ammo from their deep stockpile of primers, bullets, and powder—nothing was allowed to go to waste. "I got no idea what's for lunch, but I'm hungry enough to eat a horse," Ethan said, dropping a fistful of rifle brass with a tinkle into a small burlap bag. "I got a six-hour shift on the CQ after chow. What're you gonna be up to?"

"Al said he had some time to see if we could find out anything about my family," Melinda sighed. She had cried for days after Al gently broke it to her that Elkhorn—along with Milwaukee, Madison, and the rest of southeastern Wisconsin—had become a no man's land, demarcated by what surviving hams had taken to calling the Red Line. Al's efforts since then to find out anything about Elkhorn, or Melinda's family, had proven to be futile.

"I know how you feel," said Ethan, who had no idea if his father was alive as a prisoner of Iron Point, or dead. "Good luck."

"I'm gonna need it," Melinda muttered, brushing loose dirt from her knees. "You, your grandma, and your friends are the latest in a long line of wonderful people who've helped us—some at great risk. We made it all this way, only to find out that my home and my family probably don't exist anymore."

Ethan zipped up his tactical vest and winged the apple core into the woods as they began walking the path back to the farmhouse. "So what're you gonna do?"

Melinda waved her broken arm. "Once the cast comes off next week, I'm thinking Jimmy and I will head for my Aunt Molly's house—she lives in Sparta, right next to Fort McCoy, which Al said is super safe thanks to all the soldiers there." Besides being deployed to patrol the Red Line, the mix of active-duty and Wisconsin Army National Guard units, under the command of the reconstituted state government, were steadily restoring order in a growing radius from the base. Melinda gazed upward at the low-hanging dark clouds. "We'll be able to make it there before the first snow if we hurry—Al said he'll try to get a hold of anyone in Sparta to relay her a message."

Ethan stopped and turned to face her, taking her hands in his. "What if you had another option?"

"Like what?" Melinda asked, raising an eyebrow.

"How would you like to stay here with us?"

Melinda's mouth fell agape. "I—I don't know what to say."

"How about 'yes'?"

"I mean, I'd be lying if I said I haven't spent more than one sleepless night wondering if Jimmy and I would make it—or whether Aunt Molly's even still alive," she stammered. "But I feel like we've already overstayed our welcome . . ."

"Which won't be a problem if you're inducted as a full member," Ethan cut her off. "You've given 110 percent since you got here, without even having to be asked—you've paid us back, with interest. And your stock with Grandma was already sky high to begin with on account of you taking in Jimmy. You two'd fit in great. Also, to be honest . . ."

"You need to replace people who've died," Melinda finished his sentence; The Compound had lost a half dozen people to illness and to fighting Iron Point.

"Something like that," he conceded over the squawking racket of a flock of sandhill cranes migrating for warmer climes before winter descended on northern Wisconsin. "But even though you've got Grandma Donna's seal of approval, it's gotta come up to a vote before the whole group. And obviously, there's danger involved if you stay."

"Won't be half as dangerous as Jimmy and me dying of exposure," Melinda said, stepping closer to him. "And would it be safe to say that a certain someone also wouldn't mind keeping me around?"

"Maybe," he said in low tones, his face inching closer to hers.

"You have yourself a deal," she whispered as she kissed him, furiously chasing away the realization that she had said the exact same words to Dulcy when she implored Melinda to come with her to Mackinaw. *And look what helping me got her . . .*

***

Buck and Reaper eagerly bounded, tongues lolling from their grinning mouths, to the young couple as they exited the woods into The Compound's main clearing. Ethan and Melinda knelt to pay the guard dogs' toll of a head scratch and a tummy rub before being allowed to continue toward the duck pond where Al, Kyle, and Jimmy were fishing.

The old man proudly looked at Jimmy as he laid down his pole and folded up his camping chair. "Kid's a natural—caught more fish than me an' Kyle put together," he said, patting Jimmy on the back before looking to Melinda with sympathetic eyes. "I'm headin' to the ham shack to try to get some news about all the problems the FIBs who fled to

Door County are causing," Al told her, using the Wisconsin acronym for Illinois residents rather than the full epithet, which was not for young ears. "Stop on by when you're ready."

Ethan savored the aroma of grilled meat wafting from The Compound's mess. "I'll see you two at lunch," he said with a wink before taking his leave—he and Melinda were cautious of displays of affection around Jimmy, who was very protective of her.

Melinda sat down in the grass next to Jimmy as Al led his grandson away. "I didn't know you could fish."

"Dad taught me," he said, reeling in his lure. "He said I was good at it."

"You never cease to amaze me, Jimmy Callahan."

Jimmy cast farther into the water. "I miss him. Mom and Brittany, too."

Melinda blew out a nervous breath, staring at a raft of migrating ducks resting on the far side of the pond as she wondered whether she was abandoning her family by staying at The Compound. *No,* she reassured herself—*Mom and Dad would want you to be safe.*

"Jimmy?" she asked, putting her good arm around the boy and his oversized Bluey winter coat they had dug out from the bike trailer the week before. "You know how I said we'd never be apart, and that you could be a part of my family?"

"Can we stay, Minda? Please?" Jimmy begged with pleading eyes. "I really like it here and the people are super nice."

Melinda grinned from ear to ear, lip quivering. "I like it here, too. You wanna stay?"

"Yeah!" he exclaimed before his face suddenly became etched with worry.

"What's wrong?"

"Will Santa know where we are?" he innocently asked.

Melinda snapped her fingers. "You know what? I bet Al can get a message to the North Pole for us! Let's go ask him."

Jimmy excitedly reeled in his lure, holding Melinda's hand as they made their way to the farmhouse.

CHAPTER 46

LUXEMBOURG

"**H**ome sweet home," Josh muttered the moment his boots touched the narrow cobblestone streets of the Castle Anthrax.

Theo followed him out the rear hatch of the team's purloined French VBMR Griffon armored personnel carrier, crouching to fit his huge frame through. "Was thinkin' the same thing, dude—longest we've stayed anywhere since Rose Barracks," he grunted, staring at the former monastery's medieval stonework, which glowed in the light of the early evening sun. "Name needs some work, though."

"Colonel Stirling and his movie references," Josh remarked as Patton and Martin hopped down from the front doors. The Lost Boys had crossed into Luxembourg three weeks prior, happening upon the monastery in the forest just outside what was left of Esch-sur-Alzette on the French border. It had long been converted to a hotel and event venue—and had been filled with the corpses of flu victims who had taken refuge there in the hope that its isolation would mean their salvation. It was shortly thereafter that a foraging expedition crossed into nearby Belgium and happened upon the abandoned Griffon, which Colonel

Stirling considered nothing short of heaven-sent to help Martin's team scout a route through France without raising suspicion. Stirling had sent the cav scouts out on a week-long recon mission, but ended up recalling them after only four days.

Josh stepped to the hatch to help ease Corinne, the French linguist, to the ground—her ability to translate signs and interview survivors had proven invaluable. *"Merci beaucoup,"* she said, reaching back inside to grab her backpack and sleeping bag.

"Thank you for all your help, ma'am," Martin said, shaking her hand. "Bet you're glad to be back."

"Absolument," Corinne replied, slinging her pack onto her shoulder. "Four days seeing people who lost everything gave me some much-needed perspective about how good I have it just by having my son with me. Speaking of which, I think I'll go hold him for a few hours."

"Remember—not a word to anyone!" Martin reminded her before she disappeared among the line of parked bumper-to-bumper military vehicles.

Patton's and Josh's faces lit up as Ann-Katryn and Kira strode toward them from the thatched-roof banquet hall that served as the unit's dining facility. "Hey, babe!" Patton exclaimed, taking his girl into his arms with a whirl.

"I am so glad you are back safe—I was worried sick!" Ann-Katryn said before wrinkling her nose with a frown.

"Yeah, sorry—four days without bathing really seals in the flavor, if you know what I mean," Patton laughed as she pushed him away. "I'll get cleaned up when we're done meeting with the colonel—but don't wait up for me," he said, stealing a kiss.

With a shy grin, Kira unpinned Josh's Starfleet comm badge from her long-sleeved Army combat shirt and handed it back to him. "Thanks for keeping it safe for me," he said, pocketing it.

"I thought you guys were supposed to be gone for a week," Kira said.

"So did we," Josh replied, nodding to his teammates strolling up the road. "We're gonna be burning the midnight oil going over everything we saw, and didn't see, with the colonel."

"Too bad—it's *Star Trek* night. Original Series—Commodore Decker and the planet killer," Kira said with a disappointed shrug. "We'll save you a seat in case you're able to—"

Josh swept in to silence her with a kiss, her eyelids fluttering shut with a moan as she kissed him back. "Been wanting to do that for a while," he said.

"Been waiting for you to work up the courage," she breathlessly replied.

"I'll take a raincheck on the episode. I missed you," he blurted before jogging away to catch up with his teammates, crouching on the run to pluck a sticky note from the ground which he promptly handed to Martin. "You lost something."

"Missile alert warning," Martin read aloud from the English translation that had been taped to one of the indicators on the Griffon's passenger-side remote-control weapons station. "Yeah, we may wanna find where this one went."

"Good thing most of the Griffon's buttons just have idiot-proof pictures on 'em—especially with Patton driving," Josh ribbed.

"Not to change the subject, but have you and Kira started shopping for his and hers pointy ears yet?" Patton asked.

"Fuck you," Josh shot back.

"I thought Vulcans only did that once every seven years," Patton retorted without missing a beat.

The team's laughter echoed off the ancient stone buildings as they headed to meet with the colonel.

***

"Glad to see you boys made it back all right," Colonel Stirling said, studying a map of northern France laid across the heavy oaken table of the conference hall he had taken over as his headquarters. "Don't bother with saluting or any 'reporting as ordered' horseshit—I'm not in the mood."

"How'd it go?" Major Villa asked, moving one of the candelabra that, along with the roaring fireplace, filled the wood and stone room with light; the trio of gothic windows along the wall had their thick burgundy curtains drawn to shield the colonel's maps and easel from prying eyes.

Martin pulled a notebook from his tactical vest. "Aside from local gendarmes, we didn't see much of anything military. Looks like the colonel's hunch is right—most of their surviving military beef seems to be tied up keeping order in the big cities. But the handful of small towns we passed through practically mobbed us asking for food and stuff—the civilians could make getting to the coast an even tougher nut to crack than the French Army would."

"Well, it's this way or we stay in Europe, so we gotta make this work. I wish we could go through Belgium instead, but I wish I had a million bucks and a unicorn pony, too," Stirling quipped. "They got torn up worse than Germany, and everyone left in the Flemish and Wallonian halves are gettin' ready to kill each other over who gets the pissing statue and whatever else is left of Brussels." The colonel nodded to a silver tray of salami and freshly baked bread on the far side of the banquet table. "Sorry you had to come back on horse-cock sandwich night at the chow hall—dig in, boys, but this is a working dinner. How far y'all get?"

Martin tapped his finger south of the Belgian border as his men began wolfing down food. "After we scoped out those World War I dead zones around Verdun—which was spooky as fuck, by the way—we managed to recon as far as south of Cambrai. We were about to press on toward Arras and maybe closer to Lille like you ordered, but you reeled us in early."

"With good reason, son—the convoy set sail to bring us home, and we just now got word," Stirling said. Martin and his team stared back at the colonel like children finding out that they were going to Disney World. "They'll be here in three days, four at most, which means we gotta pull a plan outta our asses with what we know now."

"About damn time," Patton said. "Took 'em forever to scrounge up a crew."

"Wish it was that simple, trooper," Villa interjected. "Turns out the holdup wasn't so much how to bring us home as it was who gets us when we return."

"Whaddya mean, sir?" Theo asked with his mouth full.

The major glanced at Stirling, who silently granted him permission to continue. "The rumors you've undoubtedly heard are true. The president's dead. Died of the flu right at the start, along with the vice president, the house speaker, right on down the chain of succession."

"Mother of God," Martin uttered in disbelief.

"Oh, it gets better," Stirling continued. "Secretary of State Atherton's alive, and under the law, the presidency should go to him. But he's caught up in a three-way political pissing match 'cause SecDef and Homeland Security decided that *they* wanna be president. And instead of stayin' the hell out of it like they should, a number of survivin' military commands are taking sides with the various factions—even after the apocalypse, the swamp is gonna swamp. Fortunately for us, everyone settled their differences long enough to agree to get what's left of us back home."

"No offense, sir, but ain't no fuckin' way I'm gonna get goat-roped into fighting a new civil war so one of these clowns can be president. Put me up against the wall and shoot me now," Patton spat, tossing his sandwich onto the tray, his appetite a casualty of the news.

Sterling's eyes drilled into Martin. "Do you boys trust me, son?"

"I think I speak for all of us when I say that we trust you with our lives, sir."

"Then give it to me straight, no bullshit—what y'all plan to do when we get back to CONUS?"

"Go AWOL and make our way back to Wisconsin," Martin responded without hesitation. "I was set to ETS right before the world ended, but the Army stop-lossed me." He looked to his team, remembering the fateful pact they had made after stopping Patton from going over the wire at Rose Barracks. "We're all sticking together."

"Damn right," Theo said.

"So say we all," Josh chimed in.

Patton rolled his eyes. "Fuckin' nerd."

"Finally, a man of culture in an army of barbarians—*Battlestar Galactica* was one of the few times when the remake was better than the original," Stirling mused, his chuckle quickly replaced by a long face. "I was a short-timer countin' down the days just like you, Sergeant Crenshaw. Had it all figured out—was gonna retire with a nice fat O-6 pension and a seat on the corporate board of some cog in the military-industrial complex. But first, Juliana and I were gonna buy an RV and spend a year seein' the country, just the two of us, to make up for all the time

I was away. I'm done too, boys. This is it for me—the Army can keep the standard-issue Legion of fuckin' Merit."

"Roger that, sir," Martin said. "If you like, you can come with us if you're headin' our way. Might be a bit cramped in the Humvee with you and Patton's girl sharing a seat."

"Thanks for the invite, but me and Major Villa here got our own plans," Stirling said with a smirk. "The good major found out his wife and kids are safe at Fort Benning. So's Juliana. Unfortunately, our sons and daughter all followed my footsteps into the military, and I got no idea where they are or how they're doing."

"We're sorry, sir," Patton offered after a respectful silence punctuated by the crackling of the fire.

"Don't be—the fact I know my wife's alive is more than you or almost everyone else knows," Stirling said. "Anyway, enough with this touchy-feely crap—let's get down to business." He stabbed a spot on the Channel coast with his finger. "That," he proclaimed, "is the embarkation port."

Josh let out a whistle. "History repeats itself."

"For all our sakes, let's hope so," Stirling snorted as Villa helped himself to a speckled blue enameled steel coffeepot sitting on a wall table. "Freshly brewed from the colonel's personal reserve—rank hath its privilege. Help yourselves, boys—as much as you want." His finger tapped Luxembourg and looped through France. "Because we're not leaving this room until we have a plan."

CHAPTER 47

WISCONSIN

Melinda shivered in the dark, the layers of warm clothing under her new camouflage jacket doing little against the cold air seeping into the three-person LP/OP foxhole overlooking the chained front gate.

It was her first shift guarding the line since The Compound's members voted to accept her and Jimmy into the group—unanimously, Ethan later confided in her. While Donna had welcomed her with a warm smile and a hug, she had made it crystal clear that the honor could be easily rescinded, her beloved grandson's broken heart be damned, if she proved herself unworthy. *Such as by dozing off on guard duty*, she thought with a yawn, scratching her fully mended and extremely itchy forearm.

"Sucks that your first shift on the line had to be balls watch," Justin said over the frigid breeze blowing through the woods. He unscrewed his Thermos and poured Melinda a half cup of black coffee. "Have one on the house."

Melinda accepted the steaming plastic cup with a nod of thanks. "I was never much of a coffee drinker," she chattered.

"That'll change, believe me," Ethan said without taking his eyes off the gate. "That is, until we run out."

Melinda took a cautious sip, grimacing at its bitter taste as she stared past her rifle into the darkness. Branches of trees stripped increasingly bare by autumn reached into an overcast sky lit a spooky gray by the hidden waxing moon, the wind bringing down colored leaves like rain. She missed the warmth of her military surplus burlap cot, next to Jimmy's in a spartan outbuilding shared by several small families. Melinda had found it uncomfortable at first—it had made Interlochen's utilitarian bunks feel like a five-star hotel's by comparison—but after a few days of constant chores, she slept like a rock.

"What the heck?" Ethan quietly exclaimed with the stealthy *click clack click clack* announcing an incoming call on the LP/OP's military-surplus TA-1 field phone. "They didn't say anything about a patrol going out tonight!"

"That's because there isn't one," Justin shot back. The landline radio was connected to another TA-1 hidden in a tree stump two hundred meters into the woods on the far side of the road—returning patrols used it to make first contact with the LP/OP before advancing to be recognized to lessen the odds of friendly fire.

Ethan grabbed the bulky green and black phone from its recessed shelf, squeezing its large rubber hand switch to crank some power before thumbing the transmit button. "Unknown caller, please identify."

"Ethan?" a man's hoarse voice rattled through the tinny speaker. *"Dad?!"*

"Sorry, kid," Justin interrupted, grabbing the phone before Ethan could answer. "Will?! Is that you?"

"Yes it is, and we don't got a lotta time," he croaked with pain. "There's two of us, and we're comin' up to you. Don't shoot, 'cause I got no idea what the damn challenge and password is."

"Ohmigod, is it him?" Ethan gasped.

"Shut up and listen," Justin hissed, pointing at the other TA-1 connecting them with the CQ. "Get the QRF and a medic up here on the double!" He turned to find Melinda staring back at them in shock. "Don't look at me, kid—watch the damn line!" Melinda dropped the coffee and got behind her rifle as Justin keyed the phone again. "Wait one, Will—we, uh, gotta let Aunt Edith at the CQ know you're comin' up."

"No, goddammit, I don't have a gun to my head!" Will angrily spat with a cough as Justin breathed a sigh of relief. There was no Aunt Edith at The Compound; the name was a code phrase to establish whether a caller was under duress. If the caller responded with anything other than confirming that they weren't under compulsion by force, The Compound knew not to trust anything else they had to say. "Listen—we think we're being followed. We're on our way up!"

"Gotcha covered! Out!" Justin said, dropping the TA-1 to the foxhole's plywood floor and aiming his rifle down the wooded hill toward the front gate. "We got two friendlies comin' up—don't shoot 'em!" he tersely relayed as the growl of the QRF's pickup truck tearing down the gravel driveway drew closer. "Melinda, hold your fire—you're still green, and I don't want you shooting any good guys by mistake, OK?"

"Got it!" she responded with relief, the red-dot reticle of her scope jerking furiously with her heartbeat.

Justin heard them before he saw them—the unmistakable racket of panicked bolting through the forest, leaves rustling and branches snapping with no regard for noise discipline. They came into view moments later in Justin's night-vision scope, a diminutive figure helping along a larger person contrasting against the gravel of the country road. The two had just crossed the street into The Compound's woodline when a rifle cracked three times from the woods behind them, the muzzle flashes giving away the shooter's position.

"Dad! Up here!!" Ethan screamed as Justin took aim and returned fire. Flashes from two more rifles lit up the woods like fireflies—and fell silent just as quickly with the volley of return fire from the dismounted QRF.

The rustle of leaves grew louder, slowing noticeably with the uphill climb. "Don't shoot!" Will wheezed over the withering firefight before sliding through the LP/OP's front slit, Ethan and Melinda pulling him along until he fell to the floor like dead weight as Justin got off half a dozen shots at the retreating pursuers; Will's unknown companion followed right behind and landed on top of him, screaming in pain as her face caught a hot brass casing from Justin's rifle.

"Get him out here!" Donna ordered, bursting through the brush at the head of a two-man litter team that quickly unfolded an old military stretcher on the ground. Will pulled himself out with his last remaining strength, just barely making it to the stretcher with the help of Ethan and his dad's companion. Donna turned on the LED lamp strapped to her forehead just long enough to frantically give her son the once-over—he was battered and bruised, and had lost a lot of weight, but he was alive. "Don't you dare give up, William Moran! You hear me?!" she frantically yelled, slapping his face to keep him conscious. Will barely managed a weak moan as the stretcher bearers lifted him up and trotted to the waiting QRF pickup truck.

Ethan anxiously stuck his head back into the LP/OP. "Go!" Justin barked before Ethan could make the ask. "Melinda and I got this—help your dad! But keep an eye on whoever that is who came in with him!"

Ethan sprinted to catch up just in time as his father was loaded into the QRF's truck bed.

Donna turned to the newcomer in the dark as Ethan climbed on board. "Are you hurt?" she asked, all business.

"No, Mom," a familiar voice meekly answered. The olive-drab Ford's headlights sprang to life, revealing Ashley staring back at her.

CHAPTER 48

LUXEMBOURG

The anxious chatter of The Lost Boys reverberated off the rough-hewn stone walls of the medieval chapel where they had been ordered to assemble after breakfast.

Morning light illuminated the beautiful stained-glass mosaic of the Virgin Mary and the disciples mourning the crucified Jesus—but only Jesus's thorn-crowned head was visible behind the large projector screen that had been set up between the pulpit and the lectern.

"So this is it, then?" Ann-Katryn asked Patton. "The big plan that you have been sworn to silence about?"

"Yup—I mean, I coulda told you, but then I woulda had to kill you."

Theo thumbed at Clayton, who fiddled with a laptop computer attached to a projector on a small folding table. "Unless the damn presentation kills us first—looks like Death by PowerPoint survived the apocalypse right along with cockroaches an' Twinkies."

Martin glanced at Josh and Kira talking animatedly at the end of their row of folding metal chairs before taking in the scene around him. The six-hundred-year-old chapel, which the monastery's owners had rented out for weddings, was packed straight back to the ornate dark wooden doors; every member of The Lost Boys was there, military and civilian alike, save for the young children playing in the side courtyard under a young Army private's watchful eye. The slapdash unit was probably the most recent addition to a long list of occupying armies that had made themselves at home there, from Napoleon to Hitler to the Allies, Martin thought, before wondering whether they would be the last.

"Group, atten-SHUN!" Clayton's voice boomed through the chapel. Soldiers sprang to their feet, the civilians more slowly following suit, instantly snuffing their nervous conversations. Colonel Stirling's boots clicked on the smooth stone tiles as he strode up the center aisle to the screen.

"Mornin', Lost Boys!"

"Morning, sir!" the audience answered as one.

"So, y'all ready to ditch the Castle Anthrax and go home?"

"Yes, sir!"

Stirling cocked an eyebrow. "I'm sorry, I didn't quite catch that."

"Yes, sir!" they shouted, the echo almost deafening.

"That's more like it—at ease," Stirling said, motioning for his audience to be seated. The colonel's barrel chest rose with a deep breath the moment the projector sprang to life, displaying a map of France and the Low Countries, with a small blue rectangle denoting their location just inside the Luxembourg border.

"Welcome to Operation Dynamo II," he announced, slowly and deliberately staring across the room. "Exactly thirty-six hours from now, the remnants of United States Army Europe will cross the French border in force and make its way with all possible haste to the Channel coast, where what's left of the 22nd Marine Expeditionary Unit and the support ships the Navy scrounged will be waiting for us."

Martin allowed himself a swell of pride for his team's role in the audacious plan as the audience gasped and whispered amongst themselves.

"For you history buffs out there, we'll be evacuating from the port of Dunkirk, just like the Brits did in World War II," Stirling continued, the town winking to life on the map. "And the path of least resistance we're gonna take comes courtesy of the carnage of the world war that preceded it." A huge red curl like a lopsided U appeared, cutting an ugly swath west from the nearby city of Verdun before hooking north to Lille, near the Belgian border about sixty kilometers southeast of their destination.

"This, ladies and gentlemen, is *Zone Rouge*—The Red Zone. Four years of brutal trench warfare during World War I turned it into a no man's land of unexploded shells, toxic soil and water, and human remains. About a hundred square klicks of it, roughly the total size of metropolitan Paris, is still off-limits to this day—and while much of the original war zone has been slowly reclaimed over the past century, it's sparsely populated by European standards." Stirling stepped back as a thick black arrow snaked from Luxembourg, curving northwest through the zone and onward to Dunkirk. "At H-Hour, E-Day—E as in evacuate—we're gonna cut right through it to catch our boat home."

Stirling raised his hands for calm over the muted grumbles of his audience. "Don't worry, this isn't Chernobyl—it's not gonna give you mutant powers or make you grow a second head. Our cav scouts who reconned the route came back no stupider or uglier than they already were," he said, glancing at Martin and his team. "If you don't stop to eat handfuls of dirt, you'll be fine."

"Maybe so, but that shit still gave me the creeps," Theo muttered under his breath to Martin. Exploring the no-go zones at night was like something out of an indie horror movie—Corinne translating the French signs warning of the unseen dangers, beyond which lay quiet emptiness. Often the zones were just desolate forest, but a handful of them were nothing but dirt in which only the hardiest of scrub survived.

Another blue rectangle to their southeast along the German border appeared on the map. "Stepping off with us at H-hour will be another unit like ours, cobbled together from surviving soldiers, civilian employees, and dependents—with the hope that our two axes of advance will sow confusion. I'd be remiss if I didn't throw in some Baby Boomer/Gen X movie references—think *The Great Escape* meets *The Cannonball Run*. We'll mow through northern France to Dunkirk before whatever remains of the *Forces Armées Françaises* is any the wiser.

"We'll move as fast as practical," Stirling continued, the map replaced by a crude illustration of their convoy, "doing our best not to bunch up without getting too spaced apart." Stirling paused. "My goal is to deliver each and every one of you across—but in combat, ladies and gentlemen, there are no guarantees. And I have to ask you to temporarily abandon a principle we hold sacred." On the projector screen, a new slide displayed the Soldier's Creed that all Army soldiers were required to memorize from basic training. A red line slowly crossed out the sentence promising to never leave a fallen comrade behind.

The stone-faced audience absorbed the magnitude of Stirling's words. "If, God forbid, anyone gets hurt or killed, we're still gonna do our damnedest to save you or recover your body for a proper burial. But there are gonna be times where that just won't be possible. If we were a cohesive combat unit with an intact logistical chain, leaving people behind would be unconscionable. But we can't risk our annihilation—either by the French Army or by desperate and starving locals—to save a few or one. While those of us in uniform took an oath to risk our lives to bring everyone home, the civilians counting on us didn't." His dramatic pause was cut short by the squeals through the ornate side windows of the young children playing outside. "And the kids sure as heck didn't. I'm not saying this is every man for himself. But if things get heavy, know that there's a risk that you'll be on your own. And know this as well—the boat home leaves when it leaves. If you're not on it, you're staying in France."

Stirling glanced at Martin before slowly scanning his audience, which hanged on his every word. "I know some of you are through with the Army and just wanna get home, but you're worried about Uncle Sam's intentions—whether they're gonna keep you in service to either help restore order or to put down all the secessionist movements springing up like weeds. I have no idea what the people who sent the convoy have in mind; I can't speak for them. But my mission isn't to deliver the Army a fighting force. My mission, as I told each and every one of you the moment you hooked up with us, is to get you all back to the USA. If, God willing, we pull this off, what you do next is up to you, and is none of my business—stay with the Army, go AWOL, whatever. You are all free to follow the dictates of your conscience."

The projector screen went white with the end of the briefing. "We're all gonna be very busy bees until step-off time, starting immediately after this with PMCSing our vehicles the best we can—we check everything, and then recheck it, and check it again. Any downchecked vehicle gets scrapped for whatever parts we can use. Do you read me, Lost Boys?" he boomed.

"Yes sir!" his audience boomed back.

"You wanna go home?"

"Yes, sir!"

"I don't believe you—sound off!"

"*Yes, sir!*" the audience shouted.

"Follow you anywhere, sir!" Patton hollered.

Stirling eyed Patton and the rest of Martin's team. "You're not as ate-up as you look and smell, Specialist Childress. Let's get to work! Dismissed."

Clayton once again bellowed the call to attention, chairs squealing as The Lost Boys, soldier and civilian alike, shot to their feet and stood ramrod straight to the clicking of Colonel Stirling's footfalls as he left the way he came.

CHAPTER 49

WISCONSIN

Ashley rocked back and forth, head bowed and arms crossed, in the corner of the bare waiting room of the farm outbuilding turned infirmary.

Ethan and Gunnar stood against the opposite wall, making no effort to hide their contempt. Gunnar's gloved finger caressed his rifle's pistol grip above the trigger, as if to dare her to give him an excuse to do what was left of the world a favor by ending her life. Reaper sat at his master's feet, staring with single-minded purpose at the unwelcome guest and patiently waiting for the command to turn her into a chew toy.

Nothing less than I deserve, she chastised herself, staring down at hiking boots that were falling apart around her aching feet.

Donna entered through the simple wooden door set into drywall that had never been painted over. "How is he?" Ashley and Ethan simultaneously blurted.

"They banged him up pretty good, but he's gonna be OK," Donna said, turning to Ethan as she tucked her stethoscope into the pocket of her flannel shirt. "You can go see him, and then you're gonna let him rest."

Ethan flew through the door as Donna's attention turned to Ashley, her daughter's clothes hanging off a frame that was much thinner than when she had turned her away. "Looks like you've had it rough, too," she said, voice cracking. "Will told me you broke him out. Thank you."

"I'm so sorry!" Ashley bawled as she fell into her mother's arms, tears stinging the angry weal on her cheek from Justin's hot brass. "I didn't mean . . . I'm so ashamed . . ."

"It's all right, honey—it's all right," Donna whispered as she locked eyes with Gunnar, his face a distrusting scowl. She broke the embrace and cradled Ashley's face in her hands. "The Prodigal Daughter returns. We don't have a fattened calf, but we can scrounge up some leftovers and put some honey on that burn. We have to talk, right now—Will also told me *why* you did what you did."

***

The living room grandfather clock chimed four in the morning as Ashley wolfed down the chicken soup that Donna had set down at the kitchen table, a knitted blanket draped over her daughter's shivering shoulders. Gunnar had insisted that Ashley be searched, and Donna grudgingly agreed for Jane to take her outside and strip her mother-naked to ensure she wasn't carrying any weapons or a radio.

Donna watched her eat, sadly remembering making homemade chicken soup for her when she would get sick. She stroked her daughter's matted, filthy brunette hair, its shocking pink dye having long ago faded and grown out.

"Mom?" Ashley whimpered. "Have you . . . heard anything about Sonia?"

"No, but we've been trying when we can—don't lose hope," Donna reassured her, pain cleaving her heart with the mention of her missing granddaughter. Buck padded into the kitchen and sat by Ashley, wordlessly requesting a head scratch with his moist, black eyes. "Looks like Buck forgives you, too. You ready to talk?" Donna said, pouring Ashley and Gunnar coffee from the enamel pot warming on the kitchen's wood-burning stove, its aroma temporarily displacing Ashley's unpleasant stink.

Buck circled three times and curled up on the hardwood floor at Ashley's feet. "Where do I start?" she asked, wrapping her hands around the warm mug.

"The beginning would be good," Gunnar said, pulling an olive drab all-weather notepad and pen from a thick ziplock bag.

Ashley nervously exhaled, struggling to meet her mother's eyes. "I came to Iron Point and asked for help after you, um, wouldn't let me in. Like the spoiled brat that I was, I told them what happened. I'm so sorry—"

"And it's forgiven," Donna said, cutting her off with a raised palm. "We really need to know what you know. Go on."

"Mayor Allworth and Chief Beecher took a lotta interest in you and asked a bunch of questions."

"What did you tell them?" Gunnar asked.

"Everything I knew, which wasn't much—there seemed to be a lot of you, very well-armed, and that you set traps in the woods," she confessed as Gunnar scribbled. "They put me up in an empty apartment, and a coupla days later, they sent an officer to bring me in for more questioning. Both of 'em were beet red with sunburn and hobbling around on account of having to walk back after you blew up their squad car—they were *pissed*." A wicked grin crossed Gunnar's face.

Ashley turned to Donna. "They leaned on me hard, but I'd already told them everything I knew. They had me draw a map of the farm as best I could from memory, and asked me to draw the path through the woods that Will and I used to hike. When I refused—I hated you all for not letting me in, but I couldn't let them try to hurt you—Mayor Allworth punched me in the face and said they'd kill me if I didn't. So I did."

Donna gritted her teeth in fury, balling her fists on the table.

"The officer took me back to the apartment and ordered me not to leave town—like I had anywhere else to go," Ashley said, biting off a laugh. "I woulda bolted and taken my chances if I knew what was coming." She paused, wiping her eyes to the quiet chatter of the CQ desk in the living room checking in with the perimeter outposts. "A few days later, they broke down my door in the middle of the night and threw me in jail after beating the shit outta me. Chief Beecher said you killed his officer and the townspeople they sent to check out the path, and accused me of deliberately leading them into an ambush. They kept me in that hot, stifling cell, no lights or air conditioning, for two days. Until . . ."

"Until what?" Gunnar prodded.

"One morning, I woke up to the sound of gunfire. Lots of it."

"Remember that?" Donna told Gunnar. "We heard that racket from here, but had no idea what it was."

"In walk three bikers—huge guys, tattoo sleeves on both arms," Ashley continued. "They whip out the chief's keys and open my cell, saying I was all right if I'd gotten locked up. I follow them outside and . . . and the first thing I see is the mayor, chief, and a bunch of other people strung up to the flagpoles in pools of their own blood. They tied their necks with wires so tight that it nearly decapitated them."

"Dear Lord," Donna muttered.

Gunnar leaned forward. "'They' being the Devil's Warriors, I assume."

"Yeah," Ashley said. "Their bikes and trucks were everywhere. Their leader, Razor, took a liking to me—I must've looked awful after getting beaten down—and I became one of his girls. I, um . . . I don't wanna talk about that."

Donna slipped her hand on Ashley's. "You don't have to. But please—keep going about the gang and what Will said you told him."

"The gang—it's more like an army, Mom—is actually a combination of several, plus a bunch of ex-cons from prisons that emptied out when everything collapsed. Razor told me that their original plan was just to ransack Iron Point and move on, but the mayor tried begging for his life by telling them about the farm and all the resources you have—offered joining forces to take it all. I told Razor about the bomb and the ambush, and made a bunch of other stuff up, to try to convince him that you were too hard of a target. Fortunately for me, the mayor and chief apparently didn't think to tell him I was your daughter."

"How many people we talking?" Gunnar asked.

"I never counted, but hundreds, easy," Ashley said. "They tried probing you, laying ambushes, but learned real quick that you weren't to be messed with. Then you sent that spy—she got caught right away. I know what they did to her. I'm sorry. And I'm sorry for everything they put Will through—I had no idea he was the prisoner Razor kept talking about until a few days ago."

Donna nodded sadly. The only reason they hadn't killed Will was because he cracked under torture and told them who he was, and his captors realized he was much more valuable to them alive. The Devil's Warriors had twice broadcast over the police band that they had him in an attempt to arrange some kind of a ransom; Donna never responded, and had kept the news secret from everyone, including Ethan—only Gunnar and Al knew.

"Once Razor decided you were too tough a nut to crack, they started picking on softer targets, raiding smaller towns and farms. But now . . ."

" . . . they've picked everything clean out here in the middle of nowhere, and they're running out of food with winter coming," Gunnar finished her sentence. "If they don't make their move to wipe us out, and soon, they won't be able to."

"And they're about to," Ashley nervously continued. "They've gotten their hands on an armored vehicle—a big one—from the sheriff's office. Just rolled right on in and took it—and a few members of the gang are ex-military who know how to drive it." Gunnar muttered a curse seconds into Ashley's description.

"An MRAP—mine-resistant ambush-protected vehicle," he growled. "During our damn forever wars in Iraq and Afghanistan, the DoD was handin' out surplus MRAPs like candy to every podunk police department that wanted one—and believe me, a lotta departments took 'em up on the offer." Gunnar glared at Ashley. "Did they say when they're gonna attack?"

"If Razor had a day in mind, he didn't share it with me. But now they know you know, which means they're probably gonna move up their timetable. And they're, um, not coming to 'wipe you out,' as you said," Ashley said, staring down at her coffee.

"Out with it, please," Donna urged.

"Pillaging the countryside like a plague of locusts is too inefficient—Razor plans to capture the farm intact, with all of you and the handful of survivors from Iron Point working the land as slaves."

Donna's haunted eyes met Gunnar's. "What do we do?"

"If they come rolling up the driveway, we're in big trouble," Gunnar grumbled, shaking his head. "Our .50-caliber rifles'll barely scratch the paint on an MRAP, and they're built to protect the passengers from IEDs, so they'll shrug off the bombs we've laid. Shooting the tires is also out, because MRAPs are equipped with run-flats. That leaves us one option."

"Which is?" Donna pressed.

"Take the fight to them—bollix their new toy before they can use it against us."

CHAPTER 50

"Lookin' good up here," Theo called down to Martin from the VBMR Griffon's passenger-side remote weapons station, his monitor screen flaring from the evening sun just beginning to set behind the Castle Anthrax's stonework.

"No problems I can see," Martin said, studying the machine gun and its bizarre-looking underslung smoke grenade launcher slewing from left to right with a nudge of Theo's joystick. "Then again, if there was a problem, we'd have no freakin' clue how to fix it."

Theo hopped down to the cobblestone street, glancing at the dark clouds underlining the reddening sun. "Looks like rain—as if this wasn't gonna suck enough," he grumbled. "Damn, do I hate gettin' pissed on—shoulda joined the Air Force."

"If it ain't rainin', we ain't trainin'," Martin joked, slapping the big man's huge bicep as a gust of cold air from the incoming storm chilled them both. "And if it helps screen our movements tonight—and keeps the French Air Force from bombing us—so much the better. We need all the help we can get."

Their Griffon was parked at the head of a long line of military vehicles snaking through the parking lot and disappearing around the bend, their crews performing last-minute maintenance as civilians began loading up their limited belongings. Come sunset, Martin and his team would tear ass out of the old monastery to scout the route ahead, leading the way for the final drive to Dunkirk.

Martin smiled at the sight of Patton and Ann-Katryn escorting Corinne and her ten-year-old son René, bags in hand. *"Bonjour!"* he warmly greeted with a wave. *"Comment allez-vous?"*

"Je suis stresse aujourd'hui," Corinne nervously replied.

"You lost me. Wait . . . I know how to say that, don't tell me," he said, struggling to recall the smattering of French she had taught him during their recon mission. *"Comprends pas."*

"She said she's royally freaking out," René translated with a grin.

"Something like that," his mother confessed, squeezing René's shoulder with a free hand.

"Hey, li'l man!" Theo said, towering over the boy. "You wanna take a tour of our ride?"

"Yeah!" René said, excitedly pointing to the 7.62-millimeter machine gun turret. "I wanna play with that!"

Theo set his patrol cap on René's head. "Let's not an' say we did," he said, beckoning the boy to follow him.

"Don't you worry, ma'am," Patton told Corinne as they watched the boy follow Theo up the Griffon's ramp. "We'll get you both back to the States before you know it."

"Those are not idle words," Ann-Katryn said, slipping her arm around Patton's waist. "I would be dead right now if not for them."

"And what do we do when we get back to whatever's left?" Corinne nervously asked. "What if all of this is the easy part?"

"If I had the answer, I'd tell you," Martin said. "The only way to take this is one day at a time. My mom used to say that every day is a gift, which is why we call here and now the present." He trailed off with a sigh, suddenly thinking about his family, guilt washing over him that his constant responsibilities had kept him from doing it more often.

"Group, atten-*shun!*" Patton nonchalantly ordered as Colonel Stirling strode toward them.

"At ease," Stirling said, examining the Griffon. "Our little French toy ready to rock 'n roll?"

"Roger that, sir—make all the surrender jokes you want, but the French knew what they were doing when they designed this bad boy," Martin replied. "The interior's nice, too, like they actually give a shit about soldiers' comfort. After riding in this, the Stryker feels like it was designed by . . . hey, Corinne, what was the name of that French dude who got off on hurting people?"

"The Marquis de Sade."

"That guy," Martin said to Stirling's amusement.

"Colonel, sir?" Ann-Katryn ventured. "What happens if Dunkirk does not let us in?"

"Oh, they're gonna welcome us with open arms," Stirling assured her. "Our ships docked this morning, and they brought along enough food and supplies from one of our remaining replenishment depots to help the surviving townspeople make it through winter. Like Texas and the other states startin' to secede, France has regional strife no different from anywhere else—the locals are pissed that everything's goin' to Paris, and the Americans showed up in the nick of time to help 'em out."

"Nothing like a little gift-giving to grease the wheels," Patton mused.

"Something like that. So, you ready to lead the way, Lieutenant Crenshaw?" Stirling asked Martin with an infectious smile.

"First in, last out, sir!" Martin shot back with the Army cavalry scout motto. "Wait, what?"

"Come to attention, son," the colonel ordered Martin as he produced a small Velcro square with a subdued gold bar. "You're an outstanding junior NCO—best I've ever seen," Stirling said as he replaced the sergeant's stripes on his breast. "But I need an officer leading this charge. One with great instincts and a brass pair of balls. Like you."

"Hey, guys, what's—" Josh interrupted as he and Kira arrived, stopping cold the moment he saw what the colonel was doing. "Holy shit!"

"*Sssssh!*" Kira admonished.

Stirling stepped back to gave Martin the once-over. "Looks good on you—traditionally, it's an enlisted mentor or family member who does the honors, but I guess I'll have to do," he said, handing him a pin-on rank for his patrol cap.

"Thank you, sir," Martin stammered, snapping a salute that Stirling returned as the small audience clapped. "Colonel, I remember my history teacher sayin' the military did away with battlefield commissions after Vietnam."

"Your teacher was right—and if the Pentagon's still standing, any swivel-chair commando who's still alive is more than welcome to put a letter of reprimand in my file. Lieutenant Crenshaw, report to me at 2000 hours to get one last briefing with whatever updated information we've collected before step-off." His eyes caught the gold Starfleet comm badge pinned to Josh's uniform. "Never did get around to askin' you about that."

"Brings me luck, sir," Josh replied. "I can take it off if you don't want me showing up the LT."

"We need all the luck we can get, son—at this point, I don't care if you run around butt naked if it means gettin' us to Dunkirk. All of you carry on," he said, taking his leave to return to his Stryker.

"Do us all a favor and keep your clothes on, micro-dick—you'll embarrass yourself," Patton ribbed Josh before snapping to attention and saluting Martin. "Sniper check, sir!"

"Wise ass," Martin grunted as he returned the honors, peeling off his patrol cap and whipping out a Leatherman knife from his belt sheath to cut off his sergeant rank and pin the new one on.

"This is cool!" René said as Theo climbed out the front passenger door and reached up to ease the boy down. "We get to ride in this all the way there?"

"That's a roger, bud," Theo replied, stopping dead in his tracks upon spotting Martin's gold bar. "What the—?" he sputtered before coming to attention and saluting, which René aped, knocking the patrol cap off his head.

"On that note," Martin said, returning the salutes, "my first order as an officer is that no one salute me from this point forward. I don't need to be attractin' any more fire . . ." He stopped to watch his words around the boy. "I mean *attention*, than we already are."

"What the heck's goin' on, lieutenant?" Theo asked, gesturing at his new rank.

"That's what happens when you miss staff meetings," Kira joked.

CHAPTER 51

WISCONSIN

The pleasant sound of classical music greeted Melinda as she opened the creaky wooden door to the ham radio room, the complex melody sadly reminding her of the promising future the collapse had ripped away.

She found Ethan reassembling his Rock River Arms battle rifle, its components carefully laid out across the small wooden work desk under the soft white light of the desk lamp providing the room's sole illumination. "Hey there!" he warmly greeted, his smile doing little to hide his nervousness.

"Gunnar said I'd find you here. Mind some company?" she asked, the unzipping of her tactical vest signaling that Ethan was getting company whether he wanted it or not.

"Mi casa, su casa," he said, pinning the extractor of his rifle bolt in place.

Melinda cautiously leaned the rifle she was still getting to know in the corner and peeled off her vest packed with half a dozen full magazines—the months of labor she had put in at the farm had made the load slightly less tiring to lug around everywhere. "Where's Al?"

"He finally went to bed," Ethan answered, thumbing behind him at the computer monitor displaying the colorful "waterfall" of real-time activity on the twenty-meter band carrying the frequency that was playing the music. "He's been up since 4 a.m. trying to get a hold of anyone at Fort McCoy or the new state government in Wausau to send help. I'm fillin' in 'til midnight."

"Al have any luck?" Melinda asked, already knowing the answer as she pulled up a folding metal chair.

Ethan shook his head with a frown as the blood-red digital wall clock above the Wisconsin map struck 2300 hours. "Shouldn't you be trying to get some sleep before the shit hits the fan?"

"I should ask the same of you."

"Believe it or not, I tried," Ethan said, nodding to the disheveled single bed shoved against the wall under the window drawn with its thick blackout curtain—Al shunned it because it was murder on his back. "Could you sleep if you were in my shoes?"

"So you got picked for the mission," Melinda sorrowfully replied.

"No—after what they did to my dad, I volunteered. With any luck, we'll catch those bastards off-guard and take out their MRAP before they know what hit them."

"And if you can't?"

Ethan slid the rifle's bolt assembly and charging handle into the upper receiver with a loud metallic *click*. "Then we kill as many of 'em as we can and run like hell back here. How's Jimmy?"

"Worried—but then again, so's everybody. He caught on pretty quick that something's up," Melinda said. "I made sure to tire him out today, but it took forever to get him to sleep."

The swelling crescendo of the end of the orchestral piece rose from the radio's speakers. *"Thanks for tuning in to Redoubt Radio this evening, wherever you may be,"* came the voice of an older man, his mellow and measured presentation reminiscent of a pre-collapse public radio announcer. *"I'm sure most of you are tuning in for the rebroadcast of Alexandra Chase's interview with Washington State Senator Rebecca Stevenson, who barely escaped the attempt on her life at the bombing of Colville. But we still have some time to kill until then, so why not spend it with me?"*

An innocent and childlike yet haunting melody filled the room. "That's beautiful," Ethan said. "You're the music prodigy—who is that?"

"Take a guess," Melinda mischievously challenged.

"Beethoven," Ethan blurted as if he was a game show contestant with the clock running out. "If I ever hear classical, I just assume it's Beethoven."

"You're off by about two hundred years," Melinda snickered. "It's a piece from an American composer named John Adams—it's called 'Meister Eckhardt and Quackie.'"

"That's a silly name," Ethan mused.

"I have no idea why—I only heard it once."

"And you remember it?"

Melinda stepped to the wall map of Wisconsin, the music temporarily accompanied by the clicks and clacks of her boyfriend performing a function check on his reassembled rifle. She felt a pang of sorrow as she remembered her seventh-grade class trip to the Milwaukee Symphony Orchestra rehearsal where she had heard the piece, her finger slowly tracing southwest to rest on Elkhorn, and the red Dymo label with her name on it that Al used to identify the hometowns of group members. *Gone. They're all gone,* she silently lamented. "I don't just remember the song, Ethan," she sighed. "If I had my flute with me, I could perform it for you."

Ethan set his rifle on the desk, sensing Melinda's anguish as he wiped his oily hands on his camouflage trousers and rose to meet her. "You told me you can play by ear—that's really impressive."

"I didn't tell you the half of it," Melinda said, not taking her eyes off the map. "The moment I hear a piece of music, I can play the whole thing from memory, no matter how long it is. I heard this composition five years ago, and I could play it as if I had the sheet music in front of me. You're the first person I've told in a very long time." Grief welled up inside her as she remembered how her family kept the extent of her talent close to the vest, not wanting her to become a wunderkind at the cost of losing her childhood. She at times had hated her parents for holding her back, but in retrospect was glad they did—and she would never get to tell them that they were right.

"God gave you a wonderful gift," Ethan said, sliding his arm around her waist.

"It feels like a curse now," Melinda bemoaned, turning to face him. "Everyone here loves it so much when I perform, and I'm so thankful for it." She paused to wipe her eyes. "But now, this gift from God is nothing but a reminder of all we've lost."

Ethan held her face in his hands. "Do me a favor."

"Anything."

"If this fight goes bad and you think we're gonna get overrun, I want you to abandon your post and run away."

"What?" Melinda blurted before Ethan silenced her with a finger to her lips.

"If things go south, you and Jimmy grab your bikes and go. Find the cache in the woods I showed you, load up on supplies, and don't look back."

A tear ran down Melinda's cheek. "I can't—"

"You have to live," Ethan insisted. "People like me are a dime a dozen. I can homestead and shoot, but anyone can do that. People like you, Melinda . . . people like you are gonna rebuild this world."

Melinda wrapped her arms around Ethan's neck and kissed him passionately. She broke their embrace just long enough to lock the door before leading him by the hand to the cot, where they both made love for the first time.

CHAPTER 52

FRANCE

"I never thought I'd get sick of bread," Édouard Labelle said with resignation, dusting the crumbs of his meager breakfast from his *Gendarmerie nationale* tactical vest as a steady rain drummed on the roof of the Renault Mégane squad car. "But when that's all you eat, it gets rather old."

"At least we're eating, deputy—you're lucky," his partner, Brigadier Deputy Constable Nel Boivin, told the rookie as they stared at the sheets of water cascading down the windshield, beyond which was nothing but post-collapse darkness. "And be thankful that we're still here with our families on cordon duty, not stripped away to put down the riots or the secessionists."

Édouard's face flashed with the green light of his wristwatch the moment it chimed three in the morning. "You're right, of course—but having said that, I'd give anything for an espresso," he retorted with a loud yawn—there wasn't so much as a coffee bean left in the small border village of Audun-le-Roman where their station was located.

A set of headlights winked into existence up the road, heading straight for them. "What's this?!" the rookie gendarme blurted.

"We shall soon find out," Nel said, puzzled at the sight of the first vehicle in weeks to approach town. He opened the car door, gasping as ice-cold rainwater soaked through his trousers. "You will not need coffee to stay awake after this."

Édouard stepped into the wet and chilly dark with a curse as his partner began waving a flashlight signal cone over his head, which quickly became pointless as the headlights of the large military vehicle bathed the gendarmes and their squad car in chalky white light. A middle-aged woman in full combat dress popped out of the top hatch of the VBMR Griffon the moment it rolled to a halt.

"*Bonjour!*" Corinne Roberts called down in French. "I need you to move and let our convoy pass."

Nel nodded acquiescence—the military was exempt from the president's *etat d'urgence* forbidding all non-essential travel to maintain social order and prevent further terrorist attacks following the Russian strikes. "Are you here to bring us supplies?" Nel called up to the soldier, shielding his eyes from the rain.

"I'm sorry, but no—we've been recalled from the German border to help with the unrest," Corinne answered, offering both God's honest truth and a bald-faced lie in the same sentence.

"Of course—Paris has to come first, as always!" Édouard sarcastically groused over the Griffon's engine. "I bet the *parigots* are eating well!"

Corinne was about to put the young gendarme in his place before Nel tersely ordered him to start the car and pull onto the shoulder. "Sorry about my partner," he apologized.

"It's all right—you're doing your duty. Thank you for letting us do ours," Corinne said, disappearing back down into the hatch.

Patton hit the gas, just barely giving the squad car time to get out of the way. "Great job, teach!" he said over the rhythmic thumping of the Griffon's oversized wiper blades.

Corinne shivered as she handed Kira back her helmet and soaked Army Combat Uniform jacket top. "Looks like the colonel was right—our camo pattern looks enough like the French one to fool them."

"Don't sell yourself short. Nice performance," Kira said, draping a wool blanket over Corinne's shoulders as René came to sit in her lap.

Martin watched from the Griffon's center command seat as the city limits came into view, the piles of roadside trash and dilapidated homes bringing back unpleasant memories of their desperation run into Vilseck to save Ann-Katryn. "Let's hope they're just as ignorant when it comes to vehicle recognition," he said, grabbing the SINCGARS radio they had plugged into the Griffon to let the convoy know to move forward.

***

"Thank you for falling for it, Inspector Clouseau," Colonel Stirling said from the commander station of his Stryker to the video image of the oblivious gendarme as they drove by.

"What movie's that from, sir?" Clayton asked from the cramped driver compartment, his voice sounding through the padded ears of the colonel's combat vehicle crewman helmet.

"Eyes on the road, soldier," Stirling admonished, looking for the hundredth time at the route programmed into the Stryker's MAPS system. They had been dealt their first lucky break, courtesy of their French teacher who had just Jedi mind-tricked two clueless cops; Stirling prayed their luck would hold for the entire five hundred kilometers to Dunkirk. He turned to a second screen that showed the approximate location of the other convoy of Army remnants that had earlier crossed into France from Germany. *Once the French get wind of this, there's gonna be hell to pay*, Stirling thought.

✳✳✳

"Merde alors," Édouard muttered through chattering teeth, the line of armored vehicles and heavy military trucks flashing past their headlights reduced to olive-drab smudges by the thick fog covering their windshield. "Things must really be falling apart."

"Now you see what I was saying? Be thankful for what you have, and that things are not worse for you," Nel said, cranking the heat to full blast. "Although I now agree with you that a hot espresso would be welcome."

Édouard crouched in his seat to watch the last vehicle pass by as the defroster vent slowly rolled away the windshield's fog like the raising of window blinds. "Strange—I don't recall ever seeing APCs like that."

"Would you like to go back and pull them over?" Nel quipped. "Back on the road, and let's hope we don't have to go back out in this."

CHAPTER 53

WISCONSIN

Ethan stomped his boots to ward off the chill of The Compound's barn as he took one last opportunity to study the sand table laying out their mission under the antiseptic white light of a battery-powered lantern. Cardboard cartons, green Army men, and toy cars and trees roughly approximated the layout of the Kiwanis park at the edge of Iron Point where Ethan's dad had taken him as a boy to play during their visits to the farm—and where the Devil's Warriors were keeping the MRAP that had to be destroyed before it could be brought to bear against them.

The twelve-person strike team had just completed its pre-combat inspection, Gunnar's and Lukasz's eagle eyes missing nothing. Jane flashed Ethan a nervous wink as she helped her husband wrap a rattling buckle on his tactical vest with black electrical tape; all around them, the rest of the team was finishing correcting whatever deficiencies Gunnar and Lukasz had caught, or were lost in thought or prayer. Ethan glanced over at his grandmother, who was talking with Aunt Ashley next to the farm's large red Case IH Vestrum 130 tractor that Donna had taught him to drive the day he turned sixteen. Ashley, who was accompanying the strike team as a guide, looked out of her element dressed in a spare set of fatigues; unlike the rest of the team, she was unarmed at the insistence of Gunnar, who still didn't trust her allegiance.

Ethan shifted the weight of his chest-slung rifle and returned his attention to the sand table. A spray-painted red arrow indicating their travel route led to a rise in the woods overlooking the park and the MRAP, represented by a Matchbox monster truck graciously donated by Al's grandson, Kyle. The toy soldiers around it laid on their sides from Gunnar's walk-through of the mission; he had flicked them over one by one as he described how they would strike fast and hard from the high ground and wipe them out. From there, they would disable the MRAP with homemade thermite grenades—they wouldn't be able to melt through its outer armor, so they would need to get inside, where the grenades would slag the dashboard and steering column like a marsh-mallow in a campfire.

Ethan allowed his mind to wander to Melinda, and the magic they had shared just hours earlier—he desperately wished she could be there to see him off, but she and everyone else were busy adding whatever last-minute augmentations they could think of to The Compound's defenses. He watched as a father and son inspected the generator and pump on the back of a beaten-up GMC Sierra that served as The Compound's fire truck. *Please let us live through this*, Ethan silently pleaded with God. *I don't wanna die . . .*

"Hey there, soldier."

"Shit!" Ethan yelped, almost leaping out of his skin at the sound of Gunnar's voice behind him. "Don't sneak up on me like that!"

"You should consider switching to decaf," Gunnar chuckled, his laugh out of place for a dangerous-looking man equipped like he was about to clear houses in Fallujah.

"How can you crack jokes at a time like this?"

"I could whimper and cry if you'd like, but that wouldn't instill you with a lotta confidence, would it?"

"Point taken," Ethan conceded.

"Pop quiz, kid—what MURS radio frequency are we using, and what's the backup?"

"Channel five, and channel three."

"What's the signal to fall back to the ORP?"

Ethan wordlessly pointed to the green star cluster launch tube strapped to the side of Gunnar's tactical vest.

"Who has the thermite grenades?"

"You, Lukasz, and John."

Gunnar slapped Ethan on the back. "This ain't your first rodeo—you're gonna do great," he reassured the scared teenager. "Everybody on me!" he called out, his voice echoing from the barn's rafters as the strike team crowded around the sand table. "They're all yours, Big Mama," Gunnar said to Donna.

A chill ran down Ethan's spine as his grandmother stepped forward, looking and walking as if the past twenty-four hours had aged her as many years.

"I'm not gonna mince words, ladies and gentlemen—if we fail, everyone you love is going to be dead or a slave by this time tomorrow," Donna said, trying her best to keep her voice steady against the tidal wave of fear threatening to overwhelm her. "But we're not gonna fail, are we?"

"No, ma'am," the strike team responded in a grim, determined monotone; there was no macho bravado in their voices like young soldiers hyping themselves up to kick ass and take names.

"Destroy that war machine and come home—we'll be waiting, dug in to our eyeballs and ready to give these animals one helluva fight if they're stupid enough to challenge us on our own turf. This is where we make our stand." A distant beeping sounded on the night air as The Compound's small forklift burned precious fuel to reposition the concrete barriers ringing the old visitor parking area to block off the gravel driveway—if the Devil's Warriors made it past the gate, they would have to cut through the apple orchard and run a gauntlet of gunfire and traps to make it to the farm.

She paused with the cracking of her voice and cleared her throat. "Al's been working like mad to get a hold of anyone at Fort McCoy or the provisional government to send us help, and he's gonna keep trying." Donna stared, one by one, into the strike team's eyes—white slits drilling into her soul from faces painted green and brown to match the autumn foliage. "Good luck, and Godspeed," she said, forlornly staring at her only grandson.

Gunnar checked his watch and motioned toward the barn door. "Let's move, people—form up outside!" he commanded, his breath forming wispy clouds in the frigid air. As the strike team began to solemnly file out, Gunnar saw the silhouette against the quarter-moon night of Will making his way to the sand table with the help of a pair of crutches. "You got two minutes, kid—see ya out there," Gunnar muttered in Ethan's ear before following his team outside.

Tears welled in Ashley's eyes. "Mom—"

"No, honey—like I said, all is forgiven," Donna said, clutching her daughter. "Save the 'just in case' goodbye, because you're coming back."

"'Let's move out' means you too, Ashley!" Gunnar disdainfully called out from across the barn. With a weak smile for her mother, Ashley gingerly hugged Will before jogging for the exit.

"William John Moran, what do you think you're doing up and about?" Donna mother-henned.

"Seeing my son off," he grunted. "And Mom, as long as I'm spitting in the face of authority, I'm taking my place on the line tonight—I'm not hiding in a warm bed while Audie Murphy here gets all the glory." He leaned his weight on a crutch to offer Ethan his hand. "I'm damn proud of you, son—and your Mom woulda been real proud too." His lip trembled as his boy gave him a man's handshake. "Don't you go joining her, you got me?" he managed to blubber before dropping a crutch to the ground and bear-hugging Ethan one-handed, ignoring the searing pain of his battered torso from his son's muscular grip as Donna joined in.

"I'll do my best—gotta go," Ethan said and ran for the exit.

Will stared after his boy as he dashed away. "There was this poem Dad used to read at bedtime when he wasn't at the hospital—I got rather sick of it," Will sadly reminisced. "It ended with, 'You'll be a man, my son!' You remember it?"

"It was Kipling, I think," Donna said. "I don't recall the name."

"Didn't make sense then. Sure as hell does now," he said as his son disappeared from sight.

***

After a huddle to pray for success—and to warn everyone to stay single-file so as not to set off any of their booby traps—Gunnar ordered Justin to lead the group into the woods and stop for a listening halt to acclimate them to the sights, sounds, and smells of their environment.

Gunnar roughly yanked Ashley from the line as the strike team moved out. "I don't give a fuck who your mom is, Judas," he ominously growled in her face. "If you're leadin' us into a trap, there's no scenario in which you come out alive. Everyone here, even your nephew, knows to kill you if you rat us out—and I promise you it won't be quick."

Ashley met his steely glare, massaging the burning pain from his iron grip. "I'm on the right side this time—believe me," she said before returning to the pack.

CHAPTER 54

FRANCE

The dark houses of the unmarked graveyard that had once been the small village of Bras-sur-Meuse flashed by in the VBMR Griffon's low-mounted headlights.

"I wonder if this is what Vilseck is like now," Ann-Katryn mournfully said, watching next to Martin in the commander seat as Patton followed the *gendarmerie* squad car driven by the town's new masters through the cold gray drizzle. She grabbed Theo's seat to steady herself on a tight turn through the confusing warren of medieval roads laid out centuries before Europeans started embracing grid planning.

You read my mind, Patton kept to himself, grimacing at the sight of a mischief of rats scampering into a door long ago kicked open by looters. "Your mom and dad are fine, honey," he lied without taking his eyes off the road. Martin stared out into the dark night with macabre fascination; the villagers, who had all succumbed to the pandemic if the bandits who now ruled the town were to be believed, had added their bones to the millions who had perished in the First World War.

The police car guided them onto a curved road up a gently sloping hill leading to their destination at the far edge of town—the bridges over the

Meuse River and the namesake canal that ran alongside it. Patton slowed at the sight of the canal bridge, the *gendarmerie* car continuing on as a truck in the oncoming lane flashed its headlights three times to order the Griffon to stop. "Sucks we gotta bribe these lowlifes to get across instead of dispatching 'em with extreme prejudice," he said, remembering their first meeting during their recon for the colonel.

"Couldn't agree more, but we can't take the chance if they rigged the bridges to blow," Martin retorted; none of the vehicles in The Lost Boys's convoy were amphibious, which made every bridge along their route a potential roadblock that could stop them cold. "Watch our back," he ordered Theo, slapping his shoulder in the passenger-side gunner's seat.

"Always," Theo responded, cautiously limbering his fingers on the machine gun turret's joystick.

Martin rose with a crouch to Corinne, who was already standing at the rear hatch—she stared at René, who slept curled up in one of the Griffon's comfortable troop seats. "You got this," he said, slinging a heavy olive-drab duffel bag over his shoulder.

"I got this," she nervously repeated, shivering with the blast of cold, wet air that greeted them with the drop of the ramp.

The duo descended to the pavement, rounding the Griffon toward a lone man illuminated by its headlights in the middle of the road; cradling a military rifle, he was dressed in a bizarre mix of military kit and civilian outdoor clothes. "I did not think we would be, ah, seeing you again," the man said in broken English, a cigarette dangling from his mouth.

"Well, here we are," Martin said, Corinne translating for him. "We're here to seal the deal we discussed the last time we met—pay for passage for us and our friends, no questions asked," he continued, gesturing past the Frenchman to the two boxy trucks blocking both lanes of the Meuse Canal bridge.

The man wordlessly beckoned two-fingered for the toll. Martin unslung the duffel bag and tossed it at the man's feet, the German military rifles and magazines they had taken from the Hacksrode gasthaus bandits rattling inside. As the man warily took a knee to inspect the goods, Martin wondered whether their journey across post-apocalyptic America would be an endless exercise of paying tribute to one warlord after another as deserted soldiers and wannabe emperors in a nation awash with guns carved out a thousand little tinpot empires.

"No bullets?" the man asked, rising to his feet.

"Do you take me for a fool?" Martin sneered.

"Fair enough. And the rest?"

Martin slowly reached into his pocket to toss over a roll of his Hacksrode silver coins with a one-ounce Germania gold mark taped to it. "Paid in full—real money. Now, *monsieur*, please hold up your end of the deal and make way."

"But of course," the Frenchman said before swiftly leveling his rifle at Corinne as another bandit appeared from between the trucks in the distance, aiming an NLAW anti-tank missile straight at the Griffon's engine block. "Tell your people to come out, hands on their heads, or you all die!" the man triumphantly demanded in his stunted English.

"That was a mistake," Martin growled, rocking on the balls of his feet and counting down in his head from five as a rhythmic *pum pum pum* rose in the distance. "Down!" he hollered at Corinne, leaping on top of her the moment his countdown reached zero.

The volley of 40-millimeter grenades lobbed from Nick Alger's Stryker on the hilltop overlooking the bridges a kilometer away struck true, their explosive power not enough to severely damage the bridge, but many times enough to shred the trucks and slay the bandits, including the man brandishing the missile launcher, who took a direct hit and departed the battlefield in a hundred directions simultaneously. Corinne squirmed under Martin's muscular frame, screaming and plugging her ears as he scrambled to draw on their double-crosser before Theo cut him down with a burst of machine gun fire.

"Go!" Martin bellowed over the racket, pulling Corinne to run for the Griffon's ramp as Theo laid down covering fire, adding to the carnage as another volley of grenades hit their mark. Josh leaped out the rear hatch with an M240B machine gun, lying in the road to cover their rear as Martin all but heaved Corinne back inside like a baggage handler loading a plane. Martin turned to join Josh just in time for the both of them to lay a stream of copper-jacketed death into a truck rounding the corner to block them off, its driver and crew not having received the memo that their plans had been exquisitely fucked. The truck, its engine catching fire and its driver shredded to ribbons, careened off the road and plowed downhill, smashing into a thicket of trees.

"I'm OK! Mom's OK!" Corinne comforted her hysterical son as Martin and Josh scrambled up the ramp. Patton weaved through the wreckage before flooring it across both bridges to set up security on the Meuse's far-side bank; the Stryker raced down the hill and through overgrown farm fields to join them. Ten minutes later, The Lost Boys crossed the bridges in force, their tires grinding what little remained of the bandits into paste.

CHAPTER 55

Mick Kilmurray held his calloused hands toward the campfire to stay warm, the sound of country music—and the screams of one of Iron Point's surviving female residents—coming from the party in Kiwanis Park in the woods behind him.

"Sucks we drew the short straw for guard duty tonight," a lanky fellow member of the Devil's Warriors he knew only as A.J. muttered, warding off the cold with a nip of Jim Beam and offering Kilmurray the bottle. He wordlessly rejected it with an outstretched palm; he could never stop with just one drink, and Razor had literally gutted some poor son of a bitch who had been stupid enough to get falling-down drunk at his post. Kilmurray's fear of being disemboweled far outweighed his dislike of spending the evening sober.

Kilmurray had barely escaped when the shit hit the fan with a handful of other hard-cases from the maximum-security Baraga Correctional Facility in the UP of Michigan; the inmates had risen up in revolt, defeating the skeleton contingent of remaining guards who went down fighting. With a new M-16 rifle in hand, courtesy of the slain corrections officer he took it from, he had stumbled across a house in the woods, where he stole clothes and food after killing the husband and wife inside, doubling his body count on top of the pawn shop owners he had slain a decade prior that resulted in his life sentence without parole. Kilmurray joined the Devil's Warriors shortly thereafter when they sacked the nearby town of Baraga, their numbers swelling as they began their rampage across the UP and northern Wisconsin.

The woman's scream echoed again through the woods, followed by laughter and a gruff-sounding man warning her to knock it off. "Damn—sounds like they got a real shindig goin' tonight," A.J. griped, staring enviously at the bonfire's glow lighting the sky from the park where a party was in full swing around their new tank, or whatever the hell it was—he had forgotten what the veterans in the gang called it. He took another swig of bourbon before passing it to the third member of their guard detail, who almost fumbled the bottle. "Careful, ya clumsy jackass!"

"Relax, dude—ain't like The Colonel's top-shelf," the butterfingered sentry slurred, downing a gulp after the save. "Now, the folks at that farm down yonder we're finally gonna stomp? I hear they're practically swimmin' in the good stuff. Oughta be plenty left over to keep us warm after Razor an' the top dogs take their cut."

"I'm more thinkin' about those farmers' daughters, actually—I'm tired of the poontang here in this podunk town," A.J. said, wrestling the bottle back. "What 'bout you, Kill? Whaddya think?"

Kilmurray checked the time with a disappointed grunt, the firelight sparking off the gold watch that had belonged to the husband he had murdered after his prison escape. "Think I'm gonna take a piss—don't you dumbfucks shoot me by mistake," he said, rising from his lounge chair and grabbing the rifle he just barely knew how to use. His boots clicked on the decaying rural backroad they were guarding as he disappeared into the starlit darkness just far enough to get a minute of privacy before unzipping his jeans and relieving himself on the asphalt. His temper flared red-hot the moment he returned to find the other two sentries passed out—A.J. was sprawled back in his chair, his precious liquor bottle emptying at his feet next to the third sentry, who lay face-down by the fire.

"Goddammit, you assholes!" Kilmurray hollered. "Fuckin' Razor's gonna thin-slice your pricks if he catches you sleepin' on the job!" He cocked his hand back, ready to wake them up with a slap when he noticed that A.J.'s eyes were wide open, his flannel jacket soaked with blood from the wire garrote that had strangled him.

"Jesus—!" Kilmurray managed to yelp before he was silenced by the excruciating pain of a large knife plunging into his kidney. The blade's removal was the last thing he ever felt before it was shoved straight through the base of his neck with a sickening wet crunch.

Gunnar pushed Kilmurray forward, his body hitting the dirt like a fallen tree. He knelt to wipe the blood from the blade of his Ka-Bar Fighter knife on his victim's back, relieving Kilmurray of his rifle as Lukasz and Justin grabbed the other two bodies and dragged them into the woods.

No turning back now, Gunnar said to himself, sheathing his knife as Ethan dashed up to help drag Kilmurray away.

CHAPTER 56

FRANCE

Colonel Stirling rose from the top hatch of his Stryker at the head of The Lost Boys's convoy, his head poking up among the antennas and the imposing .50-caliber CROWS remote weapons system mounted on the roof.

The cold autumn rain that had been drenching northern France all night had finally stopped with the sunrise, but the dreary low-hanging cloud cover remained, promising continued safety from being spotted from the air. Chilly, moist wind stung Stirling's face, beading water on the tactical goggles shielding his eyes.

Stirling briefly spun around to check the line of Strykers and other vehicles snaking behind him, keeping twenty meters between one another on the rural French road just past the small town of Rethel; they had just crossed the A34 motorway connecting it with the larger city of Reims forty kilometers southwest, and Paris farther beyond. This was the nearest their path would take them to the City of Lights, but with all the news of rioting and unrest—and the military force assembled to bring it to heel that could easily be siphoned off to stop them—even 160 klicks seemed too close for comfort. Every kilometer they subsequently traveled would take them farther from Paris, adding percentage points to their odds of survival.

The colonel smiled in spite of himself, standing triumphantly in a fighting vehicle leading fighting soldiers across northern France like General Patton—*except, of course, we're heading the other way*, Stirling mused. *One-third of the way there—290 klicks to go. So far so good . . .*

His flicker of optimism was instantly snuffed by the thunderclap of an explosion. Stirling whirled to see a plume of smoke rising from the shoulder of the road two hundred meters behind him—an armored Humvee weaved violently back and forth, belching smoke as it spun out of control and flipped with a crash of metal and glass. Stirling was about to radio The Lost Boys to plow through the ambush, but there was no ambush—no gunfire, no rockets, no nothing.

"Everybody stop!" the colonel screamed into his helmet-mounted radio over the convoy-wide net, grabbing the hatch's handles to steady himself as Clayton hit the brakes. "Hold fast on positions!" he ordered, demanding radio silence until further notice before clicking to the internal comms with his driver. "Turn around—now!"

"Was that a fuckin' IED?!" Clayton yelled back.

"No—now shut your hole and *drive*, soldier!" Stirling thundered, cursing their sudden reversal of fortune as he got back on the net and violated his own order for silence just long enough to order the Humvee ambulance forward, realizing with growing dread that the Great War may have claimed some of his soldiers' lives more than a century after the guns had fallen silent.

***

The lifeless eyes of the young second lieutenant, the right side of her pretty face burned and mutilated, stared into the gray sky as two privates wrapped her body in her poncho. She lay dead next to the shattered Humvee, its right side peppered with shrapnel and tendrils of black smoke wafting from under the hood.

"I'm sorry I fucked up. I didn't mean to fuck up," the Humvee's driver chanted from the back of the ambulance, holding an ice pack to her head as a medic wrapped a nasty gash across her forearm. The Humvee's other passengers lay in the ambulance's two stretcher bays; they were hurt worse but could be saved, provided any of the ships waiting for them at Dunkirk had a decent sickbay.

Goddamned Iron Harvest, Stirling silently fumed. Four years of trench warfare in France and Belgium had left behind untold millions of tons of unexploded ordinance, which tractors inadvertently dug up every spring planting and fall harvest. Farmers piled whatever they upturned at roadside collection points for disposal, and anyone dumb enough to fuck with it deserved what they got. Unfortunately for the driver and her passengers, she had nodded off just long enough to swerve onto the shoulder and hit a harvested artillery shell that turned out not to be a dud. A Stryker or an LMTV running over the shell would have lost a wheel and resulted in a mobility kill, but the passengers would have been safe—*so of course it had to be a Hummer that did it*, Stirling ruefully thought.

The colonel gestured to the despondent driver. "She'll live. Get her ass on the nearest Stryker—we're moving out," he ordered the medic—survival meant staying on the move, and they were idling in place. Two privates blew past him to load the dead lieutenant's body onto the back of an LMTV like so much cargo.

The VBMR Griffon recon vehicle rolled to a halt in the oncoming lane; Martin and Josh leaped out the rear hatch, gawking at the remains of the Humvee they had stolen from Vilseck and driven across Germany and Luxembourg. *That could've been us*, Martin thought with a shudder.

Stirling pivoted to the duo before they could say a word. "Lieutenant Crenshaw, get back out front and scout ahead toward the bridge crossing at Marle in advance of our arrival. And watch where you drive if you gotta leave the hardball for any reason—y'all are screwed if you blow a wheel on some UXO out in the middle of the sticks where we can't get to you." Stirling angrily glared at the demolished Humvee. "Of all the damn rotten luck!"

"Lady Luck's not done givin' us the high hard one yet, sir," Martin said as Josh turned up their Eton radio to reveal a woman, in French-accented English, warning every American unit on French soil to turn around immediately or face destruction. "Looks like our secret's out."

CHAPTER 57

WISCONSIN

The lone sentry guarding Razor's house swore at the sight of Tex Bowman striding up the road in the moonlight, the clicking of his black leather harness boots slowly rising over the distant sound of music from the party. Whatever had happened, it had to be bad if it meant rousting a boss who hated more than anything to be bothered in the middle of the night, the sentry realized, fear gripping tight over Razor's hair-trigger temper.

"Here to see the honcho," the gang's muscled, overweight sergeant-at-arms tersely said the moment he reached the front-yard campfire keeping the guard warm on the frosty night.

The sentry motioned to the front door of what had once been the mayor's house, its façade glowing crimson from the campfire on the darkened block. "Better you than me—*vaya con Dios*," he grunted.

Tex stepped up to the front deck, angry that an otherwise great evening had turned on a dime to shit. The party had started getting good; Tessa, three sheets to the wind, had climbed onto the MRAP's hood to perform a strip tease—her face was nothing to write home about, but you could bounce a quarter off her tight bod. She had just started her grand finale when the chief of the watch pulled him aside to deliver the bad news.

The funk of trash, body odor, and pot smoke greeted Tex as he stepped through the door and up the stairs, his miniature Maglite flashlight illuminating the smashed-up living room and demolished wall-mounted flatscreen television; loud snores from the master bedroom accompanied the groan of the wooden stairs and the crunch of broken glass underfoot from the shattered wall portraits that no one had ever bothered to sweep up. Tex pocketed his flashlight upon reaching the upstairs foyer, where chalky moonbeams streaming through the windows shone like spotlights on two large patches of dried blood caked into the carpet—one from the spy sent by the farmstead after Razor had finished having his fun with her, and the other from the poor bastard who had let Razor's favorite girl slip him a mickey and escape with their valuable prisoner. Tex knew Razor wouldn't bleed him—he had ridden with him since the beginning—but he didn't savor the task of being the bearer of bad news.

Razor's rhythmic, thunderous snoring abruptly ceased with the loud creak of the bedroom door. "This better be fuckin' good," his gravelly voice grumbled from the dark, the women on each side of him stirring. The smell of the room competed with Tex's own stink after a week of not bathing.

"The three guys we had on all-night watch guardin' the back way into town through County Highway G went missin'," Tex said, scratching his long beard—dereliction of duty was on Razor's very short list of permissible interruptions.

"That's diff'ernt—never had three bail on us at once," Razor muttered, his muscular tattoo-sleeved arms appearing jet black in the darkened room. "I take it we got new eyes on the back door?"

"Yeah, but I don't think these assholes hung up their helmets. We found blood—a lot. As in someone ended up a coupla quarts low."

"Goddammit," Razor grumbled, reaching over one of the naked women to take a swig from an open bottle of Jack Daniel's on the nightstand—this wasn't the first time since staying idle in Iron Point that his bored and increasingly restless riders took out their anger on one another. "Guys are startin' to go at it 'cause there's nothin' else to do—the sooner we take out that damn farm, the better."

"Boss?" Tex ventured. "You think them farmers did this?"

"They don't got the balls," Razor retorted.

The sudden roar of rifle fire ratting the windows said otherwise.

***

"That's one!" Ethan yelled, rifle bucking as the pot-bellied biker in his sights crumpled to the ground with two well-placed shots that tore through his side. He quickly shifted on his elbows to drill another biker between the shoulder blades as he tried running for cover. "Two!" Ethan whooped in triumph, tallying his kills in revenge for what they had put his father through.

Ashley watched in fascinated horror as her nephew and The Compound's assault team turned the Devil's Warriors jamboree into a slaughter, the revelers too drunk or stupid to react. A handful of survivors made a desperate run for cover behind the MRAP, only to learn at the cost of their lives that Gunnar had set up an L-shaped ambush giving his team a clear line of fire on all sides of the armored vehicle. Ashley recognized Tessa—a real grade-A bitch—as she angrily snatched up an AK-74 and haphazardly sprayed the treeline before a thumb-sized bullet from

Lukasz's .50-caliber Accuracy International AX50 sniper rifle turned her ugly face into pink mist.

Gunnar angrily put a wounded biker crawling for his rifle out of his misery, his hope of disabling the MRAP by stealth having been shot to hell the moment they stumbled upon the party. The bikers who had managed to find shelter behind trees or the line of pickup trucks along the narrow dirt road heading back into Iron Point were beginning to return fire, and time was quickly running out before reinforcements arrived—all would be for naught if they didn't disable the MRAP, no matter how many of the bikers they killed.

Justin and Jane leaped up to make a mad dash for the armored vehicle under the rest of the assault team's covering fire, hurdling over bodies as they ran. Bullets tore into the ground around them before Lukasz sighted on the gunman behind a truck and blew him away. Headlights flared in his Leupold scope as he yanked back the bolt handle to chamber another round, and Lukasz traversed his rifle to find a Humvee bouncing down the dirt road, rushing headlong toward them. He put a round through the driver-side windshield, and the stolen military vehicle violently swerved off-road to plow head-on into a large oak tree with a satisfying crash.

"Things are startin' to get spicy, Big G!" Lukasz yelled to Gunnar, loading a fresh magazine as Justin and Jane slid to cover behind the MRAP's mammoth rear tires.

"Move your asses—we got a world of hurt comin' our way!" Gunnar screamed to the Christensens as Justin pulled a thermite-packed soda can and a Zippo lighter from his tactical vest. He stepped up onto the MRAP's right-side air tank and flung open the passenger-side door—where a biker lying in wait on the seat emptied the magazine of a fully automatic Glock handgun into Justin and his wife.

CHAPTER 58

"*No!*" Ethan screamed as he and Gunnar shot the Christensens' assailant, rounds pinging and rattling inside the MRAP. Ethan rose onto all fours to run to them before Gunnar lunged to pin him down.

"We gotta finish the job!" Gunnar hollered in his ear. "Stay put and cover me—" he began before Ashley darted past, briefly eclipsing the bonfire as she ran straight for the war machine.

Ashley sprinted for all she was worth, Gunnar's profanity-laden order for her to return drowned out by the rest of the assault team laying down covering fire with their dwindling ammunition. She deftly leaped over an eviscerated corpse, only to slip on a steaming pile of intestines and land hard on her tailbone. Seeing stars from the pain, she maniacally scrambled on all fours into the MRAP's shadow, desperately feeling around for the grenade Justin had dropped, flinching with each stray round pinging off the vehicle's armor.

A sickly gurgle caught her attention the moment her hand serendipitously slapped down on Justin's lighter. Jane, coughing up blood with a spasm, pointed with her ebbing strength at the spray-painted olive-drab aluminum can that had rolled into the weeds under the dead biker hanging limp from the MRAP's passenger door. Ashley gave a determined nod as Jane weakly smiled, her arm falling to the ground as her eyes began to go glassy.

With a disgusted shudder, Ashley slid the body out of the MRAP by its dangling and bloody arms, the mangled corpse hitting the ground next to Justin. She felt for the grenade's ten-second fuse as the firelight reflected off Justin's lighter, emblazoned with the red, white, and blue insignia of the First Marine Division where he and Jane had met. Ashley hoisted herself inside, trying not to puke as she slithered over the blood-soaked seat.

***

Razor's forehead throbbed from where it had violently struck the side of the Humvee when it slammed into the tree. He shook his head to clear his blurred vision, only to be rewarded with an agonizing headache that made the worst whiskey-soaked hangover seem mild by comparison.

He wiped a hand over his face, briefly panicking as it came away red with blood before realizing that it wasn't his—the inside of the cabin was sprayed with gore. Lukasz's shot had demolished his driver's head, and had had plenty of energy left over to pass through and blow a softball-sized hole in Tex's chest behind him. Razor pushed open the passenger door with a grunt, the knot on his head throbbing with each heartbeat as he fell onto all fours. He had just reached up into the wrecked Humvee to grab his M4 carbine when the MRAP's rectangular bulletproof windows suddenly lit up from the inside with a shower of sparks. Razor screamed with rage, ignoring the sharp pain of a cracked rib as the MRAP's windows glowed a demonic red, smoke billowing out the top hatch as the incendiary device the enemy had planted began consuming the armored vehicle from within. A green flare lanced into the sky with a *whoosh* to the grating tweet of a whistle. "*Fall back!* Ashley, let's go!" a man's voice hollered over the tapering rifle fire.

Razor's injuries disappeared in a flash of adrenaline and fury upon seeing Ashley dart for the incline leading into the woods, the light of the dying bonfire illuminating her face as she stopped ever so briefly to look back at her handiwork. He fell to his elbows on the Humvee's buckled hood and took aim at his former lover.

"You shouldn't have come back, you fucking bitch!" he roared, savoring the terror on her face as she recognized his voice. He teased Ashley with a false hope of survival, giving her a few extra seconds of life to try to make her escape before shooting her square in the back. She hit the ground face-down, the bullet lancing her heart, as Razor angrily fired the entire thirty-round magazine, one round at a time, into her body.

***

Please, God, bring Ethan home. Bring all of them home, Melinda silently prayed as she walked Jimmy by the hand into the dark and chilly barn to the sounds of battle coming from Iron Point.

Jimmy, already disquieted by the fighting and the anxiety of Melinda and the other grown-ups, whimpered at the sight of the open trapdoor in the concrete floor, the passage glowing like a spooky cave from the basement lanterns. His friend Kyle stood at the entrance with his parents and Donna, who were ushering the children down to shelter.

"Do I hafta go down there?" Jimmy whined, clutching his Bluey stuffy, his watering eyes catching the light from Donna's handheld lantern.

"Just until it's safe," Melinda said, trying to put a brave edge to her voice for Jimmy's sake.

"Can't you just stay with me instead of fighting the bad guys?"

Melinda knelt to look Jimmy in the eyes, the military surplus Kevlar helmet dangling from the back of her tactical vest knocking against the heel of her boot. "I need you to be a big boy, Jimmy. Can you do that for me?" He nodded silently as Melinda pulled him into a hug.

Kyle walked over to them, brandishing a Candy Land board game box. "Mom and Dad said we gotta go down now," he told Jimmy. "Wanna play?"

"I don't know how."

"I'll show you," he said, leading Jimmy down the concrete stairs, Melinda staring sadly after him as the crying of an infant pierced the night over the distant gunfire.

Melinda stepped to Kyle's parents, who like her were decked out in full battle gear—they would be guarding the barn as the last line of defense. "We'll watch after him," Al's daughter and Kyle's mother, Shelby, said before Melinda could make the ask that she had heard from every other parent who had entrusted them with their kids. Melinda had barely managed to blubber her thanks when Donna's radio chirped.

"They did it, Mom—they took out the MRAP and about twenty of the Devil's Warriors with it," Will reported from the CQ.

"Thank God," Donna exclaimed with a gasp of relief—the gang would still be coming, and they'd be pissed, but Gunnar's team had significantly evened the odds. "Did everyone make it?"

Will's long silence answered Donna's question. "Um, Will?" she asked, voice trembling. *Ethan!* Melinda silently panicked, jaw quivering as Donna's wrinkled hand shot out to grab hers. "Will, answer me!"

"We lost Justin and Jane."

Donna let out a sob, her heart sinking like a stone. Everyone at The Compound loved the hardworking and eternally optimistic newlywed couple; the Christensens had been planning come spring to start a family, and Donna had told them how much she was looking forward when the time came to help bring their baby into the world. "Please tell me that's all," Donna barely managed to whisper into the radio.

"No, Mom."

"Who else?" she croaked.

"It's Ashley," Will said. "She's gone."

CHAPTER 59

FRANCE

*T*he two fastest things in the universe are light and word of mouth, Colonel Stirling groused as Clayton slowed the Stryker to a halt.

At least a hundred people of all ages blocked the road at the edge of the town of Origny-Saint-Benoite, where Stirling planned to cross the Oise River and the Sambre-Oise Canal. The pathetic band, shivering in the damp morning cold, held up signs, in English, begging for food, medicine, or whatever The Lost Boys could spare; a handful of them held up hungry or sick young children.

A chill crept up Clayton's spine; the townspeople were just *standing there* in silence like zombies. He slowly crept the eight-wheeled war machine toward the desperate civilians and laid on the Stryker's horn, but they refused to budge. "What do I do, sir?" he asked the colonel over the internal comms system.

"Get ready to move," Stirling answered, overriding the controls of the Stryker's gunner and slewing the .50-caliber weapons turret to take aim at a roadside berm, the bare branches of its thin trees reaching into the gray sky. "Sending," he announced, pulling the joystick trigger to fire a seven-round burst into the dirt. The desperate townspeople immediately broke and ran for their homes.

"I woulda taken the shot, sir," Stirling's gunner said as the Stryker continued on its way.

"I know, son," Stirling said, allowing himself a brief moment of pity for the fleeing townspeople on his display screen.

"I'm gonna stick my oar in, sir," Clayton said over the rising whine of the Stryker's engine. "If these folks knew we were comin', every swingin' dick from here to Dunkirk's gonna be stopping us and begging for help."

"You read my mind, sergeant—just get us through town and across those bridges," Stirling ordered as he pondered his options. His planned route had mostly stuck to back roads, leapfrogging from one small town to the next; but with the ever-increasing odds of entanglements with both civilians and the French military, Stirling now pondered sacrificing stealth and security for speed. With a glance at the map on his screen, Stirling decided to vector Lieutenant Crenshaw and his cav scouts west to get eyes on the A26 motorway leading northwest to the Channel coast, which would cut their travel time, provided it wasn't choked with abandoned cars like the German autobahns had been.

The colonel was about to relay the order before Martin's voice blared in his ear, bearing the bad news that The Lost Boys had just been found.

***

The six-wheeled EBRC Jaguar armored recon vehicle furiously kicked up mud as it tore across an empty farm field toward a distant copse of bare trees.

Martin nervously followed the squat, turreted vehicle with his M22 binoculars from his vantage point on the roof of an abandoned farmhouse, watching as it came to a halt next to the first Jaguar they had spotted, their peculiar angular camouflage pattern having the odd effect of making them stand out against the brown autumn foliage. Not for the first time since going AWOL from Vilseck, Martin wished they had stolen an RQ-11 Raven drone to scout their surroundings; they had almost driven right up on the French recon team before ducking behind the farmhouse in the nick of time. "Make that two Jaguars—nothing else changes," Martin radioed the colonel, amending his SALUTE report on the enemy's size, activity, location, unit, time, and equipment. "Orders, over?"

"Wait one," Stirling tersely radioed back, ordering Martin to stay on the frequency and await further instructions.

"Not even one klick away," Josh said from behind binoculars of his own, the cold of the farmhouse's roof tiles chilling him through his Gore-Tex jacket. "We shoulda snagged a Raven, LT."

"You don't say," Martin grumbled, checking his Michelin map of northern France, their location ten kilometers northeast of Saint-Quentin marked with a pencil. The Jaguars had stopped smack in the way of the convoy's axis of advance; they knew The Lost Boys were coming. Martin nervously peeked over the roof's edge to their Griffon below, his mind racing to refine a contingency plan if they had to bug out fast—if the enemy saw through their deception of driving a French vehicle, the Griffon would be no match for the Jaguar, with its 40-millimeter turret cannon and four anti-armor missiles.

The revving of diesel engines interrupted Martin's pondering of worst-case scenarios. "What the—?!" Josh blurted as both Jaguars backed out and wheeled around, carving deep ruts in the muddy field before beating a hasty retreat back the way they came. Martin almost fumbled his binoculars off the edge as he scrambled to get a better look—he had barely acquired the retreating Jaguars before a tiny green-gray blob cresting a distant rise to the north caught his attention. The blob was joined by three more—Stryker fighting vehicles, all of them headed his way.

"Save your breath, lieutenant," Colonel Stirling cut Martin off before he could radio in a contact report. "You got eyes on the other unit doin' this with us—thank God they were in the neighborhood. They know to look for you—hook up with 'em and wait for the rest of us. Out."

"And me with nothing decent to wear for company," Josh joked with relief.

"Smartass," Martin snorted, grabbing a star cluster tube from his tactical vest and slamming its firing pin cap onto the roof, its bright green signal flare launching into the sky on a plume of white smoke.

CHAPTER 60

"*All stations this net, all stations this net—they're coming,*" Lukasz's voice ominously crackled from the MURS radio clipped to Melinda's tactical vest.

And I have a freakin' front row seat, the teenager anxiously told herself as she stared from her foxhole through the sepia of early sunrise at the iron front gate leading into The Compound. The distant buzz of a quadcopter drone watching the invaders' approach cut through the eerily still morning air.

"Be advised we got multiple bandits inbound," Lukasz continued, watching the procession with Donna and Will over the shoulder of the drone pilot who had joined them in the CQ. "Motorcycles and trucks, lots of 'em, heading down the road straight for us, ETA three minutes. Good hunting—and may God help us all."

The rumble of engines began rising in the distance. "Steady, kid," said Melinda's foxhole partner, an older Army veteran named Mark—Gunnar had tried his best to divide the military and police veterans as equally as possible among The Compound's defenders. "We'll wait for 'em to bottleneck at the entrance. Then we nail the coffin shut."

Melinda blinked away tears, wondering whether the frigid day would be her last—and whether she had made a fatal mistake choosing to stay at the farm rather than continuing on toward Elkhorn and taking her chances. *Like choosing whether to take the* Titanic *or the* Hindenburg *to America,* Mark had ruefully remarked upon hearing Melinda's story as they killed time, nervously awaiting the biker gang's counterattack. She closed her eyes to offer a silent prayer that she hadn't sealed her and Jimmy's fate.

"Horseshoe—don't shoot!" Gunnar hissed the running password identifying friend from foe scant seconds before he and Ethan slid into the foxhole.

Melinda grabbed Ethan and kissed him, almost yanking him off-balance. "Oh, thank God!" she heaved as the two embraced. "I'm so sorry about your aunt."

"She made it count," Ethan said with steely pride.

"Yes, she did," Gunnar said, shoving Mark to the the foxhole's alternate firing slot and taking the position overlooking the gate. "Now we gotta do the same, as many times as we can, 'cause we just whacked the fuckin' hornet's nest."

"Whacked it?! We hosed it with a can of Black Flag!" Ethan boasted, taking his place next to Melinda.

"Damn right, but don't get cocky," Gunnar admonished, popping open a thick orange plastic case to reveal an older-generation radio-controlled explosives initiator. The woods facing the road bristled with IEDs daisy-chained together with primer cord presciently bought by a Compound member with a federal explosives license. They would rip a deadly swath through the invaders bunched up in the kill zone as they worked futilely to force open the gate—which had been welded shut the night before—and the panicked survivors would find themselves in the middle of a shooting gallery of interlocking fields of fire.

Gunnar toggled his radio to the Compound-wide net as the rumble of cruise motorcycles grew louder and louder. "All stations this net, hold fire until we give 'em the warm welcome—once we set it off, you're weapons free. Send 'em to hell. Out." He grabbed his other radio tuned to the dedicated frequency for the CQ. "We're hot," he reported, turning the initiator's arming key. "Say when, Luke."

"We got a problem, boss—" Lukasz began.

"I got armor at the gate!" Mark yelled.

Gunnar scrambled behind his SCAR-H rifle's scope to see a Bearcat—a smaller, four-wheeled armored vehicle likewise stolen from a county sheriff SWAT team—roll up to cover the dismounted bikers who angrily spiked their now-useless bolt cutters to the ground in front of the welded gate.

"I thought you guys blew it up!" Melinda yelled.

"We did!" Ethan said. "They musta had another one!"

Fuck! Gunnar swore to himself, hoping the enemy's new toy was at least causing their unprotected soldiers to congregate in front of the IEDs.

"Kill zone's packed—let 'er rip!" Lukasz's voice screamed from the radio.

"Fire in the hole!" Gunnar hollered, his thumb mashing the initiator's red firing button. Flashes of white light lit the woods, followed by the roars of explosions and the thunder of gunfire from The Compound's entrenched defenders.

"Hot damn, that's what I'm talkin' about! Come get some!" Mark whooped, taking aim and firing at a stooped figure staggering between the trees. Melinda laid the green dot of her scope on one of the men who were hastily wrapping a heavy-duty chain around the gate so the Bearcat could try pulling it down. Her first shot harmlessly ricocheted off the Bearcat's armor, but her second struck true, the glowing red tracer round lancing into the man like a laser in a science fiction movie and dropping him. She shifted to take a shot at another man crawling for cover, her mind on autopilot and not caring a whit that she had just killed for the first time.

"We just wiped a bunch of 'em out, Big G!" Lukasz's voice triumphantly blared over the cacophony of battle. "I'm counting dozens, at least . . . wait . . . *oh shit everybody get down!*"

Gunnar flinched with the *boom* of another explosion—this one to their rear.

"What the fuck was that?!" Ethan screamed.

"Shut up and keep firing!" Gunnar ordered, bolting out the foxhole's back entrance and diving behind a large tree at the woodline's edge overlooking The Compound. Smoke billowed from a large hole blown in the Moran farmhouse where the front door had been. Gunnar watched helplessly as three jet-black drones with underslung cylinders dove straight for the house like Stuka bombers—one zipped through the hole and exploded inside while the remaining two scored direct hits on the window to the ham radio room and the base of the radio antenna in the side yard. Two more fireballs roiled from the woods in the locations of the closest foxholes with their sectors of fire aligned toward the main gate. The flash of a tiny green light in the sky gave away a bright orange drone, its bulbous camera aimed directly at Gunnar.

"Get out!" he screamed at the top of his lungs, running into the foxhole to yank Melinda and Ethan from their firing slits by their tactical vests and violently shoving them out the back. *"Mark! Move it!"* Gunnar yelled, catching up with the kids and tackling them to the ground as

another kamikaze drone flew straight through Mark's firing slit and detonated, blowing him to bits and bringing down the entire earthen mound roof.

Gunnar leaped off Ethan and Melinda, frantically scanning them for injuries. "You all right?!" he yelled over the piercing ringing of his ears.

Melinda violently shook her head, blind with panic. "I ... I can't hear!"

"It'll come back!"

"Ohmigod!" Ethan mindlessly screamed at the sight of his grandma's home.

"We gotta fall back! *Follow me!*" Gunnar ordered, Ethan quickly overtaking him as they ran for the burning Moran farmhouse.

A burst of sparks in the sky heralded the shooting down of the thermal drone the Devil's Warriors had used to pinpoint The Compound's forward defenses with the defenders' own body heat, but the damage was done—an enemy whose technical skill had been sorely underestimated had ripped a huge gap in their front lines.

CHAPTER 61

FRANCE

Patton watched the precocious young boy sitting in his lap wolf down the last spoonfuls of what was supposed to be his breakfast. "Don't forget the best part," Patton said, theatrically waving his hand above the MRE's open plastic pouch before yanking out a bag of M&Ms with a flourish like a magician pulling a rabbit out of a hat. "Abracadabra!"

The boy wordlessly hugged Patton and Ann-Katryn, his soulful eyes barely visible through an unkempt mane of brown hair peeking out from under a ratty winter cap. "You're welcome, little fella—now run along," Patton said, his voice thick—while neither understood the other, kindness was a universal language. The child ran off, quickly disappearing among the rows of Army vehicles lining the narrow main street of the tiny village of Gouy.

Ann-Katryn stared at the handful of desperate townspeople who had emerged from their ancient brick homes to weave among the Strykers, LMTVs, and Humvees, trying to beg what they could from the Americans like their great-grandparents had done with the Allies liberating their nation almost a century prior. "I thought the colonel said that things in France were not as bad as everywhere else."

"Looks like these poor saps didn't get the memo," Patton replied, sliding his hand over Ann-Katryn's belly, the tiny beginning of a bump hidden underneath her winter coat. "Our son's gonna want for nothing—you have my word."

She looked into his eyes and smiled. "And you know we are having a boy, how?"

Patton gave her a quick kiss. "Lucky guess."

A lone machine-gun round fell to the asphalt sidewalk at Patton's feet with a tinkle. "Mind tossin' that up here, dude?" Theo asked from the Griffon's roof, where he and René were linking ammunition belts to replace what he had burned off lighting up the bandits in Bras-sur-Meuse. Patton scooped it up, squinting into the overcast mid-morning sky as he flipped it to René. "We're gonna be leavin' the moment the LT gets back from the meeting," Theo told the boy, looking down the road to where the leaders of The Lost Boys and the other American unit were hashing out a new plan. "You gotta use the latrine, now's the time."

"Latrine?" René asked, puzzled.

"The bathroom," his mother explained from the Griffon's ramp, where she was translating a Radio France news break for Josh and Kira.

The boy gestured to a shuttered brick mom-and-pop store across the street. "Mom, all the boys are just peeing on that poor guy's wall."

"Beats peein' into a plastic bottle in front of everyone in a movin' APC, kid," Theo said, grabbing René's arms to lower him to the ground.

"We aim to please," Patton chimed in. "And you aim too, please."

"Was that—what do you call it—a 'dad joke'?" Ann-Katryn asked incredulously.

Patton laughed. "Never too early to start practicing, hon."

"Hey, everyone—get a load of this!" Josh called out, cranking the radio's volume.

"To the American forces in France—we pledge not to engage in any hostilities, so long as you do not force our hand," the radio announcer said in English. *"Please make your way to your embarkation point at Dunkirk. You will be safe unless you take any hostile action against French citizens or property."*

"Well, hot damn!" Theo said, stepping down on the Griffon's rear tire.

"About time they came to their senses," Kira quipped as the announcer lapsed back into French. "It's not like we were marching on Paris or anything."

"To be fair, if the Mexican Army started cutting across the USA because the commanding general wanted to visit his *abeulita* in Winnipeg, we probably woulda been a little bit pissed off, too," Josh said, trailing off as he noticed the look of consternation on Corinne's face. "Dare I ask?"

"The announcer just warned any 'renegade' French military units to leave us alone."

"Saddle up—time to move!" Major Villa barked farther down the line to the commotion of soldiers up and down the convoy scrambling to mount up. Martin jogged from the concluded staff huddle past a Stryker flying an Alabama state flag with the words ROLL TIDE scrawled on its armor, its crew having escaped during the Vilseck mutiny before hooking up with the other slapdash US unit.

"What's the plan, sir?" Patton asked Martin, ushering Ann-Katryn, Corinne, and René up the ramp.

"Thunder run," Martin declared, referring to the military tactic made famous in the Iraq War of a swift and aggressive armored penetration into unknown territory. "We're takin' the highway—we're done sneakin' around."

"The French are lettin' us pass—we heard," Patton said.

"Wish it were that simple," Martin shot back. "If you're wonderin' why these poor folks don't have any food, it's because some rogue French and Belgian units took it all from 'em, and they're out there somewhere between us and Dunkirk—we may end up having to fight our way through after all."

"Nothin's ever easy, is it?" Patton grumbled, hoisting himself up into the driver's seat and gunning the engine.

"The easy way's always mined," Martin replied before hustling up the ramp.

CHAPTER 62

WISCONSIN

Reaper and Buck galloped to meet Gunnar, Ethan, and Melinda dashing from the woods, their anxious barks punctuating the blaring whine of the demolished farmhouse's smoke alarms. Ethan, mad with fear, sprinted past the black hole billowing smoke from what was left of the radio room, and rounded the house to charge headlong through the gaping maw that had been the front door.

"Dad! Grandma!" he called out, stepping into a living room torn to pieces by shrapnel, the walls peppered with ball bearings and scrap metal. Lukasz sat slumped against the far wall, his face a bloody mess and his dead eyes staring vacuously at the overturned CQ desk, its radios and computer shattered. *"Dad!"*

"They're OK," the drone pilot croaked from a dark corner, his raspy voice barely audible above the smoke alarms and Gunnar's boots pounding on the hardwood as he ran to his fallen friend. "They were in the other room when . . . when the bombs went off," the young man hissed with pain, clutching his side.

"Where are they?!" Ethan exasperatedly yelled as Melinda announced her entrance with a scream at the sight of the carnage.

"Your grandma took off with Al—he got hurt real bad," the drone pilot groaned. "Your dad took off, too . . . dunno where . . ."

Thick smoke crept across the ceiling from the kitchen as Buck and Reaper barked and whined outside to warn their masters of the danger. Ethan helped the wounded man to his feet as Gunnar set aside Lukasz's dinged but functional sniper rifle and began frantically tearing open the Velcro pouches of his tactical vest. "We gotta find 'em!" Ethan screamed, wild-eyed.

"No, kid, we gotta fight!" Gunnar shot back, yanking out .50-caliber magazines and tossing them to the floor with a glance at the rounds they carried. "C'mon, Luke, hook me up—" he angrily mumbled before clenching his fist in triumph upon finding a magazine loaded with green-and white-tipped ammunition. "We're in business!" Gunnar declared, shoving the magazine in his leg cargo pocket and grabbing the hand guard of Lukasz's monster rifle. "You able to walk?" he tersely asked the drone pilot.

"I think so," he coughed, steadying himself on the couch, the air quickly becoming unbreathable with the thickening smoke.

"Make your way to the aid station. You two," Gunnar told Ethan and Melinda, "help reinforce the barn—you may be the only thing standin' between these savages and the kids."

"Where you goin'?" Ethan demanded.

"To stop that Bearcat or we don't stand a chance!" Gunnar yelled, sprinting out the hole where the front door had been.

***

The headlights of Al's white Ram 1500 Big Horn briefly flashed in the morning twilight with a click of his key fob.

"You weigh a ton!" Donna griped from under her friend's arm, her hands slick with his blood as she helped him limp the final few feet to his truck, which was parked behind the farmhouse in the old customer lot among the RVs and personal vehicles of The Compound's members.

"Never did get around to goin' on that diet," Al slurred as Donna helped him into the driver's seat, the tall Yagi-Uda antenna next to her burning house buckling with a groan of metal. "Not that it matters anymore . . ."

"Don't say that. You're gonna be—"

"We got no time for that bullshit," Al cut her off, his breathing labored as he struggled with trembling hands to connect and power up the Yaesu mobile ham radio wired into his truck. "I need you to . . ."

"Already on it!" Donna called out, throwing open the side tool box in the Ram's bed and grabbing the cylindrical omnidirectional antenna inside.

"Got the frequency set . . . I pulled 'em in right 'fore those damn bombs hit," Al mumbled, barely above a whisper. "You gotta finish what I started. For duty and humanity . . ."

"That's my line, remember?" Donna nervously quipped as she finished screwing the antenna into the discrete mount just barely sticking out from behind the passenger door. The sounds of battle grew closer as the Devil's Warriors advanced, inch by inch, toward conquering her farm and sentencing whoever remained to a fate worse than death. "Comms are up! Let's—" she said before trailing off at the sight of her old friend slumped forward, head resting on his steering wheel. She touched his neck to feel for a pulse, then caressed his bearded cheek upon not finding one.

A white-hot fury rose inside her, burning away her sorrow. Barbarians had taken her long-lost daughter and her best friend, and were about to take away everything and everyone that she had left in this ruined world—and all she could think about in that moment was making them pay.

Donna pried the ham radio mike from Al's hand and mashed the transmit button, fervently praying that the people on the other end were still listening.

CHAPTER 63

FRANCE

"What'cha playin'?"

René looked up at Martin for the briefest of seconds from his Nintendo Switch. "You talking to me, sir?"

Martin cracked a smile from the command seat set back between Patton and Theo, the fallow farms and bare trees of northern France rolling past the Griffon's narrow windshield. "No, I'm talking to the other kid playing video games."

"Mario Kart."

"So are we," Patton wisecracked, his passengers swaying in their seats as he followed the Stryker ahead of him to weave around a derelict SUV on the four-lane A26 motorway, Mario Kart's upbeat soundtrack adding a surreal feel to their race for the Channel coast. Martin looked back at his passengers—Corinne watching her son, Ann-Katryn nervously fidgeting in her seat, and Josh and Kira fast asleep, their heads bobbing as Patton dodged a small delivery truck, its rear door long ago crowbarred open and its cargo picked clean.

The Lost Boys and the other American remnant, which to Martin's knowledge had never gotten around to giving themselves a snappy name, had merged to form a single unit speeding north for Dunkirk. The all-night rain that had screened their movements at the expense of making their trek miserable had stopped. Patches of blue sky began to peek through the cloud cover, a welcome sight now that they didn't have to worry about the French Air Force blasting them into oblivion with the agreement between the French and the State Department—one of the few remnants of the shattered US government still functioning—to allow them safe passage. Colonel Stirling had let slip that the truce had much more to do with French magnanimity than the secretary of state's diplomatic aplomb; the French had deployed almost all of their military units to Paris and other major cities to their south to quell raging civil unrest—including many that otherwise would have been right in The Lost Boys's path of advance—and there was no practical way for them to catch up and try to stop the Americans.

That left the renegade units that had broken away from French command and control that could find the US convoy a tempting target—or force the American relief fleet waiting in Dunkirk to trade their food and supplies for The Lost Boys's safety.

Theo pointed to a white bedsheet tied to an overpass, the words AIDEZ-NOUS LES AMÉRICAINS scrawled on it in large block letters. "What's that say?"

"Help us, Americans," Corinne answered, standing up just long enough to peek through the windshield, her travels with the cav scouts having conditioned her like Pavlov's dog to be on call to translate at a moment's notice.

"If the locals know we're here, the bad guys do, too," Theo said. "Hope this don't get rough."

"Stay icy, soldier," Martin ordered with more confidence than he felt. The Army's war machines that struck fear in enemies around the world—the M1 Abrams tank and the M2 Bradley armored personnel carrier—had been left behind in Germany on account of their heavy maintenance requirements and the fact that they were gas guzzlers that didn't get miles per gallon, but rather literally burned gallons per mile. While the Stryker was a dependable and versatile platform, and many in the convoy were armed with anti-air and anti-armor weapons, The Lost Boys would be in big trouble if they found themselves having to fight.

"One hundred and ninety klicks to go," Theo said to no one in particular, consulting the GPS display next to the weapons screen. "Little under three hours."

"We might just pull this off," Patton said.

"Yeah—the Europe part," Theo retorted. "We still gotta get off the boat an' get home."

Patton glanced over the tall weeds of the unkempt median to a group of abandoned cars in the southbound lane, their drivers having run out of gas trying to flee Calais at the start of the collapse. "If home even friggin' exists."

Martin leaned forward in his seat. "OK, guys, that's enough."

"Don't make me turn this car around—no trip to the Dells for any of you!" Patton said in a mocking officious tone, eliciting a laugh from Theo.

"Knew you'd get the hang of being a dad," Martin said. "Eyes forward."

CHAPTER 64

Gunnar leaped from the protective cover of a raised flower bed, Lukasz's bulky sniper rifle pumping in his arms as he made a five-second rush for a concrete barrier at the edge of the tractor trail ringing the apple orchard. He slid behind it, gunfire chattering all around as the men and women of The Compound put up stiff resistance. Behind him, the Moran farmhouse became engulfed in flames, adding an evil red glow to the early sunrise.

Lowering the rifle's telescopic legs and popping open the dust covers of its Leupold scope, Gunnar high-crawled to the edge of the barrier, a large oak tree and decorative shrubbery offering the perfect covered and concealed line of sight down the vehicle-width lane that cut through the middle of the orchard. Like Normandy's infamous hedgerows, there was no way the Bearcat could bash through the thick rows of trees and wire fences; the tractor lane was the only path wide enough to accommodate it, and presented Gunnar's one chance to knock it out.

Gunnar assumed a firing position behind the Accuracy International, the gold standard of sniper rifles that Lukasz, a former SWAT sharpshooter, had paid out the nose to buy. He slid the bolt back to chamber one of Lukasz's specialty Raufoss Mark 211 explosive penetrator rounds, gritting his teeth in frustration with the black ring that appeared around the edges of his sight picture—he and Lukasz had different distances between their eye and the scope.

The Bearcat slowly lumbered into sight and turned straight toward Gunnar, several bullets from an unseen Compound member harmlessly bouncing off its side before a shaggy man in the up-armored roof turret swiveled to return fire. The string of IEDs at The Compound's entrance had dealt it some damage—a wisp of smoke from the Bearcat's straining engine drifted past its cracked bulletproof windshield, and it was running on flats—but it still lumbered forward like Juggernaut's carriage.

Gunnar adjusted the scope ever so slightly as the Bearcat crept by a purple sign indicating the type of apple cultivar in that row; one of Moran Farm's many hidden survivalist features was that the orchard signs were color-coded to denote their distance in meters from the house. Unsure of whether the Bearcat's armor could stop a Rafouss round, he aimed at the driver behind the cracked windshield, steadied his breathing, and squeezed the trigger. The thumb-sized round's tungsten steel penetrator pierced the damaged ballistic glass, annihilating the driver as the high-explosive charge followed, filling the Bearcat with hot shrapnel—the man in the turret shrieked in pain and disappeared from sight, shredded below the belt. Gunnar quickly chambered another round and fired, the roar of the mammoth rifle's report drowning out the sound of the Rafouss piercing the armor and detonating in the V8 engine—oily black smoke seeped from the hood and front slats, confirming the kill.

With a wicked grin, Gunnar safed the rifle and displaced, eager to add to his tally and avenge Lukasz's death.

***

"You motherfuckers!" Razor howled as the Bearcat died in front of his four-by-four truck, stopping cold the main thrust of his attack through the orchard.

He jumped out as the Bearcat's rear double doors swung open on a plume of toxic smoke, the turret gunner screaming in agony as he pulled himself out and fell to the ground, his ruined legs sizzling with dozens of white-hot metal shards burning him from the inside out. "God-*damn!*" Razor's driver hollered at the horrible sight and smell before his boss drew his .357 Magnum pistol and put the poor bastard out of his misery.

Razor whirled on the line of trucks and choppers now bottlenecked behind the Bearcat. *"Keep moving!"* he screamed, furiously waving his handgun forward at the crimson glow of the burning farmhouse. "Dismount and press the attack! Don't stop until you reach the farm buildings! We capture those, it's over! *Go!"*

The Devil's Warriors scrambled through the rows of trees hemming them in, the orchard lighting up with firefights. Their opponent was determined and disciplined, Razor grudgingly conceded as he glared at the wrecked Bearcat and the corpse at his feet, but his men more than made up for that with numbers and sheer brutality. Once they were victorious, Razor silently pledged, the vanquished farmers would learn about the latter the hard way.

CHAPTER 65

FRANCE

A Peugeot minivan veered away from The Lost Boys's convoy just in time to avoid getting turned into modern art, its tires squealing on the rain-slicked road to the accompanying honk of a Stryker's high-pitched horn.

Patton tightened his grip on the Griffon's small steering wheel as two more civilian vehicles crept by in the left lane of the A26 motorway ahead of the town of Setques, laying on their horns to encourage the spooked Peugeot driver to speed up. "Where the hell'd all these people come from?" he asked.

"Mein Gott," Ann-Katryn murmured at the sight of no fewer than fifty people of all ages walking as a group on the other side of the guardrail.

"They're comin' from everywhere—if I was you, I'd be more concerned about where they're goin'," Theo said, watching a bicyclist weave through vehicles left abandoned in the shoulder with more and more frequency the closer they got to the Channel coast.

Dunkirk, Martin said to himself—*word's out that the Americans dropped off a big ol' load of groceries and every starving Frenchy's beating a path to their door.* "Friction," Colonel Stirling had called it when the two American convoys had huddled in Gouy—the never-ending parade of Murphy's Law bullshit that pops up to disrupt military operations. Patton bit off a curse as he swerved to avoid a desperate refugee toeing the lane's edge, waving his arms for help. *Nothing fucks up a plan more than civilians on the battlefield,* Martin remembered the colonel's words before they moved out—*every one of whom have absolutely nothing left to lose.*

Patton slammed the brakes as the Stryker in front of him slowed to a crawl, knocking Ann-Katryn into the back of Theo's seat. As he hit the gas with the convoy again picking up speed, she turned away with a gasp at the sight of a mangled body lying in the road, a wailing woman being held back by her travel companions.

"All stations this net!" Colonel Stirling's stern voice rang in Martin's helmet headset to the *thunk* of a rock angrily hurled against the Griffon's windshield. "If you wanna get home, do *not* stop for any civvie dumb enough to jump in the way! It's you or them! Out!"

"Damn, that's cold," Theo grunted.

"Save it," Martin tersely cut him off to keep René from learning what had happened. "You copy that, Childress?" he asked Patton while ordering Ann-Katryn back to her seat with a silent point.

"Lima Charlie, sir—any pedestrian who fucks around finds out and wins the prize inside the box," Patton nervously replied. He glanced at a blue sign labeled *gare de péage*—one of the few French phrases he had picked up—listing toll prices in Euros based on trip length; the fees had been constantly updated with the runaway inflation in the weeks before the collapse. "Toll plaza's comin' up—hope the colonel brought along a shit-ton of quarters."

"Just follow the leader, wise ass," Martin said as the convoy slowed to bypass the narrow toll lanes by turning into a restricted area for the highway police and French toll authorities. The lead Stryker rammed the access gate, snapping the red and white boom barrier like a breadstick as it led the way for The Lost Boys to exit the motorway for the *routes départementales*—the French equivalent of US state highways—that would take them on the final leg to Dunkirk.

Patton waved at a lone gendarme who had stepped out of the small police station to investigate the racket. Martin smirked at the officer's incredulous stare, which comically shifted between the intruding American military convoy and his useless sidearm; he managed to breathe easy for three seconds before the lead Stryker exploded, a ball of flame shooting into the sky to announce the kill.

CHAPTER 66

*P**lease don't shoot us by mistake—please don't shoot us please don't shoot us please don't shoot us*, Ethan fervently prayed as he and Melinda sprinted for the foxhole guarding the approach to the barn, every footfall a struggle against the basic human instinct to run away from gunfire instead of toward it.

"Horseshoe! On your right!" Ethan screamed the running password, sliding like a runner stealing home behind a large sitting log from one of The Compound's overnight camp rental sites that had been hastily laid next to the fighting position. Melinda dove to the ground next to him, crawling for cover to the sound of bullets embedding into the barn's aged red sidewall.

"Thank God!" Kyle's father, Glen, hollered from the foxhole as Shelby squeezed off a round at a target. "We got the whole damn Mongol horde comin' right for us!"

Melinda's heart froze at the sight of the orchard crawling with shadowy figures advancing in the early morning light. Gunnar's disabling of the Bearcat had made the orchard's pedestrian rows the gang's main axis of advance; the barn's four heavily outnumbered defenders were holding

the line between the barbarians and the children and infirm sheltering in the barn's basement. Melinda seethed with rage, the thought of
them falling into the monsters' hands destroying what little remained of
her resistance to hurting another human being. A young woman who
couldn't have been much older than her picked up from behind a gnarled
apple tree to dart across to another—Melinda led her, firing until the
woman clutched her abdomen and fell to the ground with a scream.
Return fire continued to smack against the barn as Melinda took aim
at another man on the move—her magazine went dry after three shots,
allowing her target to take cover with a half dozen others huddled behind
a rusty red classic Ford F-2 pickup that in better times served to add a flair
of classic Americana for farm visitors.

"Reloading!" Melinda barked, thumbing the magazine release to drop
the empty from the well as she ripped open a Velcro pouch to grab a fresh
one. "There's a bunch of 'em behind the truck!"

"I know!" Ethan hollered. Another group of bikers worked up the
courage to make a run for the pickup, sensing the opportunity to make
a final charge to overwhelm the defenders in strength. "We're counting
on it! Stay down, Melinda! Low as you can get!"

"Now?" Shelby and Glen yelled in unison as Melinda hugged the
ground.

"Now!" Ethan screamed at the top of his lungs.

The trio unleashed into the ancient truck, peppering it with a dozen
rounds before the twenty pounds of Tannerite packed inside the door
detonated, instantly turning the Ford into a fifteen-hundred-pound
IED. Melinda winced with the thundering explosion and the *whoosh* of
a large slab of metal whizzing over her like a frisbee with mere inches
to spare. Grievously wounded bikers screamed and writhed in the thin,
clearing smoke among severed limbs and piles of butchered meat that

had once been human beings; Melinda gawked at the sight of a man staggering like a zombie, a huge chunk of ragged steel having cleaved him down the middle, before Glen put him out of his misery, shots pinging off the metal as he fell.

"You like that, assholes?" Ethan furiously taunted over the lull in the fighting. "Keep comin'—we got plenty more where that came from!"

"Ethan!" Melinda screamed.

He turned his head to see his girlfriend hysterically stabbing her finger at the small, shattered barn window behind them—and the unmistakable glow of a fire brightening inside.

Ohmigod—Jimmy! her mind shrieked as she leaped up and ran for the barn door around the side, ignoring Ethan's calls to stay put.

***

"Don't move!"

Donna clandestinely shoved the hand mike of Al's truck-mounted ham radio into his lap, slowly turning to find herself staring down the barrel of a .44 Magnum hand cannon wielded by a large man wearing a Devil's Warriors denim jacket. The eyes of the two bikers flanking him darted at Al's corpse, ensuring that he no longer posed a threat.

With impressive speed for his size, the man stepped forward to pull Donna's handgun from its holster. "Hands where I can see 'em."

"You're too late, sonny boy," Donna said, forcing a smile as the rear of her burning house collapsed on itself, a shower of embers roiling skyward.

"For what?" the man angrily asked.

"You'll see."

"Dude, it's her—the honcho!" one of the sidekicks excitedly said as if he was a teen sleuth solving a mystery.

"No shit!" the other spat.

"You're comin' with us," the man continued, ignoring his comrades' inanity. "We're gonna take a little walk so's you and the big guy can work things out."

"If by 'work things out' you mean choosing whether to be enslaved or executed, no thank you." *Ashley, give me strength*, she silently prayed, hoping to face the end as bravely as her daughter had. "Just get this over with."

"I *said*, let's go," the man growled, loudly cocking the hammer of his revolver.

Donna lunged in desperation for the 9-millimeter Glock handgun holstered on Al's hip before the man shot her in the chest, killing her instantly. The last thing Donna's executioner ever saw was the blinding flash of headlights coming straight at him with the growl of a diesel engine and a man's blood-curdling furious scream.

Will Moran rammed The Compound's QRF pickup truck into his mother's killer at full throttle, crushing him against the Ram. The collision further punished Will's battered body, his howl of agony trailing away with a sigh as one of his cracked ribs broke clean and pierced his lung. His suffering lasted only a few seconds more before the other two men emptied their magazines into him through the driver-side window.

CHAPTER 67

FRANCE

"*Floor it!*" Martin hollered at Patton, the screaming of their civilian passengers drowned out by explosions heralding the destruction of two more Strykers behind them.

"*Contact!* Nine o'clock, one thousand meters!" a voice boomed from the tactical net as Patton stomped on the gas to get the hell out of the kill zone, almost rear-ending the Stryker ahead of him doing the same. The Lost Boys rolled past the flaming hulk of the lead vehicle to the *whoosh* of a wireless TOW missile launched from one of their M1134 Stryker anti-tank guided missile variants, a distant *boom* announcing the destruction of an older-generation French VAB Mephisto anti-armor vehicle.

The convoy's new lead, a Stryker Dragoon, ripped through a wire fence and tore onto the ramp leading to the D942 roadway, its 30-millimeter Bushmaster cannon roaring on the move to light up an AMX-10 RC before it could bring its cannon to bear on them. Farther down the line, another Stryker loosed a Javelin anti-tank missile from its CROWS remote weapon system to finish off the small advance team that had ambushed them.

Colonel Stirling angrily slammed his hand against the armrest of his commander's gun override control as he tallied his losses on his display screen, blue icons representing the convoy's vehicles save for a gap for Lieutenant Crenshaw and his cav scouts, whose VBMR Griffon wasn't equipped with the American BLUFOR combat information system. Two of his losses were from the other contingent that had merged with The Lost Boys—the lead vehicle and the Stryker of their former commanding colonel; Stirling had taken the reins on account of his date of rank preceding his counterpart by exactly one month. But the third Stryker had belonged to Staff Sergeant Nick Alger and his boys from the Big Red One—they had made it all the way from Poland, only to get killed within a stone's throw of the safe harbor that the colonel had promised them.

So close to getting everyone home in one piece, he fumed, rocking in his seat as Clayton peeled through a roundabout. *Until these pieces of filth handed me my ass just short of the goddamn finish line.*

He breathed a sigh of relief that the LMTVs carrying most of their civilian dependents hadn't been harmed—for now. But if the renegades were able to chisel away enough of their Stryker escort, they would be helpless to be seized and used as a bargaining chip to barter for the supplies the US had dropped off—or worse.

The colonel scrolled his map north to Dunkirk, where the Navy was waiting to take them home. The intricate network of canals dug over the centuries to the vital deep-water port acted as moats ringing the city, making it easily defendable—the remnants of the 22nd Marine Expeditionary Unit and the local *gendarmerie* had sealed it off by fortifying the handful of bridge crossings over them. *Forty-five klicks—half an hour away*, Stirling said to himself, analyzing for the thousandth time the route to the A16 bridge over the Bourbourg Canal where the Marines were waiting for them. But The Lost Boys were flying blind in hostile territory through a fog of war thicker than pea soup, surrounded by non-combatants he didn't want to harm—and without satellite and drone intel, air cover, and the like, he had lost many of the force multipliers that made the US military so formidable and deadly.

Clayton laid on the Stryker's horn, just barely avoiding smashing into a slow-moving van. "Fuckin' civilians! Get the fuck off the damn road! Oh, shit—*contact*! Dismounts in the open! Ten o'clock—"

"I got 'em—*sending*!" the gunner yelled, lighting up the foot soldiers with his .50-caliber machine gun, slewing the remote-controlled turret to stay on target as Clayton circled another roundabout. Stirling switched radio frequencies with the stab of a button, hoping to increase their ever-shrinking odds of survival by instigating his second international incident of the day.

CHAPTER 68

Melinda shielded her eyes from the blinding glare of the fire devouring a stack of lumber in the corner of the barn, its flames hungrily beginning to lick at a nearby wooden workbench—and a full acetylene welding tank next to it.

Oh my God oh my God, Melinda chanted to herself over the muffled screams of Jimmy and the other children sheltering under the floor, panic swelling inside her. *Think think think think . . .*

She reflexively ducked at the sound of a bullet piercing the wall and embedding itself with a metallic *ka-chunk* into the side of a run-down GMC pickup with a large plastic water tank in the back. "The fire truck!" she gasped, grasping the discharge hose and turning the spigot to start the water flowing. She swore as nothing happened, watching in desperation as the fire grew unimpeded, a plume of acrid smoke billowing toward the rafters.

Ethan leaped into the truck bed to open the fuel valve and choke of the portable generator that powered the pump. "You need water pressure!" he hollered, revving the generator to life with a yank of the pull cord.

The hose stiffened in Melinda's hand, water shooting out its improvised PVC nozzle. "You got three hundred gallons—make it count!"

Melinda charged toward the fire, taking aim at its base as her volunteer firefighter father had taught her to do, her effort instantly rewarded with hissing geysers of steam. The blaze's radiant heat stung her face like a bad sunburn, forcing her several steps back until it weakened enough for her to press the attack. Melinda glanced nervously at the water tank, its level continuing to drop; failure meant pulling the children out of the barn and throwing them into a shooting gallery. Ethan appeared at her side with an extinguisher, snuffing the weakened fire once and for all with bursts of white chemical powder. He ran back to the truck as Melinda kept the withering water stream on the charred wood, the fleeting exhilaration over putting out the fire and saving the kids replaced with the terror of going back into combat.

"We did it!" Ethan exclaimed, killing the generator with a sputter, the sounds of battle outside returning with a vengeance. "Let's go! They need us out there—"

The deafening hammer of gunshots echoed inside the barn as bullets tore through the young man's body. Melinda had just enough time to scream Ethan's name as he fell from the truck before her world went dark with a vicious blow to the side of her head.

CHAPTER 69

FRANCE

Virginie Micheaux huddled in the corner of her small living room, clutching her grandchildren to her bosom with wrinkled hands.

What had just happened made no sense. Two Army vehicles had rolled into Craywick an hour prior, parking outside city limits and training their guns down Route 300 as if there was a war on. Instead of bringing desperately needed aid, they angrily ordered their fellow countrymen who came out begging for help to go away—and shot one who refused. Then came the sounds of guns and rockets—distant at first, but ominously creeping closer, like what her parents had said it had sounded like when the *boches* invaded in 1940, and again four years later when the Allies came to drive them out.

She held the children tighter with the rumbling of a loud engine. "Is that *Maman?* Is she back?!" granddaughter Sandrine excitedly asked, eyes lighting up—their mother, who worked in Paris, had not been heard from since the collapse.

The engine's growl grew louder, rattling the portraits on the walls and the china in her cabinet, as a large boxy silhouette crawled across the wispy drawn curtains, blotting out the light as it slowed to a halt. "I'm scared, *Mémé*," whimpered the older grandson, Julien.

"Ssshh—we're going to be all right," Virginie consoled before her ears perked up at the sound of two men yelling in English. *Americans?!* she incredulously asked herself over the back-and-forth in the alien language; there had been rumors that the Americans had come with food. She cautiously rose on shaky legs, telling Julien to watch his younger sister.

Virginie slowly opened the front door to find an idling six-wheeled armored vehicle that was almost the size of her small house. She cautiously ventured down the small brick path leading to the street as a man and a woman soldier darted out the rear of the behemoth brandishing slender olive-drab tubes. She didn't understand the jumble of words the young man rudely barked at her, but his wild gesturing for her to go away needed no translation.

An older woman rose from the vehicle's top hatch as the soldiers sprinted down the street out of sight. "Madame, please go back inside—it's not safe!" she yelled in fluent French.

"Please—my grandchildren need food!" Virginie begged. "We have nothing—"

The loud staccato of rifle fire cut off Virginie's pleas. The old woman screamed with fright, ducking down as quickly as her arthritic joints allowed as the shots were silenced by a horrible roar and an explosion, a plume of white smoke rising over the modest waist-level wooden fence circling her front yard. Her hands shot to her ears as an all-too-brief silence was shattered by a second roar, and another plume of smoke.

A pretty young blonde woman appeared, unceremoniously dumping a large cardboard box over the fence onto the unkempt lawn as Virginie struggled back to her feet. "*Entschuldigung,*" she apologized in German before following the two soldiers back into the monster vehicle, which sped away moments later.

Virginie's heart skipped a beat upon spotting the single line of French stenciled on the box among rows of English text—MEALS, READY-TO-EAT, INDIVIDUAL. She nervously glanced around, ignoring the ache in her back as she quickly rolled the heavy box inside before anyone saw what the peculiar strangers had gifted her.

***

"Gate's open! I say again, gate's open!" Martin radioed as their VBMR Griffon tore out of Craywick, letting Colonel Stirling know that the small enemy recon element they had stumbled upon had been neutralized—and hopefully was the last of the renegade soldiers standing between them and Dunkirk.

"Hey, lieutenant!" Josh breathlessly spat, pulling plugs out of his ears as Kira and Ann-Katryn plopped down in their seats. "Remember back in Germany when you said you wanted to hear it if we thought you had a dumb-assed idea?"

"Noted!" Martin replied as the colonel confirmed that The Lost Boys were on the move and would be linking up with them shortly; the convoy had stopped to reload their vehicle-mounted weapon systems after running a Mad Max-type gauntlet up Route 300—they had lost two more Strykers, but had given as good as they got.

Patton drove past the burning hulks of the two VAB armored vehicles that Josh had destroyed with shoulder-fired disposable AT-4 rocket launchers stolen from Miesau Ammo Depot. "You hit a home run, nerds—good shootin'," he yelled over his shoulder. Josh was about to fire back with an inappropriate response, but thought the better of it at the sight of Corinne rubbing her distraught son's back—all of it was getting to be too much for him.

Mammoth seaside dock cranes, idle since the collapse, rose over the trees like frozen giants as the Griffon ascended to the large roundabout connecting Route 300 with the A16 motorway, the overpass offering a commanding view of the flat coastal terrain around them. A cold, damp wind carrying the salty smell of the ocean whipped Martin's face as he rose from the top hatch to the sight of a rainbow arcing across the sky with the autumn sun shining through the breaking clouds. He raised his binoculars to scan east down the motorway, and was pleasantly surprised to find it clear of civilian traffic aside from a handful of abandoned vehicles. And four and a half klicks away, glimmering in the sunlight, was the bridge over the Bourbourg Canal—and safety.

The Griffon looped around the overpass as the whine of Stryker engines heralded the arrival of The Lost Boys streaming north up Route 300. The Stryker Dragoon that had taken the lead following the toll plaza ambush rose onto the roundabout, descending just as quickly down the single-lane on-ramp to eastbound A16. Martin smiled in spite of himself as vehicle after vehicle followed, nodding respectfully with the passing of Colonel Stirling's command Stryker.

Patton gunned the engine to catch up with the convoy. He had just reached the on-ramp when a pair of abandoned cars violently exploded up ahead, bathing the colonel's Stryker and a trailing LMTV in a rain of fire and shrapnel.

"Major Villa, keep 'em going!" Stirling's panicked voice screamed from the all-convoy net as his mortally wounded APC ground to a halt. *"Don't stop! We'll figure—"*

A high-explosive shell slammed into his Stryker, blowing it apart.

CHAPTER 70

WISCONSIN

A groggy moan escaped Melinda with the crushing pain of a man's knee pinning her to the cold concrete floor, and the sting of her wrists being flex-cuffed behind her with agonizing tightness.

A rough pair of hands violently rolled Melinda onto her back, her head throbbing and eyes struggling to focus from the blow that had incapacitated her. A large man towered over her, kicking away her rifle and tactical vest. "Try causin' any trouble and you'll end up like your friend," he grumbled.

Oh, God—Ethan, she remembered, the memory of watching him get shot snapping her out of her fog as if she had been doused with a bucket of ice water. She turned her head, her breath catching in her chest at the sight of his bloody arm sprawled out behind the fire truck.

A hulking figure backlit by the glow of the burning house streaming through the barn door circled his finger overhead to the sounds of battle continuing outside. "This'll be our prisoner collection point," Razor told the half dozen foot soldiers who had made it to the barn with him. "We'll order everyone to lay down their arms and pen 'em up with this little cherry Pop-Tart here."

"Sounds like they still got a lotta fight in 'em, boss—" a henchman said, a loud rip of gunfire from Glen and Shelby's foxhole on the other side of the barn wall interrupting him.

Razor ripped the radio from Melinda's tactical vest, the local MURS frequency still buzzing with the frantic traffic of Compound members. "Not after I make 'em an offer they can't refuse," he said with an evil stare at the basement trapdoor and the whimpers of The Compound's children. "Provided they don't wanna watch their kids get barbecued."

"No!" Melinda defiantly screamed before the goon who had subdued her stomped his boot into her shoulder and knocked her back to the floor.

"Ain't you feisty," the man taunted, Melinda's face twisting in anguish as he ground his heel into her. "I call this one—she's mine."

"Anything," Melinda pleaded, her voice choked with sobs. "I'll . . . do anything you want. Just please don't hurt the children."

"Let's hope for their sakes that your fuckin' friends share your eagerness to please," Razor said, raising Melinda's radio to his mouth.

Rifle fire suddenly exploded from behind them. Razor dropped the radio, hissing with pain as he clutched his shoulder and ran into the shadows. The scraggly man's foot flew from Melinda's shoulder as two bullets exited out his chest; she desperately pushed herself away with her legs, just barely avoiding her captor falling dead on top of her.

"Find cover!" Gunnar yelled at her, shooting on the move as he had practiced in innumerable military kill houses, having discarded Lukasz's sniper rifle for his SCAR-H. He killed a biker brandishing a sawed-off shotgun before effortlessly advancing on another who was clumsily fumbling an M-16—Gunnar shot him with the last two rounds in his magazine. He dropped the rifle on its harness and seamlessly drew his Sig Sauer P365 handgun, killing another target rounding the fire truck.

Melinda awkwardly rose to her feet and ran for the burned corner workbench to find a tool she could use to free herself. She shrieked as Razor intercepted her from behind the farm tractor, pulling her close to use as a human shield as he leveled his .357 Magnum at Gunnar.

Before he could pull the trigger, sixty pounds of Belgian Malinois flew through the air like a furry missile, Reaper's jaws ferociously clamping down on Razor's forearm like a steel trap. Reaper yanked his arm down, forcing Razor's shot to go wild as Gunnar dove for cover. Razor flung Melinda to the ground like a rag doll and began pummeling Reaper, but the Maligator was unrelenting. In desperation, Razor reached for the large serrated knife on his belt with his good arm, barely grabbing the handle before Buck jumped to sink his teeth into his wrist, his thrashing bite rending flesh and crushing bone.

With the mindless howl of a helpless animal being ripped apart by a wolfpack, Razor struggled to bring his powerful arms together to shoot Buck with the Magnum he still clutched in his hand with an iron grip. Slowly, excruciatingly, he managed to bring the pistol to Buck's head.

Melinda tightened up into a ball, jamming her eyes shut with the deafening gunshots. She screamed and thrashed as a strong set of hands grabbed her to once again take her prisoner.

"It's me!" Gunnar yelled, holstering his pistol and sitting Melinda upright to snip her plastic bindings with a Leatherman pocket tool. She opened her eyes to see Reaper and Buck growling over Razor, who vacuously stared back at her, blood gushing from a hole in his forehead. "You OK?"

"They . . . they killed Ethan," Melinda stammered, trembling as she rubbed her raw wrists.

"I know—we'll mourn later," Gunnar said, slapping a fresh magazine into his rifle. "Grab your gear—there's still fighting to do."

The barn ominously shook with the deep booming of a chain of explosions.

"What the hell was that?!" Melinda yelped over the renewed screams of the children and the clatter of wall-mounted tools crashing to the floor.

"It's the cavalry!" Gunnar whooped with the familiar sound of military helicopters. "Looks like Al got through after all!"

A Wisconsin Army National Guard UH-60 Black Hawk slowed to a hover over the barn, the downdraft from its large rotor blades buffeting the roof and kicking up clouds of dirt and straw as a door gunner raked the orchard rows with a mounted M240B machine gun, mercilessly cutting down bikers as they tucked tail and ran. A second Black Hawk rained fire as it flew by, oily explosions blossoming as tracer rounds ignited the fuel tanks of the bottlenecked trucks.

Cheers erupted from scattered Compound survivors as the battle became a rout. Melinda stared, mouth agape, at a menacing-looking attack helicopter she recognized on account of her kid brother Steve's hobby of building models—*Apache*, the name came to her as a salvo of antipersonnel rockets screamed from its wing-mounted pods to connect with unseen targets on the country road. Fireballs rose above the trees, the sounds of the explosions reaching them a second later as the Apache let rip with its bottom-mounted 30-millimeter chain gun, its aim slaved to whatever the co-pilot was looking at through the visor of his sophisticated helmet. The pilot slowed to a crawl like an alpha predator stalking prey, his co-pilot picking off individual targets unable to hide from the Apache's all-seeing forward-looking infrared radar.

Reaper padded up and sat next to his master as another Black Hawk touched down in a nearby clearing just long enough for a dozen infantrymen to jump out and hit the dirt. Gunnar squeezed Melinda's shoulder as the grunts picked up and advanced to contact. *We won—we made it*, he mouthed over the cacophony of helicopter blades.

Behind them, Buck laid next to Ethan's body, whimpering sadly as he laid down and rested his head on folded paws.

CHAPTER 71

FRANCE

Patton anticipated Martin's order before he could yell it, bringing the Griffon to a screeching halt next to the armored five-ton LMTV and the civilians scrambling to lower themselves from the truck bed. Theo slammed the button to activate the Galix countermeasure system mounted below the remote gun turret, launching eight cylindrical grenades into a wide arc that shrouded them in a thick curtain of smoke, hiding them from view and confounding thermal cameras and missile guidance systems.

Martin, Josh, and Kira charged down the ramp, the inferno of Colonel Sterling's funeral pyre burning hot on their skin as they ran for the LMTV. The truck's cabin had borne the brunt of the IED, with the butchered remains of the hapless driver and his NCO still buckled into their seats, but the side armor had spared their two dozen passengers. The handful of able-bodied men who had hopped to the ground were starting to help the others down.

"Get on board!" Martin bellowed, knifing his hand toward the Griffon as Josh and Kira moved to grab two crying children being handed down by their parents. Martin angrily kicked away a travel bag that had been tossed down to the road at his feet. "Leave your shit—we don't got the time or the room!" The passengers ducked with the zip of a rifle round cutting through the air over their heads to make Martin's argument for him. *"Go!"*

Theo and Patton stood at the Griffon's open bay, frantically guiding the civilians bolting inside and yelling for them to pack in as tightly as they could. Corinne and René hurriedly scrunched into the back, while Ann-Katryn scooted to the edge to help women and children up the ramp. A woman, her belly swollen in the late stages of pregnancy, stumbled and fell ahead of Josh and Kira, who brought up the rear with an older passenger and a man hobbling with a nasty gash in his leg. Ann-Katryn and Patton darted as one to help the pregnant woman to her feet, shoving her up the ramp to the helping hands reaching for her as Josh and Kira boarded with their infirm passengers.

Martin flinched with the loud *chink* of a stray bullet striking the Griffon's armor as the sounds of gunfire and explosions rose to a fever pitch. His order for Patton to drive them the hell out of Dodge was cut off by the explosion of a mortar round splashing on the far side of the highway, shooting up a geyser of dirt and rock. *"They're bracketing us! Get us outta here!"* Martin screamed, red-faced.

Patton spun to Ann-Katryn, who stood motionless, staring blankly forward as if oblivious to the danger around her. *"C'mon, babe!"* he yelled, pulling her by the hand before realizing to his horror that she was falling forward like dead weight. Patton screamed her name, lunging to catch her and scoop her into his arms. *"Make a hole!"* he mindlessly shrieked, her head lolling back as he bounded up the ramp.

"Shit!" Martin yelled, running to the driver's door and hoisting himself up with one step.

"LT?!" Theo yelped as Martin plopped behind the steering wheel and slammed the door. "Where the fuck's Patton?!"

"Ann-Katryn's been hit!" he barked, throwing the Griffon into drive before Theo could respond. The safety of the canal bridge was minutes away, but their lone vehicle making a run for it down an empty stretch of road would be as helpless as a target in a carnival shooting game.

Martin slammed on the brakes a second later at the sight of a hulking dark monster coming directly at them through the swirling smoke. "You want us? *Come and get us!*" Martin defiantly challenged above the screams of their passengers as he threw the Griffon in reverse. "*Catch me if you can, motherfuckers!*"

"Hold up, LT!" Theo whooped. "It's ours!"

The thinning smokescreen curled around the flat, menacing maw of an Amphibious Combat Vehicle, leading a convoy of three that, like the rest of the 22nd Marine Expeditionary Unit, answered the late Colonel Stirling's call to say to hell with their rules of engagement. The remote turrets of the two trailing ACVs swiveled to let fly with long volleys of 40-millimeter grenades that rained down on their unseen attackers, their high-explosive payloads ripping them to shreds.

"We don't got their freq—see if they got a medic with 'em!" Martin ordered Theo, who flung open his door and leaped to the pavement.

Theo ran to the front of the lead vehicle as a barrel-chested gunnery sergeant rose from the top hatch. "We got wounded!" he yelled before the NCO could speak, motioning back to the Griffon.

"How bad? Can we evac 'em back to friendly lines and treat 'em there?" he called down, his loud voice honed by a lifetime of leading Marines carrying over the battle.

"Sounds like she's hit bad—she's pregnant!"

"Corpsman!" Gunny barked below as the ramps of the eight-wheeled ACVs dropped to disgorge a platoon of bloodthirsty Marines who charged into the fields, eager to get their kill on. An AH-1Z Viper attack helicopter swooped to provided close-air support by pummeling an unseen target with Hydra rockets while in the distance, a Marine F-35B Lightning jet fighter laid waste to an armored vehicle hidden in a copse of trees with a GBU-53B StormBreaker bomb.

Theo ran back, two Navy corpsmen hot on his heels, to find the rest of his team and Kira hurriedly pulling Ann-Katryn from the Griffon and lowering her to the ground, Patton cradling her head with a bloody rag. "What happened?" a corpsman asked, dropping to his knees and unslinging his aid bag.

"Shrapnel—she caught it in the back of the neck!" Patton yelled.

"You shouldn'ta moved her!" the other corpsman reprimanded, unzipping his bag to yank out a foam cervical collar and an IV bag and tubing.

"No room!" Patton barked with a glance at the civilians packed into the Griffon, who watched them in sad silence. Ann-Katryn, pale as a ghost, began convulsing. "Hang in there, hon! Stay with me!"

The first corpsman shot two fingers to Ann-Katryn's carotid. "No pulse—she's stopped breathing!" he yelled, shoving Patton aside and raising Ann-Katryn's chin to open her airway, the danger of moving her injured head and neck now irrelevant.

"Babe?!" Patton cried out as the other corpsman chucked his equipment to unzip her coat and pullover to begin chest compressions. "You can make it! Don't give up—*you can make it!*" Josh and Theo darted to hold back their friend, who thrashed in anger at the cruelty of fate and his powerlessness to stop it as Ann-Katryn's life, and that of their unborn child, slipped away on the cold, wet road.

CHAPTER 72

Melinda sat on the cold ground, holding Jimmy in her lap as she blankly stared at the smoldering remains of the Moran farmhouse.

She shivered under the wool blanket given to her by the National Guardsmen who had made short work of the Devil's Warriors and were now doing what they could for The Compound's survivors. Snapshots of the battle flashed through her throbbing head like stop-motion nightmares—the drone attack, watching Ethan die, learning of the deaths of Donna, Will, Al Leonard, and so many other friends she had made. Jimmy flinched with the distant clap of a pistol shot announcing the summary execution of another gang member who had been captured alive; the military had neither the logistics nor the remotest desire to handle prisoners. She realized how much she had changed after chasing away a momentary fantasy of doing the honors herself.

Melinda shrugged the blanket higher on her shoulders and hugged Jimmy close to ward off the cold, which had grown more pronounced as the charred remains of the house continued to cool. Her gaze wandered to the fish pond where she and Jimmy had decided to accept Ethan's offer to stay—*we could've made a good life here*, she silently lamented. Gunnar and a number of The Compound's survivors intended to stay and rebuild, but he said he wouldn't hold it against anyone who wanted to leave with the soldiers, who offered to take them somewhere safe. Part of Melinda wanted to stay and take the gamble of surviving the winter, but she couldn't fathom putting Jimmy at risk.

The distant chop of rotors from the Black Hawks investigating what, if anything, remained of Iron Point and its residents rose above the ringing in Melinda's ears from the drone explosion and a night-long firefight with no ear protection. *Please, God, don't take music from me*, she pleaded, squeezing Jimmy as he clutched the stuffed Bluey he had grabbed from his backpack. *If that's the price I have to pay for my life, I don't want it.*

Melinda barely acknowledged the tall Hispanic soldier walking up to her, his uniform emblazoned with the black-diamond insignia of a company first sergeant. "You OK, miss?" he asked.

She looked up with mournful eyes, a tear clearing a trail down her dirty face. "No."

The first sergeant knelt in front of her and Jimmy. "I need to know whether you two're stayin' here or comin' with us."

Decision time, Melinda steeled herself. "Where would you be taking us?"

"A refuge facility—don't worry, it's a lot nicer than it sounds—that's been set up outside of Wausau. Proud new capital of the soon-to-be-independent Republic of New Wisconsin."

"What?!"

"Yeah—sounds like we're gonna be our own country, just like all the other survivin' states talkin' about headin' for the exit. The USA's done for, and we gotta take care of ourselves." The first sergeant thumbed at the collapsed and blackened Yagi-Uda antenna next to the farmhouse's ruins. "You hadn't heard?"

"I've been a little preoccupied," Melinda retorted. "We were in Michigan when the collapse started, and we've been trying to make it home or somewhere safe."

"You tellin' me you two hoofed it all this way?" the first sergeant incredulously asked.

"Well, we biked, but yeah—up and across the UP."

"You got my respect, for what it's worth. Where's home?"

"Elkhorn—near Lake Geneva and Delavan."

The first sergeant's chiseled face softened. "Miss, I dunno how to tell you this . . ."

Melinda gingerly covered Jimmy's ears. "You don't have to—I know everything out that way is gone. My Aunt Molly lives in Sparta—instead of Wausau, could you take us with you to Fort McCoy? Who knows?" she said, a flicker of hope kindling in her heart. "Maybe some of my family made it out to her."

"That's the attitude—my wife and kids managed to make it there from Mankato after everything fell apart. Yeah, I can get you two on a bird," he said with a glance at their backpacks, "provided that's the only luggage you got." He pulled a Snickers bar from his tactical vest and offered it to Jimmy. "I was savin' this for myself, but I think you need it more. Wanna go up in a helicopter, little guy?"

"Yeah!" Jimmy cheered, eagerly snatching the candy bar from the first sergeant's hand. "Can we, Minda?"

"Of course!" she said, slowly standing. "And what do you say to the nice man?"

"Thank you!" Jimmy said with his mouth full.

"Yes—thank you," Melinda added.

"*De nada*, miss—don't go wanderin' off," the first sergeant said, trotting back toward the stick of Black Hawks sitting in the harvested fields, swarms of soldiers coming and going.

Melinda began pondering how they would fit their winter clothes and other must-haves from their bicycle trailer into their packs when a friendly *woof* from Buck and Reaper heralded Gunnar's approach, his boot skittering a piece of spent ammo brass across the gravel driveway. Jimmy giggled as Buck put his paws on his shoulders for a hug.

"I figure you're leaving, then?" Gunnar asked Melinda, tilting his head at the helicopters. "No wrong answer."

Melinda nodded sadly as Jimmy frolicked with the dogs. "They're gonna fly us to my aunt's house—hope she's still there. I wish you all the luck in the world, but I have this little guy to think about now, and sorry to be blunt, but we gotta play it safe."

"I understand. We're gonna miss you."

"Likewise."

Gunnar laid a strong hand on Melinda's shoulder. "You and Ethan held your ground and saved the kids." She said nothing, silently wondering how many of those children were now orphans. "He was a good man."

"Yes, he was," she sighed with a wan smile.

"Keep in touch—and if you ever change your mind, you and Jimmy are always welcome." Gunnar called the dogs to heel, walking away to begin the arduous task of picking up the pieces.

Jimmy looked up at Melinda with round, innocent eyes. "Can I say goodbye to Kyle before we go?"

"Sure," Melinda said, taking his hands in hers and recoiling in mock revulsion upon feeling them squish with dirt and melted chocolate. "Yuck! You're filthy!" she exclaimed to Jimmy's amusement, unzipping her backpack to dig up a pack of wet wipes to clean him up. She carefully pushed aside her flute, only to stop at the sight of the kitchen towel protecting the jar of gooseberry jam that Dulcy's father had snuck into her provisions.

Just think happy thoughts and you'll fly.

Melinda twisted the jar open, running her finger along the rim and sticking it in her mouth. Dulcy was right—it was, in fact, the best thing she had ever tasted.

"I told you we'd make it," Melinda told Jimmy, wiping his hands with the towel. "We're gonna be all right."

CHAPTER 73

THE ATLANTIC COAST

"You're stayin' in the Army?! You for real, Major?"

Diego Villa smiled at Martin's incredulousness, squinting into an evening sun glowing a gorgeous red over the South Carolina coast and the flight deck of the *USS Bougainville* as the amphibious assault ship steamed toward Charleston and the mouth of the city's namesake harbor. "Serious as a heart attack, lieutenant."

"Sure you don't want me to take you to sickbay to have your head examined, sir?"

"I'm sure," Villa said, looking around at the clusters of Marines and surviving members of The Lost Boys taking in the view. "I got a wife and kids, and they're safe on post at Fort Benning, hopefully gettin' three squares a day—if I resign my commission, we end up having to fend for ourselves. Besides, my country needs me, regardless of how many stars end up disappearing off the flag."

Martin waved to Corinne and René as they passed by. "Part of me—a very small part—is jealous. I still got a hella long way to go—you'll probably be holdin' your family by this time tomorrow."

"Wish it were all wine and roses," Villa said. "I also gotta track down Mrs. Stirling and tell her about the colonel."

"It ain't fair that Colonel Stirling didn't make it. None of us would be here if it weren't for him."

Villa chuckled.

"What is it?" Martin asked.

"He said the same thing about you—on the last day, right before the highway thunder run," Villa said, gazing into the sunset. "Good luck and Godspeed, Lieutenant Crenshaw."

"To all of us, sir," Martin said, snapping to attention and saluting before taking his leave to find his team.

Martin made his way through the eerily silent gaggles of soldiers and civilians; there were no celebrations or cheers from the tired and spent men and women who knew they were extremely fortunate to be alive, and had no idea of what lay ahead for them. A handful had shot themselves or jumped overboard during the two-week transatlantic voyage, the thought of losing their loved ones too much to bear as snippets from Redoubt Radio revealed that they had no hometowns to return to. Ann-Katryn had been buried at sea the day after the fleet set sail; Martin, Josh, and Theo had maintained a discrete but constant vigilance to ensure that Patton didn't try to punch his own ticket.

He found his team near the bow of the ship, the distant hoots of tugboats waiting to steer them up the narrows of the Cooper River to US Coast Guard Base Charleston cutting through the distant chatter of seagulls whirling over empty beaches. While the collapse had run Charleston through the wringer like other major cities, it was in better shape than others its size—the *Bougainville*'s home port of Naval Station Norfolk had been smashed along with the heavily populated cities of the Northeast Corridor.

"Home sweet home," Josh said, greeting Martin with a nod.

"What's left of it," Theo grunted. He pointed ahead at a stone wall ringing a small island near the harbor inlet, a large but weathered American flag waving in the cool breeze. "Wonder what that is."

"Fort Sumter—my parents took me there on vacation the one summer that Dad made an effort to not be an alcoholic piece of shit," Patton said in a dull monotone, the wind whipping his unkempt black hair. "It's where the Civil War started. Fitting sight, seeing as how it sounds like they're gonna make a sequel."

"They'll be making it without us," Martin said, glancing to port as the navigation lights winked to life on the *USNS Red Cloud*, the thousand-foot-long roll-on, roll-off ship carrying The Lost Boys's surviving vehicles, and those of a third group of remnants that had managed to slog through Belgium and The Netherlands. "When we disembark, we fuckin' bail, just like Vilseck." *God, that was a lifetime ago*, Martin thought.

Josh shot a nervous glance at the soldiers around them. "No offense, lieutenant, but we may wanna be a little more circumspect about our plans."

"Your secret's safe with me—I'm doin' the same damn thing," said a thin young soldier who looked barely old enough to shave, but had the haunted eyes of a broken man. "Jump ship and get across the damn country before winter to find my family and my girl in Eugene—or wherever it is they fled to, 'cause the lady on the radio said there ain't no more Eugene."

"Sorry, friend. Good luck to ya," Theo said, shaking the man's hand.

"You, too," he murmured and took his leave.

"We're gonna need it, that's for sure," Martin said. "Not to be a buzzkill and ruin a perfectly good sunset, but we still got a long journey ahead of us. Our little pleasure cruise was just the intermission."

Patton sighed, breaking the silence that had fallen back across the team with their leader's cold dose of reality. "Hey, Josh—where's Kira?"

Josh gestured past a row of four Marine Corps F-35B VSTOL aircraft to the *Bougainville*'s command island. "She's below decks watching our stuff so no one helps themselves while we're up here admiring the view."

"For the record, you don't gotta hide your girl from me, dude," Patton said. "S'alright."

Josh shrugged. "Just lookin' out for you, after, you know . . . after what happened."

"Thanks."

"Don't mention it."

"Thank all of you—for everything," Patton blurted. "I thought more than once about jumping into the ocean or suck-starting my rifle—I knew you guys were keepin' your eyes on me—but I never went through with it. Because we're a team. I didn't wanna fail you like I failed Ann-Katryn's parents. I gave them my word I'd keep her safe . . ."

Josh and Theo slapped their friend on the back. "I miss her, man. So much," Patton lamented, staring at a wispy blue-gray cloud as the cold breeze stung his welling eyes. "I woulda made a good dad, don'cha think?"

"Don't do this to yourself, brother," Martin said, trying not to choke up. "Ann-Katryn would've wanted you to make it."

"Yeah, she woulda," Patton sighed resignedly.

"And we need you, buddy. We still gotta cross a thousand miles of God knows what to get back to Wisconsin, and it ain't gonna be easy."

Patton came to something approximating the position of attention and saluted. "Follow you anywhere, sir."

"We're glad as hell you're with us," Martin said, smartly returning the military courtesy.

"Good news is we're back on our home turf—that counts for somethin'," Patton said, the corner of his mouth curling into the slightest of smirks as he turned to Josh. "For starters, we don't hafta rely on Threepio here to be our interpreter."

"Fick dich," Josh jokingly shot back. "Need me to translate that?"

"There ya go again with the sexual harassment," Patton snorted. "Lucky for you we're gonna bail, or I'd file an EO complaint."

Martin smiled as his men broke into laughter. They still faced a long and dangerous trek, and even if they made it, they had no idea what, if anything, was waiting for them; aside from Josh, who grew up in the Green Bay suburbs, the other three lived well behind what Redoubt Radio now called the Red Line demarcating the surviving part of the state from no man's land.

God's will. And thank you, Colonel Stirling—rest well, he silently prayed, closing his eyes to let the weakening autumn sun warm his face as the tinny sound of the ship's 1MC intercom ordered the *Bougainville*'s skeleton crew to begin preparations to return to port.

CHAPTER 74

WISCONSIN

"Yummy!" Jimmy gleefully squealed with a lick of his vanilla ice-cream cone.

"Yeah, it's been a while, hasn't it?" Melinda said with a chuckle at Jimmy's youthful innocence before closing her eyes to savor the first sip of her vanilla milkshake. Drinking raw milk had taken a lot of getting used to, but it made the best ice cream ever.

The selections at the old-timey downtown Sparta malt shop that had just reopened with the end of spring were a pittance of what they had been before the collapse, the kindly old proprietor had explained as he handed Melinda her order, but that he expected things to improve fast with the ongoing return of commerce. Her eyes scanned the impressive pre-collapse hand-painted menu that ran the length of the counter; she had no idea what in the heck a phosphate was, but was determined to find out the moment the mustachioed soda jerker was able to make one.

Melinda sighed contentedly, the ice cream and the malt shop's working air conditioning offering a respite from the hot June day. For a fleeting moment, a sense of pre-collapse normalcy was almost close enough to touch, aside from the fact that she had paid for their order with a precious 5.56-millimeter round, and that her Windham Weaponry SRC rifle was slung over the summer dress she had borrowed from her Aunt Molly—being taller than she was, it showed off a little more than Melinda would have liked.

She led Jimmy past the small queue of customers and out the door into the noontime sun, a rivulet of melted ice cream streaming onto Jimmy's knuckles before he licked them clean; with no napkins, Melinda mused, her charge would be a sticky mess if he couldn't keep up with the heat. And after a very brutal winter, Melinda had promised during the worst of it, she would never complain about summer scorchers ever again.

Melinda and Jimmy's arduous trek had ended in Sparta, where Aunt Molly had taken them in without hesitation. They mourned Mallory's death, and lamented the uncertainty as to what had become of the rest of their family—Aunt Molly had never heard from Melinda's mother, and Elkhorn was sixty miles behind the Red Line. While Sparta had been spared from the pandemic, a lot of people succumbed to pre-existing conditions as they ran out of their medications, and the cold winter and seasonal influenza took even more lives. There had been just enough food to go around; the survivors who made it to spring were hungry, but didn't starve.

Ironically, Melinda knew more about the fates of the people who had helped her on her journey than she did her family, courtesy of an old ham radio Elmer who lived down the street and traded goods for information. He had gotten word from an operator in Mackinaw City that Nathan and Esmeralda Bowers, and Spencer and Caroline Myers, had made it through the winter. Sadly, he had had no luck contacting The Compound—all Melinda could do was pray that Gunnar and the other survivors were doing all right.

Upon learning that Melinda was a gifted musician who carried a veritable encyclopedia of music in her head, the Elmer accepted payment for his services in the form of playing duets with him on the guitar. They performed Men at Work's "Land Down Under" in honor of his late wife, who was born and raised in Brisbane and had died from diabetes after the collapse; he had even made Melinda a Vegemite sandwich, which she barely managed to choke down with the fakest of gratitude. When she told him about her adventures, he played her an Australian song she had never heard before, called "Great Southern Land," that her odyssey reminded him of. It brought her to tears, although he lost her when he explained that it came from an off-the-wall movie about Albert Einstein growing up in Tasmania and splitting beer atoms.

Melinda and Jimmy smiled and waved at other people going about their business on Sparta's tidy main drag—like Melinda, almost everyone was armed, long rifles draped over civilian clothes like photos she remembered from the streets of Tel Aviv during the Gaza war. Downtown was devoid of cars, save for the occasional Humvee from Fort McCoy—aside from farmers and a handful of prudent survivalists, the only people who had access to fuel were the military; she hoped that would change as the economy slowly returned back to health. Her free hand reflexively held down her dress with a welcome but hot breeze that fluttered the tattered American flags pathetically dangling from the old-fashioned street lamps that had just started working again with the return of grid power. New Wisconsin, as the old state minus the no-go zone was now being called, was poised to follow Texas and at least nine other states in seceding from the disintegrating Union and forging its own path.

A whistle from across the street snapped Melinda out of her reverie. "Nice legs, Mel!" yelled a stocky middle-aged woman lugging a bag of flour into the front door of the bakery where Melinda worked part-time. The owner paid her employees in baked goods and other commodities that they could barter for needed items—Melinda hoped the rumors were true that New Wisconsin would soon be adopting its own currency, based on gold and silver and redeemable on demand. "Come to give us a hand on your day off?" the owner jokingly asked.

"Not on your life!" she laughed before taking another sip of her milkshake; Jimmy was doing his best to keep up with the sticky heat, licking his hand to stop another rivulet from falling to the ground. Melinda checked the time on the slender leather watch her aunt had gifted her. "We gotta start heading back—can you eat that on the go?"

"You bet—and thanks again, Minda!" Jimmy cheerfully replied. Melinda mussed the boy's close-cropped hair; Aunt Molly for whatever reason had the magical power to get him to acquiesce to a haircut.

The duo started making their way home, where Jimmy would stay with Aunt Molly while Melinda attended a public meeting at the local elementary school, where surviving teachers and civic leaders were discussing how to resume children's education; Melinda felt obligated to homeschool Jimmy as his parents had done, but wondered if she was up to the task when she hadn't even graduated high school. After the meeting, she would spend the rest of the afternoon tending the backyard garden while listening to Redoubt Radio and its mix of entertainment and news from a shattered nation. The federal government was nothing but a pathetic paper tiger feebly roaring at New Wisconsin and the other seceding states, and the states of Montana, Washington, Oregon and northern California had devolved into armed rebellion; listening to the news made Melinda appreciate the fact that no matter how bad things were, they could always be worse.

As they rounded the corner, they accidentally barreled into a man heading the opposite direction, knocking Jimmy off balance and making him drop his ice cream. "Oh, no," Jimmy whimpered, staring forlornly at the cone, resting scoop-side down on a bed of pebbles on the loose concrete. "Can I get another?"

"No you can't, honey—that's all the money I had with me," Melinda consoled him, leaving unsaid that the treat was a splurge they could barely afford.

The handsome man looked down at Jimmy. "I'm so sorry, little guy—I should've been looking where I was going," he said, fishing two rounds of 7.62-millimeter NATO from his pocket and dropping them, one at a time, into Jimmy's sticky hand. "Go buy yourself a new one."

"Thanks, mister!" Jimmy said with a toothy smile before running back to the malt shop.

"I'll be waiting right here!" Melinda shouted after Jimmy with a hint of worry as the boy theatrically threw open the malt shop's swinging screen door. She stifled a smile upon instantly recognizing the local celebrity, despite his Milwaukee Brewers baseball cap and well-trimmed beard. "I guess I should thank you, too."

"Just fixing what I broke—what I gave him should more than cover whatever he wants," he said, adjusting the rifle slung across his back before offering Melinda a handshake. "Name's Martin. Martin Crenshaw."

"I know who you are—I don't think there's anyone in Sparta who hasn't heard about you and your friends walking all the way from Germany," Melinda said as they shook. "What a story, by the way."

"Not to tarnish the legend, but we didn't walk across the ocean—we cheated and took a boat." Martin said, tipping the brim of his hat. "You a native, or did you end up here like us?"

"No—I grew up in Elkhorn."

Martin's eyes grew as big as saucers. "So did I! You for real?"

"Wait a minute . . ." Melinda gasped, her mind piecing together where else she had seen his familiar face. "Holy crow, I *do* know you! You played football—you're Mark Crenshaw's older brother!"

"Yes and yes!" Martin excitedly exclaimed, motioning her to a nearby street bench where they could catch up, ignoring the burning heat of the black metal as they sat. "You obviously know my story—let's hear yours!"

"Mine's a lot less impressive," Melinda said, brushing a wisp of curly hair from her face before sharing a condensed version of her and Jimmy's journey, the excitement of finding an Elkhorn native overriding the sorrow at reliving the memories of losing Dulcy, and Ethan and everyone else at The Compound. "I ended up in Sparta because my aunt lives here, and . . . because Elkhorn's gone."

"Yeah, I know—probably along with my whole damn family," Martin said.

"I think Aunt Molly and Jimmy are all I got left," Melinda sighed. "My sister died of the flu, and last I heard from Mom before everything went dark, Dad and my brother Steve had gotten sick, too. For what it's worth, I'm, um, sorry for your loss."

"Thank you, and right back at you. But all this doesn't seem, you know . . ." Martin stumbled, struggling to find the right word.

"Official?" Melinda ventured.

"Something like that." Martin stared up at one of the weathered lamppost flags of the dead nation he had enlisted to defend what seemed like an eternity ago. "I've been talkin' with my team about crossing over the Red Line to see what's left of Elkhorn. Find my family and give 'em a proper burial."

"That's gonna be dangerous."

"So was fighting our way across what's left of Europe and America," Martin said, shifting to face Melinda. "So was your trekking across two states as a teenager with zero survival skills—and so was fighting off a horde of post-apocalyptic zombie mutant bikers while protecting a defenseless young boy. We've all spent the past year in danger—what's a little more?"

Their eyes locked as a feeling of purpose swelled inside Melinda, like the first night at Jimmy's house when God told her to look after him. So many people had risked so much to help her and Jimmy—but while Sparta was her home now, she realized her journey wasn't done yet. She had one last leg to complete.

"I'm coming with you," Melinda declared.

"You serious?" Martin asked, taken aback.

"Never been more serious in my life. Like you, I know the lay of the land, and two heads are better than one," Melinda said, patting her rifle. "And like you said yourself, I can hold my own—don't let the cute dress fool you."

"What about your little friend?"

"Aunt Molly can watch Jimmy while we're gone. She wants to know what happened to my family as much as I do."

Martin stared into her pleading, expressive eyes, weighing the pros and cons—and unashamedly tallying the way she filled out her dress in the pros column. "OK, Melinda Hodgson, of Elkhorn, Wisconsin, you talked me into it," he proclaimed, again offering his hand. A warm smile crossed her face as they shook to seal the deal.

"When do we go?" she asked.

"When we're ready. But the first order of business is coming over for dinner and meeting the team," Martin said as they rose from the bench. "You like *Star Trek*?"

"Not in the slightest."

"Good. Me neither. But Josh and Kira do, and they won't shut up about it, so you'll probably have to sit through an episode whether you want to or not."

"You like live music?" Melinda coyly asked.

"Who doesn't?"

"I may have a better idea than TV."

Martin returned her grin with a flirtatious one of his own. "What is it?"

"You'll see," she teased, her heart swelling with hope. The world she had known was gone and would never come back, but this brave new one rising from the ashes—the one Ethan had told her she would help build—was full of promise.

Her eyes met Martin's again for a brief magic second before he looked past her and roared with laughter. Melinda turned to see Jimmy double-fisting two king-sized cones, his face smeared with strawberry and vanilla ice cream.

"I like this guy, Minda."

Thank you for reading *All We've Lost*! If you liked it, it would mean the world to me if you take a short minute to leave a heartfelt review on Amazon (and Goodreads, if you have an account). Your kind feedback is very much appreciated, and very important to me.

Acknowledgements

Before I begin the ritual of ending this latest novel by giving credit to everyone along the way who played a role in bringing this story to life, I'd like to take a moment to thank you, the reader, for your patience. I made you wait a while for *All We've Lost*.

I was well on my way toward writing a third book in the Unraveling series last year, when I came to the realization about halfway through that I wanted, and needed, to tell this story first—and made the decision to shelve it for later and write *All We've Lost* instead. I so very much hope that it was worth the wait.

While I dedicated my first novel, *Big Sky Fallen*, to my dad, I owe him yet another debt of gratitude for his voluminous collection of classical music, which played in my head like a soundtrack as I wrote about young Melinda Hodgson and her journey. I took up playing trombone in fifth grade, and played straight through college; of all the things in my life that I've lost—not counting my mind—I miss music the most. Next to the band of brothers I met in the military, the men and women of the Northern Illinois University Huskie Marching Band were the most awesome and talented bunch of drunken and libertine degenerates it has ever been my privilege to know, and I respectfully dedicate Melinda's story to them.

As long as I'm waxing nostalgic about academia, thank you to those long-ago editors of NIU's campus newspaper, the *Northern Star*, for making the horribly irresponsible decision to hire me to draw a reckless and cynical comic strip that got me hooked on the power of words to destroy and heal; unfortunately, I was much more adept in my intemperate youth at the former than the latter. And for the tiny handful of you who remember that poorly drawn exercise in libel and bad taste so long ago, I hope you caught the inside joke weaved throughout the story of Martin Crenshaw and his team making their way across post-apocalyptic Europe.

It's hard to put into words the admiration I have for my amazing cover artist, Christian Bentulan, who almost brought me to tears when he sent me the cover for *All We've Lost*—thank you so much, my friend! I knew at first glance at Christian's immeasurable talent that I wanted him to design my book covers—and God subsequently blessed me with similar providence when it came to finding a voice artist.

The glowing reviews and ratings that you wonderful people gave *Big Sky Fallen* and *Cascadia Rising* prompted me to move up my timetable and take the plunge into partnering with a voice artist to produce audiobook versions of my novels. After finding about a dozen narrators whose biographies looked like a decent match, I started listening to their online samples—and the moment I listened to Gary Tiedemann, I knew I found the voice of the Unraveling series. His versatility, range, and the soul he brings into his work is a wonder to behold, and I very much look forward to our continued partnership.

As always, thank you to my amazing wife, Kristin, and our children, Grace and Logan, who sometimes, kinda sorta, find it in their hearts to give me time to write.

Thank you to preparedness expert David Kobler, aka southernprepper1, whose YouTube video about how to turn a four-by-four into a poor-man's fire truck cured a killer bout of writer's block regarding how to end the Battle of The Compound.

Last but certainly not least, thank you to guntuber Brandon Herrera and law enforcement YouTuber Cody Garrett, aka Donut Operator, whose videos are a constant source of entertainment and knowledge. I'll wrap up with a tip of the hat to Cody, whose off-the-cuff joke in one of his videos about turning garden gnomes into IEDs with ball bearings and Tannerite had me laughing so hard that I just had to incorporate it into this book.

Kevin Craver

May 2025

About the Author

Kevin Craver had a comfortable childhood devoid of zombies, post-atomic mutants, or cyborgs trying to kill him before he could grow up to lead the human resistance to victory. He turned a side hustle of drawing a nihilistic comic strip for his college newspaper into a living as a token conservative in the world of newspaper journalism, earning eighty state and national writing awards over his twenty-year career. Somewhere along the line, he realized that his life didn't suck enough, and spent fourteen years and two deployments as an infantryman in the Army National Guard.

When he's not writing about the end of civilization or hoarding cans of bacon in his basement—because the living will envy the dead in a world without bacon—he caters to the whims of his wife, daughter, son, and Ragdoll cat.

Visit Kevin's website at www.kevincraver.com to sign up for e-mail updates on upcoming releases.